D1526945

21 Hours

Dustin Stevens

21 Hours
Copyright © 2012, Dustin Stevens

Warning: All rights reserved. The unauthorized reproduction or distribution of this copyrighted work, in whole or part, in any form by any electronic, mechanical, or other means, is illegal and forbidden, without the written permission of the author.

This is a work of fiction. Characters, settings, names, and occurrences are a product of the author's imagination and bear no resemblance to any actual person, living or dead, places or settings, and/or occurrences. Any incidences of resemblance are purely coincidental.

For Maddie...

An Uncle is a bond of faith
That even time can't sever
A gift to last all of our lives
An Uncle is forever...
           -Anonymous

It's funny what goes through a man's mind when he thinks he's about to die.

When you live your entire life as one-half of a pair of twins, you get used to being asked an endless series of inane questions. Are you identical? Did you dress alike growing up? Could your parents tell you apart?

Seeing as how my twin is a woman, the answer to all of those is pretty straight forward.

The one I get the most though, and don't ask me why this is, is if it true that twins can sense what the other one is feeling?

I'm no scientist, couldn't be further from it. I spent the five years most people spend in college incarcerated at a correctional facility in Orient, Ohio. What I am is a man chock full of common sense, and whenever most people ask me that question I just look at them like they're crazy.

All that is why, as I was lying on the banks of the Ohio River, I was as shocked as anybody to realize it wasn't the broken wrist that entered my mind. It wasn't the half-pound of gravel ground into the exposed flesh of forearms. It wasn't the coppery taste of blood on my tongue or even the missing half of my pinkie finger.

Instead, sprawled flat on my back staring at the awakening dawn sky above, waiting for the final death knell to come my way, the last thing I remember thinking before blackness took over was...

Dear God, I hope Lex can't sense what I'm feeling right now.

Chapter One

There are very few incontrovertible truths in life.

Death, taxes, and no matter how many times you've branded cattle, it always smells like burnt ass. There's no way around it, and while wearing a bandana like an old-time bank robber may keep any residual pieces from actually entering your nose, it does nothing to keep the smell from wafting in.

I'm long past gagging from it, a skill I've acquired over many rotations on the yearly cycle of working a cattle ranch.

Sadly, I can't say the same for my cohorts.

"You boys realize if you don't move faster than this, we're going to be here all spring."

Blinking away a few drops of moisture from my own eyes I shoved the design end of my brand back into the glowing coals of the fire and waited. There'd be an excuse any minute. There always was.

"Damn Shane, can't you smell that?" Bret Hickam gasped. Beneath him, everything he'd eaten in the last two days was gathered in a half-digested heap, dust already settling over it.

"And you think adding the smell of vomit is going to make it better?" I asked, pulling a second brand free from the fire and inspecting the glowing end of it.

"Can't help it," Joe Murphy wheezed beside him. He was bent at the waist with spittle dripping from the end of his lip, a second pile looking to reveal everything he'd eaten in the last few weeks at his feet.

"Try harder. And go get the next calf. These things don't brand themselves."

In my periphery I could see Hickam scowling at me before stumbling towards the holding pen, his thin frame still doubled over. Beside him Murphy remained dumping the contents of his stomach onto the ground, continuing their two-man act solo.

Thrusting the glowing tip of the brand back into the coals I raised my eyes to the horizon just a few miles off. Stretched across the sky in a jagged shark tooth pattern sat the Big Horn Mountains, their top halves still covered in snow. Normally in May the entirety of the range is shrouded in white, but this year an abnormally warm spring has melted the snowpack much earlier than expected.

Should make for a bitch of a summer. Four long months of drought and fire watch.

Behind me I can hear Hickam grunting as he drags a second Angus calf into the ring, the critter bawling as it tries its damnedest to fight free. Turning back I cast an angry glare at Murphy, who eventually picks up on the hint and pushes himself up to give a hand.

Damn greenhorns.

Every spring the ranch is crawling with them, trust fund babies from the east coast, all dying to spend a year on a real Wyoming ranch and prove how tough they are. Old man Winters, the ranch owner and my boss for the past five years, likes to say they're full of piss and vinegar.

I just think they're full of shit.

After a considerable tussle Hickam and Murphy managed to wrestle the calf to the ground. Each of them held down a pair of legs and looked up expectantly at me.

"You have to secure the head," I remind them for the third time. "Otherwise she's going to jerk free the second I touch her."

Shifting his frame slightly to the side, Murphy pressed a hand down on the calf's neck, wrapping one thin hand around both front legs.

I can't help but smirk behind my bandana. This is going to be funny.

Giving the brand one last shake I wrench it free from the fire and position it over the calf's rear haunch. I can see her staring up at me as I stand poised with the glowing red iron in my hand, the look in her eyes exactly the same as mine would be if someone were about to brand my ass.

Without giving any warning the iron is pressed against her haunches, the smell of charred rawhide instantly filling my nostrils. On cue, the calf bucked wildly beneath it, swinging her

16

head in a wild arc up from the dusty floor of the ring. Murphy's single hand hold was no match for her as she smashed her skull into his nose, sending him tumbling over backwards. With her front half free she kicked Hickam away and bolted around the ring, her throbbing backside sending her running in circles.

From his knees Hickam looked up at me, mortified, his pale face even whiter than usual. "Joey? You alright?"

I jammed the brand back into the coals and watched as across from me Murphy slowly rose to a seated position, his hand cupped over his nose with blood oozing between his fingers. "That sumumabitch bwoke my nose!"

"Told you to secure the head."

"I did!" Murphy replied, his eyes pink with involuntary tears. Like Hickam, everywhere on his face that wasn't soaked in bodily fluids was pale white.

"Like hell. You patted her on the neck. You're lucky she didn't kick in every one of your damn teeth."

A large knot worked itself down Murphy's throat as he swallowed and stared at me, unsure how to respond. Behind him the calf continued to circle, though she'd slowed to a trot.

17

"You mean you knew what would happen and didn't warn him?" Hickam asked. His face was a mix of stunned and appalled, his jaw hanging open as he spoke.

"I did. Multiple times. And just think, now he doesn't have to smell it anymore."

Both boys sat in the dust and stared at me like I was a creature from another planet. I call them boys because despite their only being a half dozen years between us in age, I could be their great-grandfather in terms of life experience.

"You two going to get up and put that calf in the pen? We have a couple hundred of these to do today."

Slowly Murphy pulled his hand back from his face and stared at the bright red blood running in rivulets along the lines in his palm. As I expected, his eyes rolled up and he toppled straight backward into the dust without moving.

"Hey! Shane!" the raspy voice of Winters called out behind me. Keeping my back to him I rolled my eyes and slowly turned, ready for some condensed lecture on how I need to take better care of the help. I've heard it before, he knows I don't care

18

to hear it again, but he keeps giving it to save face with the other hands.

Raising a hand I slowly turned and waved to him, acknowledging I know where he's going and I don't need to hear it.

"You've got a telephone call!" Winters called out, completely ignoring the cluster playing out in the ring.

Twirling my hand in the air in a helicopter fashion, I yelled out, "We've got cows to brand. Tell them I'll call back."

"She said she's your sister and it's urgent!"

The words don't even finish leaving his mouth before the brand I was holding hit the ground. In long strides I headed straight for the side of the pen and hoisted myself over the broad board fence, dropping down on the other side.

"Get that calf put up," I said to Hickam, still sprawled in the dirt with his mouth agape. "I may or may not be back."

Moving quick, I walked straight across the opening between the barns and the ranch house, tugging the bandana down around my neck. Already a chill ran the length of my spine and a tangle of barbed wire had formed in the pit of my stomach.

19

This couldn't be good.

Chapter Two

"I didn't know you had a sister," Winters said, holding the phone away from his body with his left hand. In his right was the gnawed-on remains of a ham bone, grease staining his fingers and the bottom half of his face. A thick paunch stuck out from beneath his overalls, a green thermal finishing the ensemble. Thinning white hair and a patchy neck beard gave him the look of a bizarro Santa Clause, though he's a pretty good employer so I don't bust his stones about it too much.

Besides, right now I'm not exactly in the joking mood.

"Heck, I didn't know you had any family at all," Winters said with a twist of the neck, as if considering the topic for the first time.

"Murphy might need to go to the hospital," I said, completely ignoring the statements. I wasn't sure if they were actual questions or not, but I definitely didn't feel like getting into it at the moment.

"Aw hell," Winters said, looking past me towards the ring. "Forget to secure the head again?"

"Yup," I said, taking the cordless phone from Winters and stepping to the side. I paused a moment to let him wander down towards the ring, still gnawing on the ham hock as he went. His considerable bulk swung from side to side as he walked stiff-legged along, dust swirling around his shuffling feet.

Pausing just long enough to make sure I was alone, I slid off to the side of the porch and pressed the phone to my face. "Lex? What's wrong?"

Nobody ever calls me. I mean, *ever* calls me. On the first and third Sundays of the month I call Mama to check in. On the second and fourth I call Lex. In total, I spend roughly twenty minutes a week on the phone, a few more if Mama is feeling chatty. They both have the ranch number, but it's only to be used in strict emergencies.

This is the first time either have ever done so.

"Who the hell is Shane?" Lex asked. Immediately I could hear the strain in her voice. It sounded like she'd either been crying or the tears aren't far off. Don't ask me how I knew all this from just five words, but I did.

Maybe it was the twin thing.

"What's wrong? Is it Mama?" I'm sure she could hear the strain in my own voice, the words strung taut like guitar strings.

"Why did he call you Shane?" Lex asked again, her voice lowered another decibel.

I'm not happy about it, but I know there's no point in dodging the question. Once she gets on something, she won't let it go until she's satisfied. "That's just what they call me. Like the movie. Guy named Shane showed up alone one day, offered to stay on as a ranch hand."

"Oh," Lex said softly. "Wasn't Shane a gunfighter that ended up sticking around and saving their ass?"

My sister very rarely cussed. Hardly ever. The fact that she was cursing, and over such a random topic, had my nerves on end. "Lex," I said, trying deliberately not to yell, "why are you calling me? What's going on?"

23

"That's why I'm calling you. I need you to come save my ass."

The air caught in my chest as my eyes hardened against the horizon. In the foreground I could vaguely make out the movement of Winters and the boys, though I didn't bother to focus on any of them. "What's happened? Did that son of a bitch hit you?"

Four years earlier my sister married Ricky Borden, former quarterback of the Ohio State Buckeyes. I wouldn't say that he and I hated each other, more that we had a tacit understanding between us.

I'd stay in Wyoming, and he'd keep his ass far away from it.

"No," Lex whispered, her voice now thick with tears. I waited as she sniffed loudly and said, "I'm actually at the hospital with him now."

If she was expecting me to suddenly break into tears as well, I was sorry to disappoint. Something told me there was more to it than that though. "What's going on Lex? What happened to Ricky?"

24

"There were three of them," she said, her voice barely discernible. "Ricky tried to fight them off, but they surprised us."

I could feel my face twist into a look of confusion, agitation boiling just below the surface. "Who? Why were they fighting Ricky?"

For several long seconds, Lex said nothing. I could hear her sobbing softly over the line, punctuated every few seconds by a deep sniffle. "Please come home. We need you here. Now."

"We?" I asked, still not sure what was going on. In front of me I could see an entire corral full of calves that needed branding and two full wagons of manure that needed spreading. She knew how hard it was for me to get away in the spring.

Besides, if Ricky got his ass kicked, he probably mouthed off to the wrong people and deserved it.

"They have Annie," Lex hissed, her sobs reaching a much higher level that relayed pain like I'd never heard before. Every function in my body, my breathing, my thinking, even my heartbeat, all stopped instantly.

My mouth fell open and my eyes went glassy, the world spinning around me.

Annie was my two year old niece.

"Who has Annie?" I whispered.

"I...I..." Lex tried to mutter. "Please, come home."

Suddenly the calves and the manure didn't mean a damn anything more. Already I was calculating drive times versus flight times, working the trip over in my head. I could feel myself squeezing the phone so hard the plastic threatened to explode in my hand.

"I'm on my way."

Chapter Three

The square green sign along the road said it was eighteen miles into Columbus and the clock on the dash said it was nearing two in the afternoon when I decided to stop. It was only the fourth stop I'd made since leaving the ranch the day before, a marathon drive that started outside of Sheridan, Wyoming and was going to end in central Ohio.

I've made the trip three times now. The first two times I spent the night in Des Moines, Iowa, a town roughly halfway between the two and just small enough that I don't have to worry about leaving my gear in the truck overnight. Both times I was driving in the fall and not moving particularly fast, taking my time as I enjoyed the weather and scenery across the middle of the country.

This time, I stopped four times for gas and didn't see a single thing. Most of the trip was spent in some shade of darkness, my headlights throwing a fluorescent cone out onto the highway and propelling me forward. The rest of the trip I sat with my eyes aimed forward, chewing my fingernails until all ten of them were rimmed with blood. When I was out of fingers, I bought a pack of Wintergreen at the third gas station and started working on it.

The entire time my mind worked almost as fast as my jaw.

There was only one picture I'd ever carried in my wallet, and that was of my niece Annie. Less than a month from her third birthday, she was the spitting image of her mother at that age. Blue eyes, puffy cheeks, a head full of curls that could fill the backseat of a car. Precocious and curious, she never stopped moving, her mind constantly inquisitive of the world around her.

The day she was born was the second trip I made home. I guess you could say I've always had a protective streak in me, especially for the women in my life. Mama, Lex, even my dog before she passed. The day Annie was born, I made a vow to myself, to my sister, and to God that I would watch over her until my last breath.

The thought of her in trouble had me in a cold rage that was buried just beneath the surface. Each time I looked in the mirror I saw myself looking fairly composed, but I knew that under it flowed a torrent of anger ready to explode like a geyser.

This last stop is one I make every time I'm passing through. To be honest I had barely thought about it until I saw the sign a few miles out announcing the exit. Muscle memory pushed the truck off the freeway without my even acknowledging it, depositing me on a two-lane state route and winding through the woods.

My final destination sat only six miles off the interstate, but it might as well have been in a different country. There was no trace of the busy thoroughfare or the cluster of restaurants and gas stations around it. The road was narrow and gravel, low-hanging branches pulled at my radio antennae as I passed beneath them. There were no houses, no buildings of any kind, and only a single car was parked anywhere in sight.

Easing the truck to a stop alongside the familiar aging Jeep Cherokee, I put it in park and climbed out. The heels of my boots made small indentations in the soft earth as I approached the lone figure sitting with her back to me, rows of headstones filing by on either side. The air was chilly, damp but clear. Overhead the sky was a mottled blue, the threat of rain virtually non-existent.

"I wondered how long it would take you to get here," a familiar voice said. It was the only sound in the small cemetery, even the birds above hearing the pain in her voice. Still she sat without looking at me, her gaze poised on a particular stone in front of her.

"How'd you know I'd come here?"

"I knew you'd do the math and figure it was just as fast to drive as fly from where you were. Probably cheaper too."

"That part never entered my mind," I said, closing the gap between us. I could see a small footpath beaten out in the grass to where she now sat.

Clearly she'd still been spending a lot of time here.

Slowly she stood and turned, her full height barely coming to my shoulder. Just a few years north of fifty, she still looked like she could pass for forty. Her curly blonde hair sat high atop her head in a messy pile, a few stray ringlets framing blue eyes and high cheekbones. A wan smile traced her lips, though it was plainly evident she'd been crying. "And let's be honest, you can't pass through without stopping to see your father."

I merely grunted a response to that part, walking forward and enveloping my mother in a tight bear hug. I truly love the mountains and I love working the ranch, but I'll be damned if it doesn't get hard being away from her, Lex, Annie.

Ricky, well, him I could take or leave.

"Hello Mama," I said softly, her pile of hair crushed against my cheek. Below my chin I could hear her crying again as she clung to me, her hands grabbing at the flannel shirt inside my jean jacket.

Over her head I can see my father's tombstone, the gray marble as polished and clean as the day we laid it. Fresh flowers sat on the ground in front of it, daisies from the planters my

31

mother kept going in a greenhouse year round. Casting a glance around I can't help but notice how dilapidated the other plots are, many of them feeling the effects of winter, while my father's looks like it belonged in Arlington Cemetery.

"Hey Pop."

Against me I could feel my mother squeeze tighter for a moment before releasing her grip and pulling me down to the small bench in front of the tombstone.

"I take it Lex told you she called," I said, still holding my mother's hand as we stared at my father's headstone. Her tiny hand felt ice cold inside mine, the knuckles drawn white beneath her skin. I could hear her sniffling, but she didn't seem to be crying at the moment.

"Yeah," she whispered.

"Have you seen her?"

I sensed my mother's head bob beside me. "I was there over night with her. I left just a little bit ago to come here and wait for you."

A thousand questions, everything I'd been rolling around since leaving Wyoming, fought their way to the forefront of my mind. One by one I forced them back, focusing on what was absolutely necessary at the moment. "Why here? Why not wait for me at the hospital?"

Her grip grew a touch tighter. "She can't tell the story again. Right now she is hanging on by a very thin thread and if she goes through it again, she might snap. Especially if she has to tell it to you."

"Why's that?" I ask, already suspecting the answer.

My mother slid her eyes to my face with a look that relayed I should know the answer. "Because she wants her baby and she wants blood. Telling you that in a hospital full of people might not be the best idea."

My suspicion was correct.

"Is she okay?" Again, I know there's no way in hell she is, but okay is a relative term in these situations.

"She still hasn't slept, and hasn't left Ricky's side, but I think she's as well as can be expected. Her in-laws are there with her now."

As well as can be expected.

Again, it's all relative in these situations.

Slowly I pushed the air out of my lungs and ran my free hand down the front of my jeans. I was still wearing the clothes from the day before, dust from the ring on my Levi's and the faintest trace of burnt cowhide on my shirt. Packing wasn't real high on my list of priorities when I left.

"Alright, start at the beginning. What happened?"

My mother closed her eyes and lowered her chin to her chest. She remained that way for several long moments, obviously willing herself not to cry. When the urge passed, she spoke without raising her head or opening her eyes.

"This is exactly what I heard her tell the police when they came last night. Every Friday, Ricky gets off early and picks Annie up from daycare. Together they get ice cream and then they go to the park."

As much as I loathe the man personally, he has proven to be a good father and provider. It is part of the reason I make such an effort to stay away and leave them in peace.

"Yesterday was no different. They hit Dairy Queen, went to the park behind the elementary school by their house, went home. When they got there, Lex was sitting on the front porch waiting for them. Said she didn't notice the black SUV parked across the street at the time, but after thinking on it was pretty sure it was there all afternoon."

Reflexively my hands tightened into balls on my thighs. Just as fast I released my right hand to ease the grip on my mother's hand and jammed my left thumbnail into my mouth. The familiar metallic taste of blood crossed my tongue, but I could care less.

"Ricky pulled his car into the driveway and unstrapped Annie, the two of them bouncing across the yard towards Lex. As they did, three men emerged from the black SUV and sprinted towards them. All dressed in head-to-toe black, all wearing ski masks."

I closed my eyes as she talked, replaying the scene in my mind. I kept my mouth shut and forced air in and out through my nose, willing my heart rate to stay under control.

"Lex saw the men coming before Ricky did. She went completely rigid on the porch as Annie got to her, only gasping out a warning a second before it was too late. The first man slammed into Ricky and they both rolled to the ground in a tussle. The other two went after Lex and the baby, everyone screaming bloody murder by this point.

"The second man got to Lex as she stood and tried to run inside, caught her with a fist to the side of the head."

"Wait," I interrupted, my heart rate pounding like a jackhammer in my ears, "they beat Lex too?"

Again my mother nodded her head. "Back of her head has a hell of a knot on it. Knocked her cold. Gave her a concussion."

It was everything I could do not to swear in front of my mother. I turned my head to the side in case any mutterings slid out, making a slew of promises to myself that I would find every last one of these sonsabitches.

"That's the last thing she remembers. When she came to, Ricky was face down on the sidewalk and a neighbor was standing over her with a washcloth." A small slurping noise slid from her lips and her shoulders wracked violently against my mine. "Annie was gone."

I sat in silence for several long minutes, processing what I'd just heard. The rage inside me was threatening to burst through every available opening, but I knew I couldn't let that happen just yet. There would be time for that later. "What did the police say?"

"Standard stuff. They were doing all they can, but that with no real eyewitnesses, physical descriptions, or leads, it was going to be an uphill climb. Can you believe that? They actually told a hysterical mother it was going to be an uphill climb."

Of course I could believe it. Everything to a cop is an uphill climb. They get so bogged down in the process sometimes, they forget to use their damn common sense.

"That's when she called me?"

"That's when she called you." My mother's voice was back to flat and even. Like me, her emotion was simmering just beneath the surface, though hers was of a much different nature than mine.

"What happened to Ricky?"

"His nose is completely shattered, as are his left cheek and orbital bones. He's still unconscious at the moment and they're actually giving him drugs to keep him there. Doctor says it looks like someone hit him across the face with a crowbar or baseball bat."

Asshole or not, I didn't want that to happen to him. Not only would it make things harder on Lex, but more importantly right now it would be one less man around should I need him.

"Mama, I hate to leave in such a hurry, but-"

"Go," my mother whispered, cutting me off. "Time is crucial. You don't have any to waste."

"Are you going back to the hospital?" I asked, rising to my feet.

"I'll be there in an hour. I just ran home to change, come find you, and get some food to take back. Her mother-in-law can't cook for crap, you know that."

I appreciated my mother's attempt at levity, but couldn't find a laugh within me. Instead, I squeezed her hand once more and stared back at our automobiles parked side by side. "I'll find her."

"I know you will," she whispered, returning the squeeze but keeping her eyes down.

"You know though, it might require me to do some things. Some things a lot worse than what happened before."

Slowly my mother raised her face to me, tears again pooling at the bottom of her eyes. For the first time ever, she looked to wear every last one of her years on her face. "You do whatever you have to do son. You just bring that little girl home."

Drawing my mouth into a tight line, I nodded at her. I turned over my shoulder and raised my chin to my father, then retraced my steps back to the truck.

Less than twenty minutes after pulling off the interstate, I was back on it and headed towards Columbus.

Chapter Four

For a Saturday, Sacred Heart Hospital on the outskirts of Columbus was surprisingly busy. Not Mardi Gras on Fat Tuesday busy, but active enough that I stood at the front desk waiting a long time for someone to help me before finally giving up. After that I tried flagging down nurses as they scurried past, all dressed in garish outfits and carrying clipboards. When that didn't work either, I cornered a janitor and had him give me directions to the intensive care unit.

He was busy going about his chores and barely spoke a word of English, but he grasped my tone and broken Spanish enough to send me in the right direction.

Dwarfed in comparison to some of the medical giants in the city, Sacred Heart's entire ICU was housed on two hallways.

Each of them extended out in opposite directions from a central intersection, both carbon copies of one another.

To my right was a sign announcing it to be the long-term care wing of the ICU. The hall was largely empty, with just a pair of nurses shuffling along and a single old man staring through a glass pane. I assumed his wife of fifty years was lying on the other side of it, but I didn't have the time or the energy right now to go find out.

By contrast, the hall to my left was alive with people. Scads of nurses, orderlies, and doctors moved through, all of them in a hurry and headed somewhere. Small cadres of crying or worried families dotted the hall, clumped together and talking in hushed tones or staring stonily into space.

At the far end I recognized Ricky's sister and entered into the maze, falling in with the flow of hospital personnel as it slipped through the groups of bystanders.

I cast sideways glances to some of the people as we walked by, each of their faces wearing the same pain my family did twelve years before. For a moment, I'm right back outside that hospital room across town, a scared kid waiting to hear what the doctor would say about my father.

With a shake of my head I tossed the thought aside and walked directly up to the sister. I think I remembered her name being Bonny, but can't be certain. Definitely not sure enough to actually use it.

I looked her a question as I approached, casting my eyes between her and some guy I assumed to be her husband. Somewhere in the back of my mind I vaguely recalled Lex telling me she got married, but again, I can't be certain.

Nodding slightly, she raised a single finger and jabbed it across the hallway. Thankfully, she wasn't in any more a mood to talk than I was.

Another nod in reply and I hooked a left toward the doorway and peered inside. Ricky's parents, Jim and Sue, were both standing by his head, looking down at him. Jim stood with one hand stuffed in the pocket of his slacks, the other along his wife's back. Sue leaned slightly back against him, a handkerchief pressed to her face and a light pink cardigan enveloping her body.

I'd met them both a time or two before. They both knew Ricky and I didn't exactly like each other, though sensed the begrudging respect we gave one another. They were both nice enough people to treat me much the same way.

In the opposite corner sat Lex in a chair she'd dragged up alongside the bed. I could only see the right profile of her face in the dim light of the room, though it appeared clean and bruise-free. Her eyes were red, but dry. Her blonde hair was roughly pulled back in a tangle from her face.

She sat leaning forward in the chair, an oversized grey hooded sweatshirt swallowing the top half of her. The bottom half was dressed in jeans and running shoes as she idly chewed on her fingernails.

Something told me hers were in even worse shape than mine.

Using the back of my hand, I wrapped softly on the door twice and stepped inside. All three heads snapped towards me, the knocks sounding like cannon fire in the silent room. The only other sound was the persistent beeping of a heart monitor and the rise and fall of a breathing apparatus.

Lex was on her feet before I got a step into the room. She buried her head in my chest and wrapped her arms around me, squeezing so tight a pair of vertebras in my lower back cracked. As she did, she tried to keep her face turned away from me, but the enormous lump behind her ear and rainbow of color along her jaw were too obvious to ignore.

"O," she whispered softly.

One hand I slid to the back of her head, the other around her shoulders, and drew her in tighter. Despite standing nearly five-foot-ten she was still a half foot shorter than me, more than that in my boots. A mixture of pain and anger welled in my throat as the image of her face filled my mind.

Consciously, I swallowed it down.

"Hey you," I whispered back.

Jim and Sue Borden both watched us silently, their faces completely flat. Looking over Lex's head I slid my eyes to Ricky laying prone in the bed and asked, "How's he doing?"

Sue's face crinkled as if she were going to cry and she pressed the handkerchief back into place. Jim pulled her a fraction closer and said, "He's hanging in there. Lot of damage, but the doctor says it's mostly cosmetic."

"Good," I murmured. The first thought that came to my head was I certainly hoped that was true, because the cosmetics looked like hell. The entirety of his head was wrapped up tight like a mummy, gauze covering everything but his mouth. There, a breathing tube stuck out several inches with thick, clear tubing running over to the machine beside him.

Lex pulled back slightly away from me and said, "You look like you could use some coffee."

I picked up on the insinuation and nodded. "Drove straight through. Some coffee would be fantastic."

Lex turned to her in-laws and said, "We'll be in the cafeteria if you need us."

Both of them nodded but said nothing.

Lex led me back through the maze of people and into the cafeteria, deftly filling two cups of coffee and paying for them in record time. Clearly it wasn't her first trip down for caffeine. Normally I'd offer, or even insist, on paying, but I let it go without comment. We had more pressing matters to get to.

"You look like hell O," Lex said as way of an opening. My given birth name was Felix, and hers Alexa. Our father liked the letter X in names and decided since he had twins it was the perfect opportunity to invoke it. It didn't matter that one name was Spanish, the other Russian. We would be Felix and Alexa, the O'Connor twins.

Over time, Alexa's name got shortened to Lex. Fearful that mine might then become Flex or even worse, Lix, my parents started referring to me simply as O. To the world, we've each been known as such ever since.

"Likewise," I said, drawing the coffee over in front of me. I could see steam rising from the open top of it, but didn't care as I upended the cup. It was a little hot, but it tasted good. Over half of the cup went down at once.

"I spent the night at the hospital waiting on my husband in emergency surgery and praying my daughter was alive. Before that I got my face pounded in," Lex said. "What's your excuse?"

"Nothing that good," I conceded. I tried my best to meet her gaze as much as possible, but kept having to avert my eyes.

The sight of her face was difficult to see. "Drove straight through to get here."

"That explains the look, not the smell," Lex said, gingerly taking a drink of her coffee. Thin afternoon sun streamed in through the window beside us, illuminating our table. Outside the first few signs of spring were just beginning to show in the forms of tree buds and green grass.

"I was branding when you called. Didn't even stop to change."

Lex bobbed her head. "Thanks for coming."

Around us the cafeteria was nearly empty, too late for the lunch crowd and too early for dinner. A few stray workers wandered by with coffee or sodas in hand, but otherwise the entire corner of the room was ours. "What's going on with Ricky?"

"The doctors got his nose opened up and reset the bones. Bout all they can do until the swelling goes down and the pressure recedes. He'll probably have to have some cosmetic surgery later on to put everything back the way it should be."

Several smart remarks came to mind, but I let them pass. "At least he's stable."

"Thank you," Lex said, her red-rimmed eyes boring into mine. She didn't have to finish the sentence, her intent was plainly clear.

I shrugged. "I know we don't get along, but that's not important right now. Besides, he can be an ass, but he doesn't deserve that."

Lex raised her eyebrows and gazed out the window. Beside us, a woman with dark hair approached. She wore charcoal slacks and a blue blouse, a small handbag over her shoulder. Fairly attractive in an official sort of way, she easily picked us out of the cafeteria and walked over. "Alexa Borden?"

"Yes?" Lex said, twisting her head from the window and starting to rise. Across from her, I released my coffee cup and did the same.

"Detective Terra Watts, Missing Persons, CPD. You're in-laws told me where I could find you."

The statement was fairly open-ended and Lex merely nodded, unsure what to say.

"Can we talk?" Watts asked. Her manner wasn't exactly brusque, but she was making no efforts at sympathy either. Clearly she was a woman with a goal in mind.

At the moment, I appreciated that.

"Here's as good a place as any," Lex said, sliding over and pushing her chair towards Watts.

Chapter Five

"I'm sorry, you are?" Watts asked, her eyes on me, her implication very clear.

"I'm her brother," I replied, doing my best not to appear hostile in any way but making no attempt to leave either.

Watts ran her eyes over me, then flicked them to my sister. Lex extended her hands out and rested them on my forearm. "I called him last night. He drove here straight from Wyoming to be with me."

Watts brought her eyes back to me and let them linger a moment, finally deciding whatever question was being debated in her head. Once she determined I wasn't a threat in any way, as she continued forward without delay. "As I'm sure you folks have heard before, the first forty-eight hours in a kidnapping are the most important. Anything beyond that and the odds of finding your daughter go down tremendously."

My eyes shifted to the wall across from us in hopes of finding a clock. There was none. I had a rough idea of what time it was, but wanted to be certain.

"Normally in these situations a ransom call is made within the first couple of hours. I assume you haven't received anything since you spoke to our officers last night?"

"No," Lex said, twisting her head. Her hands were still on my forearm and I could feel them digging into my sleeve.

"Have you checked your messages at home? Might there be something waiting for you there?"

Again Lex turned her head. "We don't have a home phone. We each carry cell-phones. I haven't gotten anything, I don't know about Ricky."

"Do you know where his phone is? Can you access it?" Watts was now in full-on investigator mode, rattling off questions like a cross-examining attorney.

"Best guess would be it's still in his car in the driveway," Lex said. "I've been here since everything happened."

"Hmm. I can contact the cell-phone company and have them access his account. We really need to know if anything's been called in."

Lex lowered her eyes to the table and nodded. "Absolutely."

"What if it hasn't?" I asked.

Watts jerked her head to face me, almost incredulous that I dared speak. "Excuse me?"

Putting on my best huckster voice I repeated, "If there hasn't been a ransom demand, what happens then?"

Again she stared at me as if I had an arm growing from my forehead. "Trust me, there *will* be a ransom demand, especially given the high-profile of the family."

Already I could feel my initial opinion on this woman shifting towards disdain. "If these people wanted money, wouldn't they have gone through the house? Seeing as how both parents were unconscious in the front yard?"

Watts shifted and squared her shoulders at me. "I appreciate your concern, but I know what I'm doing. Taking a television is nothing compared to the type of money these people will likely be seeking."

I let Watts continue to appraise me like an idiot, saying nothing. My blood pressure pounded in my ears and my temper was a fraction of an inch below the surface, but I swallowed them both. Her attention needed to be on Annie, not me. "I'm sorry, just worried about my niece."

Her face softened a bit around the eyes. "I can appreciate that. I don't mean to come off as harsh, you'd be surprised how many people try to tell me how to do my job."

I pressed my lips together and nodded, but said nothing.

Watts turned back to Lex and produced a business card from what looked like somewhere up her sleeve. She held it between her thumb and index finger and slid it across the table. "Unfortunately, until they make contact, all we can do is wait. With no eyewitnesses and no leads, we wouldn't even know where to begin."

Lex's eyes went glassy again, but she said nothing. Instead, she released my arm with one hand and dragged the business card over.

"I'll contact the phone company and get access to your husband's voicemail records. In the meantime, if you hear from anybody or if anything potentially helpful comes to mind, you get in touch with me."

Lex nodded, her eyes glazed over as she stared down at the card pressed flat in front of her. Watts nodded once to me and rose, already reaching for her cell-phone as she backed away.

"Wait, that's it?" Lex asked, her head twisting to the side towards Watts. The words stopped Watts cold in her tracks, her back remaining to us for several long moments before she turned. When she did she remained several yards away from the table, making no effort to close the gap or hide the trace of annoyance on her face.

"Look, sadly, over 2,000 children go missing per day in this country. While I'd like to tell you there was a standard protocol for making sure every last one of them gets home at night, there isn't. All we can do is work with what we're given, which in this case isn't very much."

I could feel my blood reach a near boiling point beneath my skin, but kept my face impassive. Beside me I was expecting the same result from my sister, who instead seized on the volume of children taken. Again her eyes went glossy with moisture.

Content that her point was made, Watts spun on a heel and stomped through the empty cafeteria. She moved fast, out of haste to get the cell-phone trace began or just to get away from us I didn't know.

Lex waited until the clacking of her shoes against the tile floor died away before again facing front. Her eyes remained trained down at the table, her body leaning in close towards me. "Thank you for not losing your cool."

"More important things at hand right now."

"It doesn't sound like they're doing a whole lot," Lex said, her voice low but even.

"No," I agreed, shaking my head. "What gets me is she acts like a victim here. The kidnappers really screwed them by not leaving a sign with names and addresses for her to follow."

Lex winced at the word *kidnappers* and I instantly regretted using it.

"You have any ideas?" she whispered.

Drawing my coffee back over in front of me, I took a long pull. It had cooled considerably, but it was still caffeinated and that was really all I cared about at the moment. "A few."

"I'm listening," Lex said, raising her eyes to meet mine.

"What if this wasn't about money at all?" I asked. I wasn't sure of the best way to broach the topic, so I just threw it out there.

Lex's eyes narrowed, but she said nothing.

"I mean, what if there isn't going to be a ransom demand? What if Annie was what they wanted all along?"

"You mean..." Lex began, her voice drifting off as her eyes darted around. Her face quivered as she tried to hold it back, the floodgates finally giving way. I leaned forward as far as the table would allow and drew her into my shoulder, her sobs muffled against my jacket.

"I'll find her Lex. Or I'll die trying."

Lex tried to speak, but when no words came out, she settled for shaking her head against me. We remained locked that way for several long minutes, her entire body wracked with quiet sobs. When she finally pulled back, her eyes were puffy and her cheeks wet.

"What time is it?"

Lex shoved back the sweatshirt sleeve and checked her watch. "Half past four."

I did the math in my head, accounting for the two hour time difference between Wyoming and Ohio. "That puts us at a little over twenty-one hours and counting."

Again my sister closed her eyes, silent tears streaking her cheeks. "Do whatever you have to do O. Just please find my little girl."

I slid my hands out and wrapped them around both of hers. For a moment I left them there before squeezing softly and rising, the legs of my chair scraping the tile beneath me. "Do you have any cash on you? I need to pay someone a visit and I can't go empty handed."

Chapter Six

Very, very few things in life made me nervous. When you've been as many places and lived through as many battles, both literally and figuratively, as I have, things don't get to you anymore. It's not that you become unfeeling, more like unblinking.

Maybe it was the fact that this time the stakes were much higher. Maybe it was the images of my battered sister and her broken husband that kept running through my mind. Maybe it was knowing the police weren't going to be much help. Or maybe it was my sitting out in front of the Orient Correctional Facility for the first time since walking away six and a half years ago.

Whatever it was, I was nervous as hell.

Lex's fifty bucks turned into three cartons of Marlboro Blacks. I sat in the parking lot and tore into the cartons one at a time, emptying them into the paper bag they gave me at the supermarket. Once inside, they would open the cartons anyway to make sure I hadn't doctored anything and the sight of a haphazard pile looks a lot bigger in the bottom of a bag.

Don't ask me how I know either one of those things.

Working another stick of gum into my mouth, I rolled the top of the bag shut and sat it on my lap. Through the front windshield I could see the prison staring back at me, the one place on Earth I swore I'd never go again. I shifted my eyes down to the clock on the dash, another forty-five minutes gone.

This was going to be miserable.

My truck door gave a loud squawk as I shoved it open and stepped out, my head down as I went straight for the front door. I'd never visited the prison before, though I'd seen it enough times from the inside to know how it worked.

A bored twenty-something with a bull neck and thick mid-section glanced up as I walked in, a Sports Illustrated spread across his lap. Beside him was a standard issue metal detector, much like the ones found in every airport in the country. On the opposite end of it was another guard with a matching build and look of boredom. The only discernible difference was a tattoo on the back-end guard's forearm. "Visiting hours are over in half an hour."

I couldn't tell if he was just letting me know or trying to warn me off, but I didn't care either way. "That's fine. I only need a few minutes."

The young man rolled his eyes and dropped the magazine to the floor beside him. The stool he was sitting on sighed as he swung himself to his feet and motioned towards the end of the metal detector. With one hand he reached to the side and flipped a switch, the faded rubber conveyor belt grinding to life. "Place the sack and any metal objects you have on the belt. Your boots and belt buckle too there Tex."

I could hear Tattoo snicker on the opposite end, but I remained impassive. It was obvious they were trying to goad me, but I wasn't about to let them.

Not here of all places for sure.

One by one I dropped the objects on the conveyor and stepped through in my socks. Tattoo watched to make sure the detector didn't pick up on anything and asked, "Prisoner's name?"

"Roosevelt Hobbes," I said, running my belt back around my waist and cinching it shut.

In front of me Tattoo cast his eyes to his partner. He unrolled the top of my sack and dug a meaty hand through it, grunting as he went. "Is he expecting you?"

"No."

"Visiting hours are over in twenty-seven minutes," the guard up front announced.

"I only need a few minutes," I replied, sliding my boots back on over my feet.

Making a scene of sighing heavily, Tattoo unclipped a radio from his belt and made a call for Roosevelt Hobbes. A garbled response came back. Tattoo grunted and looked over at me. "Who the hell are you?"

"Tell him it's O."

Tattoo made a face and relayed the information. A moment later the radio squealed out another response. Tattoo pulled it back and looked at it before returning it to his belt. "Go on in. He'll be down in a minute."

I nodded at each of them in turn and took up the sack. The hallway from the entrance was short and narrow, ending abruptly in a small holding room. The entire room was sterile white with a half dozen round folding tables and a handful of chairs for each of them strewn about. A man in an orange jumpsuit sat at one table on the far side leaning in close to a woman and two small children. None of them even glanced my way as I walked in and took a seat in the opposite corner.

All four walls in the room were lined with windows, all reflecting the room back onto itself. Behind every one was no doubt another bored guard, waiting for a disturbance that never came.

Bile began to rise in the back of my throat as I sat and looked around the room, bad memories coming at me thick and fast. I begged Mama not to come the entire five years I was in this place, but she wouldn't hear of it. Every Sunday like clockwork.

Easily the worst half-hour of my week.

A door on the opposite end of the room jerked open, jarring me from the memories. Through it shuffled Roosevelt Hobbes, his hands and feet in shackles. Like every inmate in Orient, he wore an orange jumpsuit, though the similarities stopped there. A salt-and-pepper afro stood out several inches from his head, framing a round face with a bushy moustache and thick eyebrows. I used to joke with him that he was the black Albert Einstein.

"O," he said as he moved forward, a half-smile on his face. He was older than me by at least two decades, though I couldn't tell how much older because the man hadn't aged a day since I met him. Continuing to shuffle he stepped forward and extended a hand, shaking mine with the same heavy grip I remembered.

"Hey Rosie. Thank you so much for seeing me like this."

"Hell, thank you for coming to see me," he said, motioning towards the table.

I grabbed the bag from the table and slid it in front him as we took our seats across from one another. The half smile reappeared as he unrolled the top and peered down inside. "Are those Marlboro Blacks?"

"I'm told they're brand new on the market, figured you might be able to stretch them a little further."

The half-smile spread into a full grin. In prison, cigarettes were currency. In Orient, Rosie was often the banker. "I definitely will. Thank you."

I nodded, but said nothing.

Rosie pushed the sack out in front of him and said, "I've been getting your letters. Everybody that gets out of this shithole claims they'll write, but you actually do it."

He was right, on both counts. "You were a friend to me when I really needed it. I appreciated it."

"It wasn't quite that one-sided," Rosie said. "As I recall, having a white boy around came in handy a few times."

It was my turn to smile. He wasn't wrong about that either.

"So what's going on?" he asked. "Your last letter you mentioned you probably wouldn't be passing through until the fall. You look like hell and I can't imagine what it took to make you step foot back in this place."

Unabashedly straight-forward. Vintage Rosie.

"You're right," I said. There was no point trying to bullshit the man, he'd see right through it anyway. "I need a favor."

Rosie nodded his enormous afro softly for me to continue, but said nothing.

"It's my niece. She's been kidnapped."

The old man's face remained motionless, his features like stone. I knew the far-off look in his eyes well enough to know his mind was racing, but he wouldn't give away a thing. "How long ago?"

"Twenty-eight hours."

"Isn't your brother-in-law some hotshot quarterback? There been any ransom demands yet?"

I shook my head. "He started at Ohio State, but hurt his neck his senior year and never played again. They do alright, but definitely not high-level ransom stuff. Not that a call has come in anyway."

"Hmm," he said, rocking his head back. "What are the police doing?"

"Not a damn thing," I spat, the words coming almost too fast.

"Hmm," he said again, adding, "you'll get that. What are you doing?"

I slid my eyes to the family in the opposite corner, then along the wall of reflective glass across from us. I could almost still see myself as a nineteen year old sitting in this room, my crying mother beside me looking back in the reflections. "You're the first person I came to. You always said nothing happened in Columbus without you knowing about it."

The old man looked hurt. "O, you don't really think I had something to do with this do you?"

"Not at all," I said, shaking my head in earnest so he knew I meant no disrespect. "What I meant was, is there anybody in town in the business of moving kids?"

Again Rosie rocked his head back, his dark eyes intent, drilling into me. "You're thinking about going after them."

"I'm not going after anybody, I'm just going to find my niece."

Rosie leaned in and dropped his voice several decibels. "You've already got five years on your sheet. You do something again, and your next stint will make this last one look like a Caribbean cruise."

I matched the old man's stare, my face a mask of determination. "She's two years old, the purest thing in my life. Hell, maybe the only pure thing in my life. I'm going to find her."

The two of us held that pose for several long seconds before Rosie grunted and nodded his head. He leaned to the side and motioned towards the window behind him, moving his hand as if writing in the air. A moment later the door swung open, a guard stepped through and dropped a nub of a pencil onto the table between us.

Rosie tore a flap of brown paper from the sack and scribbled out a quick message.

"Take this to my nephew. His name is Troy Hobbes and he runs the operation for us now. Give him this note and tell him I sent you. He'll be able to help."

Rosie folded it twice and extended it towards me. I didn't open it to read, and I wouldn't. If he said this would get me in, that was good enough for me.

He also didn't bother to mention an address. It was withheld in case anybody was listening, and because I already knew where the place was. Though I'd never been there, he'd told me many times before. Despite that, it was still very necessary I went to see him first out of respect. "Thank you so much Rosie. I owe you."

Rosie shook his head and raised a hand as if I was talking crazy. "Just keep those letters coming. I enjoy hearing about your life out on the ranch."

"Will do," I promised, standing and extending my hand. "Let me know how those Blacks work out."

Rosie stood and returned the shake, but ignored the comment. "It's damn good to see you O, I'm awfully sorry about your niece."

Without another word we parted, both headed in opposite directions.

Chapter Seven

The backlight on the truck's control panel illuminated the clock's numbers against the dash as I drove south on I-270, telling me it was right at six-thirty. Counting backwards from my conversation with Lex a few hours before, the clock in my head reset to nineteen hours.

And counting.

The spring sun was well on its way towards the horizon, but still a couple inches of orange remained visible as I pushed south. Late day rays threw themselves across the highway, bouncing off the windshields of passing cars. Again I was working at the nail on my left ring finger, ignoring the taste of blood in my mouth. On my lap sat Rosie's note, the same ball of barbed wire just inches from it in my stomach.

In the southwest corner of Columbus I exited the freeway and wound my way through the suburb of Grove City, one of many non-descript bergs situated around the outer belt. The same array of chain restaurants and convenience stores greeted me as I passed through, indiscernible from a thousand other suburbs across the country. Nearly all of the restaurants were full with clumps of people standing outside the door waiting to get in, the Saturday night rush in full effect.

With the exception of another jolt of caffeine, there wasn't a food on the planet that sounded appealing at the moment.

Two miles off the freeway, on the outer edge of Grove City, sat a small airstrip. As late as the eighties, FedEx used the strip for hauling all cargo going in and out of the city, but they had long ago switched their operations to Port Columbus on the other side of town. At the time, the strip was remote enough and innocuous enough that nobody thought to tear it down.

Now, nobody really cared.

The place looked pretty desolate as I pulled off the road and through the main drive. A rusted chain link fence ran the perimeter and a gate sagged open on either end. A handful of small outbuildings dotted the place, most of them in shambles and badly in need of a coat of paint. Foot tall weeds poked up through cracks in the pavement and slapped at the undercarriage my truck as I eased through.

The row of outbuildings extended for a couple of hundred yards, offset by a crumbling runway extended out to the right. At the very back of the grounds sat what I guessed used to be the shipping warehouse for the strip. A faded FedEx logo was still stenciled on one side of it. There were no cars parked anywhere, the only signs of life being dull light poking through a pair of second floor windows.

The ball of barbed wire grew even larger in my stomach as I pulled up in front of the only door I could see and climbed out. I made a point to show my hands at all times as I walked to the door, knocked three times and took a step back. Above me I could hear the small video camera overlooking the door turn to focus on my face, but I kept my eyes locked straight ahead.

Minutes crawled by. Sweat formed in the small of my back and along my upper lip, my heart pounding in my chest. I had no idea what I was about to walk into, but I had a feeling it wouldn't be friendly. Not at first anyway.

Three minutes turned to four and then five before I could hear the slow turning of a heavy metal latch behind the door. A moment later it creaked open, nothing but darkness within.

Out of it extended the end of a double-barreled shotgun.

"What do you want white boy?" a deep voice asked. I couldn't see a single thing inside, but he sounded like a very pissed off Ving Rhames.

A lump settled in my throat as I stared at the shotgun. At this range there was no chance of him missing. At this range, there was no chance that thing wouldn't separate my shoulders from my waist. "I'm here to see Troy Hobbes."

The voice paused a second, making no attempt to lower the gun. "What business you got with T-bone?"

"His uncle Roosevelt sent me." Slowly I raised my hands and widened my fingers, then reached into my right jacket pocket. Using just two fingers I pulled the note from it and extended it forward into the darkness.

A meaty paw snatched the note away, almost taking half my hand with it. "Wait here," the voice said before pulling the barrel of the gun back into the darkness and slamming the door shut.

My heart rate receded slightly as I waited. I wasn't shot on sight, which gave me a chance. I just had to trust Rosie's note would do the rest.

He didn't disappoint.

The second time the door opened, I was greeted by a man instead of a gun. I was only half right on my earlier assessment. I thought he sounded like Ving Rhames, but this man was much, much larger than that. He was dressed entirely in black, with boots, cargo pants and a tank top. A stack of necklaces hung from his neck. He looked to weight somewhere in the high two-hundreds, all of it thick muscle.

I was right about him sounding extremely pissed off.

"T-bone will see you," he said, standing aside so I could walk through. He still held the shotgun, though he now gripped it by the barrel and let it swing by his side. He motioned with his head towards an office on the second floor, the source of the light visible from outside. "Top of the stairs," he said, slamming the door closed and wrenching the lock as I stepped through.

"Thank you," I mumbled and walked straight for the metal stairwell bolted to the side of the wall. I kept my eyes facing forward as I walked, trying not to notice the rest of the warehouse. Around me I could see rows of televisions, stereos and DVD players, all stacked high on pallets along the walls. Between them were dozens of high-end cars parked in uniform rows.

Most of the room was shrouded in darkness, the place still for the night. During the day, I imagined it resembled a small city in there.

The metal stairs groaned as I ascended them, my boots scraping against their grated tops. I counted out two dozen of them before I reached the top landing, paused, and knocked on the closed door in front of me.

"Come in."

Gently I pushed the door open and stepped inside, forced to squint by the blinding light of the office. In front of me was an enormous oak desk that extended nearly the length of the office. On either side were two black leather loveseats, both of them holding a carbon copy of Ving Rhames downstairs, complete with shotguns.

Behind the desk sat a young black man with closed cropped hair and a thin goatee. He too wore a collection of chains around his neck, accented by diamond studs in either ear. Best guess, he couldn't have been more than mid-twenties in age as he sat and stared at me.

I could see the note spread open on his desk and waited for him to speak first.

"This note says you're a friend of my uncle's."

It was definitely a statement and not a question, but I nodded anyway. "Yes."

"And that you need a favor."

Another statement. "Yes."

He gazed at each of his associates and said, "If my uncle says you're cool, we're cool. That's the only reason you're standing here right now. As far as a favor goes, I can only do what I can do."

"That's fair," I said. And it was. I couldn't ask anybody to stick their neck out on my behalf. "I'm actually only looking for information."

Again, he glanced at each of his cohorts. "What kind of information?"

The first real question he'd asked since I'd been there. Things seemed to be moving okay so far. I decided to push the boundaries a tiny bit. "Your uncle tells me you guys keep a tight finger on what happens around town. You ever come across anybody moving kids?"

Troy made a face. "Moving kids? What the hell are you talking about?"

"Kidnapping them. Selling them off."

The look slowly slid from his face. It became a blank slate for several long seconds as he stared at me. "You see anything downstairs when you walked up?"

My pulse ticked up a bit. I wasn't sure where he was going with this. "Not really. It was pretty dark." I wanted to seem as non-threatening as possible, but I knew lying to him would only piss them off. "Few electronics, couple of cars."

Troy gave me an apprising look, nodded imperceptibly. "Exactly. That's what we do here. We don't mess with no kids."

"I meant no disrespect."

The air pulled out of the room for a moment as he studied me. "Why you asking about kidnappings?"

"My niece was taken yesterday. I have a very small window to try and find her. I was hoping you guys might be able to tell me where to start looking."

Again Troy consulted each of his workers. Neither one gave any indication of even being alive except to occasionally blink as they stared daggers into me.

"When my parents died, Unc took me in as his own. For him, I'm going to help you, but I'm going to tell you right now it won't seem like help when you get there."

My eyes narrowed, but I said nothing.

"The guy you're looking for is a cat named Merric. Works out of a warehouse in Reynoldsburg."

"That's who's running the kids?" I asked.

Troy shook his head from side to side. "He's only a middle man. Pure snatch and grab guy. Sends them to

Cleveland or Cincinnati, that's where the real brains to the operation are."

As he spoke, Troy leaned forward and scribbled an address on a corner of Rosie's note. "But like I said, you won't get in there the way you did here."

I accepted the bit of paper from him and asked, "How so?"

"Let's just say nobody gets in to see him without a little initiation first."

What that meant I had no idea, but if Troy was taking the time to warn me, it couldn't be good. "Thank you."

Troy nodded and said, "Just so you know, Merric and I aren't exactly friends. It wouldn't be in your best interests to mention my name to him."

I nodded in understanding.

"And to be clear, if you did, friends with Unc or not, our next meeting wouldn't be quite so civil."

Again, I nodded in understanding.

Chapter Eight

The world outside grew darker by the minute. Inside the truck, the lights of the dash now glowed back at me. The speedometer said I was pushing seventy as I rounded the southern outer belt of Columbus towards Reynoldsburg. The clock pointed out it was almost eight.

Seventeen hours and change remaining.

I wasn't entirely sure where the address Troy gave me was, but I knew the street name well enough to know where to start looking. The first twenty-three years of my life were all spent in the greater Columbus area, albeit the last five of those I wasn't exactly out and about much. There are certain locations you come to know even if you've never seen them.

Diamore Road was one of those places, but not in a good way. The kind of place that if you found yourself there, you knew you'd made a wrong turn somewhere.

And here I was driving directly into it on a Saturday night.

When Lex first called me, I did the math and decided that driving was the obvious choice. Much less hassle, and I'd arrive in the same amount of time. Not to be discounted though was the fact that in my truck, I could bring along a few extra supplies I might need along the way.

As I drove, I inventoried the list in my head.

Behind the front bench seat was a Winchester 30.06, a beautiful model I purchased in Cheyenne to hunt antelope with. Thank God for Wyoming and its lax gun laws.

In the glove box was a Luger .9mm the ranch gave me to carry when riding fence lines. So far I'd only had to use it once to fire on a rattlesnake, but I knew it was sighted in up to fifty yards. Anything past that was a crap shoot.

Common sense told me I couldn't walk in to see Merric carrying either of those. I pushed them from my mind and went on down the list, making notations of the more primitive weapons I had on hand.

In the bed of the truck was my oversized toolbox, complete with a chisel, a couple of screwdrivers and a pipe wrench. All solid weapons in a jam, but nothing I could carry in with me.

That left only the tire iron stashed under the seat and the ceramic switchblade I'd had nearby every day since leaving prison. Press button release with a four inch blade, it was made somewhere in Germany and easily passed through any metal detector on the planet. So far the only blood it had ever drawn was my own, an accident that occurred once while opening a Christmas package from my mother. It was the first time I'd ever used the knife and I didn't expect it to tear through the package tape quite so easily. One good tug sent it straight through and back against my leg, gashing my thigh and ruining a perfectly good pair of Wrangler's.

Lesson learned.

I could feel the sweat again return to my face and back as I hooked a left onto Diamore and headed north towards the interior of the city. With a shift of my weight I pulled the knife from the jacket of my coat and slid it into the top of my sock. I dropped the leg of my jeans back down around it and could feel the elastic holding it in place between my calf and boot.

The numbers on the buildings slowly ticked by as I held the address up and looked for the number Troy gave me. Based on the street I was on and the place I had just been I paid special attention to the dark corners along the roadway, thinking I was looking for a warehouse tucked away in a shady back alley.

What I found instead was nothing short of an Atlantic City casino.

The warehouse was lit up like a Christmas tree. A series of neon lights announcing various alcoholic offerings lined the windows, the parking lot packed with automobiles ranging from decrepit Pintos to high-end Escalades. A steady stream of people, as varied in their appearances as the cars they drove, all moved together towards the front door.

Sliding into the back of the lot I checked the address and craned to see the building numbers on either side of me. I definitely had the right place.

My heart beat receded for a moment before picking back up again. This wasn't what I was expecting at all. On one hand, there were plenty of witnesses around to whatever might be lying inside. On the other, there could be many, many more enemies than I anticipated.

Easing the truck into the back corner of the lot, I checked to make sure the knife was still wedged in place and climbed out. Ignoring the stares of people around me, I fell into the flow moving towards the front door.

Two men standing a few inches above five and a half foot tall manned the front door, each of them standing several feet in width. Both wore ill-fitting suits and dark sunglasses, their faces locked straight ahead as people passed by. Between them was a set of double doors standing open, spilling light and sound out into the parking lot.

I wasn't sure how to approach the situation, but this seemed like as good an opportunity as any. I peeled myself off to the side from the flow of foot traffic and slid to a stop next to one of the bouncers. Up close I could see he was much younger than I originally thought and his face was pockmarked with acne scars. No doubt the result of years of steroid abuse.

"Excuse me," I said, pulling to a stop several feet away from him. The man made no effort to turn and face me. "Excuse me."

The man continued to gaze straight ahead, no indication that he even knew I was there. If not for how damaged his skin was, I might have thought him made of wax.

It was time to try a different tactic. I moved closer so that my face was less than a foot from his. "I need to see Merric."

For the first time, the man moved. A muscle twitched in his neck, followed by a small arch in his left eyebrow. Still he made no attempt to respond or even look at me.

Instead, he raised his right wrist to his mouth and said, "We've got one for Peka." Just as fast he dropped his hand back down and grasped it in front of him.

"Excuse me..." I asked, confusion of my face.

A moment later a man emerged from the double doors, the only one moving against the flow of traffic. He wore a black pinstriped suit with a pink shirt beneath it opened at the collar. Thick dark hair was combed straight back against his head and his face was clean shaven. He extended a hand to me as he approached, his dark features shaped into a broad smile.

"Welcome, welcome," he said, shaking my hand vigorously. His voice had the slightest tinge of a European accent, somewhat masked by faux enthusiasm. "My name is Vincent. Please, come with me."

Never in my life had I been to Las Vegas, but the interior of the building resembled what I'd always imagined Sin City to look like. The entire first floor was a cornucopia of slot machines and gaming tables, sights and sound spilling in all directions. A wide staircase stood before us, leading up to a second floor that housed much the same.

Massive throngs of people grouped up around nearly all the tables. Many plainly wore how well they were doing on their faces. The ones that weren't doing well were even more obvious.

Vincent noticed my jaw go slack as we walked and smiled. "Quite an impressive sight, no?"

"For sure," I mumbled. "I had no idea anything like this existed in Columbus."

"Technically, it doesn't," Vincent replied. "But we're only breaking the law if the law shows up to say so, right?" he added with a wink. The implication was readily apparent.

I nodded, but said nothing.

"So you are here for Peka?" Vincent asked, apprising me as we swung by the lights of the casino and exited through a metal door along the wall.

"I have no idea what Peka is," I answered. "I merely asked to speak with Merric."

A small smile grew on Vincent's face. "Same thing."

I made no attempt to hide my confusion. "What the hell's going on here?"

Vincent stopped and pointed to a second door in front of us. It was painted entirely in black save a red X through the center. "Go through that door and wait. It will take a few minutes for us to get things ready."

"Get what things ready? What is all this?" I asked. Apprehension welled inside me. I was in no position to lash out right now, but every nerve in my body told me something was afoot.

Vincent again smiled and held his hands in front of him. "Do not worry my friend. Right through that door and Merric will see you shortly."

This was bad. There had to be another way to find what I was looking for. I was of no use to Lex or Annie dead. "Um, maybe I should just go. Merric seems like a very busy man."

The smile slid from Vincent's face and he pulled back the left tail of his jacket to reveal a snub-nose revolver tucked into the waistband of his slacks. "Right through that door. Merric will see you shortly."

Chapter Nine

A narrow hallway extended away from the door. The walls were made of cinder block, the floor and ceiling from concrete brushed smooth. Every few feet a single bulb hung down, housed in a wire cage that threw a random pattern of shadows across everything.

The door slammed shut behind me and a thunderous echo reverberated off the walls. I already knew the door would be locked tight, but I turned to check just the same. Not even a doorknob stared back at me.

This was very bad.

My boots made a knocking sound against the floor as I walked forward, the hallway sloping downward before me. With each step a dull buzzing grew in the distance, starting almost inaudibly and rising in volume. The ground continued to fall away until I was certain I'd descended over a story underground before leveling off.

Ahead of me loomed a second door, this one much different than the one I'd just passed through. It looked to be made entirely of wood and had cross pieces in the shape an X on the bottom with several horizontal slats spaced evenly across the top. Just a day before I was back in Wyoming staring at cows through a similar gate, now I was in a casino on the worst street in Columbus doing the exact same thing. Something told me whatever was on the other side of this one was going to be a lost more hostile than a bovine.

This was really not good.

The gate in front of me grew ever closer as the sound grew louder. It escalated from a hive of bees into an anxious crowd, the distinct din of voices drifting in through the wooden slats.

I pressed myself tight against one side of the hallway and crept up to it. With a jut of my head I gazed between the top two slats to see the gate opened into a wide earthen ring. Straight across from me was a matching wooden gate with polished concrete walls poured in a circle connecting them on either side. The floor of the ring was soft dirt, the ground lying in uneven humps.

Above the ring, at least a dozen rows of bleachers extended straight up like some sort of gladiator arena. Already they were over half full of people, with more streaming in by the second.

It didn't take a genius to see what was about to happen.

I'd never been one to back down from a scrap. In high school football I was so willing to throw down, the coaches changed my nickname to KO, short for knockout. In prison, well, nobody gets out alive without having been through a few scuffles.

That being said, I had no absolutely no interest in fighting. Best case scenario, I beat down whoever the hell Peka was and royally piss of Merric. Worst case, I end up face down in the soft dirt of the ring. Neither one would help find Annie.

"Ladies and gentleman," a voice boomed over a microphone so loud it bounced through my tiny hallway. It was thick with a Gaelic accent which I guessed belonged to Merric.

"We have a very special treat for you here this evening. Peka has been issued a challenge!"

A shower of cheers rang out from the nearly-full bleachers. Many stomped their feet on the wooden rails beneath them, producing a deep rumbling sound. Others whistled or clapped their hands overhead.

"Our challenger tonight comes to us fresh off the farm and is currently listed as a fifteen-to-one underdog. Please put your hands together and welcome Cowboy!" As he finished the introduction, Kid Rock's *Cowboy* came on over the loud speaker. The volume was at full blast, but it failed to drown out a chorus of boos as the wooden gate swung open in front of me.

The knot was firmly back in my stomach. For them to have already pegged me as a fifteen-to-one underdog after a brief walk through the casino floor meant I either looked like an easy victim or Peka was a force to be reckoned with.

In my boots I measured nearly six and a half feet tall and weighed 210. I did not look like an easy victim.

I gave one last glance around the hallway to make sure there was no other way out before stepping onto the arena floor.

As soon as I cleared the gate it swung back into place, leaving me standing very much alone under the blinding lights of the arena. Above I could see people continuing to boo, many making exaggerated thumbs-down gestures while a few even laughed.

My gaze hardened as it swept around the room. I didn't want to fight, but if that's what it took to get to Merric and on to Annie, that's what I would do.

The time for concern was over.

"And his opponent, a man you all know and love, coming to us with a perfect nineteen and zero record...Peeee-kaaaa!" Merric called over the PA, his voice echoing through the hall. Instantly the crowd broke into pandemonium, chanting Peka's name again and again.

Across from me the gate swung open, revealing a darkened hallway. From deep within it a man slowly emerged, his enormous frame almost scraping the walls on both sides. My eyes bulged a bit as he stepped into the light of the ring, his stare locked on me.

The crowd went into a frenzy as Peka walked out to reveal a Samoan man standing just shy of six feet tall with a pointed nose and chin. Thick black hair was shaved into a Mohawk on top, the rest pulled back into a ponytail that disappeared somewhere down his back. A web of tribal tattoos covered both shoulders and one side of his face.

None of that bothered me. It was more the fact that he must have weighed somewhere close to four hundred pounds.

Overhead Peka's tribal entrance music came to a stop. Merric again took up the microphone and said, "The only rule here is the fight continues until one of you can't. Go!"

On cue the crowd shifted from mindless cheering to focused banter, lobbing comments and encouragement at the ring. I glanced down at my attire and instantly wished I was better equipped for a fight. My mind wandered over the knife tucked away in my boot, but I decided to leave it there for the time being. If I did somehow get out of here, I didn't want Merric to know I was coming to see him armed.

I did my best to keep my face impassive as I stared at Peka. In my mind I kept trying to conjure Annie's face and remind myself why I was there, but all I could manage was the twisted smile of the massive Islander as he cracked his knuckles and circled right.

So this was actually going to happen.

If prison taught me anything, it was to always err on the side of aggression. I matched Peka's circle for three steps before shuffling forward and snapping a hard left jab, followed by a quick 1-2 jab-cross combo.

All three punches landed square. None had any effect.

The noise of the crowd faded away as I shuffled backwards and came in again, shot out another jab followed by a hard hook. Both of these landed as well and the hook snapped his head to the side. When it came back around, his expression had changed from bemused to angry.

Angry can be good. Angry sometimes causes people to be overly aggressive. I only hoped he would do something I could take advantage of.

Again I retreated out of arm's reach and bounced on the balls of my feet. I could see venom welling in his face as he rolled his body into a fighting stance and charged towards me. I waited until he was just a couple feet away before springing straight forward into a roll and narrowly ducking under his thick outstretched arms. In one fluid movement, I rolled to my feet and aimed the toe of my boot at his ribs as hard as I could.

My boot slammed into his doughy abdomen, the blow producing little effect but to send a ripple through the thick belt of fat wrapped around him. Peka bent to the side and slammed his arm down across my calf, pinning my leg to his side. He grinned menacingly as he clutched it there and watched me hop on one foot.

He jerked forward to pull me off balance and swung in with a heavy overhand blow from the opposite side. Balled up, his hand was the size of a Thanksgiving turkey and I lowered my head to keep it from slamming into my nose.

Instead, it connected right at my hairline. I could feel blood running down the side of my face as I went down flat on my back. The lights above drifted out of focus for a moment before snapping back and a dull hum settled in my ear. Before I could move, Peka swung in hard with an open handed swat across my jaw that sent my face hard in the opposite direction. A plume of spittle and blood sprawled out across the dirt in front of me.

Time seemed to slow down. My head spun and I could feel blood dripping down my cheek and chin. Peka's massive legs stomped in a circle around me, no doubt playing to the crowd as I laid there. I forced myself to roll in two tight revolutions to the side and retook my feet, my head spinning as I stood.

Across the ring Peka had his back to me, his arms outstretched over his head. A renewed sense of purpose welled within me and I charged hard at his exposed spine and launched myself through the air. My shoulder slammed into him just below the kidneys and shoved him forward, his face meeting the concrete wall unceremoniously.

Peka turned and snarled at me, blood dripping from his nose. I hopped to my feet and swung a vicious left uppercut at him, the punch landing square across his cheek. The sound of bones popping rang out as it connected, both from his face and my hand. Stifling pain rippled through my arm as I stumbled backwards and my hand flopped uselessly by my side.

In a flash of speed I didn't expect from a man his size, Peka rushed forward and grabbed me by my shirt. Before I could move he hefted me over his head and launched me across the ring like I weighed nothing at all. My body smashed into the wooden gate I'd used just a few minutes before, wood splintering around me.

For several long seconds I remained on the ground as my body attempted to process what just happened while Peka stomped around and rubbed his broken jaw with a dour expression on his face.

Very slowly I rolled to all fours and stared at the floor beneath me as my eyes came back into focus. The knife tucked in my boot again entered my mind, but was replaced by the jagged piece of two-by-four pinned beneath my body.

I stayed on my knees, my focus on the board, as Peka marched around in the ring. I watched through my periphery as after a few seconds he tired of waiting for me to rise and moved for me, anticipation creeping in, waiting for him to stalk closer.

When his thick legs were just a few feet away, I grasped the makeshift weapon and shot forward. Holding it like a poker, I smashed the flat end of it up under his chin. The broken jaw

97

twisted grotesquely across his face as he stumbled back a few steps and his eyes began to flitter.

I shifted my grip down to that of a baseball bat and hefted it over my head, slamming it down flat against his forehead. Peka wobbled in place before dropping to his knees, his tremendous bulk bouncing in place as he settled into the dirt. With one quick step I shifted to the side and swung as hard as my hand would allow across his cheek.

The two-by-four splintered into a thousand pieces as pain coursed through my left arm. Blood and shards of wood fluttered into the air as Peka's eyes rolled up into his head and he fell to his side. A puff of dust rose around his enormous body as he lay in the center of the ring, unmoving.

I stumbled several steps, dropped to a knee and lowered a hand to the ground to steady myself. Above me the crowd of the sound of the arena returned, a mixed reaction of amazed delight and bettors angry at their loss.

While bent over, I slipped the knife from my sock into my left hand and stood. I made a show of letting the left hand appear useless as I stared up at the crowd, watching as they

showered cups and betting slips into the dirt around me.

Chapter Ten

The switchblade was palmed in my left hand, my right hand cupped around it as I followed Vincent up a back stairwell. Every few steps he glanced over me, his face somewhere between impressed and annoyed. My guess was he was a little of both.

On my end I focused my eyes straight ahead and kept walking. I made no effort to meet his gaze or even let him know I could feel his eyes on me. Instead I locked my jaw and followed, my head and hand both aching.

At the top of the stairwell was a single metal door. Vincent took out some sort of card and waved it in front of a sensor on the wall. A moment later the red light in the corner of it flipped to green and an internal lock released, the sound loud in the empty concrete stairwell. I made no effort to reach for it, keeping my hands folded in front of me and waiting for Vincent to pull it open.

Right now they thought my wounded body was essentially useless. Better to let them keep on believing it.

The door opened into a wide landing on the second floor. Oval in shape, the left side of the landing held a row of dark tinted windows looking out over the parking lot. With a quick glance I could see that more people were arriving by the second, cars now parked haphazardly along the road.

The right side of the landing was taken up by a single room. A cream colored wall bowed out halfway into the foyer, a wooden double door standing in the middle of it. The entirety of the foyer was decorated in red and gold, the colors swirled into a pattern on the carpet and mixed in several tapestries hanging on the wall.

Not the colors I would have associated with a man named Merric, but what do I know about interior design?

My eyes scanned the room as we walked across the carpet. Two cameras hung above either stairwell entrance, but there were no guards in sight. This was a good thing.

Vincent wrapped twice on the wooden doors and paused, again glancing my way. "Bring him in," a voice barked from within.

A gust of icy air burst into my face as I stepped into an enormous office. Shaped like a football, one side was comprised of the wall I'd just passed through. On either side of the door were banks of video monitors, all of them showing different angles of the casino floor and parking lot, at least thirty or forty in total.

The opposite wall housed two enormous windows, separated by a gap of wall just wide enough to hold a framed Irish flag. Behind one window I could see the flashing lights of the casino floor below. Through the other, I could see a handful of men working to revive Peka in the arena floor.

An enormous desk sat in front of the Irish flag, the dark wood stretching nearly ten feet in length. On one end of it was an oversized computer monitor. On the other were the polished black boots of Merric.

There was nobody else in the room but us three. I guess he thought the cameras and the keycards were enough security for his inner sanctum.

Major advantage for me.

"Well then, that was quite a show you put on," Merric said. His accent was even thicker in person, some of the words almost indecipherable. He had medium length red hair spiked out from his head and skin so pale it was almost albino. He wore a purple dress shirt with a black vest and slacks. Several large rings adorned his fingers.

I nodded, but said nothing.

"Any man willing to go through all that must really wish to speak to me."

I considered the question. I couldn't give a damn about speaking to him, I just needed information I knew he had. "Yes, sir."

Merric smiled at my use of the word sir. "And what's your name?"

"Cowboy will do," I said. If he really wanted to know it wouldn't take long to find out, but I wasn't going to offer up that information if I didn't have to.

The smile faded just as fast. "Normally I like to know with whom I'm speaking, but we can do it that way if you'd prefer. What can I do for you Cowboy?"

The next words out of my mouth would no doubt determine how much longer somebody in that room lived. I could sense Vincent move to just off my left shoulder while Merric continued to eye me. "I understand you're a man known to locate certain things from time to time."

"Depends on the things," Merric said.

"Children."

The word had the effect I intended. His face fell flat as he lowered one foot at a time to the floor. He leaned forward and rested his forearms on the desk and his voice dropped a decibel. "I don't know what it is you think you know, but I promise you've been misinformed."

Beside me, Vincent edge a little closer. Good. I needed him within arm's reach. I twisted my head at Merric. "I don't think so. The information came from a pretty reliable source. They tell me you're the guy I talk to about getting my hands on a kid."

Merric shifted his gaze to Vincent. "Jesus Vinny, you brought a damn cop in here. Take this asshole out."

Vincent moved to just a couple of feet away and went to grab me. "I'm not a cop for Christ's sake," I spat. "If I was a cop I'd have walked in here with a SWAT team and taken the place apart. I sure as hell wouldn't have wrestled around in the pit with that gorilla of yours."

Vincent stopped mid-movement and stared at Merric. He clearly wanted to obey his boss's demands, but found it hard to argue with my simple logic.

"If you're not a cop, you're a pedophile and I don't deal with your kind either. Meeting adjourned. Vincent, see his ass out of here," Merric said, leaning back in his chair and tossing a dismissive wave of his hand in my direction.

A surge of adrenaline burst through me as I pushed the knife into my right hand and pressed the blade release. I heard the familiar snap of the blade pop open and jammed it into the left side of Vincent's chest. No further parlay, no waving the blade around and trying to scare them.

Always err on the side of aggression. Besides, something told me these guys didn't scare easy.

The razor sharp ceramic blade slid through his suit and into his heart without opposition, buried clear to the hilt. Vincent's eyes bulged as a small rasp escaped his throat and he toppled over backwards. As he went, I released the knife and snatched the snub-nose from his waistband, twisting and holding it at arm's length towards Merric.

The entire altercation took less than five seconds. He didn't even have the chance to look surprised, let alone make a move.

"I'm not a cop and I'm damn sure not a pedophile."

Merric's slack jaw worked up and down several times. "That...he...you just killed my second-in-command."

"And you kidnapped my niece. I'd say we're even." For the first time since leaving the hospital, I had the upper hand in a situation. The feeling of empowerment was a welcome change.

Merric continued to stare at Vincent lying prone on the floor. His eyes stared vacant at the ceiling above as a small rose of blood crept outward from the knife handle protruding out of his chest. "You're dead. You're so fucking dead. I've killed men for a lot less than that."

"Does it look like I care?" I asked. His gaze shifted back to me and studied my face, still stained with blood.

"What do you want?" he asked.

"I want my niece."

"Does it look like I have her here?" Merric asked, fanning his hands on the desk and looking around. "I'm a business man for Christ's sake!"

I twisted the angle of the gun and shot a hole through his left hand. The sound of the revolver was nowhere near as loud as I feared in the small office, paling in comparison to Merric's pained screaming as he clutched his hand. Bits of the wooden desk dotted the front of his vest as blood dripped between his fingers. "You crazy son of a bitch, you shot me!"

"I broke my hand fighting in your little game down there. Again, we're even," I said. "I want my niece."

He continued to rock back and forth in his desk chair, moaning as he cradled his hand. "I don't have your damn niece you bastard!"

"But you know who does, and you're going to tell me."

"I'm not going to tell you anything," Merric, a renewed flash behind his eyes. "What I'm going to do is push the button under my desk and watch as my men come in here and tear you apart."

I took a hard step forward and thrust the gun out towards him. "I wouldn't recommend that."

He stared at the barrel of the gun and then at me, his gaze switching from one to another. He continued to cradle his hand in front of him and I could see his tongue slide out over his bottom lip.

Three full seconds passed before he lunged for the button.

The first shot caught him in the chest and launched him back into his chair as a look of shock filled his pasty features. "I...I..." he whispered.

"Shouldn't have messed with my family," I finished. The second shot was three inches removed from the first, slamming into his heart in the same place I stuck the knife in Vincent. He made no more sounds as he settled back into the chair, his eyes focusing on nothing as blood dribbled down the front of his vest.

I turned and did a quick scan of the cameras to make sure nobody was coming and slid around to the other side of the desk. Merric continued to stare into space as I pushed past him to the computer. With my right hand I reached out and snatched the pocket square from his vest and dropped it over the computer mouse. Holding it there I quickly scanned through the files on his desktop.

Three minutes of searching turned up nothing of use.

I left the pocket square where it laid and fished Merric's cell-phone out of his pocket. Thumbing through it, I went for his outgoing calls and saw a list of numbers originating in the 513 area code.

Cincinnati, just like Troy said.

I pressed end to clear the phone and started again, this time headed straight for the text messages. There were only three, but that was enough.

Once more I picked up the pocket square and wiped the snub-nose clean. I dropped it into the trash beneath the desk and retrieved my knife from Vincent's chest, wiped it clean on his suit and returned it to my sock. Something told me there wouldn't be a full investigation into this, but if there was I couldn't afford to leave a trail of fingerprints behind me.

I was definitely in the system. It wouldn't take them long to find me.

I opted for the same stairwell Vincent brought me up just ten minutes before. My feet hit the main floor on the far side of the casino and I moved quickly through the crowd for the front door. Several people stopped and stared at my busted face as I walked by. A few others even tossed token congratulations my way.

I did my best to mumble thank you's to them as I went, but I'm sure I missed a few.

The last person to offer congratulations was the steroid infused doorman as I stepped out into the night air. I didn't even pretend to acknowledge him as I made a direct line for my truck and put as much distance between me and Diamore Road as I could.

Chapter Eleven

The next thirty minutes passed in a blur. The first half of it was spent tearing through southern Columbus, hell bent on making sure I wasn't followed. By the time I could breathe easy that Merric's clan wasn't following me, I realized I had blown through three red lights and was pushing sixty on city streets.

On a Saturday night, that's practically asking for the cops to flag you down. I was an ex-con with a broken wrist, blood covering half of my face, a murder weapon stuffed in my sock and a truck full of guns I'd brought across state lines. The last half of the thirty minutes was spent as the slowest car on the freeway, checking every mirror to make sure I wasn't about to go back to jail.

Lucky for me, there weren't many cops out on the roads. Not so much for me, my trip to Merric's and back cost me almost two hours. It was ten o'clock. Evening had slipped well into night.

The lights of Sacred Heart Hospital still burned bright as I pulled into the parking lot. For such a late hour the lot was almost full and I parked in the same spot I'd used earlier in the day. I checked my reflection in the rearview mirror and considered trying to scrub the blood from my face, but decided to leave it.

I bypassed the intensive care unit, followed the signs to the emergency room and prayed for a thin crowd.

For the second time in twenty minutes, luck was on my side. A small handful of elderly people sat scattered around the waiting room, none of them in any visible trouble. I clutched my hand in front of me and limped up to the front counter where a harried looking woman in her mid-thirties sat pecking at a computer. Lank brown hair hung straight down to her shoulders, framing a thin face that appeared aged far beyond her years. She looked up as I approached and gasped. "Oh my, are you okay sir?"

I offered a small smile and said, "Got rear-ended getting off the freeway. Hit my head on the steering wheel, jammed my wrist trying to catch myself. I think it might be broken."

It wasn't a foolproof story, but it seemed plausible enough. There was no way anybody in there could refute it, and that's all I was concerned with.

The woman grabbed up two clipboards and shoved them my way, then pulled them back. She leaned in close and whispered. "Tell you what, why don't you follow me and you can fill these out while you wait to see the doctor?"

"Thank you so much," I whispered back. I even glanced out at the waiting room to let her know I was in on the ruse before following her to the back.

Two parallel hallways ran straight back from the nursing station, both of them full with patients. Most appeared to be parents there with sick children as the sound of their screaming filled the air. A few of the rooms housed elderly people hooked to breathing machines.

As we walked by one man was having nails removed from his calf. A doctor leaned in close with a pair of pliers and

114

pulled the long metal daggers out while a pair of orderlies held him down. Blood ran from the open wound as he threw his head back and howled in pain, thrashing against them.

Of everybody we passed, it was the only one I would even vaguely classify as an emergency.

The nurse led me back to the x-ray room and had a tech run a scan of my hand. As soon as they were done she took me to an empty bay and left me with the clipboards and the promise that a doctor would see me soon. I muttered my thanks and started in on the forms.

Soon turned out to be over half an hour before a middle-aged man with close cropped hair and a heavy beard of the same length burst through the curtain and into the room. He wore a striped tie loosened at the collar and a long white coat, the same as most every other physician in the country. He even had the matching set of dark circles under each eye to really look the part.

"Good evening, my name is Dr. Niedermeyer," the man said, thrusting a hand in my direction. His skin was soft and dry from years of scrubbing, the grip weak.

"Felix O'Connor," I said, returning the grip.

"Says here you were in an accident this evening," Niedermeyer said as he consulted the chart.

"Yeah," I offered, shaking my head. "Rear ended."

"Oh," he said without looking up. "Get one of those through here every couple of days it seems like. You ought to see what it looks like when there's a little rain out there."

"I bet," I managed, already wanting the encounter to end.

Neidermeyer rose, ducked outside the curtain and grabbed the x-rays from the plastic bin along the wall. He tugged out a large film from the envelope and held it up to the light, then tossed the envelope onto the bed beside me. He pulled a pen from his jacket pocket and used it as a pointer. "Yeah, you can see here that the second metacarpal is fractured. Looks like the break doesn't go clear through, which will keep us from having to reset it."

He fell silent and studied the film for another moment before stuffing it back in its envelope.

"So that's good news?" I asked.

116

"Well, you won't be flipping anybody off with your left hand for awhile, but yes," Neidermeyer said, "that's good news. Far less painful, far less swelling. I'll have one of the nurses put a cast on there for you and you'll be on your way."

"Thank you," I said to his back as he whisked out of the room.

I'm pretty sure he didn't actually look at me once the entire minute and a half he was there. If he did, he didn't seem to notice the lattice of blood covering half my face.

Another fifteen minutes passed in the silence of the small room. I found some gauze in a top drawer and ran some water from the sink. I used them to scrub my face until the gauze no longer came back pink, finishing just as a nurse came in pushing a small cart. Her dark black skin shined beneath the bright overhead lights and a nest of small, tight curls were showing signs of heavy graying. A pair of glasses with thick lenses hung from a chain around her neck as she shuffled in.

"You the guy with the broken hand?" she asked, her voice fatigued and graveled.

"Yes ma'am," I said, holding my hand up for her to see. Nearly two hours had passed since the break and my body's natural defenses had taken over. Bone marrow had leaked into the surrounding area and numbed up my entire hand. I knew it wouldn't be long before it hurt like hell again, but for the time being I was alright.

She nodded and pushed in the cart, piled high with thick strips of plaster and a pan of water, the same as I'd seen used before. It wasn't my first broken bone, odds were it wouldn't be my last.

Neither one of us said much as she worked. I watched as she wrapped my hand in heavy gauze and began applying the strips of plaster. It started to harden almost instantly, the heavy white wrapping encasing my hand to several inches past the wrist. I wasn't thrilled at the idea of losing mobility, but reasoned that the cast would provide more support than a broken hand ever could.

When she was done she piled the remnants of her work high on the cart and shuffled out, no doubt headed off to the next poor bastard that had spent his Saturday night fighting. I slid the insurance forms from the clipboards and showed myself out of the ER, but when I got to the front the nurse's station was empty.

I paused for a moment to wait for the nurse with the thin face to return. The same small cluster of elderly people sat in the holding area and the same children screamed down either hallway. While I stood there, I glanced up at the clock on the wall and realized another hour was already gone. Eleven o'clock, fourteen hours and counting.

Without a word, I stuffed the forms into my back pocket and disappeared. Nobody so much as glanced my way.

Chapter Twelve

Rather than try and find my way through the maze of hospital hallways from the emergency room to the intensive care unit, I walked outside and circled the building. The night air was cool against my skin and I made a mental note to grab my jacket from the truck next chance I got. Overhead only a handful of stars dotted the night sky, most of them blotted out by the ambient glow of the city.

I looked down at the new club attached to my left hand, slowly rotating it. The white plaster of the cast was now completely hardened and stretched from above my knuckles down past my wrist. I flexed the top half of each of my finger, the limited range of motion awkward as my hand tried to curve into a fist.

A stabbing pain rocked through my palm as I flexed the fingers, forcing me to relax the grip. The numbness was wearing off. I couldn't afford to take any real painkillers, but I'd ask Lex for something when I saw her.

My boots clomped against the concrete sidewalk as I swung around to the intensive care unit doors and entered. A young man not much older than twenty was seated at the nurse's station as I approached, his nose buried in a text book on the counter in front of him. "Can I help you?" he asked.

"Yeah, I was here earlier, I'm here to see Ricky Borden."

"I'm sorry, general visiting hours ended hours ago sir," the young man said, his voice pleasant and official. He had short dark hair gelled straight forward and wore light blue scrubs with a nametag that said Skip.

Definitely a male nurse in the making.

I took a sharp breath and slowly pushed it out. Skip was going to make me say something I really didn't want to.

"I'm family."

He gave me a quick once over, from my clothes to the cast to the bruises I was sure dotted the side of my face, and nodded slowly. "You were here earlier, so you know where they are?"

"I do," I said, already sliding off to the left. If that was supposed to be some sort of test, it was weak at best.

I didn't wait for him to say another word as I pushed down the hallway. Everywhere I looked there seemed to be another clock reminding me what time it was. My pace unconsciously picked up, my boots the only sound through the deserted corridor.

The harsh sterile look and feel of the hospital receded under the dimmed evening lighting. I could see patients sleeping in their rooms as I passed and picked out a few family members sitting quiet beside them. Every one of them wore the same tired expression of worry, the trials of the day etched on their faces.

I prayed Lex didn't look the same, but knew she probably did. It was the same way we all looked years before.

The final corner of the hallway came into view and I leaned in against the wall and rounded tight against it. Ahead of me, a flurry of activity was at hand. Several people were grouped together, many of them gesturing frantically. On one side of the hall was Lex and the Borden's, on the other was Watts and a pair of uniformed police officers. Although all six spoke in hushed tones, urgency was evident in the air.

I made a direct route for the group and unrolled my shirt sleeves as far as they would go. I snapped the cuffs in place by my wrist to hide the cast the best I could and ran a hand through my shaggy hair, dragging it across my forehead. There was no way I could hide my injuries, but I could at least make them appear less severe.

All six people looked my way as I approached, my boots again giving me away.

I really needed to find a pair of stealthier shoes.

The Borden's turned right back, dismissing me within seconds. To be fair, it was longer than they usually give me.

Lex kept her eyes locked on me a bit longer as her gaze did a quick inventory of me. She met my eyes for just a moment, her eyes again rimmed with red, before looking away. Something new was going on.

Something bad.

"What the hell happened to you?" Watts snapped in my direction. Beside her the uniforms stopped and looked at me. Both looked to be in their mid-twenties with matching crew cuts and very poor attempts at facial hair. Neither one was even as tall as Watts.

"Got rear ended," I said. As with the doctor, I offered as few details as possible. My story was flimsy at best. I didn't want to give her any loose strings to tug on.

"Mhmm," Watts said, her facing relaying disbelief. "Just in the last few hours?"

I made a confused face. "Yeah? The doctor said most accidents happen during storms or on Saturday nights."

"And they happen during a kidnapped child situation? Involving a concerned uncle?" There was no doubt where she was going with this. I had to cut her off and get the attention back on whatever was going on. I needed details and I needed them fast.

Otherwise, I was headed to Cincinnati.

I held the cast up for her to see. "If I was out playing vigilante, would I have gone to the emergency room to get my hand looked at it? I got rear ended making a dinner run. So what's going on?"

The irony of my excuse wasn't lost on me, given that I had done that very thing.

Watts gave me one last look before turning her attention back to Lex. "We'll give you some time to figure out finances. I'll be in the lobby. Come find me as soon as you're ready. I'm going to start putting things in place."

Lex nodded as Watts stomped away, her lackeys right behind her. Square toed heels reverberated against the tile floor as she stomped off, making my boots sound like slippers by comparison.

"What's going on?" I asked again, conscious that Watts ignored it the first time.

"Where the hell have you been?" Jim asked.

It was my turn to ignore a question. "Lex?"

Lex looked even smaller inside her grey sweatshirt than she had that afternoon. The sleeves were pulled down over both hands, her left arm folded across her stomach. The right was vertical by her side, a bloody thumbnail protruding as she

125

gnawed at it. She twisted at the waist towards the Borden's and said, "Can you give us a second?"

Both of them stared daggers at me as they departed, slowly retreating back into the room.

"Did Ricky take a turn?" I asked.

Lex shook her head. "What the hell happened to you?"

"You don't want to know," I replied. It was true, as was the fact that I really didn't want to retell it.

Her eyes again ran over each of my injuries. "Was it worth it?"

I honestly didn't know the answer to that question yet. Long ago I vowed never to lie to my sister. Now didn't seem the time to start, even if it was a situation I would have never dreamed possible. "It's progress. We'll see how much later. What's going on here?"

"We got a ransom call," Lex said. She said it in a flat and even tone, very little life in her voice. I knew my sister well enough to know she was past emotional and headed towards catatonic. I only hoped she wasn't already there, or worse yet, had resorted to some form of self-medication.

I moved forward and put my hands on her shoulders. "This is a good thing. It means Annie is alive."

She nodded dully. We were losing her fast. She wasn't equipped to deal with everything that happened, let alone the omnipresence of her in-laws.

"How much do they want?"

"Fifty thousand, cash," Lex responded. "They want it by one, or..." She let her voice trail off. Her body wracked once with a shudder, but no tears came out.

"Is that doable?"

"Fifty thousand? Not even close. We don't have that kind of cash on hand, less than half. His parents far less than that."

A hundred thoughts ran through my head. I made less than forty thousand dollars a year and didn't have access to more than five hundred dollars in cash a day through my ATM card. Mama lived tighter than all of us. "Where the hell do they expect us to get fifty grand in cash in the middle of the night? And tomorrow's Sunday, the banks won't be open again until Monday morning."

Lex nodded again. That's why she was going catatonic. She'd been given a straw to grasp at, but couldn't quite wrap her fingers around it. It was the ultimate cruelty to lay on a mother.

I clenched my fingers down on her shoulders, ignored the burning that rippled through my left hand. I lowered my face so it was even with hers and said, "Lex, Ricky was an Ohio State football player."

Her eyes flicked up to mine, but remained glassy. "*Was*, past tense. And that didn't pay him anything, it just lets every person in the state interrupt our dinner for autographs when we go out."

"I know," I said. I'd heard that rant repeatedly from my sister over the years. Fans, especially Buckeye fans, have an extreme sense of entitlement when it comes to connecting with their heroes. "But he played with some guys that are now in the NFL. Is there anybody you can call and get a loan from?"

A small flicker passed over Lex's face. "Right now, I don't think anybody even knows Ricky's in here. Can you imagine calling someone in the middle of the night and asking for fifty thousand in cash?"

"Can you imagine not calling them?" I replied, trying to be as gentle as possible while getting my point across.

A quiver passed over Lex's face and for a moment I thought she might cry. She was coming back from the edge. The wheels were turning again. "There's only a couple he keeps up with with any regularity. One plays for the Raiders and lives in California."

Most likely she was referring to Drumaine Hicks, a tight end. "No help there."

"Another is in Alabama having his knee operated on," Lex said, her mind going through the list. I knew this to be Carl Paxson, All-Pro tackle for the Vikings.

Even in Wyoming, they have *Sportscenter.*

"What about Coach Tinsley?" I asked, running through the list of people that might be in the area. I knew it was unlikely that a sixty-five year old man kept that kind of cash on hand, but reasoned he made north of a few million a year. Fifty grand might be walking around money to someone with those kinds of pockets.

Lex shook her head. "Ricky hasn't spoken to Tins since he graduated. They never really got along after what they did to him his senior year."

What they did to him was sit him in favor of a freshman that was a far better player. Now didn't seem the time to bring it up though.

"So who does that leave?"

Lex's eyes traced the opposite wall before shifting back to me. "Fuego."

Already a feeling of dread welled inside me. "Please tell me there's someone else."

"With fifty grand in cash on hand?" Lex said. "There's not."

"How do you know he'll have that kind of money lying around?" The words were just out of my mouth and already they sounded ridiculous. Everybody knew he dropped that kind of money on trips to the strip club or race track. Fuego spent as much time on TMZ as he did on ESPN. "Alright Lex, let the police handle this and I'll go to Cincinnati. I have a lead there."

"No," Lex snapped, her bloody hand on my forearm. "I need you here. If I can find Fuego, I want you to pick up the money and make the delivery."

The barbed wire in my stomach grew an inch in size. "Look, Lex, this is what the cops do. Watts is already looking at me like a convict. She could easily pull my records if she hasn't already. I need to stay out of sight on this."

Her hand slid from my arm and went back to her side. "I don't trust them," she whispered. "You promised to do everything you can to help Annie. They didn't."

For just the briefest of moments I considered showing her the cast on my hand or Merric's cell-phone in my pocket, but I didn't. She was right. If going to retrieve the money from Fuego helped us get Annie home, so be it.

"Make the call."

Chapter Thirteen

I was staring at the dashboard clock when Saturday slipped into Sunday. With the passing of one minute the countdown to finding my niece became thirteen hours. My stomach continued to knot at the thought of her out there somewhere, no doubt scared and crying.

The last time I saw her was several months before. The weather was unseasonably warm and we spent the day in the sunshine, going to the park and fishing at the lake. She made me go down the slide over fifty times while carrying her on my back and insisted on holding the blue gill in her tiny hands before we threw it back. Standing there with the sun splashed across her tangle of blonde curls and her tongue pushed into the corner of her mouth, I was certain I had never seen a more beautiful moment in my entire life.

It might have even made up for the years of ugly ones that preceded it. I knew for a fact it was making up for everything that happened in the last two days. I hadn't ate or slept, had a broken hand and face that was actively turning purple, but it didn't matter.

Annie was all that mattered.

The stoplight turned to green and I angled the truck through the empty streets of Worthington, a suburb on the northeast corner of Columbus. The entire town had a community beautification policy that required every building to be made of brick and well-landscaped, from mortgage brokers to McDonald's. It housed the few elite athletes, actors and musicians that called the city home as well as the executives from Nationwide Insurance and Abercrombie & Fitch.

Even at such a late hour, the town exuded an air that warded off outsiders. Every car in sight was on the higher end of the spectrum and all of the homes went for several hundred thousand minimum.

Needless to say, my dented truck and I didn't exactly fit the mold.

Perhaps even more out-of-place in Worthington though was Fuego. A first generation Mexican-American, Fuego was born Hector Lopez in Arizona. A gifted receiver, he earned a full-ride to Ohio State and became an All-American for the Buckeyes. Right after being selected in the first round of the NFL draft, he bought an enormous house in Worthington and moved his entire family into it. During the season he lived two hundred miles north in Detroit, but the rest of the year he resided here in this polished suburb.

The son of immigrant parents, Lopez began his career as a polite young man that was known to outwork anybody put across from him. Over time the work ethic remained, but the polite part was cast by the wayside. He fell in the love with the cameras and all that they brought with them, slowly turning himself into a media machine.

The truck groaned as I idled to a stop in front of a large iron gate, a small community guard booth to my left. As I approached, the door to the booth slid open and a middle aged white man with a weak chin and a receding hairline stepped out. He wore the uniform of some no-name security company designed to resemble police officer regalia. "Evening."

"Evening," I replied, propping my elbow up on the window ledge.

"What can I do for you this evening?" the guard asked, his voice carrying a trace of Wisconsin in it. Minnesota, maybe.

"I'm here to see Fuego."

The guard raised his eyes to me, then ran them the length of my truck. "Are you on the list?"

"I'm not sure, but he's expecting me. Felix O'Connor."

The guard made a quick pass over the list, but found nothing. Lex had just spoken to Fuego less than a half hour before and I didn't expect him to remember to put me on the list. I just hoped he remembered talking to Lex at all. "Are you sure he's expecting you?"

"Definitely," I responded.

He pulled a walkie-talkie from his hip and depressed a button. A moment later I could hear ringing, the walkie-talkie acting as a cell-phone with a loud speaker.

"Yo," snapped a self-important voice I recognized from television to be Fuego's.

"Um, hi, Mr. Fuego, this is Jerry at the front gate. I have a Mr. Felix O'Connor here to see you?"

There was no response for several seconds, the line filled with party noise from inside. This was going to be worse than I thought. "Who the hell is Felix O'Connor?"

"Ricky's brother-in-law," I shouted at the walkie-talkie. "You talked to my sister Alexa a little while ago."

This time Fuego responded without delay. "Oooh, yeah-yeah-yeah," he rattled off rapid fire. "You the fool here to pick up fifty G's. Come on up playa!"

This was going to be way worse than I thought.

Jerry's eyes grew a bit larger at the sound of fifty thousand dollars, but he said nothing. Instead, he retreated into the booth and opened the gate, waving as I eased through. "Last house on the left. Can't miss it."

I followed the winding path past a handful of homes, all of them with finely manicured lawns and darkened windows. If not for the blinding light coming from the last house on the left, the world would have been completely at peace.

My truck pulled to a stop on the curb in front of a house that was as garish as its owner. The stucco of the exterior façade was painted in vibrant red, yellow and orange, all mixed into a mosaic of color. The hedges were shaped to resemble flames rising into the air and the front yard had three enormous red-rock gardens through it, also in the shape of flames.

Light poured from every window in the house and the persistent sound of music bumping floated down to the curb. A series of expensive sports cars filled the driveway, ranging from a Cadillac Escalade to an Aston Martin.

For a moment I paused and took in the scene before me. If given the choice between facing Peka again or walking up to the front door I would go to the front door, but I would have to think about it first.

I pushed a long breath out through my nose and ascended the driveway, my head down as I headed for the door. I pressed the bell and waited nearly a full minute, then pressed it again and waited almost two. I could hear music and people talking just on the other side, but nobody made any effort to let me in.

I considered a third ring, but opted against it. Instead I tried the doorknob and finding it unlocked, let myself in. I had no idea a single door could mask so much chaos.

The door opened into an expansive wooden foyer with a large staircase extending straight up in front of me and large common rooms to either side. To my left, a half dozen people were busy playing video games on a seventy inch flat screen, all of them engrossed and screaming at the television. To the right a DJ pushed out urban hip hop music while several handfuls of people gyrated to the beat.

I stood motionless, shifting my eyes from the left to the right, unsure of where to go next. A young woman with mocha colored skin and her hair pulled back into hundreds of tiny braids descended from the stairwell and I extended a hand towards her. "Excuse me, do you know where I can find Fuego?"

The girl gave me a disapproving look and said, "He's out back in the hot tub." She was dressed only in a tiny pair of underwear and a bikini top, most likely headed in that direction, but made no effort to show me where to go.

I pushed through the foyer, past the main stairwell and on into a massive kitchen. Several people were huddled up around an island in the middle of it, all snacking on chips and pizza. None of them looked to be older than twenty-five, the entire group openly staring at me as I walked by.

The kitchen gave way to another pair of living rooms, these two quieter than the ones up front. To one side a home theater was set up with several people watching some new action movie and to the other were two tables of people playing cards. More stares as I passed through, though nobody said a word.

After walking for what felt like a mile, I found the back door and let myself out onto a deck that stretched the entire length of the house. More people were grouped around a couple of kegs set up along the left rail. Beside them, a large hot tub threw a steady tendril of steam into the air.

I took a deep breath and walked straight to the hot tub, the world seeming to slow down while everyone present turned to stare at me. As I approached, I could see a handful of men press in from either side.

In the rear of the hot tub, with his arms stretched out wide to either side, sat Fuego. Flames of red, blue and yellow tattooed both his forearms and a heavy gold chain hung around his neck. His hair was dyed platinum blonde and spiked into a Mohawk and his front teeth were covered with a gold grill.

He watched me as I approached, his eyes hidden behind mirrored sunglasses. He was the only male in the hot tub, the rest of the free space filled with scantily clad women. "Who the hell invited the cowboy?" he asked as I approached, an uneasy laugh sliding out from the crowd.

They might not know who I was, but they knew to laugh at the boss's joke.

I smiled lightly at the comment, hiding my disdain over being called cowboy again. Hadn't this state ever seen boots before?

"Hi, I'm Felix O'Connor, we spoke just a moment ago."

Fuego pursed his lips and twisted his head, but said nothing. Beside me, I could feel several men inch even closer.

"My sister Alexa Borden called you," I said, waiting for some sign of recognition out of him. There was none. "On behalf of her husband, Ricky Borden..."

Fuego held the pose for several long seconds before breaking into a broad smile. As he did, everyone around the hot tub seemed to collectively release their breath, myself included. "Man, I'm just messing with you. Ramon, give this man his money," Fuego said, motioning to a wiry young man beside me with a shaved head.

Without moving, Ramon reached down to his feet and picked up a black leather bag with flames embroidered onto it and thrust it my way. Classy.

"Thank you so much," I said. "We'll have the money back to you first thing on Monday."

I turned towards the door.

"Man, what you in such a hurry for? Stay and have a drink."

I paused, the bag clutched in front of me. I did not want to offend him, but I damned sure didn't want a drink. "I appreciate the offer, but I really can't. I have to be going."

Fuego turned his head to the side and gazed at Ramon. "You believe this cat? Shows up asking for fifty G's, then refuses to even have a drink with me. You know what that is?"

"That's some shit?" Ramon asked, glaring across at me.

"Yeah, that too," Fuego said, "but I was thinking that's disrespectful."

Sweat broke out on my brow again. This was the last thing I needed right now. One, because I didn't have the time, and two, because I had no way of walking out of there alive.

"No, no, nothing of the sort," I stammered. "I'd love to have a drink, but I can't. Ricky's on a tight time table. I have to get this money back to him."

Fuego looked at me, not believing a word I said. "If you won't have a drink with me, you at least gotta tell me what he's up to. What's he need all that scratch for?"

I was standing there when Lex called him the first time. He hadn't asked for any details and Lex hadn't offered them. Even now I was uncertain how much I could divulge. At the same time, Fuego was offering me a fair trade so we could both save face.

142

"He, uh, well, he's not doing so well."

"I know," Fuego said, "fool couldn't even call and ask me for the money or come pick it up himself. He's really gonna be not well next I see him."

"Um, no," I said, gripping the bag in my hand. "I mean, he's in a coma. He was attacked by some people on his front lawn yesterday."

Every person visibly tensed, their eyes shifting to Fuego, who leaned forward from the rail behind him. With his left hand, he slid the sunglasses from his face. "You kidding me right now? Cause that's pretty messed up if you are."

"No."

"Is that what that money's for? Not strippers or gambling or something?" he asked, jutting his chin towards the bag in my hand.

My head twisted from side to side. "His daughter was kidnapped. This is the ransom money to get her back." I knew I was probably sharing more than I should, but he was asking me a direct question and seemed genuinely concerned. He was also the bag man on what might bring my niece home. He'd earned the right to know.

Fuego dropped his head to the side. "Take that money and get out of here. You need any more, or anything at all, you give me a call. We'll be here all night."

For the first time, the men on either side of me took a step back and nodded their agreement. This was a side of Fuego that never showed up in the tabloids. His reaction took me by surprise.

"Again, thank you so much," I said, holding the bag out in front of me. Without another word I spun on my heel and jogged back through the house and out the front door, leaving dozens of staring people in my wake.

Chapter Fourteen

Lex was pacing outside of the hospital as I drove up. I didn't bother pulling into the parking lot, instead sliding to a stop in the loading zone before her. A handful of police cars were parked in the first row of the lot, over a half dozen in total. Despite the clear presence of a significant number of people, Lex and my mother were the only two outside.

Mama sat alone on a wooden bench looking out across the front lawn, a tan cardigan sweater wrapped around her body. Lex paced a steady path on the asphalt, working on a thumbnail as she went. As I climbed from the truck, both looked up at me.

"You get it?" Lex asked.

I pulled the bag across the front seat and held it up for them to see. I slammed the door shut behind me and circled around to the front with it gripped in hand.

"Oh thank God," Lex whispered and rushed forward, her arms extended. I handed the bag over without pause and she tugged the zipper open and rifled through it. "Did you thank you him profusely for us?"

"Yes."

"Did you tell him we'd have it back to him first thing on Monday?"

"I did. He just waved a hand and said to call if we needed more."

"Must be nice," Mama snorted. Her eyes held the same glazed red look as Lex, but her cheeks were dry. Her clothes and hair were different than when I'd seen her earlier, meaning she'd cleaned up before returning.

Once when we were kids, she was working in the garden and nearly sliced her thumb off with a hand trowel. Before bringing her to the hospital, my father insisted she make herself presentable before going to town. It was a maxim that had stayed with us all ever since.

"What happened to your hand?"

I held up my casted left hand and rotated it for her to see. "Broken bone. Nothing serious."

Normally she would have demanded a detailed account and asked if I wanted homemade soup. Now, she just nodded. "And your face?"

"Same nothing serious."

Again, she nodded. "Did it help?"

I offered a slight twist of my head. "It's a lead. If this money drop doesn't work..."

Beside me Lex drew in a sharp breath, a small whistle escaping her. She made one last pass through the bag and once content it was all there, zipped it up. "How much does he know?" she asked, ignoring my comment.

"More than I wanted to tell him," I admitted. "He was a little upset Ricky didn't call or come by himself, even more so when I refused to stay and have a drink."

"You told him so you could get out of there," Lex whispered.

"I'm sorry," I whispered. "It felt a lot better than trying to fight my way out with their money."

147

Lex shook her head. "No, you did the right thing. I just haven't really told anybody yet. I keep hoping this thing will resolve itself before it gets out and gets any more...*real*."

I knew exactly what she meant. I'd spent every minute since branding a day and a half before laboring under the same thought.

"Why are you guys out here? What's going on?"

Lex pulled the bag in close to her chest and wrapped both arms around it. I could see fresh blood lining both of her thumbs as she plopped down beside my mother and stared out over the parking lot. "I couldn't take any more of the Borden's. The longer this drags on, the more comments they make."

"Comments? About what?"

Lex continued to stare straight ahead, but said nothing. Instead she shook her head, her ponytail swinging behind her head.

My mother followed her gaze and said, "They think this happening and you showing up here aren't a coincidence."

My eyes bulged forth so hard they pulled me towards the bench. "They think *I* have something to do with this?"

I made no effort to hide the vitriol welling inside me or the incredulity oozing through my voice.

Both my sister and my mother stared straight ahead, saying nothing. My right hand balled into a tight fist as I turned and gazed out with them. I drew my mouth tight to keep from saying anything and breathed through my nose.

Up until thirty-six hours before I was tucked away in rural Wyoming branding cows. I barely ever returned to Ohio and only interacted with four people there with any regularity. Two of them were within three feet of me. One was sitting in jail. The fourth I was currently trying to find.

"I would kill myself if it meant keeping that little girl safe," I seethed, just loud enough for them to hear. "Hell, I've spent all night damn near doing just that."

"I know," Lex said.

"Nobody's blaming you," Mama whispered.

"It's sound like those sonsabitches are!" I shouted, extending a hand towards the hospital. Both of them fell silent, their gaze remaining on the parking lot. I lowered my arm and hooked my thumbs in my pockets, staring hard at the ground.

I had to calm down. People tend to get out-of-control when they're angry. I couldn't afford that right now. Those bastards would get told, just not right now.

"What about the police?" I asked. "It looks like they've got an army hidden around here somewhere."

My voice sounded a lot more even than I felt.

"They've set up shop in the cafeteria," Lex said. She pushed back the sleeve on her left arm and checked her watch. "It's a little after twelve-thirty. We should go in. They'll be waiting for us."

I nodded and stepped aside to follow them. Neither one made any effort to move. Both stared up at me.

"What?" I asked, casting my eyes from one to the other.

"We got another call while you were gone," Lex said.

The ball pushed itself back to the forefront of my stomach. I tried to keep the anger that was already just beneath the surface from bursting forth at not telling me sooner. The fact that they hadn't meant bad news. "What did they say? Did they up the asking price?"

My mother shook her head.

"No," Lex said beside her. "They said they want the money in a single bag dropped into the dumpster behind the Sawmill Road Applebee's. One person. Alone. No cops."

The line sounded like a cliché. Something didn't feel right.

"These guys watch too many movies."

"They also said they're already in place and they'll know if we try anything," Lex said. Her voice broke just a bit on the last line, the pain evident.

My eyes flitted from one to the other. "Okay?"

"It's got to be you," my mother whispered.

I made a face before I never realized it. "What do you mean it has to be me? There's a room full of police in there. This is what they're trained to do!"

"The caller said no cops," my mother replied.

"So I'll loan one of them a pair of jeans! You think these guys know every single officer on the force?"

"What if they do?" Lex asked. The comment stopped me in the middle of my rant, my right hand still in the air. Her face turned to me, moisture stinging the bottoms of her eyes. "What if this is a major child abduction ring? What if they have people on the inside?"

I swallowed hard and blew a breath out through my nose. This was not my role. I had to make my sister must see that grief was clouding her judgment.

If she wasn't going to listen to me, I would try a different tact. "There's no way Watts will go for this."

Lex hugged the bag closer to her chest. "Does that mean you will?"

"It means what I will do is a moot point. There's no way she'll let this happen."

"But does it mean if she says yes, you will?" Lex pressed.

I exhaled again. Two pairs of eyes studied me, neither person moving at all. This was not my place. There were professionals sitting not fifty feet away trained for this. There was an investigator in there that already had her eye on me.

"Yeah, I'll do it."

Chapter Fifteen

Lex handed the bag back to me and led all three of us inside. She kept her arms folded, but moved purposefully, a woman on a mission. My mother fell in right beside me, her hands holding the tan sweater closed in front of her.

The hall was completely deserted as we walked through, the three of us spread like geese in a V. One out of every three lights in the ceiling above was on, the others dark. Long shadows stretched across everything, conveying a sense of both silence and apprehension.

My boots echoing off the tile was the only sound in the hallway as we marched past a deserted information desk and on towards the cafeteria. A generic plastic sign affixed to the wall directed us where to go, but my sister's practiced feet led without even bothering to glance at it.

The door to the cafeteria parted easily as we pushed through, a small groan rolling out of its hinges. At once the room turned to look at us. Over a dozen officers in black uniforms stood in a loose circle going over a large white printout spread flat on a table. In the center of the group was a young man in jeans and a Radiohead t-shirt, his hair buzzed into a tight crew cut. His cheeks were ruddy and he repeatedly rubbed his palms along the front of his jeans as he stared at us.

Beside him was Watts, her suit jacket off and her sleeves rolled to the elbow. She regarded us warily as we approached, her eyes settling on me and the bag in my hand.

I tapped Lex on the shoulder and handed it off to her. With a jerk of my head I motioned towards the front of the cafeteria. "I need coffee. Be back in a minute."

"You just don't want to be the one to break the news," Mama hissed.

"You're right," I agreed. "It has to look like it came from Lex. I'll be back."

We were both right. The idea had to start and end with Lex. As the grieving spouse and concerned mother she was the only one with enough juice to convince Watts to let me go. Of course, I also wanted no part of that woman staring me down as Lex made the request.

After seeing the greenhorn they planned to use though, I had a much better feeling about the odds of the switch going down without a fight.

The cafeteria was deserted as I walked in. Empty coolers stretched along both walls and a barren salad bar ran through the middle of it. A soda machine and coffee machine stood side by side, each humming and throwing soft light out into the space.

I fished a dollar from deep in my pocket, fed it into the machine and ordered a large black. A second later a cup dropped down into the dispenser and a steady stream of liquid ran into it, filling it just shy of the brim. Without pause I grabbed it up and took a long pull. It tasted more like the swill we made while riding trails than the high-end stuff I had earlier with Lex, but it was hot and caffeinated.

My body reacted the way I hoped it would.

Armed with a fresh jolt of energy I walked out into the cafeteria. On one side my mother and Lex stood, their faces firm. Across from them was Watts with her hands on her hips, looking stern. Behind her was a legion of officers, all casting looks between one another. Everyone looked nervous except for the young man in jeans, who seemed relieved.

I walked up slowly to the group, careful to shuffle my feet so my boots didn't reverberate against the floor. I could feel several sets of eyes boring into me as I approached, but pretended not to notice. Instead I took another long pull of coffee, sliding in beside my mother.

"This is my daughter and this is my money," Lex said, her voice hard. "I would feel better knowing that we're not violating the only rule this guy laid out for us."

"With all due respect ma'am, you have to let me do my job," Watts countered. "And my job, the job I was trained for and have spent years doing, is to bring your daughter home."

"I'm not saying you don't know what you're doing," Lex shot back.

"In order for me to bring your daughter home, you have to let me run this investigation my way," Watts said, her voice rising to drown out Lex's comment.

Big mistake.

If there's one thing that is never a good idea, it's to talk down to an O'Connor. I took another swig of coffee to hide the small smile on my face. Beside me, my mother coughed into her hand. Watts was about to get her ass chewed and we both knew it.

Lex took a long breath and leveled her eyes on Watts. "You're investigation? *With all due respect*, so far I haven't seen any sort of investigation. I've seen a dozen people sitting around, drawing a check from my tax payer dollars, waiting for a phone call. A phone call that came to me. A phone call you claim couldn't be traced."

"Now Miss Borden..." Watts tried to interject.

"So far I can't see where you've done a damn thing. If I'd never called you at all, we wouldn't be one inch further away from finding my daughter. This is my money, she is my daughter, and that is my husband lying in a coma in there."

157

Tears began to line her cheeks as she swiveled and motioned to me. "And he is my brother! If I say he's the one that drops off the money, then he's the one that drops off the damn money!"

My mother stepped forward and wrapped her arms around Lex, drawing her in. Lex folded herself around the bag and pressed in tight to my mother's chest, trying to stem her crying. I remained motionless.

A tall man wearing Sergeant's bars and a clipped moustache turned to Watts and said, "He's just the drop-off guy. Somebody has to walk the money up there and put it in the dumpster."

Watts sighed, but said nothing. She was obviously steaming and trying to keep from tearing into Lex. She couldn't let the men see her back down, but she couldn't fly back at a woman facing everything my sister was.

A pudgy guy with thinning brown hair and a poor excuse for a beard added, "The caller said no cops. There's no way in hell anybody's mistaking this guy for a cop."

Under normal circumstances I would have taken offense to the comment. At the moment, I was finding it hard not to find the entire scene a little humorous. The tough detective tried to squash the wrong person, got steamrolled, and now her team was trying to cover for her.

If finding Annie wasn't the most important thing in the world at that moment, I might have let it all play on a little longer. As it were, I didn't have that luxury.

"Look, I'm not trying to step on any toes here. I don't know what I'm doing and I don't even know where the Applebee's on Sawmill Road is. Detective Watts, why don't you drive my truck? I'll ride shotgun and make the drop."

Every eye turned to stare at me except for Lex. Her face was still buried in my mother's sweater.

Watts studied me. I could tell she didn't like it, but knew there wasn't a ton of options.

"Lex?" I asked.

Lex pulled herself free from my mother's grasp and nodded. Her face was red and shiny as she wiped the back of her sleeve across her nose. "Yes," she whispered.

I glanced up at the clock on the wall. It was a quarter to one, a little over twelve hours to go. If all went right, it wouldn't take nearly that long. "Detective?"

Watts stared at me for several long seconds. She pursed her lips and put a hand on her hip, doing her best to relay extreme agitation. It was working. "Do I have a choice?" she asked.

I said nothing. I knew she wanted to bait me into being the bad guy here. I had extended her enough courtesy on this one, I wasn't going to make myself a sacrificial lamb.

She grabbed her jacket up from the chair back beside her and turned to the others. "You all have a two minute head start. The plan is still the same. Get into position. I'll be right behind you with Cowboy in his truck."

The room scattered like flies, all of them swarming every available exit. She waited until they were gone before turning her ire on us. "I don't appreciate you putting me in that position in front of my men."

I ignored the comment and jumped in before she further angered my mother or sister. "You're welcome for me giving you an out."

Her mouth dropped open to respond, but I cut her off again, tossing her the truck keys. "Time's up. Let's go."

Chapter Sixteen

"Jesus, how the hell do you drive this thing?" Watts snapped. I watched as she swung the truck through a wide left turn, arms flailing as she went. She handled the thing as if it were the wheel on a clipper ship, wildly over-correcting in both directions as we fishtailed down the road.

Thank God everything was deserted at this hour or we would have really been in trouble.

"You realize this is an automatic with power steering..." I said, letting my voice trail off. It's not like I was asking her to drive a five-speed tractor or a racecar with a hot-foot shifter.

"It's also the size of a damn bus," Watts said.

A small smile grew on my face in the darkness. Outside, an Arby's and a couple of branch banks slid by, all of their windows dark for the night. "So that's what it is. You're used to driving a Matchbox car. Let me guess...Miata?"

Maybe I was playing to stereotypes a little bit, but I purposely picked a known male car. She wore a suit, carried a gun, worked as a detective. She might not be the most badass woman I'd ever met, but she was in the top five.

Watts gave me a nasty sideways glance, picking up on the insinuation. "Funny. How about we spend these next twenty minutes in silence and then I can dump you back at the hospital and be on my way, huh?"

I was under her skin. Good. She'd spent the day holding no bones about her low opinion of me, now I could take a few minutes to repay the favor. For some reason, despite where we were going, I had a feeling it wasn't going to amount to anything anyway.

"Are you still upset you pissed off the wrong woman and got your hand slapped in front of a room full of people back there?"

The scowl was still there, but she didn't bother turning to look at me. "No, I'm more pissed about having to *work* with an ex-con."

So there it was.

She'd gone through my files that afternoon, saw what was in there. Lucky for me, I'd spent enough time around law enforcement in prison to see the ploy coming. She was setting a trap, trying to flip the power dynamic back in her favor. "Well, you know what they say, best way to catch a criminal is to use a criminal."

Watts glanced my way, fighting the truck as she made a left onto Sawmill Road. "You've seen too many movies."

"As have you if you think one little comment was going to make me lose my cool or start spilling my guts," I fired back. My eyes were focused outside the passenger window but I could feel hers on me.

So much for a working relationship. I was just hoping to keep things civil moving forward.

"What really happened to your hand?" Watts asked.

So much for civil.

"Car accident."

"I took a look when we got in. There's not a scratch on this rig. Nothing big enough to cause a gashed head and broken hand anyway."

"Wasn't in my truck," I said. "Don't you know how badly these things handle in city limits?"

"So who's car were you driving?"

"My sister's."

"I pulled the reports from this afternoon, there was no reporting of any accidents involving an O'Connor," Watts fired back.

"Well then, you had a busy day," I said. "I wonder, did any of that work actually pertain to finding my niece?"

My voice was flinty. I was not in the mood for this back-and-forth. I'd done nothing to provoke Watts, yet she was treating me like I was the kidnapper. One day I would have to thank Lex for putting me in this situation.

Watts pulled my truck to a stop along the curb. Less than a block away I could see the darkened neon road sign announcing Applebee's to the world. A few blocks ahead I could

165

see a single car sitting on the opposite side of the road. Another slowly drove by. I assumed they were both with us, but had no way of knowing for sure.

Watts kept both hands on the wheel, gripping it so tight her knuckles showed beneath her skin. I could tell she wanted nothing more than to reach out and slap me, the feeling quite mutual at the moment. "Unfortunately, there are no cameras on the backside of the building. I have a team in a van three blocks away monitoring the traffic cameras a block over in either direction, but it's doubtful they'll see anything."

I nodded, but said nothing.

"There are teams hidden in the area. I don't know how close they were able to get and if they'll have a direct sight line on you. Odds are you'll walk through an empty parking lot, make the drop, and walk back. Whoever is waiting for the money will watch for a few hours to make sure the coast is clear before retrieving it."

"And if they don't?" I asked.

"Yell like hell. Somebody will be there fast. I can't promise it'll be me, but somebody will be." A slid my eyes across to her and for a second thought I saw the faintest outline of a smile.

A bullet travels at several hundred feet per second. If something went down, they'd be responding to a possible homicide, not me yelling. "Comforting."

"Hey, you're the one that volunteered for this," Watts said.

I opened the passenger side door and stepped out into the night. I grabbed my jean jacket from behind the seat and slid it on. My eyes leveled on Watts as I hefted the bag up from the seat in front of me. "Is that what you seriously think?"

The sound of the truck door slamming followed me down the sidewalk.

Chapter Seventeen

I left the scene in the truck behind me. Make no mistake, I was still plenty pissed at Watts and the audacity she had in assuming she knew anything about me, but that wasn't important at the moment. Again, this was about Annie. I could not afford a misstep.

My breath came in even gasps as I walked forward. My heart rate increased to a steady hammer and a thin film of sweat encased my entire body. The numbness was beginning to recede in my hand and I could feel my pounding pulse first passing through my swollen hand, again as it reached my head.

The sidewalk receded to driveway as I hooked a turn and walked around the edge of the building. I could feel the lump of the switchblade still wedged in my sock. I desperately wished I could have brought the Luger along out of the truck, but there would have been no way to get to it with Watts sitting there. I could only hope she didn't get bored and start snooping while I was gone.

With each passing second, I wished more and more that Lex hadn't bothered to involve the cops at all. I was unarmed, carrying fifty thousand dollars, and had no visible backup. The best I could hope for was shouting range.

Great.

My heart raced even harder as I walked around the side of the building and swung a wide turn. I held my breath as I peered around the corner and spied a dumpster with a stack of empty wooden pallets stacked beside it. A single security light threw a hazy yellow sheen down over everything and a waist-high hedge ran behind it.

There wasn't a sign of life anywhere.

Slowly my breath evened out as I cut a direct path across the asphalt to the dumpster. Yellow lines passed diagonally beneath my feet as I walked on, gaze swinging from side to side. Ahead of me the dumpster loomed, a plastic flip-top resting down atop it.

For a moment I considered fishing the knife out from my boot before opening the lid, but decided against it. If someone were foolish enough to be waiting in it, they were either armed or they weren't. If they had a gun, there wasn't much a switchblade could do to stop them. If they didn't, there wasn't much they could do to stop me.

Just as fast as it had receded, my heart began to pound again. I switched the bag into my left hand and jerked up the lid with my right, head swinging about to inspect the contents of the dumpster. There wasn't a single thing in it. The garbage collection had already ran for the night, leaving behind only a thin layer of congealing sauces and creams. A handful of napkins and small paper items remained stuck to it, but otherwise there was nothing else inside.

Somewhat disappointed, I tossed the bag in and dropped the lid over it. The sound of it slamming echoed through the night as I turned on my heel and walked away. I jammed my fingers into the pockets of my jacket and moved fast, making no attempt to hide the disdain on my face.

I could see Watts behind the truck windshield as I strode from the parking lot and headed towards her. She lifted her hand to her face as I approached, no doubt speaking to her men positioned nearby. I still had yet to see a single one anywhere around, though another car did roll by.

Across the street, the lone parked car was gone.

The truck creaked as I jerked it open and climbed inside. My hands were still jammed deep into my pockets and my face wore an open scowl.

"What happened?" Watts prompted. Her voice was tense, more professional than confrontational.

"Nothing," I spat.

Watts lowered the handheld phone from her face and dropped it against her leg. "Look, I know we don't like each other, but right now-"

I cut her off. She was right, I didn't like her, but that wasn't the point. "No, I mean nothing happened. The dumpster was completely empty. Not a car in the lot or a soul to be seen."

"Oh," Watts said. She lifted the phone back to her lips and said, "The drop has been made. Be on the lookout for any suspicious behavior or persons attempting to enter the parking lot."

There was a few muted responses back. Watts didn't respond to any of them.

"What do we do now?" I asked. The sound of my breathing filled the cab. I was fuming, pushing it out through my nose in heavy bursts.

"Now we wait a while," Watts said. "You'd be amazed how many people circle back within the first half hour."

The clock in my head was already counting again. Another half hour would put us at almost two returning to the hospital, eleven hours before the artificial deadline expired. "And if they don't?"

"Then I'll take you back to the hospital and my men will wait as long as it takes."

I nodded. My heart and breathing slowed, but were both still racing. This entire situation wasn't sitting well with me, waiting in the dark even less so.

"So you're still pissed at me?" Watts asked. Her tone was even, her eyes aimed straight ahead.

"What?" Confusion crossed my face. The question seemed far from left field, even for her. "No...I mean, yeah, I'm plenty mad at you...but that's not what I'm thinking about right now."

"So what are you thinking?"

I turned to glance at Watts. I couldn't tell if she cared what I thought, or was just amused and wanted to tear it to pieces. "I'm thinking none of this adds up. We don't hear a word for thirty-some hours, then we get one out of the blue?"

"Hmm," Watts said. "I've seen calls come in over a week later before. Kidnappers think the longer they hold the kid the more paranoid the parents will get, more they'll pay."

"Okay, so then why ask for fifty grand? Yeah, that's a lot of money, but that's not *ransom* money. That's more like student loan or new car money."

Watts weighed it. "I wondered that too. Maybe that's all they thought they could get in cash on short notice?"

"So then why grab her on a Friday afternoon? Why not do it on a Monday? Or why not wait to make a ransom demand until Monday?"

"Maybe they hadn't planned on Mr. Borden going into a coma. That changed their plans."

"Yeah, but how do they even know that?" I countered.

We paused and looked at one another. We were both playing devil's advocate and we knew it. Not one word uttered between us wasn't something the other hadn't already considered. We were basically testing each other, a battle of wits to see just how much the other knew.

"Why are you doing this?" I asked.

Watts opened her mouth to answer, then closed it, visibly wrestling with how to proceed. "Maybe there was a kernel of truth in what you said earlier. The whole criminals helping catch other criminals thing."

"If you've seen my files you know I didn't have anything to do with children, kidnappings, ransoms, nothing," I said. As we spoke, we both continued to watch the deserted street.

"No, but how's the old saying go? Prison is the best education a criminal ever receives?" Watts countered, raising her eyes and rolling her head towards me. I matched the glance, surprised at her sudden candor. Maybe it was the late hour or the current situation, but she was close to being downgraded from Heinous Bitch to Moody-As-Hell.

I smirked in response. "You have no idea. I saw and heard things that would make your head spin. Incarceration isn't only a massive expenditure of government funding, it creates super criminals."

"Is that what it did to you?" Watts asked.

We both knew she was pressing. It's not like she was even attempting to hide it. I decided to play along anyway. I was tired of her riding my ass all night, and if this played out the way I thought it would, I was going to need a little separation from her. "Prison pushes people one of two ways. It either scares them straight or makes them even worse."

Watts nodded in the darkness, her eyes locked forward. "A friend of mine used to work counseling inmates. She swore that nobody ever left jail the same as when they arrived."

"Not even close," I agreed, shaking my head. "I always tell people every person sent to jail should be re-evaluated after a week. That's all it takes to sort through the pile. After that, you send the ones that have learned their lesson home. No need to worry about them again."

"And you would have fallen into this group?" Watts asked.

I paused before answering. A handful of answers came to mind, none of which felt right. I was still an ex-con and she was still a detective. One civil conversation wasn't changing that. "I did my time. No need to dredge it back up."

Watts nodded again as silence settled in over the car. It was still uneasy in the cab, but there was much less tension than just a short time before. We weren't friends, but we weren't about to come to blows anymore either.

"And one more thing," I said.

"Hmm?"

"Whoever named this as the drop-point knew when that dumpster gets emptied. That's why they picked one o'clock and not midnight."

Chapter Eighteen

Watts pulled my truck to a stop in the front row of the parking lot. The crowd had thinned in the hour since we'd been gone, a couple handfuls of cars scattered around the lot were all that remained. What the difference was between midnight and two a.m. on a Saturday night I didn't know, but it must have been substantial.

She twisted the keys to off, pulled them from the ignition and dropped them into my lap in one movement. Neither one of us looked at the other as we sat there, the truck engine ticking.

"What happens now?" I asked. The keys rested in a tangle on my left thigh, but I made no effort to grab them.

"Now, we wait," Watts said. "My men are in position and will continue monitoring everything. The minute they hear something, I'll pass it on."

"And what are you going to do?" I asked.

Watts sighed and looked out over the lot. She dropped her gaze towards her lap, then lifted it to look at me. "Did you know a child goes missing every forty seconds in this country?"

I matched her gaze, but said nothing. Already I didn't like where this was going.

"That's over two thousand per day, almost eight hundred thousand per year," Watts continued.

I had never stopped to consider the numbers. There was only one child I cared about, and she was missing. "So you're telling me this is futile?"

Her brown hair twisted against her shoulders as she turned her head. "No. I'm just saying, when you stop and think about the sheer vastness of it, it seems rather daunting."

I considered responding with some bit of encouragement, but opted against it. She needed her head clear on finding my niece, she didn't need a pep talk. "So what are you going to do?"

I knew the point she was getting at, and it was a valid one to make. I just also needed her to know that while I respected it, my chief concern was on Annie and nothing else.

She turned her head back to the front windshield, almost a silent acceptance of our half spoken conversation. "I'm going to go back in there and get another cup of coffee, then I'm going to climb into my car and go be one more set of eyes at Applebee's."

"Hmm," I said, mulling her response.

"Like I said before, I still think this guy shows up soon. This feels amateur, for all the reasons we discussed earlier."

"Agreed," I said without pause. "I don't suppose there's any chance I can get a half hour alone with this guy when you do grab him?"

Watts coughed out a laugh and swung free from the truck. "That's assuming he actually has your niece."

I climbed from the truck across from her, weighing the response. "Not really. If he does, Heaven help him. If he doesn't, he just wasted a lot of time for everybody."

We walked side-by-side through the main entrance. Our shoes beat out a steady two-man chorus against the tile floor as we went, the halls still dark and empty. We went as far as the main desk before parting to go our respective directions.

"What are you going to do now?" Watts asked, turning to face me while walking backwards towards the cafeteria.

I matched the pose, my pace staying even as I headed towards the intensive care unit. "I'm going to go check on my sister," I said.

It was true, if only a small fraction of the truth. Already my mind was running the numbers on a trip to Cincinnati and how much time I could afford to wait for someone to show up at Applebee's.

Watts nodded. "I'll be in touch if I hear anything," she said before disappearing into the cafeteria.

I started to respond, but let it go. She was already gone. Instead I turned on a heel and continued towards the ICU, my stride never breaking.

The clock above the department front desk said it was a few minutes after two, putting me at eleven hours and counting. After the intensity of my early evening, the last few hours had slowed tremendously. I knew in my heart that this was the best route for Annie, though I was having a hard time convincing my mind of that.

I don't do well with idle time. Never have.

The desk was unmanned as I swung past it. The halls were still only a third-illuminated and aside from my boots, the only sounds were the muted intonations of monitors and breathing machines throughout the hall. A young nurse with bloodshot eyes and a ponytail of straw-like hair stared at me as I walked by and opened her mouth as if contemplating stopping me, but said nothing.

Either she recognized me from earlier or decided it wasn't worth the effort. Which one, I can't be sure.

The sound of my approach had already pulled Lex into the hall as I rounded the final corner. She wasn't slouched in a chair or continuing her frenetic pacing, but instead stood with her arms in front of her staring my way. "Well?"

I held my hands out by my side, palms up. Behind her my mother lifted herself from a chair and stood at her shoulder, rubbing sleep from her eyes.

"I made the drop. That's all I know."

Lex pressed her lips tight and closed her eyes. I was proud of how well she'd handled the last thirty-six hours, but the strain was beginning to show. She was cracking, little by little, before us.

"Was anybody there?" my mother asked.

"No," I said, shaking my head. I could see Jim Borden nudge his head out from the room to listen, though he made no effort to join the conversation. Sue was nowhere to be seen, nor was Ricky's sister, who's name I still wasn't sure about. "There wasn't a soul anywhere. I walked through a desolate parking lot, dropped the bag in an empty dumpster, and walked back."

"You were gone a long time for all that," Lex whispered.

"Watts and I waited a half hour to see if they would show up. After that, she brought me back here and left her men to watch the area."

"And where is she now?" my mother asked.

"She's headed back there," I said. I omitted her stopping for coffee, which felt a little strange. I had no reason to be protecting her, but still felt the need not to mention that part. Lex needed to believe every available person was looking for her daughter. "Any change here?"

Jim disappeared back into the room as Lex resumed her pacing. She was up to round two on her right ring finger, the skin around it as raw and bloody as her thumbs. My mother looked at me with tired eyes and said, "No change here."

The three of us stood in silence for a moment, all unsure what to say. There was no new information any one of us could offer and nothing anybody could do. It was a feeling we all despised, none more than me.

My mother retreated back into her chair while Lex continued to pace. I could hear the heart rate monitor pinging from inside Ricky's room and could hear his breathing machine rising and falling. Otherwise the entire scene was silent.

I made it three minutes, a full two minutes longer than I anticipated.

"I'll be back," I said and turned down the way I'd just come. I heard a pair of mumbled responses from behind me, but neither made any attempt to stop me. They sensed the way I felt. I'm sure in their own way they wished they could move about as well.

The nurse was gone as I rounded through the ICU and towards the front desk, my feet taking me towards the cafeteria. I had eaten almost nothing the last couple of days and each successive cup of coffee had a diminished effect on me. It was already time for a caffeine refill.

The front desk was unoccupied as I slid past it and reached for the double doors of the cafeteria. A moment before my hand got there they burst open, a very startled Watts standing on the other side.

Her phone was in her left hand, a coffee cup in her right. A stream of brown liquid ran over the back of her thumb and dripped to the floor, the consequence of running into me unexpectedly.

"Sorry," I mumbled, standing to the side for her to pass.

"Never mind that," she hissed, motioning for me to follow her. She pressed the phone tighter to her head and said, "No, that wasn't for you. Haul his ass to the station right now. Nobody talks to him until I get there!"

Adrenaline surged through my temples, doing a far better job of getting me going than any coffee on the planet could have.

I took three quick jog steps to draw even with her and matched her pace back out into the cool night air. A hundred questions pulsed through my mind, all of them waiting for her to get off the phone so they could pour forth.

They never got the chance.

Watts snapped her phone shut without signing off and tossed her coffee into a trash can as we stomped by. Her face was grim and her eyes locked on the front row of cars ahead of us.

"This time we're taking my car," was all she said.

Chapter Nineteen

"There's a flasher on the floor behind your seat. Grab it," Watts said. It was definitely an order. There was no wiggle room on her intent. This was a good thing, we were finally getting somewhere. Movement was back afoot.

I rotated in my seat and fished the hard plastic light up off the floorboard, throwing aside a mountain of empty coffee cups. They fell away without objection as I lifted it free, landing with the sound of empty cardboard rolling around. Swinging back to face forward, I ran my sleeve over the clear plastic to wipe away a few errant streams of liquid and flipped the switch on the base of it, filling the car with a pulsating blue and red strobe.

Watts operated my window from her door, lowering it as a blast of cool night air flooded in. I ran a hand over the suction cup along the bottom of it before jamming it down against the hood. It was probably done harder than it needed to, but I wasn't taking a chance at it flying off behind us.

As we were climbing into the car, Watts told me that the call had just come in that her men grabbed someone trying to sneak into the parking lot. He was a young male, alone, and put up only a token flight attempt before being arrested. Both he and the money were waiting at the police station for us to arrive.

Well, for Watts to arrive. I don't think my presence mattered much to anybody. She only invited me because I almost ran her over going to the cafeteria.

Watts angled her BMW 3-Series through the empty streets on the west side of Columbus. The strobe light allowed us to pass through every stop sign and traffic light unabated, though it wouldn't have mattered. At this time of night, there wasn't a soul around to stop us anyway. Her tires screeched in protest every time she made a turn, the car traveling at a rate of speed far exceeding safe maneuvering within city limits.

Neither one of us cared.

The Hilliard branch of the Columbus Police Department sat in an enormous brick building on the corner of Moore and

Whittier Streets. First a school house, it had been converted years before when the department grew too large to be housed entirely downtown. The building still contained the red brick façade and evenly spaced windows, but that was about all of the school that remained. The entire front lawn had been converted into a parking lot and an enormous flag pole sat in the middle of it. A concrete retaining wall encircled the pole, a thick tangle of flowers within.

Several lights burned bright from the building as we approached. A large church and a bank stood on either side of it, both dark. A handful of police cruisers filled a quarter of the parking lot, all of them aligned in a haphazard row oblivious to the stalls painted on the ground.

Watts joined the club by slamming the BMW to a stop diagonally across two handicapped stalls. She ripped the keys from the ignition and we both hopped out, the flasher still going strong atop the car.

Neither one of us even gave it a second glance as we headed inside.

I let Watts pull a half step ahead of me as we entered the building, both as a sign of deference and so she could lead the way. She took me straight past an unmanned desk and used her key fob to get us through a glass door crisscrossed with chicken wire. Not once did she glance back to make sure I was still with her or pause to ensure I followed. It would have been a waste of effort if she did. I had to will myself to slow down and not fly right past her.

Behind the door a hallway led us straight back through a row of identical offices, each one with a name and rank stenciled on the window. I noticed Watts's as we walked past, three down from the Branch Chief. Not the top dog, but she definitely had some clout.

At the end of the hallway we hooked a hard right and went past a row of holding cells. All three were empty, as was the guard desk that sat overlooking them. My guess is whoever was assigned to it was down watching the festivities with our guy next door.

Watts continued to stomp straight ahead, her gait and face both urgent. She keyed us through another door just past the holding cells and into a small hallway, this one alive with

189

voices. We walked forward a few more steps and circled into a viewing room housing every single officer I'd seen in the cafeteria a couple of hours earlier. In addition there were a couple of new faces in the crowd, no doubt whoever pulled the night shift at the precinct.

Probably the most action they'd seen around there in a long time. Had to be more interesting than putting up with drunks like most Saturday nights.

A few of them gave me sideways looks as I entered behind Watts, stopping just inside the door. Their gazes lingered for a moment as she took center stage in the room, reverting to her the moment she began to speak.

"Alright, give me everything we've got," she said. She stood with her hands on her hips as she addressed the room, her suit jacket bunched behind her wrists. Her left leg jutted out to the side and she scanned the room, entreating someone to speak.

A middle aged cop with bright orange hair and a healthy smattering of freckles took a half step forward and extended a small Steno pad in front of him. "This young man was apprehended thirty minutes ago cutting through the parking lot of the mini-mart adjacent to Applebee's. He was on foot, dressed in black cargo pants and a black zip-up hooded sweatshirt. He was found carrying a portable music player. No phone, no identification of any kind."

He kept his eyes diverted from her as he spoke, reading the words in front of him in a monotone voice void of emotion. Despite that, I could see a few droplets of sweat forming on his forehead and his budding paunch moving with quick breaths.

"Officers spotted the perpetrator as he slid through a bank of shrubs separating the two properties. A brief attempt at flight was made before the perpetrator abandoned the idea and was arrested without incident."

"Has he said anything?" Watts asked.

"Not one word," the Sergeant with sandy brown hair and the moustache said. As he spoke, Red retreated back into the crowd. "Has refused to answer any questions. We don't even know his name."

"Has he lawyered up yet?" Watts fired back.

"Hasn't said anything," the Sergeant echoed. "He appears to be in a state of shock and is almost catatonic. Doesn't look around much, just kind of sits and stares."

Watts swiveled towards the enormous bank window on the opposite side of the room. She twisted her head to examine it a few seconds before turning back. I knew enough to know it was one-way glass and that the perpetrator was sitting somewhere on the other side of it. From where I was though, I couldn't see a thing beyond the mass of uniformed humanity in front of me.

Watts started to speak again, but thought better of it. Without a word she strode over and disappeared through a side door. A murmur arose from the crowd as they pressed in tight, all jockeying for position at the viewing window. I remained where I was, glad to just be present. This entire situation had not sat right with me. Any second now it would be over, I just had to trust Watts knew what she was doing in there.

The room quieted down in expectation as I assumed Watts had entered. A cop with a head shaved clean and a prodigious stomach hanging over his belt pressed a button along the wall allowing her voice to stream into the room. I still couldn't see anything, but remembered my own time spent in a room like that enough to know what was going on. If given the choice between viewing or listening, I was fine with the current arrangement.

"Good evening," Watts said, her shoes clacking against a solid floor. All evening I had found the sound of boots to be rather annoying, but at the moment I realized they could also be quite imposing.

No response.

The sound of a chair scraped back across the ground. It moaned a bit as Watts lowered herself into it. "What's your name?"

No response. A few heads glanced back and forth amongst the crowd. Nobody even knew I was there.

"You realize it is in your best interests to cooperate, right?" Watts pressed, her voice even. "As it stands, you're looking at kidnapping, child endangerment, attempted murder and extortion. If you don't want to go away for the rest of your natural life, it would be in your best interest to talk to me right now."

The room leaned forward almost as one. The air sucked out in a collective gasp, everyone anxious to see how the perpetrator would react to that.

Again, he said nothing.

"I'm going to let you sit here and think about all that for a few minutes," Watts said. I could hear her shoes cutting a path across the floor again and a moment later, she was back with us.

From what I've seen on TV and read in books, it was classic interrogation technique. Get a young kid, throw a huge stack of charges at them, threaten them with the prospect of going to jail for the rest of their life. It usually doesn't take long for them to have a sudden change of heart.

Thankfully, I never went through the spiel. In truth, it was probably a good thing I didn't. No telling how differently things might have played out.

"Anything?" the Sergeant asked as Watts strode into the room. She slammed the file she was carrying down on the table and paced, her suit jacket back behind her wrist as she put one hand on her hip and the other to her forehead.

"Where is the money now?" Watts asked, ignoring the question.

Red motioned with his chin towards a table off to the side. My eyes slid to follow his motion, landing on the patent leather bag embroidered with Fuego's trademark flames. That thing really needed to go.

Watts sighed and resumed pacing. "One of two things. Either (A), he's really catatonic like you said, or (B), he was just a rabbit for someone that scares him a helluva lot more than we do."

Shit. The thought of him being a rabbit never entered my mind. Maybe he was nothing more than some kid told to walk through the parking lot just to see what would he happen. Maybe he wasn't saying anything because he didn't know anything.

Maybe the brilliant plan of the CPD just got my niece killed.

The ball returned to my stomach in a violent way, roiling uncontrollably. Sweat beaded across my upper lip and my breath grew short in my chest. I had to see this little bastard and get some idea for myself.

Careful to drag my feet so they didn't sound against the concrete floor, I began working my way to the left. I slid behind a pair of uniforms watching Watts' every move and skirted the outside of the room. As I walked, the viewing window came into sight little by little.

By the time I could see the young man sitting on the other side, I abandoned any attempt at being covert and walked straight for it. An inexplicable expression crossed my face, confusion replacing the anxiety of just a minute before.

Around the room, several heads turned to watch me. None of them said anything at first, but as I walked they began to stare. By the time I reached the window, many were gawking.

I could have cared less.

"Hey, partner, what the hell do you think you're doing?" a man snapped. I didn't recognize the voice, wasn't about to turn around and answer him.

Watts appeared by my side. "What is it?"

I raised a finger and tapped it against the glass. "I know this guy."

Chapter Twenty

Watts pressed a finger against the glass just inches from mine. Her head snapped towards me and her jaw dropped open. "What do you mean you know this guy? You mean..."

Clearly she was asking if this was somebody I had come in contact with in prison. I appreciated her not broadcasting that information to the group. Few things in life happen faster than a mood shift when people find out you're an ex-con. I don't even want to speculate how pronounced it is when those people are a room full of cops.

"I mean, I don't *know him* know him," I said, gazing at her and then back through the glass. "He was working the front desk at the ICU earlier this evening."

Behind me I could hear a buzz go through the crowd.

"Do you know his name?" Watts pressed.

I shook my head. "He wore a badge that said his name was Skip, but whether or not that's true I don't know."

Watts instantly shifted back into attack mode. "Mezner, get on the phone with Sacred Heart. Tell them we need everything they have on Skip from the ICU. I don't care what time it is or who you have to wake up."

She left me standing at the glass and strode right back through the side door. A wall of cops crowded in around me as she emerged on the other side of the window. A few of them nodded in my direction, while others glared. I guess they took umbrage with an outsider giving them a hand.

The early reports were right. Skip looked catatonic as he sat at the table. He was still dressed in black, his hooded sweatshirt zipped clear to his throat. His dark hair looked disheveled from having been under a hood earlier and dark circles hung beneath both eyes.

His gaze flitted to Watts as she entered before refocusing on the smooth grey table top in front of him. He made no movement as the door slammed shut behind her or as she tossed the file back down between them.

"Soooo, *Skip*," Watts said, settling herself into the chair across from him.

The comment hit home. He winced at the use of his name, the skin around his eyes tightening. "That is your name isn't it, Skip?"

His mouth dropped open a fraction of an inch, but he said nothing. Instead, he took in deep gulps of air.

"That's what I thought," Watts said. She tilted the file up towards herself and pretended to read through it. From where we were standing we could see there was nothing in it, though she did an excellent job selling it otherwise. "Also says here you work the graveyard shift in the intensive care unit over at Sacred Heart."

Sweat poured down Skip's face. All visible signs of color were gone, his face a ghostly white pallor.

"Is that how it goes Skip? You seek out families in the area, get some of your boys together, make a play on them? Beat up the dad, punch the mom, swipe the kid? Make a little money? Rinse and repeat?"

Skip was cracking. We could all see it. I only prayed she finished the job before he uttered anything about a lawyer.

"You messed up this time though, didn't you Skip? You trust your boys to punch the mom, grab the kid, but you don't trust them to pick up the money, do you? Had to be there to handle that part yourself?"

Skip's bottom lip started to tremble. Still, he said nothing.

"Right now, you're on the hook for that entire list I gave you earlier," Watts said, turning the screws further. "You give up your accomplices and you tell me where the kid is, we can talk. I can get the charges knocked down. If not, we're going to throw the book at your sorry ass."

Watts slapped the empty file closed and smacked it flat onto the table in front of her. "And when they send you away for a nice long time, I'm going to make sure everybody knows it was for kidnapping a little girl. I might even tell people you were using her for your own sick pleasure. You know what they do to guys like you in prison, Skip?"

I closed my eyes and set my jaw tight at this. I knew what Watts was getting at, but hearing the words that someone might be violating Annie made my blood run cold. For both our sakes, I kind of hoped Skip was clean. His because he was too young to die, mine because killing him in front of a roomful of cops would more or less end my life too.

Watts stood up and leaned forward over the table, her palms flat. She moved in until her nose was just inches from his and twisted her head to stare into his eyes. "In prison, you'll be the little girl Skip. And there won't be anybody for you to call out for."

Watts kept her face directly in front of his before sliding to the side. She let her hands linger on the table top as she pushed away, dragging them along and taking up the folder with her left. Every eye was glued to her as we all leaned in, waiting for some response. She made it almost to the door before Skip muttered his first words of the night.

"I didn't take the girl," he whispered. His eyes remained focused downward, glassy.

Watts stopped in front of the door, but said nothing. She made no move to turn around or return to the table either.

Skip swung his eyes to her, now red as moisture lined the bottoms of them. Catatonic had been replaced by wanton fear. "I don't have any boys, and we didn't punch anybody or put anybody in a coma."

Watts dropped her chin to her shoulder. "So who did?"

"I have no idea," Skip said, swinging his head from side to side. The flood gates were opening. Watts had cracked him. "I swear to God I have no idea."

Watts turned and folded her arms across her chest. She kept the folder tucked beneath her right bicep and stared down at him. "You're not making much sense Skip. We got a ransom demand while you were at work, which just so happened to be right down the hall from the family of the victim. Later you were grabbed going to fetch the money."

"All I know about is the money, I swear," Skip said, staring up at her. His eyes were wide, imploring her to believe him.

Watts narrowed hers. "And what do you know about the money?"

Skip's mouth dropped open and he shook his head. "I heard about what was going on when I came in to work tonight."

Dammit. Already I knew where this was going. My hunch from earlier was right. We'd just wasted almost three hours with this kid. For a moment, I weighed going in after him, roomful of cops be damned.

"You *heard* about what was going on?"

"Yeah, you know, from the staff. Nurses talk, so do techs and doctors. Everybody knew all about it. They were all too happy to fill me in."

I saw it the moment it clicked with Watts as well. Slow realization crept over her, replaced almost instantly by contempt. "So you heard we were waiting for a call, decided to make a little money huh? Told them to drop the money at one, you get off at two and head on over?"

Tears began to run down Skip's face. His face crinkled as he shook his head. "My mother's in a nursing home. I work at that Applebee's during the day and at the hospital at night to pay for it. I figured, this guy used to be a star football player, he's got money to burn. It's only fifty grand..."

His voice trailed off as he cried harder. He raised his head and said, "But I didn't hurt anybody. I swear to God I didn't hurt anybody."

Watts glared at him, but said nothing. Instead she strode out and slammed the door behind her.

The room seemed to stand still for a moment, unsure how to proceed. Several glances were cast from one to another as I retreated back to my corner by the door. I didn't need to look at Skip a moment longer. Nothing good could come from it.

Watts barged back in, the entire room cowering in front of her. "I want this kid booked right now. The first second we can get him into county lockup, do it. And keep him there as long as we can."

A couple of men disappeared through the door Watts just used. I assumed they would appear behind the glass a moment later, but my view was blocked. Also probably a good thing.

The room milled about for a full minute before filing out. Many of them had been called in to handle the ransom situation and now that it was over, they were no longer needed. With a few exchanged nods or half waves, they drifted off.

Watts stood with a hand to her head, rubbing her brow. Several pairs of eyes continued to watch her every move as she stomped back towards the far side of the room. She took up the garish black-and-flame bag from the table and gripped it by the handles on either side, holding it out in front of her.

With purposeful strides she exited the room, hissing "Come with me" under her breath as she passed. I said nothing, didn't even bother to look up at the remaining men watching, and slid out into the hallway behind her.

"Where we going?" I asked, jogging several quick steps and falling in beside her. She was moving fast and I had to almost run to keep up with her.

"Back to the beginning," she said, cutting a direct course back towards the parking lot. Through the front windows, I could still see the red and blue strobe light circling atop her car.

Chapter Twenty-One

Watts waited a moment for me to hit the passenger seat before dumping the money bag in my lap. The dead weight of fifty thousand dollars landed with a thud against the front of my jeans, a momentary swell of nausea rolling through my stomach. It receded just as Watts slammed the car into reverse and peeled away from the parking lot.

"Should I leave the flasher up top?" I asked, my voice neutral. Unlike her coworkers and underlings in the precinct, I wasn't afraid of her. I was just happy to be doing something again.

"Leave it," Watts said. Her hands deftly maneuvered the steering wheel as she hooked a left back towards the hospital. If even possible, the route was more deserted than an hour before.

There's a reason they say people working the three a.m. shift pulled graveyard duty, because that's exactly what the world is.

Lifeless.

With the flasher leading the way above us, Watts cut through the night, ignoring traffic signals and the lanes painted on the road. During normal daytime hours the drive between the two places took fourteen minutes. Earlier, she'd covered the ground in ten minutes. This time it was more like six.

We slammed to a stop in front of the main door. Watts left the car in the drop-off lane, turned on the caution lights and grabbed the keys from the ignition. I slid out opposite her and flipped the switch on the flasher but left it suctioned to the roof. No reason to wake a hospital full of sleeping patients.

Also no reason to be too hasty in taking it down. We might need it later.

I kept the money bag in my right hand as we went, making it look like I just held on to it without thinking. Already there was a plan forming in the back of my mind. I prayed it wouldn't come to that, but knew better than to rule it out. That's just kind of how the night had gone so far.

"Alright, so we're back to the beginning. What's the plan?" I asked, the two of us falling in side by side. Together we cut a path for the ICU, both oblivious to the loud sounds of our shoes echoing through the halls. We each had a dozen thoughts running through our minds and there wasn't anybody around to tell us to quiet down.

"We're going to go talk to your sister again. To your in-laws. There has to be something," Watts said. She too was beginning to show signs of strain. I guessed she was fast approaching a full twenty-four hours on her feet, punctuated by several stiff jolts of caffeine. Her mouth was drawn into a tight line and her eyes were bunched revealing crow's feet at the corners.

I glanced at the clock again as we swung past the ICU nurse's station. "Little bastard cost us three hours," I muttered. We were now just inside ten hours remaining. Single digits. Something needed to break, and fast.

Watts grunted some form of response and continued speed walking forward. Her fists were balled tight and the tail of her jacket swung back and forth as she headed for the final corner and made the turn.

At the opposite end of the hall Lex and my mother were both on their feet, watching us approach. Both of them had their arms folded across their torsos and Lex had her thumb up beside her face. She was going to be gnawing on the bone by the time I got Annie home to her.

A range of emotions crossed both their faces, spanning everything from hope to fear in a matter of seconds. The last they knew I said I would be right back. Now here I was well over an hour later with Watts and the money in hand. From where they sat, it couldn't look good.

"False alarm," I said in a loud faux whisper, holding a hand up for them. I could see Lex's chest lower as she exhaled a long breath and my mother reached out and laid a hand on her arm. From inside the room the Borden's both appeared, each looking like they'd just awoken from a nap.

Watts shot me a sideways glance. For a moment she looked hostile, but it passed as she realized what I'd done. Almost imperceptibly she nodded my way. "He's right. Turns out the ransom demand was made by a hospital employee who thought he could take advantage of the situation."

"*What?*" Lex asked, her face flat. Beside her, my mother pulled her hand from Lex's arm and held it to her agape mouth.

"The young guy who works the front desk here," Watts said, motioning back over your shoulder. "He heard through the hospital grapevine that we were waiting for a ransom call. Everybody in Columbus knows who Ricky Borden is, so he thought he would make a little money on the side."

"When this is over we're going to own this hospital," Sue Borden said, her eyes flashing. All four of us in the hallway turned to glance before facing back to one another.

Grief is one of the most dissected human emotions. Apparently Sue was already past denial and firmly entrenched in the anger stage of the process. It was just not something any of us needed right then, especially not my sister.

Lex ignored Sue and asked, "What does this mean? Are we any closer to finding my daughter?"

Watts opened her mouth to speak, but closed it and shook her head. "No. This guy's personal greed set us back a few hours. We're no closer, but we're no further either."

"This is all your fault you know," Sue spat. Again all eyes turned to face her. A snarl appeared on Watts' face and she raised a finger to respond before realizing Sue wasn't looking at her.

She was looking at me.

The entire bunch fell silent as Watt's finger lowered to her side. The comment was so unexpected, it took several seconds for it to sink in. When it did, I gave a hard twist of my head and made a disbelieving face. "*What?* My fault?"

"Well, she's right you know," Jim said, folding his arms across his chest and leveling the same accusing stare on me as his wife.

I could feel the veins in my forehead throbbing. If these people had any idea what I'd been through tonight they'd be on their knees kissing my ass right now. Instead they were hurling accusations my way. I balled my right hand into a fist so tight I could feel the fingernails digging into my palm. "How...the...hell...do...you...figure?"

I drew out every word so they could feel the malevolence dripping from them. These people had no idea how ugly this could get in a hurry.

Across from me I saw my mother put on a face that matched my own. She was in full-on Mother Lion mode. Nobody messed with her children, especially not right in front of her. Watts made a face that was part confused, part disciplinarian as she looked from one side to the other.

Lex remained between us, her gaze vacant as she stared at nothing particular on the wall.

"We all know what you did," Sue said. "It's no secret that's why you hide in Wyoming playing cowboy."

"He's not hiding from anything you self-righteous bitch," my mother seethed.

I appreciated knowing my mother had my back, but this wasn't her fight. It wasn't particularly one I wanted to have either. I knew the look on Lex's face to know this would send her over the edge in a hurry. I needed her in the moment to help me find Annie.

"Now wait just a minute there," Jim said, raising a hand and pointing it towards my mother. I was between them before even one more word could slide out. Like with Skip earlier, I knew I was hanging on by a thin thread. Part of me almost dared him to continue, the other part knew nothing good would come from it.

"No you wait," I said, swatting his hand down. "I haven't even been in Ohio in months. Your son's one of the biggest assholes in the country. The odds are he pissed off the wrong person and that's what this is all about, don't you think?"

"Our son isn't a murderer!" Sue spat, her voice rising just shy of a yell.

It took every fiber of my being not to club them both to a pulp with my cast. Instead of responding, I stood quivering with anger in the middle of the hallway.

My mother pressed tight against my back to let me know she was there. I could feel her trembling as well, no doubt wanting to tear Sue Borden limb from limb. Watts stood off to the side, a hand raised in either direction.

"She's still not wrong," Jim said. "Our son may be an asshole, but everybody knows you spent five years in prison for killing a man in cold blood. You were evil before you went to jail, no telling what you picked up inside."

I stared at the floor, my body still trembling. It didn't matter where I looked at that particular moment, all I could see was red. "And that's what you think this is about?"

"This is karma!" Sue said, her voice breaking as she started to cry. "This is you having to answer for your sins!"

"Go to hell!"

I couldn't take it anymore. I felt my mother's arms wrap around my wrist as I cocked my arm and prepared to shatter Jim's jaw. I wasn't going to hit Sue, but I was going to pound him so savagely she'd feel it. I didn't care if Watts arrested me right then.

Before I got a chance to throw that punch though, Lex stepped in. She didn't put herself between us, she didn't move at all in fact. What she did was far more powerful. She simply turned her head towards all of us and said, "They weren't his sins."

Chapter Twenty-Two

"Lex, don't," I whispered. All the air had sucked out of the hallway. Everyone stood staring at her, not knowing what to do. I wasn't sure what she planned to say next, but I prayed it wasn't what I thought she might.

Not here, not now. Not after so long.

"O, it's time," Lex whispered. Her eyes were glassy with tears as she turned to face me. Slowly I lowered my fist back to my side and my mother's hands freed themselves from my waist. The hostility of just a few moments before was already dispelled, waiting to see what she would do.

"Lex, *don't*," I said, casting my eyes towards Watts. A thick knot settled in the back of my throat. I would rather let Watts see me pound both the Borden's to within an inch of their lives than hear what Lex might say next.

"It doesn't matter," Lex said. "It's been twelve years. You served the sentence. It's time the truth came out."

I shook my head from side to side, but said nothing. This was not at all what I wanted. Annie, Annie was the most important thing right now.

"Alexa, what are you talking about?" my mother asked. "What's been twelve years?"

"You know," Lex whispered.

My mother's eyes glassed over to match Lex's and her hand went to her chin. "You mean the accident."

Lex shook her head. "It wasn't an accident, but you always knew that too."

I closed my eyes and lifted my face towards the ceiling. Every bit of my being wanted her to stop, but just as surely I knew she wouldn't.

Lex turned her attention past me and my mother to the Borden's. Watts had lowered her arms back to her side and stood off to the left, watching the entire scene unfold. "Twelve years ago, just after our high school graduation, our father was killed. He'd worked a double shift that day and was coming home around midnight. It was dark and it had been raining."

My mother reached out and tried to take my hand. When her hand found the cast, she wrapped it around my forearm instead.

"A group of high school kids from Marysville were out at the same time. They'd been to some graduation parties, had been drinking, lost control of their car and did a complete one-eighty into oncoming traffic. Our father slammed into the rear end of their car going sixty miles an hour. He died on impact, none of them got more than some bruises."

My mother's nails dug into me. That night was over twelve years past, but it still burned hot within us all. He was only forty at the time.

"The two passengers in the car were given citations for underage intoxication. The driver was released on bail and given a court date for later in the summer. At a time when we should have been going on a senior trip and celebrating, we buried our father and waited for trial."

Lex stopped for a moment to clear her throat. Part of me was desperate for her to stop talking. Another part didn't want her to quit. Somewhere, deep down, I knew I needed to hear it.

"Turned out the kid's dad was some kind of big-time attorney downtown. Worked for Nationwide, knew all the prosecutors in the area, even the judge. He bargained it clear down to some community service and a little bit of probation. Not even a slap on the wrist."

Up until this point everything she'd said was public knowledge. As much as I wanted to hear it, I couldn't let her say it. "Lex, don't do this. Leave it be. Let these assholes think what they want."

She turned her tear-filled eyes to me. "But what if they're right? What if this is all happening to right some long-standing wrong?"

"You don't believe that," I said. Everyone else watched us like a crowd watching a tennis match, their heads swinging back and forth. Confusion was splashed across every one of their faces.

"But what if it is?" Lex continued. "What if my little girl is in danger right now to get back at me? For what I did to that boy? What I did to you?"

My mother's nails dug so hard into my arm I thought they would tear the fabric of my clothes. She pressed tight against my hip and whispered, "Go on honey."

"The day we found out, O was beside himself. Our father was his hero, one of his best friends in the world, and his killer was going to go free without ever seeing the inside of a jail cell. He couldn't bear the idea. He stole a bottle of Jack Daniels and a shotgun from the house and set off to even the score."

I felt a tingle run down the nape of my neck. These were details that had never seen the light of day. I wasn't sure I wanted them there.

"I don't know why, but I went with him," Lex continued. "I knew when he left that he was in a bad place. I couldn't bear the thought of losing my dad and my brother just a month apart, so I went to try and talk him down.

"Somehow, O'd figured out where this guy lived. He drove straight to the end of his street and parked at a playground looking down towards his house. We got there early in the evening and stayed through the night. We talked a lot and watched everybody that came and went.

"By morning, O was completely wasted. He'd finished the entire bottle of Jack, and he never drinks. As far as I know it's the only alcohol he's ever had in his life."

She slid her eyes to me and I nodded. She was right. To this day that evening is the only time in my life I lost control of myself for even a minute.

"Shortly after dawn, O broke down and cried. He told me how much pain he was in and how much he missed dad. By the time he was done, it was clear the plan was never going to happen. He had no intention of harming that boy, he just needed somewhere to aim his frustrations.

"After that, he passed out. Cold. He slumped to the side and fell across the front seat of the truck. Back then he was a lot bigger and it took me almost twenty minutes of pulling and lugging to get him off to the side. By the time I did, the sun was rising."

Every eye was focused on Lex. I could literally hear my heart pounding in my ears and feel my chest rising and falling with each breath. She was actually going to do it.

" I have no idea why I did what I did next. The entire truck smelled like whiskey and dad's shotgun was lying behind the seat. I had just gotten O wrestled into the passenger seat and was sweaty and pissed off. I'd never seen my brother cry, I'd just lost my father, and unfortunately for that poor bastard he chose that moment to pull out of his driveway."

Lex lowered her chin to her chest as heavy tears slid down her cheeks. "I aimed the wheel at him and gunned the engine as hard as I could. We slammed into him head on and killed him instantly, just the way he did dad.

"The impact woke O, though he was still pretty drunk. The boy's father heard what happened and came running down, saw O staggering around. They took one whiff and figured out he was drunk. By the time the cops got there, they swore they'd watched the entire thing from the front steps as they waved their son off for the morning."

221

Lex sniffed and raised her eyes. Her face was red and puffy, glistening with tears. My mother continued to grind her nails into my flesh, the entire group hanging on every word.

"The judge gave O five years for vehicular manslaughter. He would have gotten less, but since he was drunk and the guy's dad was an attorney, he got the higher end of the sentence. O never once said a word to anybody that he wasn't the one driving that morning. He swore me to secrecy and said he'd lie and tell everyone he did it anyway. Shortly thereafter, he went to prison and I went off to college and met Ricky."

She leveled her eyes on the Borden's. "And that's why he's here now. He gave up his life for me, and I knew he'd give up his life for Annie. None of this is his fault. It's mine."

Chapter Twenty-Three

Lex covered her face with her hands. She remained stone still for a few moments before her shoulders started to wrack with silent sobs. After several of these, she broke into violent crying that rang through the hallway. Across from us the Borden's looked at each other dolefully and retreated into the room. My mother moved forward and wrapped herself around my sister, who remained rigid before hugging her back.

Within seconds, they were both sobbing. The floodgates were open, from the situation we now faced and the pain that we had all locked away long ago.

A small ripple of emotion passed through me, replaced just as fast in my mind by an image of Annie. There would be time for this later. Right now I had a task to complete and I had nine and a half hours to do it.

I motioned with my chin towards the front door to Watts. She began to drift that way as I put an arm around Lex and my mother and pulled them tight for a moment. I kissed the top of both their heads and whispered, "I'll be back."

Each of them nodded, but said nothing. They were crying too hard to speak.

I took off back down the hallway in a quick march, Watts moving fast to keep in stride. We said nothing until we cleared the ICU. Once our boots found the tile of the front foyer I said, "I need to hang on to this money."

It wasn't an order, but it definitely wasn't a question.

Watts picked up on the message and cast a sideways glance to me. "That money's technically evidence in a crime."

"It technically belongs to my sister," I countered. I knew we were both right, though hers trumped mine by quite a bit. I just hoped she'd be willing to overlook it.

We walked out through the front door to the BMW still sitting in the loading zone, caution light affixed to the roof. She put her hands back on her hips and said, "All that she just said in there..."

I looked at her, knowing she was thinking she'd just been handed a full confession. Hopefully she'd be willing to overlook that for the next few hours as well. "I don't suppose there's any way you can un-hear that can you?"

Watts waved a hand at me. "That's not what I meant. Did you really go to prison to protect your sister?"

I gave her one long look before turning away, saying nothing.

She studied me as if debating something before nodding her head. "Where are you going?"

Telling her where I was headed was the last thing I wanted to do. I might not have been guilty the first time I went to prison, but I'd already done some things tonight that would land me back there. More were bound to come.

At the same time, I was asking her to overlook a full confession and let me walk away with a giant bag of evidence. "Cincinnati."

She raised a questioning eyebrow. "What's in Cincinnati?"

I sighed and lifted my gaze back to her. At this point, I had nothing more than a hunch and a prayer. "I don't know. I talked to someone earlier that told me I might find what I'm looking for down there."

The other eyebrow raised to form a matching set.

"I know it's vague and it sounds like I'm hiding things, and I probably am. The information I got came from some very off-the-record conversations with some people I wish I'd never met. I don't know how accurate it is, but it's all I've got. I have to try."

Watts nodded her head, comprehension sliding over her. "The old Brothers-Behind-Bars network."

"Those men were never my brothers," I replied.

And I meant it.

"How big is it? Should I be riding shotgun?" she asked. "Or better yet, should I leave you here and go check it out myself?"

I didn't want to tell her about Merric's phone still locked in my truck and I damned sure didn't want her showing up down there in full-on cop mode. Something told me an operation like this had a fail-safe in case the police showed up. She went in through the front door, the kids disappeared out the back.

Again though, I couldn't very well just tell her that.

"I truly don't know. If it is something, it should be you. If it's not, you should be here working the pavements, not wasting four hours on a round trip."

Watts stood motionless for several more moments, mulling it over. She knew as well as I that she had no further leads in Columbus. The only option she had was standing in the ICU crying her eyes out. At the same time, following one crazy hunch to Cincinnati wasn't a very efficient use of her time.

She pulled a hand from her hip and fished a business card from her jacket pocket. She held it between her index and middle finger and extended it to me, the same as she had to Lex hours before. "You call me if you find anything. And I mean *anything*."

"Yes ma'am," I said, accepting the card.

"I can have Cinci PD there in five minutes flat. Do not do anything stupid and go charging in somewhere like, well, a cowboy on a horse."

I smirked. These Midwesterners really loved that imagery for some reason. "I won't."

She jerked her head towards the bag in my hand. "I'm inclined to hang on to the money just to make sure of that, but I won't. You might need it."

"Thank you," I whispered. She was going out on a limb for me. I had no idea why, but I wasn't about to question it. I nodded once more to her and headed towards my truck.

Behind me I heard her softly say good luck. I made no effort to turn and respond, only offering a small wave of my left hand as I strode away into the night.

Chapter Twenty-Four

I put Merric's cell phone on the dashboard and stared at it all the way from Columbus to Lebanon, just north of Cincinnati. With the truck set on cruise control I alternated glances between the clock on the dash and the phone. The clock inched on towards five a.m., ratcheting up the pressure inside of me. There was just eight hours to go. Something had to happen fast. The phone kept telling me I wasn't entirely sure what that something was.

I worked at my right index fingernail for twenty minutes as I rolled into the northern suburbs of Cincinnati, the metallic taste of blood filling my mouth. It wasn't as good as a cup of coffee, but I was already so wired it was probably better for me at the moment. The first signs of morning traffic were starting to dot the highway as I pushed the truck off the right shoulder and followed an exit onto Kings Mill Road.

The truck whined as I turned into a Shell station parking lot and grabbed up the phone from the dash. Outside a single man in jeans and ball cap filled his oversized Dodge pickup with gas, paying me no mind. Otherwise there were no signs of life around, despite blinding lights bathing everything in a fluorescent glow.

I flipped the phone open and saw there were six missed calls. All from the same number, all matching the one I'd noticed before with the 513 area code. That was a good sign.

Using my thumb I cleared the screen and went back to the text message menu. There were still only three there. The first was nothing, a simple greeting. The third was a farewell. The second one was what I was after, a confirmation of a time and place. Pier Twelve, nine a.m.

That was still four hours away, and a worst case scenario. If I could find whoever this was, maybe I could make a deal long before it came to that. At the very least I could figure out if Annie was even down here. I didn't have time to waste, certainly not four hours to catch a boat that might have God-knows-what loaded aboard it.

I took a deep breath and watched as the lone customer climbed into his truck and drove away. The muffler roared as he swung out onto the road, announcing for the world that he was a big man with a truck.

The corner of my mouth curled in a smirk before I even realized it.

Going back to the phone, I pulled up the call log and paused. I stared down at the same number listed several times in succession and practiced my best Gaelic accent. It sounded like shit. I could only hope whoever it was wouldn't notice. I pressed the call button and held the phone to my ear.

It rang only once before someone snapped it up. The voice was deep and clearly pissed. "Where the fuck have you been?"

These guys were business partners. I knew from Troy that Merric was lower on the totem pole, but not a complete nobody in the structure. "It's Saturday night, where the hell do you think I've been?"

I spat the words out in my best accent, wincing and holding my breath.

"What the hell's wrong with your voice?" the man snapped.

Dammit. I kept the accent in place and went with it. I was out of options. "I've got a cold, what are you, my mother?"

The man paused for several seconds. "What's the name of your right hand man?"

"*What?*" I snapped, my voice almost betraying me. The question was genuinely my own and slid out before I realized I was asking it. No choice but to keep playing the angle. "What kind of shite is this? You're testing me now?"

"Answer the question," the man breathed back.

"Vincent. His name is Vincent and he's sitting right here, would you like to talk to him?" I filled my voice with incredulity, almost shouting in the empty parking lot.

The line was silent for several long seconds. I held my breath and prayed I hadn't overplayed my hand.

"Look man, you disappeared all night and when you finally call you sound like some dick giving me a fake accent, so don't go running your mouth to me!"

I was on thin ice, but at least I was still on ice. "Sorry," I mumbled. "Long ass night."

"That's better," the man replied. His voice wasn't quite as deep as Ving Rhames's back at Troy's, but it had a lot more bravado to it. This was clearly someone used to getting their way. "Everything good for this morning?"

So that's why he was calling. This was my opening, if I was going to make a move, this had to be it. "Actually, I've got a couple more for you."

Silence. I held my breath for several long seconds, staring hard through the front windshield. Outside, I could see the dark outlines of roller coasters across the street at the King's Island amusement park against the morning sky, all standing silent.

"You shitting me? It's already five o'clock man, the unit is loaded. You know I don't like last second deliveries."

He wasn't yelling, but his voice was hard.

"You'll want these," I said, my voice trying to convey confidence despite it fleeing from me by the second. "And my guys are already en route. They'll be there shortly to make the delivery."

Again, silence. "I don't like this, man. I told you about this before. Switching the orders at the last second is asking for trouble."

"This is the last time, I swear. The guys grabbed a group I wasn't expecting, so I thought I'd add them on. Free of charge," I had no idea what I was doing. Hell, I didn't even know who I was talking to. The odds of me seeing tomorrow were going down by the second.

Oddly enough, I didn't care.

"Don't tell me they're free like you're doing me some damn favor," the man said. "You know that's not how this arrangement works. I tell you to get me a load, you get me as many as you can."

I *really* didn't like whoever was on the other end of this call. It would be better for both of us if we never met.

"Well, I got some more," I said, trying hard to maintain the adopted accent through gritted teeth. "You want them or not?"

"Course I want 'em!" the man snapped. "If your boys are here in the next hour, just bring them by the shop. If not, take them straight on over to the dock."

Here it was, the moment of truth. I didn't want to go anywhere near this guy's shop, which probably looked something like Troy's place from earlier. At the same time, I couldn't afford to wait four more hours. I was already down to eight. "They'll be there in a few minutes. What's the address again?"

"Man, who the hell is this!?" the man bellowed. "Merric, *the real Merric,* knows damn well where my shop is!"

Shit.

I'd managed to play it off the first time, I had to hope for another miracle. "I know *where* the damn shop is! It's on the waterfront! I just asked for the street address. I gave my guys a GPS, not a damn road map. This isn't 1985 anymore!"

The line went dead. I waited several seconds before flinging the phone against the passenger door and going inside to get another cup of coffee. It looked like I had a much longer morning ahead of me than I anticipated.

Chapter Twenty-Five

It was nudging six o'clock by the time I found Pier Twelve. It was tucked along the riverfront just beneath the Brent Spence Bridge, the cantilever structure carrying interstates 71 and 75 into Kentucky. Out to the left sat Paul Brown Stadium and Great American Ballpark, home to the Bengals and Reds respectively. Both sat empty and resting along the river like bullfrogs brooding in the morning half-flight.

I was down to eight hours and counting. Part of me wanted to call Watts and see if she'd gotten anywhere in Columbus, but the more prudent part of me staved off the idea. If she had anything, there was an entire police force to back her up. If she didn't, she might be tempted to come join me.

A thin grey light blanketed the world as I pointed my truck down Pier Twelve. I hadn't spent much time around water in my day, but it looked pretty close to what I'd always expected a dock to look like. It was over a hundred yards wide at the base, made entirely of concrete. A few warehouses lined the outer edges while a series of smaller buildings filled in the gaps between them and dotted the landscape through the middle. Industrial sized dumpsters sat in haphazard patterns around the grounds and a few overhead cranes stood silent, their hooks pointing down. A couple of gas pumps were interspersed as well.

The entire scene looked like it could use a good cleaning and a coat of paint.

The wide base extended out about eighty yards before giving way to a series of long docks. Also made of concrete, they jutted out into the Ohio River like fingers from a palm. All of them were lined with metal shipping containers stacked in even rows. I couldn't see any forklifts around, but knew they must be close by.

I pulled the truck about halfway down the pier and backed it up against a dumpster along the far left side. At six o'clock on a Sunday morning the docks were dead, a fact I hoped to use to my advantage. One quick glance around revealed there was no way I could check every container by hand in the next few hours, and that was assuming there was no surveillance around to wonder why some *cowboy* was walking around banging on doors. My best bet was to wait for movement and hope it pointed me in the right direction.

My right hand reached into the box of mini donuts on the bench seat beside me, grabbed two and crammed them into my mouth. After not eating for almost thirty-six hours, the chocolate covered pastries tasted divine. A few swigs of the extra large coffee resting between my legs helped them go down. As soon as they were gone, I repeated the process until both containers were empty.

A dull buzzing filled the truck, setting my nerves on edge. I remembered Merric's cell phone was buried somewhere inside the littered cabin and dove down to the opposite floorboard. With my right hand I tossed aside mounds of cups and wrappers until I found the phone resting against a knotted pair of bungee cords.

I thumbed it open to see the same number I'd just spoken to looking back up at me. This was going to go one of two ways fast. I stared at it for a moment as it continued to vibrate against my palm before exhaling and flipping it open. I was going to continue playing Merric and hope for the best.

"Yeah?" I let annoyance show. Nobody hangs up on Merric and take forty-five minutes to call back.

"Who the hell is this?" the same heavy voice demanded.

"What? Who the hell do you think this is? You called me, remember?"

"No, I called *Merric,*" the voice snapped. "I asked who the hell you are."

I made a pained sound into the phone. This was not good. Part of me was already starting to wish I'd tossed the phone in the trash back at the Shell station. "What do you mean who am I? I'm Merric you idiot."

"Fuck you!" the man screamed. "Merric's dead, and so are you when I get to you."

The knot of barbed wire in my stomach expanded through my chest and into my throat. Not only had I not learned a damn thing about where Annie was, I had possibly outed myself as Merric's killer to his business partner.

My eyes rolled to the glove compartment, my thoughts on the Luger stashed away in there.

I dropped the accent. There was no point in it anymore. "I didn't kill him," I said. Even I had a hard time believing the words as they left my mouth. There was no way he was going to believe me.

"Bullshit," the man said. "You know Vincent, you have his phone, and you answer with a piss poor imitation of him."

True on all points. I was already starting to wish I'd called Watts on this. "Yeah, I went to see him last night and yeah, I met Vincent. But I didn't kill anybody. They were already like that when I got to them."

"Man, you lying bitch, who the hell do you think you're talking to?" Worse than thinking I'd killed his partner, he now felt disrespected. This was getting worse by the second.

"Actually, I have no idea," I said.

I could hear him draw in a sharp breath to yell again, but he stopped short. "Wait...*what?*"

"I don't know who I'm talking to," I said again. "But I want to meet you."

He exhaled every bit of breath he had on the opposite end. "You got some nerve you know that? What the hell could you possibly want to meet me for?"

"I want to make a trade." I was on thin ice. Not because I didn't think he'd meet with me. I knew he would. More to the point that I would be walking right into a trap.

"You got to be shitting me," he said. "You kill my partner, try to pretend to be him, disrespect me, then want to do business with me?"

When it was all listed out that way, it did sound like I was shitting him. Nobody was that crazy.

"Yeah," I muttered. I closed my eyes and pictured Annie. I thought of her the winter before playing in the snow for the first time, her mound of curls bunched up under a hand-knit cap my mother made. "I want to do business with you."

The man laughed. Not in a haha, somebody-just-said-something-funny sort of way, but in a it's-my-lucky-day sort of way. It was a trap. There was just nothing I could do about it. I was out of options, and I was even lower on time. "Well alright then. You know where Pier Three is?"

I was sitting less than a mile from it. "You mean down on the waterfront?"

"Where the hell else would a pier be?"

I exhaled. I was playing his game now. I couldn't lose my temper and pop off. "Yeah, I have a good idea where it is."

"A good idea huh?" the man said. "Well how long do you think it'll take you and this good idea of yours to get here?"

I considered the question. Just like with Troy and Merric, I knew I couldn't walk up carrying a gun. It would be best to be in the truck as long as possible, which meant driving. At the same time, if I did somehow live to get out of there I would want my truck and the guns left untouched if I needed them. I glanced again at the dashboard and did the math backwards in my head. "I can be there in half an hour."

"You have fifteen minutes."

The line went dead before the words were even out of the air.

Chapter Twenty-Six

I parked at Pier Six. The drive from Twelve was quick and simple, the piers descending in numeric order every few hundred yards. Parking three away left me somewhere between a quarter and a half mile out, which was close enough to get there in time and get back quickly if I somehow survived. Far enough away to be seen arriving on foot without them taking my truck.

Each of the piers had a little different makeup as I slid past them, though the basic premise was the same. A wide concrete base housing whatever building was needed offset by several long docks extending into the water. I remember seeing an old picture from the fifties that showed every single dock busy hauling metals and textile goods downriver towards the Mississippi. Now, they looked to be less than half active.

Better than most industries, all things considered.

Pier Six looked like it was still fairly active hauling lumber. A few split rail trucks were parked beside enormous cranes, their back ends filled with rough hewn logs ready to be hoisted into containers. A few piles of bark and sawdust sat in random spots around the yard and a couple of lean-to's had pallets stacked high beneath them.

Unlike the others, there were no gas pumps anywhere. Too much of a fire hazard.

I pulled the truck to a stop behind one of the log wagons, tucked in tight between it and a small outbuilding. The wagon looked like it had been parked for a couple of days and a heavy layer of sawdust rested against its tires. The building's front door stood sagging open and one of the windows was broken, shards of glass hanging down in a haphazard arrangement.

Clearly nobody had been here in quite some time. The odds of anyone showing up at dawn on a Sunday were pretty low.

I left the keys above the visor. Somebody was bound to search me when I arrived and I didn't want them getting any ideas. My shotgun called to me from behind the seat and I contemplated trying to sneak in the Luger from the glove compartment, but I opted against them both. Whatever comfort I might feel from having them with me would be offset by the ire I would raise by walking in armed.

My eyes fell on the black money bag on the seat. For a moment I considered taking it with me, but decided against it. Any man with the kind of juice to own multiple piers and leave them sitting empty wouldn't blink at fifty thousand dollars. Besides, taking a bag that sized into a hornet's nest would almost certainly raise suspicion.

Carrying only the ceramic switchblade still lodged inside my sock, I stepped out into the damp morning air and began walking. The layer of sawdust coating the ground muffled the sound of my boots as I crossed the pier and made my way back to the street, the clock ticking down in my head. I had been given fifteen minutes. I was down to just under ten.

Piers Five and Four passed by in order, neither of them looking like they'd been touched in eons, which made sense. If this guy was running an enterprise out of Pier Three, he probably owned the ones on either side just to make sure there weren't too many people around.

This wasn't a small timer I was dealing with here.

Great.

The clock ticked down to five minutes as I crossed onto Pier Three. I kept a steady pace going with my head angled down in front of me, my eyes flicking from side to side.

For all their efforts at trying to remain isolated, these guys didn't know a damn thing about being inconspicuous. The pier resembled a small city. Two large warehouses lined the outer edges of either side. All four stood three stories high and were painted black, easily in the best repair of any building I'd seen all morning. Each of them was lined with fresh washed windows tinted so dark they almost matched the black paint of the exterior.

At the back, sitting right in front of me, was a building that looked like a miniature version of Tony Montana's house in *Scarface*. It stood two stories tall with wrap around porches on both levels and thick columns supporting them both. A small fountain sat in front of it, shooting water ten feet into the air in a wide fan. A tangle of SUV's and trucks sat in front of the house and as I approached, I could see a handful of men begin to dot the second floor porch.

Like the warehouses on either side, the house and fountain were painted black. Every vehicle in front of them was as well and the men standing guard were dressed in matching outfits of the same midnight hue.

Not much imagination with this crew, that's for sure. It's not every day I'm the most colorful thing in sight.

I rocked my weight forward so the boots hit on the balls of my feet and walked straight across the pier towards the house. It wasn't hard to figure out where this guy would be holed up, it was the only building with any signs of life. The fact that those signs of life were carrying automatic weapons made it all the more obvious.

After a moment I lowered myself and let my feet hit the ground as normal. It didn't matter how loud my heels were against the concrete, they could already see me coming.

Behind the house docks jutted out on either side, the low concrete rows barren. A healthy swath of dark rubber skid marks darkened the ground covering them, paths diverging towards each of the warehouses spread about the pier. There was no telling what each of them housed as they stared down at me, but it was very apparent they didn't want it sitting out in the light of day.

The front door of the house opened long before I got there. I couldn't see it, hidden behind the peacock-tail fan of the fountain, but I could hear the hinges on the door creaking. Dawn was just beginning to break over everything, though overhead it was still dark enough for handfuls of stars to be seen.

I swung out to the left of the fountain and circled around it, my hands by my side. I made sure to keep them out of my pockets and in plain sight as the fountain slid from my field of vision and the front door came into sight. In front of it three men stood in a tight line, only a couple of inches separating each of their shoulders. They were all white, with very pale skin and hair shorn close to their heads. All three wore black cargo pants and lace-up boots. The men on either side wore Spandex shirts and the one in the middle wore a black ribbed tank top.

Together they stood and watched as I approached. It was impossible to get a good read on their faces as they hid behind mirrored sunglasses, though their body language was somewhere between disdain and indifference. None of the men were overly bulky, instead cut from corded muscle interspersed with veins.

All three carried some kind of assault rifle in front of them. I wasn't quite sure what they were, just knew they definitely weren't M-16's.

Maybe Israeli, possibly Russian.

I raised my hands a few inches, walked up the two short steps onto the porch and paused in front of them. Part of me wanted to say I was there for a meeting, but I had no idea who I was meeting with. Besides, they knew who I was. I was doing everything on their terms now.

"You the dumbass here to see Rif?" Tank Top asked from the middle. He snapped the words out like a challenge. It was obvious he thought my showing up like this was just plain stupid.

He was probably right.

"Yeah, he's expecting me."

Tank Top smirked. "We've all been expecting you."

He jerked his head in an upward nod and two more men materialized from either side. I hadn't even noticed them positioned behind the enormous porch columns and wondered how many more were roaming the place. They were dressed like the others, but carried no visible weapons as they gave me a quick pat down. It was brusque and much rougher than it needed to be, but they found nothing.

I didn't say a word. I didn't let on that I even noticed. I sure as hell didn't show any relief that they missed the knife tucked low against the inside wall of my boot.

The men disappeared again to either side as Tank Top nodded and retreated through the front door. The Spandex Twins on either side of him parted for me to pass, then fell in behind us, encircling me in a tight triangle. As a group, we marched in lockstep through the front door and into an enormous foyer.

The inside of the house differed in every way from the outside. Though it had the facade of a residence, functionally it looked more like a warehouse. The entire first floor was open, save a dozen or so thick support columns equally spaced throughout. The ground was concrete brushed smooth and the walls were unfinished, formed from either block or exposed wood frames. Small rooms were sectioned off in various places by chain link fence, some containing video surveillance monitors and others with boxes piled high. One even had a dozen or so cots lined tight, many of them filled with inert objects rolled in blankets.

This wasn't an office, it was a compound.

Tank Top led me through the center of the space, as much to show me what I was up against as to reach the elevator tucked against the back wall. He stepped inside and pressed a button to send us up one floor while the Spandex Twins stopped short and stood guard on either side. From what I could see, it was the only way in or out of the second floor.

The door slid apart, opening me into yet another different world. Gone was the dark décor of everything else on the pier, replaced by a spacious floor plan with walls painted white and fixtures all in gold. Tank Top stepped forward onto a sparkling white tile foyer and nodded as a new pair of Spandex Twins fell in on either side of me. Off to the left was a dining room with a polished oak table and chairs, a full kitchen just beyond it. To the right was a master bedroom suite, a four poster bed just visible through the ajar door.

As a triangle we walked forward towards a set of wooden doors. Made from some kind of dark hardwood they were hand carved with the word Lucio spelled out in script letters on the left and Rifkin on the right. They parted as we approached to reveal a sprawling office that extended the entire length of the floor in both directions.

Bookshelves lined the wall to my back and sides, giving way to windows facing out towards the parking lot. Contemporary office furniture, sofas and arm chairs, were positioned to either side and an enormous desk sat right in front of me.

Behind it was a diminutive man in a wheelchair. He wore a pair of tan linen pants and a white shirt buttoned to the collar, his pale head shaved clean. His fingers were steepled in front of him as we approached, his dark eyes tracing over me.

Not what I was expecting in the least.

His eyes searched over me for several long seconds, the room silent. "So you are the gentlemen that killed my business partner, then had the audacity to call and ask to meet with me?"

His voice was the same deep and booming baritone from the phone, seeming out of place on a man of his appearance.

I paused before answering. The question was phrased so as to be a trap. "I didn't kill your partner, but I am the man that called and asked to meet with you."

Rifkin stared at me for several long moments before shifting his eyes to the side. I followed his gaze to the far wall where a forty-two inch plasma television was mounted between two book cases. For a moment, the screen was nothing but dark fuzz before an image came into view.

The video showed the interior of Merric's office, the image taken just hours before. On it, I could see myself shooting Merric before taking his cell-phone and reclaiming my knife from Vincent's chest. The video started just seconds before I dealt the fatal bullet to Merric and ended just as I was leaving, my face frozen in front of the camera.

The barbed wire in my stomach began to twirl like a hamster on a wheel as a heavy sweat engulfed my body. All moisture fled from my mouth as I did my best to turn an impassive gaze back to Rifkin.

Still, I said nothing.

"So again I ask," Rifkin said, "so this is the man that killed my business partner, then had the audacity to call and ask for a meeting with me?"

My tongue felt like a wedge of sandpaper in my mouth. "Yes."

Rifkin kept his fingers pointed upward in front of him. "So you lied to me."

I said nothing.

He kept his eyes locked on me for several long seconds, a morose look on his face. Finally he turned his gaze to Tank Top and nodded.

In one quick movement Tank Top shot a flat palmed strike into my stomach. All of the air escaped my lungs in a burst as I doubled at the waist, the smooth hardwood floor filling my vision. He jerked my right arm back behind me, extending my hand up and away from my body. I tried to stand and pull my arm free, but the Spandex Twins appeared on either side and forced me to continue staring at the ground.

"You see, I do not deal with men I cannot trust," Rifkin recited as if scolding a child. "You chose to start this off by lying to me, so until I have wiped the slate clean there is no way I can trust you."

I felt Tank Top grab my pinkie by the base and squeeze it tight, a practiced move that extended my finger to full length as the nerve's inside it screamed in protest. A moment later a metal sleeve slid down over it and clenched.

Excruciating pain tore through my arm as I gasped, stars dancing before my eyes. My entire body wracked with shock as I remained bent at the waist, four boots staring up at me. Just a second later, Tank Top released his grip and my arm fell back to my side. The boots slid back away from my field of vision, replaced by the bottom half of my pinkie lying bloody on the floor.

Twenty-Seven

My body's first reaction was to cradle my hand. I jerked my right hand down and attempted to wrap my left around it, only to have it jam it against my cast. The room swayed in several tight revolutions as my eyes bulged and I gulped in deep breaths of air. Without realizing it, I dropped to a knee and drew in ragged gasps, droplets of blood hitting the floor in a random pattern beneath me.

"Maurice, take care of that," Rifkin said from somewhere above me. His voice still possessed the same rich baritone, though it sounded bored.

A pair of hands grabbed me beneath the armpits and roughly hauled me to my feet, my boots slamming down beneath me. A moment later Tank Top appeared and stuffed a wad of fresh gauze into my hand, motioning for me to cover the wound.

Beneath me, the other Spandex Twin sprayed some sort of solution on the blood droplets and wiped them up with paper towels.

Despite the pain searing through my body, this display told me two things. One, that Rifkin was OCD about cleanliness. Two, this was not the first time this sort of thing had happened.

My mind alternated between courses of action. The initial shock subsided a bit, giving way to the throbbing pain. Incredulity pulsed through me and I wanted more than anything to leap over the desk, dump the bald bastard on the floor and use my knife to smear his blood over every square inch of the place. Another part of knew they were three armed men surrounding me that would cut me down before I even made it to, let alone over, the desk.

The final part, the part that spoke louder than the others, was telling me this wasn't about me right now. This was about Annie.

I pinched the insides of either check between my teeth and wound the gauze around the stump of my finger. Blood soaked through the first few layers and it wasn't until the padding was over a quarter inch thick that it remained white. I used the entire ball that Tank Top gave me and tucked the end down inside the previous layer.

"You are right Mr. Rifkin. I shouldn't have lied to you."

The words surprised him. I could tell by the look on his face that it wasn't the reaction he was expecting and I silently chalked up a point in my favor. At this point, I would take anything.

His eyebrows rose in unison. "Usually it takes at least two fingers before people receive the message."

"No need for that," I assured him. "Message received." The words tasted bitter coming out of my mouth, but I managed to say them with a straight face. I'd been through too much to do something stupid out of pride or anger.

Rifkin nodded to the men and they retreated a half step away from me. Close enough to still keep me from trying anything, far enough that we could talk freely. He opened his mouth to speak, then closed it and regarded me again. His eyes lingered over my attire, the state of both of my hands and the robin's egg protruding above my left temple. "What the hell are you doing here?"

I paused to consider my answer. Given that half my pinkie was gone, I'd lost the ability to bullshit him even a little. He would see right through it, and my own seething anger wouldn't allow it. I decided to cut right to the chase. "I'm here for the same reason I went to see Merric."

At the mention of Merric, Tank Top and the Twins all tensed, but moved no closer as Rifkin watched me. "I've seen the video. If you think you can defeat all four of us and then walk out the front door, you're full of shit."

We both knew that already, he just felt the need to say it aloud. Despite his appearance of being in control, he was OCD and had Little-Man Syndrome, compounded by being in a wheelchair.

"I didn't come in here thinking that," I said. "I came in here because I was told you're the man to speak with. I didn't seek out Merric to kill him and I got no pleasure from doing it."

"So then why'd you do it?" Rifkin asked. There wasn't near the anger in his voice that I expected. The tone belied more annoyance than intensity.

I studied Rifkin for a moment, my mind trying to piece together his reaction. "You don't actually care that I killed Merric."

Rifkin made a face. "Merric was a piece of shit. A mid-level crony that thought he was big-time. I can have him replaced by lunch. I'm more annoyed that I have to go the trouble than I am that you took him out."

So this was business. Clearly one didn't amass what Rifkin had here by being a hot head and making rash decisions. He was pissed I messed with his operation. Maybe he would be willing to negotiate after all. For better or worse, I decided to lay my cards on the table.

"He stole the wrong kid."

Rifkin's eyes flicked between his men and back to me. A muscle in his cheek twitched, but he managed to keep his face even. "He did what?"

"I killed Merric because he stole my niece. I went to him to try and negotiate her return. He wouldn't talk business and he threatened to kill me, so I did what I had to do."

Rifkin returned his hands back in front of him. He shook his head and muttered under his breath. "That stupid son of a bitch. Wouldn't listen to a thing I said, always thought he was so much smarter than everybody else."

I shook my head. "Stealing the daughter of a local hero isn't very damn smart."

His eyes shot to me, narrowing a bit. They ran over me again, a tiny trace of confusion on his face.

"Oh no, not me," I said. "She's my niece, but her father was a very famous football player in Columbus. Merric's men put him in a coma and made a hell of a mess of things."

Rifkin shot his eyes to Tank Top and shook his head again. "That son of a bitch got off easy getting shot in the chest. How many times have I told him about keeping a low profile and covering his tracks?"

I realized I was pressing my luck, but I inserted one more comment. My hand hurt like hell and if I could hurry this along before my steaming hatred for everyone in the room exploded, I needed to do so. "His tracks were so obvious I managed to track him all the way to this room in a couple of hours."

His eyes shot back to me, hard. I kept wondering how he found himself confined to that wheelchair and how much I would like to finish the job for him.

"So you did," he said. "And now that you're here, what the hell do you want?"

"I want my niece," I fired back without pause.

Rifkin lowered his gaze to his desk. He reached out with his left hand and straightened a row of pencils lined up in the middle of it, his OCD on full display again. "I realize you probably are a really big man wherever it is you come from, but allow me to make a few things clear. One, I'm the only one that gives orders in my office-"

"I wasn't giving a order, just answering your question," I inserted. Yet again, the image of Annie was the only thing keeping me on the level.

Rifkin held up a finger to silence me, a move that always makes my blood boil.

"And two, nobody messes with my business. You've already caused quite an inconvenience for me tonight by removing one of my major suppliers."

"I just want my niece," I said. "I can pay you."

"Stop interrupting me!" Rifkin shouted, his voice reverberating off the walls. Beside me all three men took a half step closer, all of them within arm's reach now. In theory I could snap a quick series of moves, divert one of their guns to hit another, take it and clean house.

In reality, I was about to become a human punching bag. I still didn't really care. Despite that, I said nothing, nodding instead.

"There is no negotiating," Rifkin said. "The clients that come to me offer far more than just their money, they offer their trust and they offer silence. If I fail to deliver, I will have lost all three."

I paused to make sure he was done speaking and said, "Only two. I can pay you, and I'm sure you can have another child here in no time." I almost said he could have it here by nine, but I caught myself in time. I wasn't sure if he knew I'd seen the text message, but I couldn't afford to tip my hand.

I felt like a first-class asshole even insinuating that he find another child and put their family through what he'd done to ours, but I didn't really care. Just like I don't believe people should be sending all their money to starving people overseas when there are starving people down the street, I believe in taking care of your own.

Annie was my own.

"You're not getting it," Rifkin said. His tone was really, *really* starting to grate on me. "These people are buying far more than just a child. They are buying peace of mind and they are buying a relationship. The people I do business with aren't just interested in children, they are interested in drugs, cars, merchandise. The amount of money they represent is worth far more to me than your entire life."

Again he felt the need to put into words what we both already knew. "So there's nothing I can say?"

"Nothing at all," Rifkin said, shaking his head. A smug smile traced his lips. "But thanks for stopping by. Tracking down Merric's killer would have been a pain in the ass."

I lowered my eyes to the ground as Rifkin laughed aloud. He raised his chin towards Tank Top and made a flippant motion with his hand. "Get his ass out of here. Take him down to the water, you know the spot. Be sure to weight him down so the catfish take care of the remains for us."

I raised my eyes to stare in malevolence at Rifkin. Every nerve in my body stood on end as I squeezed the bloody stump of my pinkie tight in my hand. Across from me he stared back and smiled, even going as far as to wave as the Spandex Twins tugged me backwards.

I let my gaze linger on him halfway across the room before turning and heading for the door. The Twins fell in a few feet behind me as Tank Top led the way, parting the doors in the middle for me to pass through.

Just before I got there, I shuffle stepped to the side and pulled a thick volume from the bookshelf. Rotating on the ball of my foot I flung it as hard as I could, the book rotating through the air like a makeshift Frisbee.

The back covers fluttered open as it flew, a few pages flapping in the air. Rifkin flailed with his arms to try and move his wheelchair but was too slow as the book slammed into his shoulder, knocking him to the floor. His chair went to its side in a clatter, the sound of cursing and fumbling limbs filling the air.

The Twins both sprinted around to the backside of the desk as a cocksure smile crossed my face. I opened my mouth to make a smartass comment to the bald bastard flopping on the ground like a seal, but I never got the chance.

The butt of Tank Top's gun beat me to it, connecting flush with the base of my skull. One second I was enjoying Rifkin getting a tiny sliver of comeuppance, the next the world was completely black.

Chapter Twenty-Eight

A splash of lukewarm water hit me square in the face, waking me from my slumber. It soaked the front of my hair and washed across my face, dripping down onto my shirt. A few droplets found their way into my nostrils and the familiar smell of ammonia came to mind.

Piss.

The bastards threw piss on me.

I shook my head hard to the side to throw the vile liquid off of me, a poor decision on my part as the world started spinning. I stopped moving and stared straight ahead for a few moments, willing my eyes to focus on the toes of my boots in front of me. When finally they receded from three pairs to just one I exhaled hard, sending a plume of urine and spittle into the air.

"That was pretty fucking stupid on your part," Tank Top said, standing over me with a small bucket still in hand.

I was seated against a short concrete wall behind the house, my back flush against the cold blocks behind me. Dawn was now upon us, the sky lightening towards gray as a heavy swath of clouds overhead kept the sun from peeking through. The docks to my left were void of life. I could see a few faces looking out the windows of the second floor towards us, but we were the only two people around. The sounds of the river lapping against the docks and the occasional call of a gull were the only sounds.

"Why's that?" I grunted. I made no effort to stand, as it was hard enough just to mutter those two words. The back of my head throbbed so badly, it wasn't until I noticed the wad of white gauze wrapped around my pinkie that I even remembered it wasn't there anymore.

Tank Top stared down at me for a moment, his nostrils flaring. Then he did something that was far more chilling than anything he could have said.

He smiled.

Two gold teeth poked out behind his thin lips as a sadistic smile spread across his face. "On your feet."

He didn't have to say what he was thinking, the message was already received. If I had gone easy, he would have shot me in the head. As it were, he now got to beat the hell out of me first. He was far from the biggest guy I'd crossed paths with in the last twenty-four hours, but I had no doubt he was more than capable of handling the job. One doesn't ascend to the right hand post of a guy like Rifkin without being able to handle himself in a scrap.

And let's be honest, I was far from one hundred percent. It wouldn't exactly be a fair fight to begin with.

I considered a smart ass remark, but the words eluded me. The only things I could think of were the pounding in my head and the impending situation I was about to find myself in. I rolled to my side, braced my hands on the ground and pulled my feet up beneath me. I rose to full height as slowly as I could, but a massive bout of spinning still hit me full on. Unable to steady myself I staggered several steps to the side before sagging against the wall. Behind me I heard Tank Top smirk as I took in deep breaths and waited for the pressure in my head to recede once again.

Unlike earlier in the evening, it didn't really subside but more like evened out. I guess there are only so many shots one can take in a night and expect to keep bouncing back. Once I was content that I could walk without keeling over, I stood to full height and turned to face Tank Top. "Where to?"

He swapped the bucket in his hand for the automatic weapon I still couldn't identify and held it across his torso. With a small jerk of his head he motioned to a set of concrete stairs towards a mud path leading down to the water's edge.

Filled with dread, I started walking.

The path descended a half dozen concrete steps before giving way to a muddy trail. It extended in a loose serpentine pattern along the water's edge past the raised concrete landing of Pier Three and on towards Pier Four. The ground to the right was littered with chunks of driftwood and bits of garbage bleached clean from exposure to the elements. To the left the river lapped up onto the bank, a thin layer of slime covering the clay lined edge.

A putrid smell hung in the air, though I couldn't tell if it was from something outside or my shirt still damp with piss.

In silence we walked past Pier Four. Rifkin's base and the warehouses of Pier Three slid from view behind us as we pushed forward. Every few steps I threw a glance up at Pier Four as it passed by, hoping for some sign of life that never showed. The view from the water's edge was even more hopeless than it had been from the street.

The pounding in my head receded a tiny bit as we walked, the blood heading south and dispersing itself in places other than the backs of my eyes. The cool morning air felt good on my skin and several times I glanced up at the grey clouds and hoped for a few drops of rain. I continued to take deep breaths as we walked, trying in vain to clear my head and devise some sort of plan.

For all my effort, nothing came to mind.

Tank Top allowed me to take the lead as we pushed on past Pier Four, making no effort to hurry me along as we went. I guessed that killing me was probably the only thing on his to-do list for the morning. He'd already let me know that he intended to enjoy this, that smile on the back porch telling me everything I needed to know. It was not going to be quick and it was not going to be painless.

272

The concrete wall of Pier Four passed by to our right. Ahead of us Pier Five rose in a matching construction, a narrow alleyway stretching between the two. Measuring almost twelve feet across, the ground was the same clay as the bank. Small piles of wood chips and flotsam were heaped in various locations and two deep ruts wound through it, heavy tire tracks pressed into the mud.

"Stop," Tank Top said behind me. I did as he ordered, glancing around. The concrete piers extended up on either side of us, their walls stretching up almost ten feet high from the muddy river bottom. A heavy iron gate stood closed over seventy yards down at the other end of the alley, the front of it covered in black tar paper. No weapons of any kind were visible and we were completely hidden from the world.

My mind recalled the knife buried inside my boot, but quickly reasoned there was no way to get to it before Tank Top unloaded an entire clip into me. I was as good as dead.

I raised the remains of my hands from my side and turned to face Tank Top. "You don't have to do this you know."

The smug expression on his face morphed into something bordering on disgust. "Come on now. Incredible stupidity aside, you've been pretty damn ballsy this morning. Don't ruin it now by being a bitch."

In any other situation, I would have thrown myself across the muddy ground at him. After the night I'd had and the situation I was in, the words barely registered with me. "Like I told Rifkin, I don't give a damn about any of you guys. I just want my niece."

"And like Rifkin told me, he wants you dead," Tank Top said.

"I can pay you," I said. "Fifty thousand. Cash. We can go get it right now."

Tank Top made a face. "First off, if I wanted your money, I'd just make you go get it and then kill you. Second, you really thought you could buy Rifkin for fifty g's? He makes more money than that before he eats breakfast every morning."

I shook my head. "Not trying to buy Rifkin. Trying to buy my niece."

Tank Top ignored the statement and took two steps back. He lowered the weapon and leaned it against the concrete wall behind him, barrel pointing up. The same sick smile spread across his face as he stepped forward and rolled his shoulders, stretching his neck from side to side. "Let's do this. I don't have all day to stand here talking to you."

My hands dropped by my sides. I had expected him to shoot me a few times in various places, stand and watch as I bled out. Maybe use a knife to remove a few more digits or appendages. Some more fingers, an ear, maybe my nose. I knew all along he would take a few swings at me, but I wasn't expecting him to actually beat me to death.

My mind rifled through my options, telling me what I already knew. I had no options. I was going to stand here and try to fight this sadistic bastard and hope he ended it quick.

Tank Top bounced on the balls of his feet a few times, then fell motionless. His hands swung back down to his sides and he stared at me full in the face. "And just to make sure this is a bit of a challenge for me, we did some digging while you were unconscious. It didn't take long for us to figure out which child was the daughter of a former Ohio State football player. Ricky Borden, I think it was?"

The barbed wire tangle leapt into my throat. Blood began to pump hard through my body and for the first time since I'd woken up, I didn't notice it tearing through the back of my head. My gaze hardened, but I said nothing.

The corner of his mouth turned up. "Judging by your reaction, that must be it. And yes, her little ass is on that boat."

I knew the son of a bitch was pressing my buttons, but I didn't care. If he wanted me fighting mad, he had it.

A guttural yell erupted from deep in my throat as the heels of my boots dug into the soft mud and hurtled me forward. I was bent at the waist and covered the ground in long uneven strides, resembling a raptor as I made my way straight for him. He watched me approach with a face that bordered on amusement, easily stepping to the side. As my momentum carried me past he dropped the side of his fist down between my shoulder blades, a sledgehammer blow that almost folded me in half.

"That's the spirit boy!" Tank Top goaded, his hands formed into loose fists by his side as he bounced on his feet. I glared up at him with heavily lidded eyes, his very visage coming to represent everything I'd been through in the past few days. Another cry poured from me as I charged again, aiming for center mass.

This time my shoulder landed square in his stomach. I tried to form my right hand into a fist to throw at him, but the balled up knob of my pinkie left it jutting high into the air. Before I could think to make another move at him his hands were under my armpits and he jerked to the side with one quick movement.

My body rotated as I passed through the air, landing on my right hip and rolling through to my knees. I tried to push myself to a standing position, but he was already on me, snapping down a hard right to my cheek.

The familiar metallic tinge of blood filled my mouth. The blow barely registered through my adrenaline fueled rage as I spit a stream of red spittle into the mud and pushed myself to a standing position.

Tank Top continued to bounce across from me. It was obvious he was toying with me, but I didn't care. This bastard would not be the reason Annie never went home.

A third time I moved forward, though much slower. I balled my right hand up the best I could and kept my left extended out like a knife, ready to strike with the cast at the first opening. An inch at a time I went forward towards Tank Top, who made no effort to engage me. It would have been easier to play defense against him, but he knew better than to give me that option.

I moved in with a left-handed stance and shot my right hand out in a couple of quick jabs. The ball of white gauze still stood up off the end of it, flashing in the dull morning light. Tank Top dodged the first one and batted away the second, pushing my fist off to the left. Using the momentum I pivoted and whipped the cast through in a hard slice that would have shattered my hand and his face if it connected.

It caught only air.

My body tailed away to the side, the cast jerking me off-balance. I stumbled several heavy steps, fighting to stay upright, when a combat boot slammed hard into my thigh. The shot wiped my legs out from beneath me, pitching me forward into a roll that deposited me flat on my back in the mud. For a moment I lay still before the sole of that same boot appeared above me. I rolled hard three times to the left, coming up onto my knees as Tank Top's stomp landed an inch deep in the mud.

The shot would have snapped every bone in my face. My neck wouldn't have stood a chance.

He stood with his boot buried in the mud and stared at me. His face creased as laughter spilled from his lips and he jerked the boot free. "Go ahead, delay the inevitable," he said. "I'm going to kill you, and then somebody else is going to kill that little girl."

The familiar swell of anger filled me, but I paused before moving. I looked down at the shattered remains of my hands and instead of rushing him like he wanted, I fished the knife from my boot. Holding it in my right hand I flipped opened the blade and stared venom at him.

For the first time, the haughty expression left his face as he bounced around, his eyes locked on the blade. I resumed my right handed stance and slid forward, my feet sideways, pushing me forward like a fencer. I held the blade out in front of me and slashed it from side to side, knowing that would do more damage than a simple jab.

If I was going down, I at least wanted to leave my mark, for me and for Annie.

Sweat dripped off the end of my nose and my breath came in rapid gasps. I moved to within a few feet of him and swung the blade through in a quick arc. As soon as the blade whipped past him he stepped forward and pinned my arm against his hip. He snapped two hard left crosses into my jaw and swung his knee up hard into my groin.

The world began to spin as the knife fell from my hand. Dark haze drifted in on the edges of my vision and a wave of nausea passed through my body. I stumbled against him, unable to stay upright.

"Actually, I hope she ends up with one of the pedophiles," Tank Top said. He raised his arm high above me and drove his elbow down into my back, dropping me to a knee. "One of those sick fucks that gets off doing things to little kids."

I wheezed for air, trying to scream a retort, to fight back, but my body betrayed me. I was at his mercy. He buried another elbow high between my shoulders, just inches from the base of my neck. The darkness crept in a little further as he bent down, grabbed me by the waist and tossed me end over end towards the wall behind him.

My entire body flipped forward, the momentum carrying me in a full flip and depositing me just inches from the wall. My hands were useless to break my fall as I landed in a heap, my legs sprawling out in either direction.

I didn't feel my right leg slam into the rifle leaned against the wall. Instead, I heard the sound of metal clattering against concrete. Barely able to keep my eyes open I rolled at the waist and grabbed up the weapon. Behind me I heard Tank Top grunt, followed by his heavy boots pounding across the muddy ground.

My damaged hands could hardly hold the thing, but it didn't matter. I dropped the barrel top down across my left wrist and steadied it with my right. Holding it upside down I squeezed the trigger, sending a spray of bullets in an uneven line towards the wall across from me. Chunks of concrete dust and mortar flew into the air as most of the bullets smacked into the retaining wall.

All except the three etched across Tank Top's tank top. I wobbled in place as he looked at me with complete shock on his face before falling forward to his knees and then his face.

A moment later I followed suit, as my eyes rolled back in my head and I passed out on the soft mud bank of the Ohio River.

Chapter Twenty-Nine

I have no idea how long I was unconscious. When I awoke, it wasn't of my own volition but from the heavy raindrops falling upon me. Even after they wormed their way through the fog of my brain I laid there with my eyes closed, fearful to open them and see where I was and what was going on around me. My entire body felt like it was on fire, the cumulative weight of my injuries melding into one unending throb.

In that moment I thought of home. I thought of the last time I felt that bad, after I was in a motorcycle accident in high school. I remembered my mother bringing me homemade chicken noodle soup every few hours and my sister reading to me from the rocking chair beside my bed.

Lex.

My mind shifted from the young girl sitting beside me to the grown woman she'd now become. My DNA match in female form. My best friend in the world. She needed me. Her daughter needed me.

The rain began to fall harder upon my face as I opened my eyes and raised myself to a seated position. My head spun as my upper body reached vertical and I braced myself with my left hand, held my head with the right. For several long seconds I remained still.

Shielding my eyes from the rain, I cast a quick scan of the grounds around me. The world was just the way I'd left it an indeterminate amount of time ago. The assault rifle lay motionless by my leg and slick clay ran beneath me. Chunks of concrete block were spread out in a haphazard pattern and Tank Top lay face down in front of me. His body was in the exact same position it was before the world went black, two dark circles having formed against his tank top. A third hole peeked out from his pale white skin along his left shoulder blade, a thin rivulet of blood running towards the ground. It mixed with the rain water as it descended down his back, washing the wound almost completely clean.

A quick look to the sky told me nothing about how much time had passed. The rains had brought dark clouds with them, the day even less bright than it was before. The storm seemed to extend for miles in both directions with no sign of letting up any time soon.

Best guess was it hadn't been very long or Rifkin would have sent someone to look for Tank Top by now. He knew his guy would take his time and really work me over good, but he also knew that wouldn't take hours, especially in a thunderstorm.

One at a time I drew my feet up beneath me and stood. I felt like a baby colt as my legs wobbled beneath my weight, fighting to steady themselves under me. I picked the gun up from the ground and stared down at the inert body of Tank Top. For a moment I considered dragging it into the river, but decided against it. I had no way of knowing how much time had passed and couldn't take a chance on missing that boat.

Besides, they knew where we were going. If he didn't return, they'd know something was wrong whether his body was here or not.

I rested the barrel of the gun atop my cast, cradled the butt of it in my right palm and walked around Pier Five as fast as my legs would allow. At Pier Six I walked the length of an alley identical to the one Tank Tap was now lying in, the clay becoming slick with rain. Sliding my way along I managed to reach the chain link gate and peeled back the tar paper to make sure nobody was nearby. Content I was alone, I shot the lock off the gate, brushed the rusted shrapnel aside and emerged onto the pier.

My truck was just where I'd left it, wedged between the log truck and an outbuilding. I jerked the door open and went straight for the clock on the dashboard. The illuminated block digits stared back at me informing me it was a few minutes after eight. One hour until the ship left Pier Twelve, five hours until she was gone forever.

I had been out for over an hour. Thank God the rain woke me up when it did.

I tossed the gun over the seatback and swung in behind the wheel. I didn't have to be back on Pier Twelve just yet, but I needed to put some space between me and Rifkin. It was only a matter of time before he started sniffing around and I was still just little more than a half mile from his bedroom.

I glanced in the rearview mirror as I pulled a K turn behind the log truck and eased back out onto the road. The entire left side of my face was puffy and covered in blotches. Right now they were faint purple and blue, but by this evening it would look like a paint-by-numbers. Lines of dried blood separated each of my teeth and a piece of my lower lip was gone.

In truth, it wasn't as bad as I expected.

I pushed the truck back along the row of piers, watching the numbers ascend as I drove. There was nominal activity on Pier Eight, a skeleton crew that looked to be doing maintenance on a couple of containers. Pier Ten had a small cluster of men standing beneath a lean-to in orange vests watching the rain fall. There was nothing urgent about their posture or the dock around them.

The only one pier with much life at all was Pier Twelve. A trio of forklifts buzzed about the place as I eased by, rooster tails of water sprouting behind them. They lifted small metal containers painted brown and grey, all headed towards one particular barge stowed at the end of the far left dock. Overhead a loading crane hefted full-sized containers onto the deck of the barge, the entire operation oblivious to the steady fall of rain going on around them. I could only see a handful of people in the few seconds it took me to drive past, but not one of them so much as looked my way.

If Rifkin was spooked, he hadn't alerted the docks yet.

I glanced again at the clock on the dash. It was almost eight-twenty. There was too much activity on the docks to approach from the front. I needed a plan, something I could pull off fast, quiet, and unseen. The same aching pain rolled over my stomach as I exhaled through my nose. I tried to keep my heart beat at an even rate and watched the windshield wipers beat out a steady rhythm as I rolled past Pier Twelve and back towards the main street that would eventually run up onto the freeway.

I stayed the course a full half mile before pulling off the street and parking behind an old milk truck in an alley. Another five minutes had ticked by according to the clock on the dash. Whatever I was going to do, I had to decide and do it fast.

Chapter Thirty

She sounded tired, irritated. I tried holding Merric's phone up to my face, but it was a pain balancing it on my mangled pinkie. Instead, I put it on speakerphone and laid it in my lap. I didn't bother to say anything the first time she answered, waiting until she snapped, "This is Watts," a second time before responding.

I still wasn't sure I was doing the right thing, but I was out of options.

"You find anything?" I asked, my voice much rougher than I remembered it being. The beating I'd received over the previous twelve hours was permeating through every aspect of my being.

Watts' voice remained hard. "Who the hell is this? How'd you get my number?"

I glanced at the crumpled business card she's given me resting on the front seat beside me. Fishing it out of my jeans pocket with a mangled finger was a major pain in the ass, but I'd eventually gotten it free. "You gave me your number a couple of hours ago."

This time, her voice softened. "Jesus, you sound like hell."

"I look the part too."

Another glance in the mirror told me hell might be a nice way of putting it.

"Where are you?" she asked. I couldn't hear any background noise on the line, though that didn't mean much. It was still just eight o'clock on a Sunday morning.

Outside, the rain settled into an even pace. It hit the windshield in a steady rhythm, the heavy drops running south along the glass before being pushed to the side every so often by wipers. The world was still dark grey with the low hanging clouds. I was yet to see another living creature in the alley or on the street in front of me.

"I'm still in Cincinnati. Did you find anything?"

Watts exhaled. "Not a damn thing. You?"

My eyes focused on a particular droplet of water and watched as it joined with several others to form a downward rivulet before disappearing against the wiper blades. I followed the path down a few inches further and settled my eyes on the clock in front of me. Half past eight. It was time to start moving.

I turned the wiper speed up, cleared the glass and eased back out on the street. I hooked a right and went higher up the string of piers, coming to a stop at Pier Fifteen.

"Did you find something?" Watts asked again.

Pier Fifteen was nearly identical to Pier Eight. A series of low-slung out buildings encircled the pier with three large grain bins arranged in a row through the middle. The same four docks as the others extended off the back end, though the middle were piled high with pallets and seemed to be used for little more than storage.

I eased the truck as far back onto the pier as I could and slid it under a building that resembled an ancient carport. The left side of it was filled with pallets stacked high with hundred pound sacks of grain while the right had a large plastic bin that was filled with some sort of liquid fertilizer. An oil slick on the ground gave away that this was a spot usually reserved for a vehicle, though none seemed to be in sight.

"I found her," I said simply as I turned the truck off and stashed the keys above the visor.

"You *found* her?!" Watts shouted, her voice filling the cab of the truck. "She's sitting there with you now?"

I dug the Luger out of the glove box and checked to make sure the clip was full. I jacked a round into the chamber and set it down on the seat beside me. "No. But I know where she is."

"Felix, do *not* go in after her alone," Watts said, her official voice out in full force. She had no doubt heard the slide of the gun. There was no room for discussion in her tone, though I wasn't really asking. There was a reason I waited until the last possible second to call.

"Get on the horn with Cincinnati Police and tell them the guy they're looking for is Lucio Rifkin. He's operating out of Pier Three along the riverfront. Trust me, they can't miss it."

292

As I spoke, I fished the tire iron out from beneath my seat and stared at it. It was one of the few things I still owned that had been my father's. An odd thing to hold on to for sure, but he'd always referred to it as the Golden Equalizer, named for the spray paint job he'd done on it years ago. He always said it helped him more times than he could remember over the years.

I don't think this is quite what he meant, but let's hope it had the same magic for me just the same.

Watts voice took on a different tone, almost distracted, as she scribbled down the information I gave her. "Never heard of him. Who is he and why do we care?"

"He's a high end guy in a low end hole," I said. "He runs everything in and out of these docks from kids to drugs."

"You're sure of this?" Watts pressed.

"Seen it with my own two eyes. Guy seems connected too. I wouldn't be surprised if he has someone on the payroll, so be careful who you take this to."

I could hear Watts continue to scribble notes. "Don't worry, I have a friend there I went through the Academy with. He's legit."

"Good." I turned and stared at the assault rifle behind the seat. It was enormous and loud, would slow me down. I could barely handle it with my hands the way they were. It had to stay behind.

"O'Connor, I'll call him right now. Do *not* do anything. Stay where you are and I'll call you back after talking to him. Let us take this from here."

I let her words sink in for a moment, a small part of me thinking she was right. The other part pushed my eyes back to the clock and knew she was wrong. I unwound the giant wad of gauze around my right finger until it was just a couple of layers thick, stained almost black with dried blood. It wouldn't be as obvious to someone watching and should allow me to handle the Luger.

Should.

"There isn't time," I said. "I'm not working against you, but my niece needs me now. I'll call you as soon as I can."

I could hear her protesting as I thumbed the phone off and tossed it onto the seat beside me. I stuffed her business card down into my pocket and wedged the Luger into the back of my jeans. Inch by inch I slid the tire iron along the inside of my cast, the curved handle resting flush inside my palm. With one final glance at the clock I swung free from the truck and out onto the pier.

I had twenty-four minutes to get down three piers and onboard a barge. The first part was pretty straight forward. The second part I still wasn't sure how I was going to pull off.

Chapter Thirty-One

I kept the gun tucked into the back of my pants. I wasn't crazy about having a loaded weapon pointed at my ass, but I didn't want to be seen flashing a gun in the open. My face was smashed to hell, my hands were mangled and I smelled like piss. If I ran into anybody my plan was to pretend to be a bum and try to slide by them. Doing that with a gun in hand just didn't seem possible.

I didn't have time to walk clear back out to the main street and sneak up through one of the alleys. I was too close to Pier Twelve to risk firing my weapon to blast through the lock on the gate. Instead, I walked out from beneath the makeshift carport I was parked under and went directly to the edge of the pier. Rain continued to fall in a steady pace as I dropped to my knees and slid my feet over the edge. I lowered myself as much as my hands would allow before losing my grip on the wet concrete and dropping into the alleyway below.

The heels of my boots sunk a full three inches into the soft mud as I hit the ground, arms flailing to remain upright. I flung myself forward against the concrete wall to steady myself and tugged my feet free of the mud one leg at a time.

Part of me should have been pissed to be stuck in the mud, but I was just happy I didn't land on my back and send a bullet through my ass.

I kicked each of my feet against the wall to shake away the sludge and set off down the alleyway. My boots made deep impressions in the wet clay with every step. By the time I reached the bank of the river, my hair was plastered to my head and my shirt hung heavy with water.

Despite being three piers away, the barge loomed large in front of me. It was an aging wreck, the top half painted black and the bottom painted red. The two colors looked to be in roughly equal portions before disappearing into the muddy waters of the river, both faded and peeling from years of service. The name SEA HORSE I was stenciled down the side in white block script, a series of letters and numbers tattooed smaller beneath it.

I increased my pace to just shy of a jog, thinking the wreck looked more like a sea mule and wondering if there was a SEA HORSE II anywhere nearby.

Like I said before, it's funny what comes to mind in these situations.

I kept as close to the concrete piers as I could and moved past both Fourteen and Thirteen, counting them off in descending order. In front of me the barge grew larger with each passing second, though it was apparent I wasn't dealing with the Titanic. The entirety of the barge stretched maybe eight yards in length. The deck rose only about six feet above the water line, the cabin of the boat just ten or twelve feet above that.

Several rows of containers were lined up on the deck, painted in various shades of grey, brown and green. Most of them sat stacked only one row high, none more than two. It seemed clear that this was not a usual working barge, but a much smaller one used for private purposes. Anybody looking to turn a profit wouldn't bother loading such a small boat less than half full on a Sunday.

I approached the far corner of Pier Thirteen, stopped and pressed my back against the concrete. By my best estimation I had a little more than ten minutes before the boat departed. Above I could see a last few forklifts carrying items onto the barge, though the flow had slowed a great deal from when I first drove by. A couple of errant voices floated on the wind as dock workers shouted things back and forth, though I couldn't make out what they were saying.

Pressing my luck I inched forward and watched as a few men walked back and forth on the dock. Each one of them was dressed in matching brown rain slickers and tan jeans. Nobody seemed to be carrying any weapons, though that doesn't mean they weren't stowed beneath the rain gear.

If this was Rifkin's boat, it bore to reason these were all his workers as well.

The traffic on the dock above seemed to settle into a one-way flow, all of it heading away from the barge. Two forklifts exited and headed down the dock as the overhead crane deposited one final full-sized container and receded back onto the pier as the captain let out one short blast on his horn.

My head told me I should still have ten minutes before the boat departed and the blast was a warning shot for everybody that was coming to get onboard. Everybody else should get back.

I closed my eyes and again thought of Annie. Of the first time I saw her, held her in my arms, made that promise to my sister. Now, this very moment, was the time to prove that I meant it. That everything I'd done the past two days, hell, the last ten years, wasn't for nothing.

A small surge of purpose went through my body. The pain receded into the background, the fatigue I felt fell by the wayside. In their place was complete clarity as I traced my eyes over the docks ahead, seeking anything that might resemble a plan.

There was no way I could board the boat from the dock. I didn't have time to walk the length of the alley and back up, and even if I did there's no way I wouldn't get stopped a hundred times by people wanting to know what the hell I was up to. There were no stairs up on to the docks from where I stood, and even if there were, there was no way to get up and onboard without being seen.

That left a water assault. I wasn't the world's greatest swimmer to begin with, even less so with mangled hands and mud covered boots.

Great.

I kept my back pressed against the wall and ran my eyes the length of the boat. The hull was made from steel plates welded onto a body, the seams all water tight. It rose only eight feet or so out of the water, but there still no way I could scramble up the side. I would drown trying to flail my way up the slippery fuselage.

I shifted my gaze a little further down and rested it on the rusted chain extending down into the water at the head of the deck. Thick lengths of solid steel interlocked and hanging down from the side of the boat, disappearing into the dirty water below.

The anchor.

Cliché as hell, but in this case just maybe crazy enough to work.

I remained where I was for several long seconds, studying the anchor. The lengths were shaped like oversized footballs, all lined up end-to-end and disappearing into the hull of the boat. They wore a color somewhere between the red and black of the barge, no doubt from a heavy coat of rust. They were also soaked from the rain that continued falling in steady torrents. It wasn't ideal, but it was all I had.

Drawing in a deep breath, I looked up to make sure nobody on the docks was visible and ran headlong towards the river. I covered the short expanse between the pier and the bank in a dozen steps and dove headfirst into the river. The icy chill tore at me, setting every nerve in my body on fire as I remained underwater and breast stroked as hard as I could.

The cast on my left hand swelled until it felt like it weighed a hundred pounds, the plaster soaking up the water like a sponge. Inside it I could feel the tire iron dig into my flesh, the cast growing tighter by the second. I gave up trying to stroke with my left hand and held it out in front of me, swinging my right arm and kicking my legs hard.

I remained submerged as long as possible before rising for air. I stopped kicking for a moment and allowed my body to slow, raising only my head from the water like some kind of wannabe Navy SEAL. My first push had taken me almost halfway to the anchor, though it still seemed far away across the rain-spattered surface. I listened hard for any sounds of alarm from above, but there were none.

For the time being, I was still unnoticed.

Drawing in a deep breath, I slipped back under the surface and resumed my swim. I didn't have near the momentum as I did the first time and stroking with only one arm made it tough to get moving. My boots felt like lead as I kicked them behind me, willing my body forward. When my lungs could take no more, I again rose from the depths and wiped river water from my eyes.

I was still over twenty yards from the anchor. I had no idea how much time remained, but it couldn't be more than a few minutes.

Opting to keep my head above water I continued pushing forward, my strokes somewhere between a breast stroke and a dog paddle. My lungs became raw as I drew in uneven gulps of water and air. Every muscle in my body burned.

Beside me the enormous coal-powered engine on the barge kicked into a higher gear. I could feel the vibrations of it rolling through the water, rattling my body. They were picking things up. Departure was going to be any second now.

Ahead of me, the heavy links of the chain moaned before slowly starting to rise up out of the water.

Chapter Thirty-Two

There is only one thing I've ever found that can light a fire under me more than adrenaline, and that's panic. It started with a horror-struck face as I watched the links rise from the depths, dark water dripping down in a heavy stream. The moment my mind pug together what was happening my arms went to work, pawing at the water. I didn't care about the club on my left arm or how much noise I made as I went, I just paddled.

One by one the links rose out of the water. I didn't know how deep the river was, but this close to shore it couldn't be more than fifteen or twenty feet. I was running out of time. Fast.

The inches crept by as I continued swimming for the chain, my form an ugly hybrid of three or four different strokes. My lungs gasped for more air and my body temperature ran hot, despite the frigid water I was submerged in. Every sound of the world died away, replaced by my heart racing in my ears.

Five yards away, the top of the anchor pushed itself up out of the water. My hands pawed furiously as the top of it extended into a shaft, followed by two claw-like hooks. The entire structure slid up out of the water like some kind of ancient sea creature, a torrent of water falling behind it. Wrenched free from the weight of the river it swung free, banging against the side of the barge.

I covered the last few yards as fast as I could, the anchor continuing to climb. I got there just as it hung several feet above the water and leaped up at it, my hands coming together above my head in an attempt to grab hold. They got halfway up the side of it, but couldn't reach the top of the hooks. Without having something to wrap around, my hands slid down the side of the wet iron.

The anchor shrugged me off and continued its ascent as if I wasn't even there. My arms splashed down to the water beside me, the momentum carrying me under. For a split second I considered just staying there, letting the weight of my clothes and my cast and my sister's expectations drag me to the bottom.

Instead, I kicked myself back to the surface. The vibrations from the engine were growing stronger, but the ship remained idle. I still had a chance.

My head burst through the surface as I drew in a deep gulp of air. I gave a sharp twist of my head and sent my lank hair out of my eyes, the wet tendrils flying to the side in a spray of dirty water. My eyes and throat both burned as I spit a stream of the Ohio River from my mouth and continued moving forward.

I knew there was no place back the other direction to get onboard, told myself there had to be something up ahead. Going forward meant possibly getting run over by the barge once it started moving, but it was a chance I had to take. I'd promised Lex and Annie both I'd die before I let anything happen to them.

After the night I'd had, I knew I was on borrowed time anyway.

The sound of iron meeting steel rang out above me as the anchor found its home against the hull of the ship and settled into place. A stream of water continued to fall down from the base of it as I passed underneath, all four limbs swinging in wide circles away from my body. The moment the anchor was in place

307

a second, longer blast erupted from the air horn and the vibrations in the water rose to a frenzied pitch.

It was shifting into gear. It was about to start moving and there was only one direction it could go.

Straight at me.

The level of panic within me rose again as I kicked hard and made the front corner of the barge. Without slowing down I swung a tight turn and kept pressing forward. Every muscle in my body screamed in protest and my lungs burned for more oxygen.

Finally, mercifully, I saw what I looking was for.

Just a few yards ahead, rising in a straight line from the water, was a row of metal rungs up the ass-end of the barge.

The very sight of the makeshift ladder pushed a renewed vigor through me as I kicked hard. The ancient diesel engine made a loud coughing sound as the boat downshifted and pushed away from the dock, the water churning along the edge of the barge. I changed to a freestyle stroke and pounded out the last few yards as the front of the boat twisted away from the dock, meeting me half way. With my last bit of energy I hefted myself a few feet up out of the water and latched onto the closest rungs.

Despite just starting to move, the force of the boat bounced me against the front of it causing every vertebrae in my back to pop. I slid my right hand behind the lowest rung and cradled it in the crook of my elbow, the momentum of the boat pinning me against the hull as it pushed out into the river. For several moments, I made no effort to move.

I waited until we were out of sight from the pier and the pressure of the oncoming water began to build before unhooking my arm from the rung and pulling myself up. The metal rungs, constructed from twisted rebar, were wet and slippery beneath my boots, the going slow. I hauled myself up one rung at a time, heart pounding as I ascended.

After more than a dozen rungs, I peeked my head up over the side of the deck and swung my gaze from side to side. I was on the front edge of the barge, a full sized shipping container just a few feet in front of me.

As quiet as my protesting body would allow, I crawled onto the deck and fell onto my side. I pressed my back against the container and lay there for several long minutes, drawing in

deep breaths and letting the cool steel of the deck calm my

protesting body.

Chapter Thirty-Three

I rose to a seated position with my shoulder blades pressed against the container, but made no attempt to go any further. Instead I sat with legs sprawled in either direction, the heels of my boots just inches away from the edge of the deck. Rain continued to fall from the sky, though I was so wet it didn't even register with me.

To my right the city of Cincinnati slid by, the high rises disappearing behind us and giving way to a sprawling expanse of factories and suburbs. Somewhere over there was the state line separating Ohio from Indiana. To my left was Kentucky, the entire area a suburb of Cincinnati. The whole scene seemed to still be asleep, nothing more than a rainy Sunday morning in the Midwest.

As the cityscape began to thin beside me, my heart rate and breathing receded to normal. I lifted the club attached to my left arm and examined it, the area from my forearm down looking like the Michelin Man's. I used my right hand to wring out as much excess water as I could from around the edges of it, though it did little to relieve the pressure. Inside it I could feel the tire iron digging into the underside of my forearm, but for some reason decided to leave it where it was.

I don't know why, but I had a feeling I might need it later.

I pushed myself to my feet and went through a quick progression to make sure everything still worked. Despite serious protest from every muscle in my body and my internal clock telling me it had been days since I had a proper meal or rest, all important functions still seemed to be working. I only hoped I could say the same in an hour.

Pushing away from the container, I slid the Luger from the waistband of my jeans and checked the slide. It spit the live round out at me cleanly and racked the next one into place, a sure sign that everything was still in working order. Later on I would have to clean it thoroughly to make sure it didn't rust, but that was the least of my concerns at the moment.

The world around me shifted to the familiar farmlands that dominated much of the Midwestern states. We were now out of the city. Any guards onboard would be easing up on how alert they were, especially with the rain still falling in a steady pattern. It wasn't pouring, but it was above a drizzle, more than enough to make someone that wasn't as wet as I was uncomfortable.

One more deep breath and I edged towards the center of the barge. I kept my back pressed tight against the container and dropped to a knee, then peered out around it towards the control tower. Staring back at me was nothing but the next row of containers, their uneven pattern blocking the main deck from view. I was going to have to swing up the side.

I knew I was going to have to get closer if I wanted to have a reasonable shot at anyone, but I was hoping to at least have an idea of how many there were first. It was hard enough trying to concoct a one man plan, not knowing how many I faced didn't help.

I gave a quick glance around and went back in the direction I first came on board. The wet steel of the deck was slick beneath my feet and I moved slow, the ping of raindrops hitting the deck around me. I made it to the far corner and dropped to a knee again, the Luger poised against my waist.

"Hey!" a voice shouted from behind me, a thick baritone cutting through the morning wind. My breath stopped cold and my heart went into hyper-drive, but I did not move.

"What the hell are you doing here?" the voice demanded, followed by the unmistakable sound of a round being locked into the barrel of a rifle.

I didn't pause. I didn't try to respond. I didn't even think. Instead I rotated on my knee, brought the Luger up and squeezed off three quick shots in succession. The first one skidded off the side of a green container, a small spark igniting in the air before being extinguished by the rain. The second two found the chest of Rifkin's guard.

Dressed like one of the Spandex Twins, a look of shock filled his face as the impact of the shots took him backwards. His lips moved in silence as if he was trying to respond before he ran out of deck space and tumbled backwards over the edge of the barge. The last things I saw were the heels of his boots and the barrel of his assault rifle as he fell into the river.

That was one down. I had no idea how many there were in total, but I couldn't imagine there being more than a half dozen or so. There would be more at the destination, but it wouldn't take that many to guard a ship in transit.

At least that's what I told myself.

I remained still for a full two minutes, the Luger poised in front of me and my eyes scanning in both directions. When nobody came running, I retook my feet and started back down the outside of the deck. They may not have seen the guard go over, but they would damn sure notice when he didn't come back.

One half step at a time I walked down the outside of the barge, placing my boots heel to toe against the metal. Around me all I could hear was the rain continuing to fall.

At the edge of each container I stopped and scanned down the thin aisle ways between the rows. Only a few feet separated each of them, darkness filling the gaps in between. I had no way of knowing if anybody was patrolling those few empty spots, but I pushed ahead anyway. After six successive rows of full-sized containers, I came to the final row of cargo. It was filled with several smaller containers, less than half the size of a regular one. They resembled small dumpsters lined up on the open expanse of the deck, each of them painted steel grey.

Again I dropped to a knee and surveyed the deck in front of me. Onboard, it looked just like it had from the shore. The entire deck was flat, stretching eighty yards long and measuring about twenty yards wide. A large cabin and holding area took up the rear twenty yards, the structure painted the same faded black as the top half of the hull. It rose two stories above the deck, the lower one encased in glass where the ship's controls were. The top one was open, with only a metal awning protecting it from the elements.

There was no sign of human activity on the top level. The glass windows on the bottom level had wipers moving in perpetual motion, clearing arc shaped swaths across the tinted glass. There was no way of knowing how many people were inside it, though I had to figure on at least the captain and one other.

On the far end of the deck were the containers I'd just passed, thirty yards of silent cargo. That left the middle thirty yards of the deck open.

Well, open except for the two guards standing with their backs to me.

They were both clearly Rifkin's men, their pale white skin shining under a heavy sheen of rain. One was dressed like Tank Top, the other like one of the Spandex Twins. Despite the dire need for these guys to diversify their wardrobe, their fashion choices weren't what concerned me. The assault rifles they both held slung across their waists did.

Both of them stood to the far side of the deck, peering down along the edge towards where their compatriot disappeared. For a moment I considered just shooting them where they stood, but I didn't trust my rain soaked, mangled hands enough to make that shot across twenty yards of open deck. I'd gotten lucky the first time. If I messed up even a single shot this time, one of the guards was bound to mow me down.

I studied the layout of the deck once more and slipped back the way I'd came. I slid my body between the first two rows of full-sized containers to the mid-point of the ship, then dropped to my knees and inched forward. Containers rose high on either side of me as I nudged my way forward, careful to remain concealed in the deep shadows they provided. In front of me the cabin of the ship stared back, the two cleared windows looking at me like oversized eyes.

Gritting my teeth, I worked the tire iron free from my cast. With every fraction of an inch it came, I could feel the screwdriver tip digging into my flesh, no doubt leaving a trench through my skin. Little by little it worked its way out, the inflated and waterlogged cast fighting for each millimeter. It took every bit of my concentration not to gasp out in pain as I worked it loose, fresh blood staining the shaft as it extended upward.

Once it was out I remained on my knees for several long seconds, gulping in air and allowing the searing pain to subside. When it fell away to a numb pounding, I gripped the crook of it in my hand, the Luger just inches away in the deck by my knee.

"Alright Pop, I need you on this one."

Aiming at a spot a little ways out into the open deck, I cocked the tire iron by my ear and launched it into the air. For a moment I watched the golden projectile turn end over end through the gray morning sky before dropping to the deck with a clatter just fifteen yards away. I snatched up the Luger from the ground beside me and held it at the ready, praying my spot in the shadows was good enough to keep me hidden.

Both of the guards appeared a moment later, each of them with guns poised. Spandex walked to the tire iron and looked it over while Tank Top scanned the silent containers. If he could see me, he didn't let it show.

"What the fuck is that?" Tank Top asked, his voice the same deep din as the others.

"Looks like a damn car jack," Spandex said, turning his attention towards the containers and sliding up beside his partner. "Better question is what the hell's it doing here?"

Tank Top's eyes scanned everything in front of him. I could tell he was nervous and more than a little trigger happy. Not a good combination. "It didn't just fall from the sky," he said, moving forward a foot at a time. His rifle was pinned to his cheek and his finger was inside the trigger guard. I was hoping they would move a little closer, but I couldn't wait any longer.

From the shadows I fired five quick rounds in succession. I started with Tank Top and put two rounds in his chest, one in his cheek. Before Spandex could move I put one between his bulging eyes, another in his chest for good measure.

On the whole, they looked like five perfectly placed shots. In reality, only the first chest shot to Tank Top went where I wanted it to.

I pushed myself back a little further in the shadows and remained still. There was no way anybody in the cabin didn't see what just happened, not with both of their bodies still lying out in the open. Blood ran from their wounds and mixed with the gallons of rain water splashed across the deck, spreading a bloody trail around them like a spider's web.

For several long minutes I remained in place and waited, my gaze shifting between the bodies and the cabin above. It settled on the tire iron lying motionless on the deck between the two and I couldn't help but smirk.

"Thanks, Pop."

Chapter Thirty-Three

Part of me wanted to remain motionless. Where I was gave me a full vantage of the cabin and the shadows concealed my body. The more prudent part of my brain told me I had to move. It had to be evident to anybody watching where the shots had come from. All they would have to do is starting emptying clips into the narrow aisle way between the containers and I was as good as dead.

Even easier than shooting fish in a barrel.

I left the bodies and the tire iron where they were and nudged my way back a few feet. Focus still on the silent deck in front of me, I rose between the first and second rows of full-sized containers and ran back to the far edge of the deck. Only the balls of my feet hit the deck as I went, pushing myself high into the air between steps to keep the heavy boot heels from echoing.

I don't even want to know what I must have looked like prancing around between the rows like that, but it was effective. I barely heard my own footsteps over the rain still pinging against the steel of the barge.

I slid to a stop at the end of the container, my right calf skidding across the surface before pulling to a stop just a few feet from the edge. I remained seated and pushed myself forward to a spot behind the smaller containers and waited, watching the deck. From where I sat I could see the bodies of Tank Top and Spandex lying prone, blood continuing to flow from them. A little further up the tire iron rested on its side, the gold paint standing out against the sea of grey.

The Luger remained poised in my hand, the barrel pointed at an angle in front of me, waiting for any sign of life. I'd used three bullets on the first guard and five on the next two. Counting the live round I ejected earlier, I still had eight bullets in the magazine and one in my pocket. I hoped that would be enough and that I wouldn't have to use near that many.

My head ticked off five full minutes without the slightest sign of movement. The boat continued to steam down the Ohio River, working its way around a bend, meaning there must be someone at the helm controlling it. There was no way they hadn't seen what happened.

Only two explanations seemed even quasi-plausible. One was that the crew was legit, that the guards were the only ones working for Rifkin. They didn't care, and might even be relieved, to see the guards taken out. The other, more likely, scenario was that the remaining guards were all pressed tight against the front windows waiting for me to show myself.

I decided to wait them out.

I was already soaked and chilled to the bone, so sitting out on the deck didn't bother me in the slightest. Curled up against the back edge of a smaller container, I was shielded from the rain and most of the wind. Fatigue was a condition I was used to by this point, any drowsiness pushed away by remembering why I was there. To find Annie and bring her home.

My adversaries didn't possess the same patience. It took almost ten minutes, but a fourth guard emerged from the cabin.

I heard him long before I saw him, the protesting steel of the cabin door hinges screeching across the barge. My nerves went on end and I raised myself from my haunches to a knee, pressed even tighter against a container. My eyes worked in rapid-fire fashion across the deck, checking the cabin from end to end in a relentless loop.

The fourth guard emerged from the far side, inching his way forward. The largest gun I'd ever seen a man carry was cradled against his shoulder, a double barreled number with one stacked on top of the other. The top one was long, no doubt a rifle capable of firing a massive round. The bottom one looked to be a couple of inches in diameter and probably held some form of explosive shell.

Whatever that thing was, it was looking for me.

Clearly I had gotten their attention.

The man was a carbon copy of every other Rifkin guard I'd encountered so far, dressed in head-to-toe black. His face was shaved smooth and pale skin stared peeked out above the gun stock. The only thing differentiating him from the others was the long sleeves of his form fitting black shirt. Quite the rebel.

This made four heavily armed guards, my mind reasoning that had to be all of them. There was no way Rifkin could foresee needing more muscle than what he had on board. Hell, the gun this guy was carrying alone should do the trick.

I wasn't foolish enough to believe that my niece was the only cargo of any value present, but I couldn't think of anything that needed more protection than what was on hand.

It's not like there were pirates floating along the Ohio River.

Unlike the two guards before him, Long Sleeves gave only a passing glance to the tire iron and the two bodies lying on the deck. He must have figured I would relocate after shooting them and kept to the far side of the deck, soon disappearing along the opposite side.

A mixture of sweat and rain droplets rolled down my face as I remained concealed behind the container. There was no way I could hope to survive a duel with him, not with me carrying a Luger and him carrying a bazooka. Optimally I would draw him out in the open, but it wasn't going to be as easy as the first time. I eyed the front of the ship to make sure he wasn't looping back on me, then scanned the deck once more.

My gaze settled on the two assault rifles lying motionless by Tank Top and Spandex. My hands weren't up to the task of handling them with any kind of accuracy, but they gave me a hell of a lot better chance than the pea-shooter I was carrying. I cast my eyes back towards the cabin and a plan formed in my mind. It was choppy and it was risky as hell, but it was the best I could do.

My only other option was to stay where I was, keep playing shadow games and hope my luck didn't run out. Judging by the size of the gun he was carrying, the odds saw me coming out on the losing end of an ugly situation.

I kept the Luger gripped tight in my right hand and pushed myself between the row of smaller containers and the first row of the full-sized ones. There were enormous gaps between the smaller ones and anybody still left inside easily could have seen me running behind them. No way was anybody going to mistake me for one of Rifkin's guards, running on my toes in blue jeans and cowboy boots.

Water splashed up with every step, flailing about in all directions as I covered the fifteen yards as fast as I could. The soles of my boots skidded a bit as I stopped to grab up Tank Top's rifle, the ground beneath me worn slick from years of forklift and container traffic.

The gun was too large to carry in my casted left hand. I jammed the Luger into the small of my back and held the rifle in front of me, the stock in my right hand and the barrel rested across my left fingertips. I paused just long enough to give one more quick look around before tearing for the opposite end of the cabin.

Bloody water splashed up onto me as I went, dotting my jeans with pink speckles. The burning reappeared in my lungs and my legs screamed in protest at the exertion. Stride by stride I pounded forward, the awkward bulk of the gun swinging back and forth in front of me. With every step I expected a spark to bounce up beside me or worse, a bullet to slam into my back. Total fear, of who was behind me, of who might be waiting for me, of what would happen if I didn't make it, propelled me forward.

It was the longest twenty-five yard dash of my life. To anybody watching from the sidelines it probably looked I was barely moving, but in the moment it felt like I had never ran faster. I slid to a stop just past the edge of the cabin, riding in on my legs. I extended them out in front of me and hydroplaned forward, twisting myself onto my stomach and laying out flat, the gun extended behind me. For several seconds I remained still, my lungs fighting to expand while I lay face down on the deck.

My eye found the sight along the top of the barrel and focused in on the far corner I'd just came from. I waited long enough to make sure the guard hadn't seen me before rising to my knees and then my feet. I kept the rifle trained out in front of me and stepped backwards, turned and leapt up the stairwell towards the lookout deck above the cabin.

There was no way that anybody watching inside had not just seen me. I could only hope there wasn't another guard in there or that they couldn't radio out to the one patrolling the deck.

My boots touched soft against the grated tops of the metal stairs, hollow tings ringing out beneath me. Rain dripped from every ledge as I moved upward, covering the dozen or so steps two at a time. My boots hit the steel landing at the top and swung out from beneath me, my body hanging suspended for several seconds before crashing down on to my side. My entire left side screamed in agony as I gasped in ragged breaths and scrambled forward on my knees, the gun still gripped tight.

My left hand throbbed inside the clumsy implement that had once been a cast and my left hip bone protested beneath me as I fell flat onto my stomach. I ignored them all, remaining several feet back from the ledge of the overlook and positioning the rifle. With every fiber of my being I pushed the various pains from my mind and focused down the barrel, aiming a few feet above where I was sitting just a couple minutes before.

I've never been in the military. Jail was the closest thing to a structured organization I've been affiliated with in my entire adult life. But in that moment, lying there staring down the barrel of a rifle and counting seconds until an enemy showed himself, I felt like a sniper. I was protected from the rain and I was out of sight. I could stay there all day waiting.

It only took another two minutes.

Chapter Thirty-Three

I probably should have felt something resembling remorse. Regardless what my rap sheet might say, violence really wasn't my nature. I was always a bit more cerebral about these things, a result I think of growing up with a twin sister. If we were angry with one another, striking her wasn't an option. Instead, I learned how to assess things, to manipulate them to my advantage. Even in prison, I aligned myself with people like Rosie to keep from having to fight my way through.

Lord knows I got in my fair share over the years anyway, but it was never something I sought out.

This was different though. My mind was locked on a singular objective, the end justifying any means necessary. I had already killed six people and engaged another in arena-style combat. I was lying prone on the roof of a barge staring down the barrel of an assault rifle, waiting for someone to show themselves, and I didn't even care. This asshole was going to get mowed down, along with anybody else onboard that stood between getting my niece back.

One of the first things that happened when I went to prison was what they called delousing. I removed all my clothes and they sprayed my entire body with a spray chemical meant to kill all lice, crabs, or other bodily contaminants they didn't want inside. Once I was dripping with the foul smelling solution, I took a hot shower and passed through to the inside, where I received my prison uniform. They said it was to ensure cleanliness in the facility.

Funny thing was, I hadn't felt clean since the moment that spray hit my skin. I knew in that very instant that I would never be the same sincere kid I was just an hour before. It was the lowest point of my life. If killing every man on this ship ensured that my sister never felt anything resembling that or that my niece could continue living the life she was meant to, then I was going to do it.

And I wasn't going to think twice about it.

After two minutes, Long Sleeves grew impatient and showed himself. Not on the edge of the boat where I expected him to, but creeping from the shadows between the containers in the middle. He must have seen that I wasn't hiding along the far edge and inched his way inward, inspecting where I'd hidden and how I'd done it. I could only see the front few inches of his gun barrel, but I knew he was crouched right where I'd been.

I thought for a moment he was going to continue moving forward to check on his cohorts, but he never emerged from the shadows. It was clear to the world that both men were dead, if not from the gunshots then from the massive amount of blood that now painted the deck around them. His weapon nudged its way out almost a foot before it stopped, swung side to side, and started to retreat back into the shadows.

I had a choice. I knew where he was and could easily make the shot from where I lay. He was in the exact same position that I feared being in, stuck in a narrow alley with limited retreat options. I could fill the gap with an entire clip of bullets and bank on at least a couple of them cutting him down. At the same time, in the off chance I missed I was exposing my position.

The image of that massive weapon filled my mind and small shudder passed through. Once he knew where I was, it wouldn't take more than for him to lob a couple of explosive rounds up here and I was toast. He might destroy part of the cabin in the process, but something told me that didn't matter at this point.

Besides, it's hard for anybody to shoot once they're dead.

I watched the tip of his gun withdraw to the last few inches of the barrel before I pulled the assault rifle tighter against my body and squeezed the trigger. There was no recoil at all from the big gun as a dozen fast rounds blew out in quick succession. I sprayed along each side of the gap, paused, added a second spray in a zigzag pattern just to be sure. Once almost two dozen bullets filled the narrow void between the columns of containers, I paused and waited. I waited for a return hail of bullets and I waited for some kind of propelled grenade to fly up out of the shadows at me.

What I got instead was a thick tendril of bloody water. It ran in a winding pattern beginning somewhere in the darkness and extended out towards Tank Top's body. The dark red of the fresh mixture was much brighter than the faint pink of the previous kills. There was blood, and there was a lot of it.

That was four.

This time I rose without waiting. If there was anybody else, they would have joined Long Sleeves or they would have shot me as I ran across the open deck. Cincinnati was now far behind me. It was time to find Annie and get the hell off this boat.

I considered leaving the assault rifle on the deck because it was enormous and unwieldy in my decimated hands, but I decided to hang on a little longer. It had the ability to unload two dozen bullets in a matter of seconds. Perhaps even more important, it had the ability to scare the hell out of somebody standing in front of it.

If anyone inside the cabin had watched me cross the deck, they knew which stairwell I'd climbed to the roof on. I opted to go back down the opposite side, hoping if they were lying in wait for me I would be able to catch them looking the other way.

I stepped from beneath the awning and back out into the rain, fat drops landing on my soaked scalp. One at a time I descended the staircase, feeling along with the toe of my boot to make sure I had secure footing before heading down.

The metal was soaked and slick and I was carrying two loaded firearms. I was too close now to afford having an accident.

At the base of the stairs I pressed my left shoulder against the cabin wall and again watched everything on the deck. I could see the two bodies lying prone, the tire iron and the fresh river of blood framing them on either end. Otherwise, there was nothing but shipping containers and an endless torrent of rain.

The rifle felt heavy in my hands as I took one last deep breath and turned to face the door into the cabin. It was solid metal, painted the same faded black as everything around it. There was no window or glass of any kind, just a simple silver turn handle.

Anything could be waiting on the other side of that door.

For a moment I considered walking around the front and sending a spray of bullets through the front window. I might hit an innocent and I might destroy some necessary electronics, but I at least I would know what I was looking at.

Of course, that also meant they could look at me.

I took one last glimpse at the landscape around me. Any signs of city life, or life at all, were long past. In their stead were nothing but rolling fields and hardwood trees just starting to bud for the year. I had been on the boat for half an hour. Only three and a half remained before my self-imposed window was up.

Anybody that could possibly know I was on board already did. If not, they only had to look out at the bodies lying in the middle of the deck. At least if I burst in through the back door like this, I stood a chance of catching them off- guard.

One more deep breath.

I balanced the barrel of the gun across my cast and nestled the stock against my stomach. With one fluid motion I reached out with my right hand, twisted the handle down and jerked the door open. I grabbed up the butt of the weapon, brought it to my shoulder and took two quick steps inside.

The cabin was overly warm, the sound of the heating vents working in overdrive above me. They replaced the sound of rain falling against metal and the air met me like a wall as I stepped inside.

The front of the cabin looked like one unending countertop, a series of buttons and controls spanning the length of it. A steering column was positioned dead center of the tangle of graphs and sensors. The rear wall was covered with charts and maps, pins and post-it notes covering all of them. A single door stood in the middle of the wall, slightly ajar. Everything inside was done in black, including the faded tile floor underfoot.

Standing in the center of it all was one man, his arms raised by his head as if he were signaling a touchdown. His hands faced me with all ten fingers pointing upwards, motionless. He was the first person I'd seen in several hours not dressed in all black. Instead he was wore jeans and brown hiking boots, a blue zip-up hooded sweatshirt over a red and blue flannel. A blue knit cap was pulled down atop his head and a tangle of white hair stuck out from his face in every direction. He looked to be somewhere in his fifties, though his trim build could have put him up or down a few years.

"Please don't hurt me," he said, his voice almost soft. Between that and the attire, he clearly wasn't one of Rifkin's men. "I'm not one of them."

"How many of them are there?" I asked, my eyes swinging around the room. There was nobody else there, nowhere for anyone to hide. The open door into the living quarters was the only possible spot for someone to be tucked away.

"Only four," the captain said, his eyes locked on mine. As he spoke, he balled his left hand into a fist and flicked his eyes towards the right hand. Five fingers remained outstretched. There was one still inside.

I nodded and shifted my eyes towards the door. He couldn't nod his head to confirm, but instead shot his eyes straight to the ceiling and back to the floor. As good as a nod. There was one more hiding inside.

Adrenaline surged through me as I raised the rifle tight to my cheek and shuffled forward. I had barely moved when the door swung open and a man dressed just like Long Sleeves stepped through carrying a rifle matching my own. Our eyes locked at the same time, our fingers pulled in unison.

The only difference was as I squeezed, I flung myself down towards the left.

The sound of gunfire reverberated through the tiny cabin, buffeted by bullets shattering glass and slamming into doors and walls. A searing pain tore through my left arm as I went down, that entire side of my body erupting in agony. Across from me the guard convulsed twice as if having a seizure, a pair of rounds slamming into his body. His rifle clattered to the ground, though he managed to stay on his feet.

The moment my body hit the ground I snapped the Luger from my jeans with my right hand and fired four quick shots in succession. All four found their mark, tearing into his body and sending splashes of blood down onto the floor. He took only a single step before pitching himself face first onto the tile, his body hitting it with a wet smack.

I kept the gun held out in front of me and watched as the blood pooled out from his body. It wasn't as fast as those on the deck, but there wasn't any rain water in the cabin to speed up the process.

My left arm continued to scream at me as I shifted the gun to the captain, his entire body rigid. His hands were still raised by his head, his left hand still held into a ball. "That's all of them. I swear to God that's all of them."

"You're sure?"

"Yes," he whispered. "Just please don't shoot me."

"Please don't make me," I replied, grunting as I shifted myself from my left side up onto my knees. I lowered my gun to the floor and pushed myself to my feet, my left arm hanging limp by my side. I looked down to see a small plume of blood on the outer half of my arm. An inch down and he would he have hit an artery. Five inches to the right and he would have hit my heart.

The captain kept his arms raised above his head and said, "You've been hit. I have a first aid kit in my room."

I ignored the comment. "Who are you and how do I know you're not involved with these guys too?"

The man bobbed his head slightly, as if agreeing these were fair questions. "My name is Seamus Smiley, Captain of the

Sea Horse. Formerly I was a Chief Petty Officer, United States Navy."

My arm throbbed. It replaced all the other pain in my body combined. "What the hell is a retired officer doing mixed up with this lot?"

"You see the guns those guys were carrying?" Smiley responded. "When that walks on your boat and tells you you're carrying some cargo for them, you don't really have a choice in the matter."

I damned sure didn't want to give this guy too much leeway and let my guard down, but what he was saying made sense. He certainly didn't look or act like the rest of them. "Call it in," I muttered. "I don't even know who patrols these waters, but if you're really a captain I'm guessing you do."

Smiley's eyes grew a size larger as he shook his head. "Rifkin will kill me if I call this in. He knows where I live, where my grandson goes to school. At the very least I'll go to jail for what they find on here."

I shook my head. "Cincinnati PD should be at Rifkin's as we speak. He won't be bothering anyone. Just in case, you can spread the word that I killed his guards and called it in. He already knows and hates me."

He continued to shake his head. "I still don't want to go to jail. I don't know what the hell in those containers, but they send five armed guards with me every week. It can't be anything good."

"You won't go to jail," I said. "I have a friend on the force there. Just make the call." She wasn't quite a friend and she wasn't technically on the force there, but I didn't care. I just wanted the call made.

Smiley kept his eyes on me and lowered his hands. He lifted the receiver from his a.m. radio alongside the steering column. His eyes never left me, or more aptly the gun in my hand, as he raised the receiver to his lips and said, "This is Captain Seamus Smiley of the *Sea Horse I* calling for the United States Coast Guard, over."

A burst of static shot out at us, followed by the mechanized voice of a young male. "This is Seaman Erick Wynn, USCG Cutter *Greenwood*. Go ahead *Sea Horse I*. Over."

"Ship requesting immediate assistance. Coordinates 38°41' North, 83° 33' West. Over."

"Roger that *Sea Horse I*, what is your emergency?"

Smiley looked at me with heavy eyes. "You'll see when you get here." Without another word he clicked off the radio and returned the receiver to its hook.

Chapter Thirty-Three

The bullet passed clean through my arm. The size of the caliber gave it so much power it didn't even notice a few inches of flesh standing in its way. It entered halfway between my elbow and shoulder, a perfect circle roughly the size of a dime. It exited three inches to the left through my triceps, the hole enlarged to about the size of a penny. The edges of both were raw. Blood oozed from each of them, running in thick crimson droplets down my arm.

Smiley stood at the wheel and watched me, his eyes dancing between me and the dead guard on the floor. We both wanted to drag his body outside and dump it over the side, but for all intents and purposes this was now a crime scene. The Coast Guard might not take kindly to us tossing casualties into the river.

Instead, Smiley pulled the barge as close to shore as the water depth would allow and dropped the anchor. Every so often a strong push of the current swung us a few feet from side to side, but the enormous implement held true. We were right where he'd said we be, waiting for the law to show up. Everything in my being told me to get away before they did, but I remained where I was. As soon as I made sure the bleeding was stopped, I was finally going to find my niece.

The first aid kit sat open atop the control panel in front of me, a collection of individually wrapped supplies splashed across the controls. My flannel was unsnapped almost to my navel, the left side of my torso exposed. My ribs were light blue and growing darker by the moment. The comically oversized, waterlogged cast dangled from my left hand. Blood ran from the holes in my arm.

Smiley took in the injuries and let out a slow whistle. "Damn boy, what did you do to piss off Rifkin?"

I shook my head and wadded several strips of gauze into a ball. Starting at the elbow I wiped it upward in long strokes, stripping blood away from my skin. "Rifkin was just one of many this weekend," I said. I wiped away as much of the blood as would come free and tossed the soiled strips into the trash. "Can you give me a hand here?"

I held a clean patch of gauze against the front hole with my thumb and a second patch over the rear hole with my middle finger. I bent over so my limp arm hung down by itself and watched as Smiley unwound over a foot of elastic tape from a roll. Starting on the underside of my arm, he wrapped the roll around three times, the thick tape covering every bit of the gauze. It was a little tighter than I would have liked, judging by the way the tape dug into my skin, but at least I knew the patches weren't going anywhere. To be honest my entire body was numb, so I couldn't feel it anyway. Once the initial shock wore off, I was going to be miserable.

Smiley tore the tape off atop my bicep and put everything back into the kit as I stood up, worked my arm back into my shirt and buttoned it. The numb feeling permeated my entire body and I couldn't help but notice that the temperature of the previously warm cabin had dropped precipitously.

I didn't have much time.

"Where would they keep the kids?" I asked, my voice low, a bit uneven.

Smiley stopped what he was doing, his hands frozen above the open kit. "What kids?"

"The ones they kidnapped, plan to sell off."

His eyes pressed closed and he twisted his head. "Oh sweet Jesus, what have I done?"

I couldn't imagine the feeling of guilt that must have been going through him, but I didn't care. The clock was still running and my strength was fading fast. I slapped the palm of my hand down on the top ledge of the control panel. "Where would they be?" I said, my voice louder but still lacking much life.

His eyes remained closed, his head continued to shake. "I don't know. I really don't. The first two rows are all his, has to be one of them."

I nodded twice and went back outside, the cold air cutting straight through my soaked clothes. My teeth chattered as I stepped away from the cabin and a fresh wave of rainwater washed over me.

So much for keeping my arm clean.

Everything outside remained just as it was. In total, less than fifteen minutes had passed, but it seemed much longer as I trudged across the open deck towards the containers.

The water around Tank Top and Spandex was now clear, the blood having washed over the sides. Their pale skin was fast turning blue as their lifeless eyes stared up at the sky. Beyond them, a reddish puddle sat between two smaller containers. I walked forward into the shadows to see Long Sleeves flat on his back, over a half dozen gouges torn into his body. Once dark red and bleeding, the rain had washed them clean, leaving nothing but torn clothes and holes the size of dimes in various locations.

I stared down at him for a few seconds as I walked past. Thankfulness filled me that my bullet holes were only through my arm. Nothing resembling guilt came near me.

I left the bodies where they laid and went back out to the small containers, four of them sitting in a row. They were all of the same general size and design, standing seven feet tall and measuring about the same across. The top of the front of each one opened up with a pair of double doors, a heavy padlock clasping them together. My eyes swung to the tire iron still lying on the deck, but my numb left arm made me think better of it.

348

Instead, I pulled the Luger from the small of my back and fired at the thin metal latch piece of the lock. It shattered and fell away with a sprinkling of metal shards.

Using my right hand I shoved aside the remnants of the lock and jerked open the door. A musty smell hit me full on that reminded me a lot of the horse barn back in Wyoming. Pallets lined all three walls of the interior, each stacked high with green bricks wrapped in saran wrap.

Marijuana, and lots of it, all piled up like bales of hay.

My stomach turned at the thought of the men that had held my niece for the last two days. She didn't need to be anywhere but at home with her mother, let alone out with men running drugs and carrying automatic weapons. A sour taste rose in the back of my throat as I stepped back and surveyed the other three small containers. Odds were they contained the exact same cargo as the first one.

I turned and glared over my shoulder at the front window. I believed Smiley when he told me didn't have anything to do with this, that he was nothing more than an unwilling accomplice in Rifkin's business, but that didn't make it much better. He still knew what he was doing was wrong, and never once did he try to stop it.

As much as I wanted to stomp and scream and cuss the wind, my body wouldn't allow it. Precious heat was leaking out of me with each passing second and a dull prod was forming in my left shoulder. It wouldn't be long before the pain settled in, after which it was just a matter of time before I was out cold, flat on my back like the guards heaped around me.

With the Luger in my hand I stepped through the row of smaller containers to the two larger ones sitting behind them. Smiley said the first two rows were Rifkin's. Annie had to be in one of them.

I stepped over Long Sleeve's outstretched legs to the door of the closest one. I wanted to drag his body away and dump it oversee so Annie and any other children inside wouldn't have to see it, but I just didn't have the strength.

Both containers were the standard shipping sort, with a pair of parallel doors comprising one end of the unit. Everything else was sealed tight. The container on the right was shit brown, the one on the left forest green. Both were positioned so their doors pointed inward.

Gun in hand, I went to the left and shot away a pair of heavy padlocks holding latches at the top and bottom in place. The small metal implements fell away with ease. Using my right hand I jerked the latches up and swung one half of the door open.

A tiny bit of light filtered in through the door, though it was apparent there were no children inside. Rows of wooden crates lined one wall, all of them stacked high with uniform precision. Across from them was an even row of long black plastic boxes. Stenciled across the side of them were the letters RPG, a string of numbers behind them.

Rocket Propelled Grenades. Weapons. This entire container was a weapons cache.

The barbed wire returned to my stomach. What if I was wrong about all of this? What if Tank Top was just screwing with me when he said Annie was onboard, toying with a dying man? What if I'd killed a half dozen people and made an enemy of a very powerful man for nothing?

What if I was no closer to finding Annie than I was yesterday and now here I was, running on fumes and out of ideas?

I swallowed the thoughts back as best I could as I walked from the container. I didn't bother to look at the cabin, instead keeping the gun poised in front of me. The top lock blasted away without resistance and I pointed the gun at the bottom one.

Click. Nothing but empty air.

I exhaled and tried not to think of the symbolism an empty chamber represented. I shoved aside every one of the questions that were running through my head and pulled the single round from my pocket. I held it up for a moment and stared at the polished brass casing, the rain droplets running over it. My entire torso in a knot, I slid the bullet in, pulled the slide and blasted the lock away.

Out of habit I kept the empty gun poised in front of me, lifted the latch and slowly the door open.

Two single bulbs hung down from the ceiling, attached to orange extension cords that ran the length of the roof and connected to a small generator on the far wall. It purred in a graveled tone, light but not indiscernible. The bulbs threw harsh yellow light down on the interior, illuminating everything.

An elderly woman sat in a wooden chair across from me, her eyes locked on mine. She wore a long plaid jumper and a wool cardigan. She had silver hair and tired eyes and when she realized I wasn't one of Rifkin's men, a look of genuine relief spread over her face. Around her right ankle was a heavy metal cuff, a silver chain snaking away from it and disappearing behind the generator.

On either side of the room were two long rows of cots, all of them with matching green blankets and thin pillows. They were shoved head-to-foot tight against one another, none of them more than three or four feet in length.

Each of the beds was filled with lumps of indiscernible size, all of them curled up tight beneath their blankets. I stood in the half opened doorway and swept my gaze over the room, trying to find the one precious object I was there to receive.

A few heads popped up to examine me as I stood there, their eyes heavy with sleep.

"Annie?" I called aloud. At the sound of my voice several more heads raised from their pillows. A pair of little girls began to cry. "Annie?"

My heart pounded as I walked into the room. I stuffed the Luger back into the waist of my pants and walked forward, hands by my side, head swinging from side to side.

"Unka O?" a tiny voice asked, a small mound moving to the old woman's left.

My heart surged into overdrive. My tongue swelled to twice its normal size and I covered the length of the container in just a few quick steps. "Annie?"

"Unka O!" she squealed, thrashing her little body atop the mattress. I was beside her in two long bounds and tore back the heavy blanket.

There, lying in a plain white onesie, was Annie, staring up at me with enormous blue eyes. She wasn't crying, but she was clearly terrified. She wriggled like a seal atop the mattress, trying in vain to get me. Padded cords were wrapped around her feet and wrists, keeping from her moving. "Unka O!"

I dropped to the bed and lifted her onto my lap. I started with her feet, using my damaged hands to unwrap the cords from her as fast as I could before moving on to her hands. The minute she was free she stood on the bed and leapt her small body onto me. Her arms wrapped around my neck and her mop of blonde curls cascaded across my face. I wrapped my right arm around her as tight as I could.

For the first time in eighteen hours I felt no pain whatsoever.

For the first time in twelve years, I wept like a baby.

We both did.

Chapter Thirty-Four

All told there were nine children in the container. Nine children with families just like mine, all somewhere nearby worried sick about their young ones. All but two of the children were girls, none older than four years old.

I shuddered at the fates that would have awaited them. To think someone like me spent five years in jail when bastards like that walked free.

The old woman didn't even bother to watch me as one by one I untied the children. Many of them were petrified for me to even touch them as I unwound the padded straps. A few bore the telltale bruises that told me why. I worked as fast as my hands and my dropping strength would allow, Annie never more than a few inches from my side. When the last one was free, I gathered them by the door and told them to follow me. I gave one last look into the container that had served as a carriage into hell for untold numbers of children and watched as the old woman opened her eyes, raised her head and murmured, "Thank you."

I didn't bother to respond in any way.

Before I went out I grabbed a handful of green blankets from the beds and dropped them across the bodies of the fallen guards. I motioned towards the cabin for Smiley to do the same and paused a few seconds for him to do so. The rain had lightened up a bit, though it continued to fall in a steady drizzle over everything.

I bent at the waist in front of the children, all of them staring back at me with eyes wide and fear on their face. "Okay everybody, we don't like it in here do we?" I shook my head from side to side and watched as many of them matched it. "And we're ready to get out, aren't we?" I bobbed my head this time, the gesture matched by almost all of them. "Okay, I want everybody here to hold hands with one other person and follow me, okay?"

I grabbed Annie up from the ground and held her in my right arm, her head resting against my shoulder. Behind us the children paired up and as a group we walked out into the rain towards the cabin. I covered Annie as best I could, my left arm hanging useless by my side. I turned my shoulder into the wind and walked sideways across the deck, shielding her and watching to make sure the other children followed. Beyond them I stared at the green blankets tucked tight beneath the guards, praying they wouldn't blow free.

Smiley held open the cabin door as we approached. Every bit of color had drained from his face and his mouth hung agape as he stared at the children marching into the cabin like soldiers. All of them were paired up, tiny hands clinging to one another, their faces plastered with tears and rain. Annie and I stood to the side of the door by the stairs until the last ones entered before sliding in ourselves. "You look like you've seen a ghost," I said to Smiley as we walked through.

"I'd rather see an army of ghosts than what just walked in here," Smiley said. He blinked fast as he stared at me, looking like he might cry as well.

"You really didn't know," I murmured.

He shook his head without saying a word.

"How about the woman chained up out there?" I asked. "Any idea who she is?"

His mouth dropped open even further. "There's a woman chained up in there?"

It was clear he knew nothing about any of this. Being blackmailed into shipping some contraband paled in comparison to what he now realized he'd been doing.

I glanced past him to the light blue quilt covering the guard's body on the floor. The children milled nearby in a tight cluster, but none gave the misshapen blob a second glance. "Do you have anywhere to put them?"

He looked at me with mournful eyes and nodded. I lowered Annie to the floor and immediately she wrapped her arms around my leg. My strength was almost gone and my vision was getting blurry. I had one last thing to do, and I had to get it done before I went under. I could feel it coming, I just had to do what I could to stave it off as long as possible.

Smiley looked down at the tiny figure wrapped around my leg. "Yours?"

"Niece," I replied. "Do you have a cell-phone I can use?"

He grabbed an ancient Nokia from atop the steering column and handed it to me. He didn't ask why I needed it or who I was calling, just began to shuffle the children past the guard on the floor and into his living quarters. I had no idea what was on the other side of that door, but I trusted he would see to the children as best he could in there.

The bottom half of the oversized phone folded down to reveal the keypad. I still had Watts' card in my pocket, but I didn't bother digging it out. I pressed out the numbers from memory and slid myself to the floor beneath a map of the tri-state area. Annie released her grip on my leg until I was situated, then crawled into my lap and rested her head against my chest. My entire body was cold and wet, but she didn't seem to mind.

I was thankful she didn't. Even though her tiny frame was just a fraction of mine, her body warmth helped tremendously.

The phone rang just twice before Watts picked up, her voice tired and irritated. She sounded annoyed to be fielding a call from an unknown number, but I was just glad she did it at all. "Watts."

"Where are you?" I asked. My voice was thin. The lights were going out. I knew it, and I couldn't do anything to mask it.

Her tone shifted from annoyed to concerned in an instant. "Where the hell are *you*? My guy says they swarmed Rifkin's place a half hour ago. Drugs, guns, prostitutes, they found everything in there except you."

"Or my niece," I whispered.

Watts drew in a sharp breath of air. "Did you find her? Is she with you?"

"She's with me," I said. The soft curls of Annie's head rested against my chin. I wanted so much to wrap an arm around her and pulled her tight, but my left arm refused. My right had to hold up the largest cell-phone I'd ever seen.

"Oh, thank God," Watts whispered.

"So are eight other children," I added.

Watts tone downshifted. Not all the way back into cop-mode, but at least half way there. "Eight others? Are they alive?"

"Everyone's okay," I said. "Well, everyone but me." I tried to chuckle, but the sounds caught in my throat.

"Where are you?" Watts asked. "Are you going to make it?"

"I'm on a barge somewhere on the Ohio River. The Coast Guard is en route, I'm sorry but I don't know any more than that."

"Are you going to make it?" she repeated. In her voice was genuine concern. If I was more alert, I would have been touched.

"I'll see you soon," I said and flipped the phone off. I let it drop to the floor, the sound making Annie flinch against me. She pulled back, her blue eyes looking me over.

A stubby finger pointed at my arm. "Booboo?"

"Yeah, that's a booboo."

She pointed at the side of my face. "Booboo."

"Booboo," I confirmed.

Finally she looked down at the cast on my hand. "Big booboo."

I smiled. "Yeah sweetie, big booboo."

Outside, a Coast Guard horn sounded. It whooped twice, followed by someone giving instructions over the a.m. radio. I couldn't make out a word of it. I stayed awake just long enough to see Smiley emerge from the back room before I finally

succumbed to the darkness.

Chapter Thirty-Five

I awoke to see bright lights above me. Not the kind of lights at the far end of a tunnel that people claim to be walking towards as they experience their last few moments on earth. The kind of fluorescent hospital lights that are three feet square with a frosted plastic plate over them. The kind that bathes everything they touch in an unnatural white light.

I blinked several times. My mind was foggy, though not the same kind of exhausted foggy it had been just a short time before.

Drugged foggy.

A dull beeping sound worked its way into my consciousness, followed by the drone of voices not far away. I rolled my head to the left to see my entire arm looked like it had been mummified, save a few inches around my elbow and shoulder. A new cast encased from mid-forearm down to my hand and a thick swath of bandages covered my entire upper arm. Dull pressures registered at several different places around my body, though none approached anything resembling pain.

I was going to be in a world of hurt once the painkillers wore off.

"Annie?" I whispered, my voice coming out like a croak.

"Unka O!" a voice exclaimed beside me, pulling my head to the right. Seated there beside the bed was Lex, Annie cradled in her arms. Behind them was Watts, leaning with one shoulder against the door. She held a cell-phone pressed to her face and looked like she'd been talking when Annie drew her attention into the room.

"Hey sugar," I whispered. "How are you?"

"I good," she said, offering me an oversized grin. "Look, it's mommy!"

"I see that," I said, dropping my right hand out the side, palm up. Lex reached out around Annie and it took it in hers, tears pooling beneath her eyes.

"Thank you," she mouthed as Annie slapped both of her hands down on ours and laughed with delight.

"Is she okay?" I asked.

"She's fine," Lex said. "They all are."

I let my head fall back against the pillow. It wouldn't have taken much for me to close my eyes right then and not wake up for days. The thought of finding Annie, of helping Lex, had been fueling me since I left Wyoming. Now that she was safe, the full extent of what I'd been through was taking hold.

I was really going to be miserable when the meds wore off.

Watts snapped her phone shut and walked up behind Lex and Annie. She gave me a look resembling a smile as I rolled my head to the side to look at her without raising it from the pillow. "Wait until the boys back on the ranch here about you in a gown," she said. I sensed it was her trying to be funny, even if her timing was a bit off.

I decided to humor her attempt nonetheless.

"They better not have messed up my boots," I said back with a small smile.

366

"I think if they did, the CPD ought to be able to pitch in for a new pair," Watts said. "You did us quite a service last night."

I brushed off the compliment. I never was very good at accepting them, probably because they so rarely came my way. No point to start pretending now. "How did I get here? And where is here?"

"Valley Memorial Hospital, Carrollton, Kentucky," Watts said. "The Coast Guard brought you here from the *Sea Horse I*. You were in pretty bad shape when they found you."

I nodded. They had no idea. "How did you guys get here?"

"When you called earlier, I was just leaving the hospital. I ran into Lex as I was headed for the parking lot and told her I was headed to Cincinnati to follow up on your call," Watts said.

"I knew when she said that she wasn't going without me," Lex added. "There was no way you'd call unless you'd found something."

"What about Ricky?" I asked.

"They put him in an induced coma for the next two days until the swelling in his head goes down," Lex said. She added a smile that was almost pure embarrassed. "I knew if I had to sit there for two more days with his parents, I would go insane."

"Needless to say I wasn't too happy about it, but I let it happen," Watts said. "We got to Cincinnati just as the CPD was clearing out the last of Rifkin's henchmen. Place was a gold mine. Mayor is talking about handing out citations to everybody involved, the whole nine."

Rifkin was nothing short of an asshole. I hoped they'd throw his ass in jail and forget about him for a good long time. Something told me he'd made enough enemies over the years to make his stay very, very uncomfortable. "What about the boat?"

"The Coast Guard found the drugs, the weapons, and of course the children," Watts said. "Captain Smiley told them what he could and Edna Iris, the old woman acting as caretaker in the container, added what little she knew. There wasn't a lot between them, but it sound like that boat was headed for Louisville. After that, those kids were in the wind. No telling how many came before them. They want to talk to you when you're up for it, but it doesn't have to be right now."

"Good," I whispered. "And the guards they found?"

Watts shook her head. "I've been monitoring the situation as close as I can from here. From what I can tell, there's no intention to bring charges. Saving a boatload of children seems to have that effect on people."

I lowered my head to the pillow and looked up at the bright lights above. Lex's warm hands still gripped mine as Annie patted the tops of them.

The people I cared about were safe. I was content.

"What time is it?" I asked, my eyes unfocused on the bright orbs of light above.

Lex made a show of trying to look at her wrist, but it was buried beneath the long grey sleeves of her sweatshirt. She glanced over her shoulder at Watts, who raised her phone and thumbed on its touch screen. "It is...twelve-fifty. Why?"

It only took a few minutes for my mind to do the math. I couldn't help but smile.

"Two days ago you sat in the Sacred Heart cafeteria and told us we had twenty-one more hours to find Annie. I did it in twenty hours and fifty minutes."

I rolled my head to the side and smiled. Lex squeezed my hands and drew her mouth into a tight, toothless smile, tears back in her eyes. Behind her, Watts smiled, shaking her head from side to side.

Epilogue
Three Weeks Later

A wide array of cars filled the driveway and spilled out onto the street. All of them seemed to be some form of mini-van or mid-sized SUV in colors ranging from light blue and greens to black. The entire scene screamed soccer moms, which made me even more uneasy than I already was. To be fair, that's what the scene was for, but that didn't do a lot to ease my nervousness.

Push a herd of longhorns across a river on horseback? Not a problem. Walk into a yard full of housewives and make small talk? Lord, help me.

I pulled the truck to a stop behind a silver hybrid Toyota SUV with a Winnie the Pooh sun visor pressed to the rear window. I shook my head twice and wondered again what I was doing here. With a final sigh I picked up the box wrapped in bright green and yellow wrapping paper from the passenger seat and climbed out. Inside it was an assortment of toys and clothes, all emblazoned with Dora the Explorer. I had no idea who Dora was or what she was exploring, but the woman behind the counter assured me they were what every little girl desired these days.

Hard to argue with logic like that.

My new Ropers clicked against the asphalt as I walked down the middle of the street and cut across the front yard to the sidewalk. I could hear the sound of children playing coming from the backyard and followed the concrete path around the side of the house, the noise growing louder as I walked. A small tinge of nervousness rolled through me as I pushed forward, the backyard coming into view bit by bit.

An inflatable bounce house covered the back corner of the lot, filled with a half dozen young children bounding to and fro with smiles on their faces. A mid-sized above ground pool stood to the side of it with a couple of children bobbing in the water, their arms or waists encased in inflatable rings and floaties. The middle of the yard was an open expanse of green grass with a large handful of children running back and forth. Every imaginable outdoor toy on the planet was strewn across the grass around them. A smattering of parents were spaced throughout, keeping a close watch on everyone.

A full wooden deck stretched the length of the house, stained a deep russet color. Twin picnic tables sat on the end closest to me, one covered with gifts of every shape and size, the other loaded with all the makings of a classic Americana barbecue. Beside them stood an industrial sized stainless steel grill with the lid closed, steam rising from its side vents.

The heavenly aroma of charred meat hung heavy in the air.

Beyond the picnic tables were several large clusters of folding chairs, nearly all of them filled with parents drinking tea and lemonade. They conversed amongst themselves and watched the children, several of them pointing or laughing.

How in the world a three year old could know so many people was beyond me. I was ten times her age and could count everybody I would invite to a party on one hand.

"Unka O! Unka O!" a little voice squealed from across the yard. I looked up to see Annie running towards me as fast as her little legs would carry her, sunlight bouncing off her white-blonde curls. She ran with arms stretched out in front of her and I set the box down on the ground and lifted her up high into the air.

"I heard that somebody had a birthday today," I said, using a voice I reserved only for her and my dog before she passed. From the deck several heads turned and openly stared at us. I couldn't be sure, but it even kind of felt like the conversation died away for a moment, everybody turning to see who the guy in jeans and cowboy boots was. "You wouldn't know anybody like that would you?"

Annie dropped her teeth over her bottom lip in a smile and bobbed her head.

"And tell your uncle how old you are today," a familiar voice said from across the deck. Annie held up three fingers in front of herself, smiling wide. Lex matched the smile and approached from the side, wrapping her left arm around my waist in a half hug. "Hey there, didn't expect to see you here today."

"Somebody told me there was going to be a party," I responded. "And kind of suggested I had a duty as an uncle to be around a little more."

Lex stepped back and said, "I think you've more than fulfilled any duty you might have, but I am glad you came. Another all-night drive?"

"I stopped in Des Moines," I said, smiling. Sometimes it was a little eerie how well she knew me.

Annie wriggled a bit in my arms, her three year old attention span already beginning to wane with adult conversation. I gave her a big kiss on the cheek as she squealed again, then set her down to disappear into the tangle of children playing on the lawn.

Lex and I both stood and watched her for several seconds, smiling. "How's she doing?" I asked.

Lex sighed and bobbed her head once. "She's doing alright. She's a kid, they're resilient. She's lucky she hasn't reached the age of hanging on to things too long yet. A couple of times she's asked questions about it, but she seems to still be herself."

I nodded. While getting her home alive was the most important thing, getting her home in the same pristine condition was a close second.

"How you coming along?" Lex asked. "I see the cast is gone."

I held up my hand revealing a small tan brace, but thankfully no cast. "Damn thing was a real annoyance on the ranch. Twice I got it wet and had to have it redone. After that I just told them to give me a brace and be done with it. They were as tired of seeing me as I was them, so they agreed."

"And your other hand? Your arm?"

I held up the nub of my pinkie, the end of it covered with fresh skin stretched tight. The line were it was closed was still very apparent, but what was left of it did move. "Healing," I said. "Arm still aches a little, but it's coming along. Nothing that time won't fix. Ricky?"

Lex folded her arms across her torso. "He's getting better. He's up and walking again. Still has horrible headaches and is really sensitive to light. The doctors say it'll take time, but he'll get there."

"Is he here?" I asked, looking past her to the people lined up on the deck. A few were still watching us, though most had turned back to their previous conversations.

Among those staring were the Borden's.

"He's upstairs," Lex said, twisting and motioning up towards a second story window overlooking the lawn. "He can't take the sunlight, and he's still really sensitive about the way he looks."

"That bad huh?"

"It's going to take several reconstructive surgeries to get him looking the way he did," Lex said. "I know he'll be glad you're here though. I told him everything that happened once he woke up. He was sick he couldn't do anything, but he was genuinely thankful for everything you did. You should go up and see him in a little bit."

"I will," I said. I knew what happened would never completely change the way Ricky and I felt about each other, but it would remove some of the lingering animosity. We didn't have to be best friends, but we could at least share a common affection for Lex and Annie. We'd both proven that time and again.

To guys, that was enough.

"Mama around?"

Lex smiled. She knew I was changing the subject, but was kind enough not to call me on it. "She'll be here at four once she's done at the diner. She have any idea you're here?"

I matched the smile. "You really think I would have spoiled the surprise by telling her?"

Our mother, for all her wonderful qualities, was a horrible liar and even worse at keeping secrets. Both were well known facts that she received endless ribbing for.

"That's true," Lex said. Her smile then shifted to mischievous. "I have a bit of a surprise for you too." She turned back over her shoulder and scanned the crowd, her eyes settling on someone resting on the far opposite corner of the deck.

I looked around her to see Watts sitting in a lawn chair looking every bit as out of place as I did. "Aw hell, what's she doing here?"

Lex turned back and smiled. "She's been around a lot the last few weeks, become something of a family friend. I think she showed up today hoping you'd be here, but you'll never get her to admit it."

"None of that," I said, giving Lex my exasperated tone. She'd been trying to play match maker for me since we were kids. None of them ever worked out very well. "We pass at being civil to one another. That's good enough."

"Oh, I don't know," Lex said. "You know how women like the bad boy types."

"I also know cops don't generally go for the ex-con types," I countered.

Lex raised her eyebrows, but let it go. She looked out over the back yard and watched Annie running in circles with two other girls. All three were giggling, not a care in the world. "I'm just saying, having another reason to get you home more often wouldn't be such a bad thing."

I slid an arm around Lex's shoulders and together we walked up on to the deck, past the tables of food and presents and by the grill still steaming. I took in the banner hanging along the back of the house wishing Annie a "Happy 3rd Birthday" and watched as the little one continued to bound across the yard. "With or without her, I have plenty of reasons to get home more often."

Lex dug her fingers into my ribs. "Is that a fact? We're going to be seeing more of you around here moving forward?"

I paused as Annie stopped mid-stride and smiled, sunlight settling on her golden curls, and waved to us. We both responded without thinking.

"I'm here now aren't I?"

BCPL
Baltimore County
Public Library

66305254R00212

Made in the USA
Lexington, KY
10 August 2017

Anne Graham Lotz
In God We Trust

D1526946

John 8th Patmos

Tribulation 2020 Cycle
by John M. Patmos (pseudonym)

Table of Contents

The Apostle John Cycle

The Holy Bible is a wonderful road map for life; past, present and future. Its verses are deep enough to puzzle scholars, yet simple enough for children to memorize. Its food for the soul. It is also full of fascinating prophecies that have come true and many that have yet reached the time of fulfillment. There are many fulfilled prophecies throughout the Bible including the first coming of Jesus. This book focuses on The Book of Revelation with an emphasis on tribulations and the second coming of Jesus. Many Christians and even some Pastors shy away from talking about this book of the Bible because it talks about the end times with frightening descriptions of Gods wrath upon a world full of sinful people whose wicked ways have led them away from God. As Christians we should not be afraid, the Bible tells us this over 350 times throughout scripture. Some say we should not explore prophecy, but I am reminded of 2nd Timothy 3:16 "All scripture is given by inspiration of God, and is profitable for doctrine, for reproof, for correction, for instruction in righteousness."

The Book of Revelation – also called the Apocalypse of John, Revelation to John or Revelation from Jesus Christ – is the final book of the New Testament. Its title is derived from the word apocalypse that means "unveiling" or "revelation". The book is written by the Apostle John who was banished to and exiled on an island in the Aegean Sea. According to later writings of Tertullian, this was after being plunged into boiling oil in Rome and suffering nothing from it and all in the audience of the Colosseum were converted to Christianity upon witnessing this miracle. This event would have occurred in the late 1st century during the reign (AD 81-96) of the Roman Emperor Titus Flavius Domitian, who was known for his persecution of Christians. In the Book of Revelation, John tells of how Jesus came to him and said to write things about the past, present and future. Jesus tells John in Revelation 1:18-19, "I am he that lives, and was dead; and, behold, I am alive forevermore, Amen; and have the keys of hades and of death. 19 Write the things which you have seen, and the things which are, and the things which shall be hereafter".

He then describes a series of prophetic visions, including figures such as the Four Horsemen, the Seven-Headed Beast, the Red Dragon, and the 2nd Beast, all which culminate at the Second Coming of Jesus. The obscure and extravagant imagery has led to a wide variety of Christian interpretations. Some see The Book of Revelation as a broad view of history, while others treat it as a reference to John's own times and events of the Apostolic Age (1st century), or, at the latest, the fall of the Roman Empire. Futurists, meanwhile, believe that The Book of Revelation describes a future event, where the seven churches have grown into a body of believers throughout the world. Could the Book of Revelation be an omnificent formula for describing multiple tribulation events past, present and future remarkably using the same words? Maybe the obscure imagery John describes is designed to fit any one or all of many frames of time period. Could it be that the Book of Revelation describes tribulation events that reoccur in cycles? Could the severity of these tribulation cycles or the final occurrence of this tribulation event be conditional upon the measure of repentance and returning to God of people during that cycle? How many of these cycles could there be? I'm reminded of 1st John 2:18, "Little children, it is the last hour; and as you

2

have heard that the Antichrist is coming, even now many antichrists have come, by which we know that it is the last hour."

I'm also reminded of Mark Twain's quote "The past does not repeat itself, but it rhymes."

The famous so called profit Michel de Nostredame or "Nostradamus" is said to have used obscure imagery for a different reason. He used this as a literary technique to protect himself during the Inquisition from being persecuted as a heretic for writing his prophecies "Les Prophéties" that was published in 1555. Interestingly concerning cycles, Nostradamus is said to have used his Jewish great-grandfathers Astrolabe to calculate future events based on the judicial astrology method. Judicial astrology is the art of forecasting events by calculation of the planetary and stellar bodies cycles and their relationship to the Earth.

Another example of cycles can be found in the books *Generations* and *The Fourth Turning*, devised by William Strauss and Neil Howe. They describe a theorized recurring generation cycle in American history and global history as follows.

Strauss and Howe use the term "turning" as a time period lasting about 20–22 years. Four turnings make up a full cycle of about 80 to 90 years, which the authors term a *saeculum*, after the Latin word meaning both "a long human life" and "a natural century". Generational change drives the cycle of turnings and determines its recurrence. As each generation ages into the next life phase (and a new social role) society's mood and behavior fundamentally changes, giving rise to a new turning; therefore, a relationship exists between historical events and generational personas. Historical events shape generations in childhood and young adulthood; then, in turn, shape history as those individuals become parents and eventually the older generation. Each of the four turnings has a distinct mood that recurs every saeculum. Strauss and Howe describe these turnings as the "seasons of history": the High, the Awakening, the Unraveling and the Crisis. At one extreme is the Awakening, which like the seasons could be summer, and at the other extreme is the Crisis, which is like winter. The turnings in between are transitional seasons, the High and the Unraveling are like spring and autumn, respectively. Strauss and Howe have discussed 26 theorized turnings over 7 saecula in Anglo-American history, from the year 1435 through today. At the heart of Strauss & Howe's ideas is a basic alternation between two different types of eras, Crises and Awakenings. Both are defining eras in which people observe that historic events are radically altering their social environment. Crises are periods marked by major secular upheaval when society focuses on reorganizing the outer world of institutions and public behavior. They say the last American Crisis was the period spanning the Great Depression and World War II. Awakenings are periods marked by cultural renewal when society focuses on changing inner values and private behavior. The last American Awakening was the "Consciousness Revolution" of the 1960s and 1970s. During Crises, great peril provokes a societal consensus, an ethic of personal sacrifice, and strong institutional order. During Awakenings, an ethic of individualism emerges, and the institutional order is attacked by new social ideals and agendas. According to the authors, about every eighty to ninety years a Crisis occurs in society. Roughly halfway to the next Crisis, a cultural Awakening occurs. *What Strauss & Howe refer to as the Awakening might better be described as Decline.*

Also, a popular cycle described by many philosophy scholars is

The Eight Stages of Decline Theory

1- From bondage to spiritual growth
2- From spiritual growth to great courage
3- From courage to liberty
4- From liberty to abundance
5- From abundance to complacency
6- From complacency to apathy
7- From apathy to dependence
8- From dependence back to bondage

Stage 1 – Great civilizations are formed in the crucible. The Ancient Jews grew from escaping bondage in Egypt. The Christian faith and the Church came out of Roman persecution. American culture was formed out of the injustices and sufferings in colonial times which in turn inspired a spiritual growth and wisdom that demanded justice for America.
Stage 2 – Steeled in the crucible of suffering, courage and the ability to endure great sacrifice come forth. Anointed leaders emerge and people are summoned to courage and sacrifice to create a better, more just world for succeeding generations. People become willing to live for something more important than themselves and their own pleasure. A battle begins, a battle requiring courage, discipline and devotion to righteousness.

I'm reminded of Joshua 10:25, "Then Josh
said to them, Do not be afraid, nor be dismayed, be
strong and of good courage, for thus the Lord will
do to all your enemies against whom you fight."
Stage 3 – As a result of the courageous fight, the foe
is vanquished. Freedom and liberty emerge and at
this point a civilization, rooted in its greatest ideals,
develops. The United States Constitution derives
from the principles of the Bible. At this stage of the
cycle many who led the battle for freedom and
liberty are still alive, and the legacy of those who
are not is still revered. Heroism and the virtues that
brought about liberty are still esteemed. The ideals
that were struggled for during the years in the
crucible are still cherished. I'm reminded of Romans
8:21 "because the creation itself also will be
delivered from the bondage of corruption into the
glorious liberty of the children of God."
Stage 4 – Liberty ushers in greater prosperity
because the civilization is now functioning with the
virtues of spiritual discipline, sacrifice and hard
work. I'm reminded of Deuteronomy 30:9, "Then
the Lord your God will prosper you abundantly in
all the work of your hand, in the offspring of your
body and in the offspring of your cattle and in the
produce of your ground, for the Lord will again
rejoice over you for good, just as He rejoiced over
your fathers."
Tragically then comes the first danger: The
temptation of becoming complacent with
abundance. possessions that are in too great an
abundance tend to occupy all our time and take on a
life of their own. At the same time, the struggles that
engender wisdom and steel the soul to spiritual
discipline move to the background. In Luke 12:15
Jesus said, "Take heed, and beware of covetousness,
for a man's life does not consist in the

abundance of the things he possesses."
People in a culture that is living on the fumes of earlier sacrifices become less and less willing to make such sacrifices. Ideals diminish in importance. The sacrifices, virtues and spiritual discipline responsible for the thriving civilization become increasingly remote from the collective conscience. I'm reminded of Deuteronomy 8:14 "be careful that your heart doesn't become proud and you forget the Lord your God who brought you out of the land of Egypt, out of the place of slavery."

Stage 5 – If complacency takes root, then foundations, resources and infrastructures begin to crumble. As virtues and ideals become ever more remote, those who raise alarms are labeled by the complacent as "Haters" or "Domestic Terrorist" and considered extreme, harsh, or judgmental. The complacent call for censorship and punishment of anyone who tries to raise alarms. This is when Christians must remember Ephesians 6:13 "Therefore take unto you the whole armor of God, that ye may be able to withstand in the evil day, and having done all, to stand."

Stage 6 – Complacency invites a growing lack of attention to disturbing trends. This apathy advances to outright dismissal of wisdom (or common sense). Many seldom think or care about the sacrifices of previous generations and seek to erase or change history. Civilization's virtues of prudence, justice, temperance, courage, faith, hope, and charity is replaced by pride, greed, wrath, envy, lust, gluttony and sloth. Spiritual apathy is fertile ground for moral decay. Civilization grows increasingly divided between righteousness and wickedness.

Stage 7 – Increasingly, peoples spiritual apathy lacks the zeal necessary for righteousness. The suffering and the sacrifices that built the culture are now a distant memory. As self-discipline declines, dependence grows. The collective culture now tips in the direction of dependence. Having lived on the sacrifices of others for years, the civilization now insists that "others" must solve their woes. This ushers in growing demands for government to provide solutions instead of personal and family virtue based solutions.

Stage 8– As dependence increases and seeking a savior, people look to a centralized nanny government. But centralized power corrupts. This tends to usher in increasing intrusion, injustice and corruption by the government. Freedom and liberty are soon replaced by a dark and tyrannical government, hungry for more and more power. If the people no longer have the virtues necessary to fight, the civilization will give way to Marxism, Socialism, Communism and ultimately Fascism. This also could enable a more powerful nation to invade and destroy the decadent civilization and replace it with their own culture.

All these stages of decline can be minimized or avoided with a devotion to God and a personal relationship with Jesus. Gods' kingdom is the only one that will last forever. I'm reminded of Luke 17:20-21, "Now when He was asked by the Pharisees when the kingdom of God would come, He answered them and said, The kingdom of God does not come with observation; 21 nor will they say, 'See here!' or 'See there!' For indeed, the kingdom of God is within you."

There are also stages within the Tribulation described by John in The Book of Revelation, like the Seven Trumpets and Seven Bowls. Why does God not deliver his wrath all at once? Maybe so the generation of people will have a chance to repent along the way just as in the Old Testament of the Bible, Pharaoh was given the chance to repent by God through Moses during the 10 plagues of Egypt.

Words and names are very important. God often changed people's names to serve his purpose like Saul to Paul, Jacob to Israel and Abram to Abraham. Now, John's vision in Revelation describes the Beast as performing evil things and the number of his name is 666. Revelation 13:18, "Here is wisdom. Let him who has understanding calculate the number of the beast, for it is the number of a man: His number is 666."

Gematria is a Hebrew alphanumeric code or cipher that was used in ancient times and later adopted by other cultures. John used Gematria to enable important calculation of the important name of the Beast. It works by adding up the numerical values of letters in a word or phrase. The following is the English version.

A=6 B=12 C=18 D=24 E=30 F=36 G=42
H=48 I=54 J=60 K=66 L=72 M=78 N=84
O=90 P=96 Q=102 R=108 S=114 T=120
U=126 V=132 W=138 X=144 Y=150 Z=156

Words That Calculate to 666
Mark of Beast = 666   Image of Satan=666   Islamic Lies=666   Witchcraft=666   Lustful=666 Sharia Laws=666   Book of the dead=666   Satan's Seal=666   Satan Cult=666   A Satanic Mark=666

9

Words that calculate to 444

Jesus=444   Messiah=444   Cross=444
Gospel=444   Jewish=444   Menorah=444
Joshua=444   Obedient=444   Increase=444
Forgave=444   English=444   Church age=444
The Key=444   The Lock = 444

Words that calculate to 888

Divine Presence = 888   Omnipresent = 888
Messiah Jesus = 888   Law of Liberty = 888   King
of the Sabbath = 888   The Lion of Judah = 888
Scriptures = 888   The King Jesus = 888   The
Passover = 888   Saved in Jesus = 888   Righteous
God = 888   Healing Numbers = 888   Coming
Truth = 888   A Holy Truth = 888   Finished Cross
= 888   The Lord's Time = 888   The House of God
= 888   The Doings of God = 888   Morning Star =
888   Biblical Prophet = 888   Forgiving King =
888   Gods Anointing = 888

Words that calculate to 906

Jesus is Lord = 906   Jesus Christ = 906   Jesus
Power = 906   Son of the Lord = 906   Lord's Prayer
= 906   Holy Spirit = 906   Lord of Hosts = 906
Through Love = 906   Jesus Glory = 906   Jesus Is
Alive = 906   Redeemer From God = 906   Jesus
Sacrificed = 906   Shed Blood For Man = 906
Prophetic King = 906   Unconditional = 906   Love
is the Law = 906   Healing Promise = 906

When John wrote The Book of Revelation, he lived under the persecution and reign of Titus Flavius Domitian, Roman Emperor from 81 to 96 AD. The number of his name is T F Domitian=666. Could Domitian be the Beast of John's current time? Could we calculate Tribulation cycles measured about every 80 years from this point in time? Emperor Domitian, the self-proclaimed "Lord and God" and ruthless dictator, reigned from 81 to 96 AD. He was the son of Emperor Vespasian and the brother of Titus, the conquerors of Jerusalem in 70 AD. Domitian was very superstitious. In fact, on the day before he was murdered, he consulted an astrologer and Apollo (the so called god of truth and prophecy). Previously the emperor had even minted coins depicting Apollo on one side and a raven, associated with prophecy, on the other. The Romans believed a bird's flight could foretell the future and Domitian looked to the raven to foretell his immediate future. Ironically, Suetonius, a Roman historian and senator, records, "A few months before Domitian was killed, a raven perched on the Capitalium and cried, 'All will be well,' an omen which some interpreted as follows: . . . a raven . . . did not say, 'It is well,' only declared 'It will be well'. Emperor Domitian died soon after and all was well! The Book of Revelation is a rebuke against Emperor Domitian and the Roman world. While Domitian looked to Apollo and the raven to foretell the immediate future, the omniscient Lord Jesus Christ revealed the future of the world in this book. John describes the Beast in Revelation 13:5-8, "And there was given unto him a mouth speaking great things and blasphemies; and power was given unto him to continue forty and two months. 6 And he opened

11

his mouth in blasphemy against God, to blaspheme his name, and his tabernacle, and them that dwell in heaven. 7 And it was given unto him to make war with the saints, and to overcome them: and power was given him over all tribes, and tongues, and nations. 8 And all that dwell upon the earth shall worship him, whose names are not written in the book of life of the Lamb slain from the foundation of the world."

In addition to the descriptive imagery in the Book of Revelation, could John's experience with Roman Emperor Domitian be the first example of what to look for in future Tribulations? With Tribulation prophecies applying to multiple time period events beyond John's time, what other Tribulation event cycles could there be from history that pertain to the United States of America? Perhaps we are in a Tribulations cycle now. I'm reminded of that old saying, "Hindsight is 2020".

The Knights Templar Tribulation Cycle

The Poor Fellow-Soldiers of Christ and of the Temple of Solomon, also known as the Order of Solomon's Temple, the Knights Templar or simply the Templars, were a Catholic military order founded in 1118, headquartered on the Temple Mount in Jerusalem. The Templars became a favored charity throughout Christendom and grew rapidly in membership and power. They were prominent in Christian finance. Templar knights, in their distinctive white mantles with a red cross, were among the most skilled fighting units of the Crusades. Non-combatant members of the Order, who made up as much as 90% of their members, managed a large economic infrastructure throughout Christendom, developing innovative financial techniques that were an early form of banking, building its own network of nearly 1,000 command post and fortifications across Europe and the Holy Land.

After the First Crusade captured Jerusalem from Muslim conquerors in 1099, many Christians' made pilgrimages to various sacred sites in the Holy Land. Although the city of Jerusalem was relatively secure under Christian's control, the rest of the area was not. Bandits and marauding highwaymen preyed upon these Christian pilgrims, who were routinely slaughtered, sometimes by the hundreds, as they attempted to make the journey from the coastline at Jaffa through to the interior of the Holy Land.

In 1119, the French knight Hugues de Payens approached King Baldwin II of Jerusalem and Warmund, Patriarch of Jerusalem, and proposed creating a monastic order for the protection of these pilgrims. King Baldwin and Patriarch Warmund agreed to the request, probably at the Council of

Nablus in January 1120, and the king granted the Templars a headquarters in a wing of the royal palace on the Temple Mount in the captured Al-Aqsa Mosque. The Temple Mount had a mystique because it was above what was believed to be the ruins of the Temple of Solomon. The Crusaders therefore referred to the Al-Aqsa Mosque as Solomon's Temple, and from this location the new order took the name of *Poor Knights of Christ and the Temple of Solomon*, or "Templar" knights. The order had few financial resources and relied on donations to survive. Their emblem was of two knights riding on a single horse, emphasizing the order's poverty.

The impoverished status of the Templars did not last long. They had a powerful advocate in Saint Bernard of Clairvaux, a leading Church figure, the French abbot primarily responsible for the founding of the Cistercian Order of monks and a nephew of André de Montbard, one of the founding knights. Bernard put his weight behind them and wrote persuasively on their behalf in the letter 'In Praise of the New Knighthood, and in 1129, at the Council of Troyes, he led a group of leading churchmen to officially approve and endorse the order on behalf of the church. With this formal blessing, the Templars became a favored charity throughout Christendom, receiving money, land, businesses, and noble-born sons from families who were eager to help with the fight in the Holy Land. Another major benefit came in 1139, when Pope Innocent II's papal bull *Omne Datum Optimum* exempted the order from obedience to local laws. This ruling meant that the Templars could pass freely through all borders, were not required to pay any taxes, and were exempt from all authority except that of the pope.

With its clear mission and ample resources, the order grew rapidly. Templars were often the advance shock troops in key battles of the Crusades, as the heavily armored knights on their warhorses would set out to charge at the enemy, ahead of the main army bodies, to break opposition lines. One of their most famous victories was in 1177 during the Battle of Montgisard, where some 500 Templar knights helped several thousand infantries to defeat Saladin's army of more than 26,000 soldiers.

Although the primary mission of the order was militaristic, relatively few members were combatants. The others acted in support positions to assist the knights and to manage the financial infrastructure. The Templar Order, though its members were sworn to individual poverty, was given control of wealth beyond direct donations. A nobleman who was interested in participating in the Crusades might place all his assets under Templar management while he was away. Accumulating wealth in this manner throughout Christendom, the order in 1150 began generating letters of credit for pilgrims journeying to the Holy Land: pilgrims deposited their valuables with a local Templar preceptory before embarking, received a document indicating the value of their deposit, then used that document upon arrival in the Holy Land to retrieve their funds in an amount of treasure of equal value. This innovative arrangement was an early form of banking and may have been the first formal system to support the use of cheques; it improved the safety of pilgrims by making them less attractive targets for thieves and contributed to the Templar coffers.

Based on this mix of donations and business dealing, the Templars established financial networks across the whole of Christendom. They acquired large tracts of land, both in Europe and the Middle East; they bought and managed farms and vineyards; they built massive stone cathedrals and castles; they were involved in manufacturing, import and export; they had their own fleet of ships, and at one point, they even owned the entire island of Cyprus. The Order of the Knights Templar arguably qualifies as the world's first multinational corporation.

Philip IV also called Philip the Fair was King of France from 1285 to his death in 1314. The number of his name King Philip=666. Could he represent the first beast that John wrote about in the Book of Revelation? Deeply in financial debt to the Knights Templar, King Philip, with the assistance of Pope Clement V, conspired to destroy the order, erase his debt and steal the Templars massive wealth and property.

Pope Clement V born Raymond Bertrand de Got also spelled de *Goth*, was head of the Catholic Church and ruler of the Papal States from 1305 to his death in 1314. The number of his name Pope de Goth=666. Could he represent the second beast from the Book of Revelation?

At dawn on Friday, October 13th 1307, King Philip with the support of Pope Clement had many of the order's members in France arrested, tortured into giving false confessions, and burned at the stake. False claims were made that during Templar admissions ceremonies, recruits were forced to spit on the Cross, deny Christ, and engage in indecent kissing; brethren were also accused of worshiping

16

idols, and the order was said to have encouraged homosexual practices. These allegations were highly politicized without any real evidence. Still, the Templars were charged with numerous other offenses such as financial corruption, fraud, and secrecy. Many of the accused confessed to these charges under torture and their confessions, even though obtained under duress, caused a scandal in Paris. The Templars were accused of idolatry and were suspected of worshiping either a figure known as Baphomet or a mummified severed head they recovered, among other artifacts, at their original headquarters on the Temple Mount that many scholars theorize might have been that of John the Baptist, among other things.

As for the leaders of the Knights Templar order, the elderly Grand Master Jacques de Molay, who had confessed under torture, retracted his confession. Geoffroi de Charney, Preceptor of Normandy, also retracted his confession and insisted on his innocence. Both men were declared guilty of being relapsed heretics, and they were sentenced to burn alive at the stake in Paris on 18 March 1314. De Molay reportedly remained defiant to the end, asking to be tied in such a way that he could face the Notre Dame Cathedral and hold his hands together in prayer. According to legend, he called out from the flames that both Pope Clement and King Philip would soon meet him before God. His actual words were recorded on the parchment as follows: "God knows who is wrong and has sinned. Soon a calamity will occur to those who have condemned us to death". Pope Clement died only a month later, and King Philip died while hunting before the end of the year.

Could King Philip and Pope Clement be the first and second Beast of this cycle as described in Revelation 13:1-18, "And I stood upon the sand of the sea, and saw a beast rise up out of the sea, having seven heads and ten horns, and upon his horns ten crowns, and upon his heads the name of blasphemy. 2 And the beast that I saw was like unto a leopard, and his feet were as the feet of a bear, and his mouth as the mouth of a lion: and the dragon gave him his power, and his throne, and great authority. 3 And I saw one of his heads as if it were wounded to death; and his deadly wound was healed: and all the world marveled after the beast. 4 And they worshiped the dragon who gave power unto the beast: and they worshiped the beast, saying, Who is like unto the beast? who is able to make war with him? 5 And there was given unto him a mouth speaking great things and blasphemies; and power was given unto him to continue forty and two months. 6 And he opened his mouth in blasphemy against God, to blaspheme his name, and his tabernacle, and them that dwell in heaven. 7 And it was given unto him to make war with the saints, and to overcome them: and power was given him over all tribes, and tongues, and nations. 8 And all that dwell upon the earth shall worship him, whose names are not written in the book of life of the Lamb slain from the foundation of the world. 9 If any man has an ear, let him hear. 10 He that leads into captivity shall go into captivity: he that kills with the sword must be killed with the sword. Here is the patience and the faith of the saints. 11 And I beheld another beast coming up out of the earth; and he had two horns like a lamb, and he spoke as a dragon. 12 And he exercises all the power of the first beast before him, and causes the earth and them who dwell therein to worship the first beast, whose deadly wound was healed. 13 And he does great wonders, so that he makes fire come down from heaven on the earth in the sight of men, 14 And deceives them that dwell on the earth by the means of those miracles which he had power to do in the sight of the beast; saying to them that dwell on the earth, that they should make an image to the beast, that had the wound by a sword, and did live. 15 And he had power to give life unto the image of the beast, that the image of the beast should both speak, and cause that as many as would not worship the image of the beast should be killed. 16 And he causes all, both small and great, rich and poor, free and slave, to receive a mark in their right hand, or in their foreheads: 17 And that no man might buy or sell, except he that had the mark, or the name of the beast, or the number of his name. 18 Here is wisdom. Let him that has understanding count the number of the beast: for it is the number of a man; and his number is six hundred three score and six."

Most of the Templars escaped with the Templar treasury along with their 15 sailing ships to Scotland, Portugal and some say to the "New World", later known as The United States of America. The Order changed its name to the Order of Christ, among other names. For the most part the Order went under-ground. There is a definite connection from the Templars to Freemasonry, whom many of the founding fathers of the United States were members. Many of the signers of the Declaration of Independence were Freemasons. Many US Presidents up to recent day, were Freemasons. It seems the United States of America may have arisen from the ashes of the Templars to start a new cycle. Evidence shows that Christopher Columbus had married into a Knights Templar family and was on a Templar mission to found the "New Jerusalem" when he sailed to what he already knew was America, not India. He flew the Templar flag on his 3 ships, the Pinta, Nina, and Santa Maria. Christopher Columbus also signed his name using a hooked X symbol associated only with Templar cipher code symbols. There is other evidence that shows the Templars already knew of America.

Henry I Sinclair, the Jarl of Orkney and Lord of Roslin was a Scottish and a Norwegian nobleman and was a Knight. There is possible evidence that say he led the Templars on a voyage in 1398 to North America 100 years before Columbus did. There is an engraving of a Templar Knight on a glacial boulder in Westford, Massachusetts, known as the "Westford Knight", possibly carved by Sinclair's group to commemorate the event. Also, according to the Mi'kmaq tribe (a First Nations people of the Northeastern Woodlands), a great friendship developed with the Sinclair group and the Mi'kmaq people. As a result, the Mi'kmaq tribe adopted the Templar banner (white background with a red cross) into their culture and have used it since then until now.

It is also interesting to note that currently the country of Switzerland has become known as the financial banking capital of the world and uses the Templar banner as its national flag. The exchange currency that it uses and is also recognized globally for trading in all countries around the world is the US dollar.

The American Revolution Tribulation Cycle

The American Revolution was a violent ideological and political revolution that occurred in colonial North America between 1765 and 1791. The Americans in the Thirteen Colonies formed independent states that defeated the British in the American Revolutionary War (1775–1783), gaining independence from the British Crown and establishing the United States of America, the first modern constitutional republic.

American colonists objected to being taxed by the British Parliament, a body in which they had no direct representation. Before the 1760s, Britain's American colonies had enjoyed a high level of autonomy in their internal affairs, which were locally governed by colonial legislatures. The passage of the Stamp Act of 1765 imposed internal taxes on the colonies, which led to colonial protest, and the meeting of representatives of several colonies in the Stamp Act Congress. Tensions relaxed with the British repeal of the Stamp Act but flared again with the passage of the Townshend Acts in 1767. The British government deployed troops to Boston in 1768 to quell unrest, leading to the Boston Massacre in 1770. The British government repealed most of the Townshend duties in 1770 but retained the tax on tea in order to symbolically assert Parliament's right to tax the colonies. The burning of the Gaspee in Rhode Island in 1772, the passage of the Tea Act of 1773 and the Boston Tea Party in December 1773 led to a new escalation in tensions. The British responded by closing Boston Harbor and enacting a series of punitive laws which effectively rescinded Massachusetts Bay Colony's privileges of self-government. The other colonies rallied behind Massachusetts, and twelve of the thirteen colonies sent delegates in late 1774 to form a Continental Congress for the coordination of their resistance to Britain. Opponents of Britain were known as Patriots or Whigs, while colonists who retained their allegiance to the Crown were known as Loyalists or Tories. I'm reminded of a Thomas Jefferson quote "Whenever any form of government becomes destructive of these ends [life, liberty, and the pursuit of happiness] it is the right of the people to alter or abolish it, and to institute new government..."

Open warfare erupted when British regulars sent to capture a cache of military supplies were confronted by local Patriot militia at Lexington and Concord on April 19th, 1775. Patriot militia, joined by the newly formed Continental Army, then put British forces in Boston under siege by land and their forces withdrew by sea. Each colony formed a Provincial Congress, which assumed power from the former colonial governments, suppressed Loyalism, and contributed to the Continental Army led by Commander in Chief General George Washington, who would later become the first President of the United States.

King George William Frederick was King of Britain from 1760 to 1820. UK Frederick=666. Could he represent the Beast in this cycle? The Continental Congress declared King George a tyrant who trampled the colonists' rights as Englishmen and pronounced the colonies free and independent states on July 4th, 1776. The Patriot leadership professed the political philosophies of liberty and republicanism to reject rule by monarchy and aristocracy. The Declaration of Independence proclaimed that all men are created equal. This also was a beginning step to ending slavery in the US.

The Bible states in Revelation 12:3, "And another sign appeared in heaven: behold, a great fiery red dragon having seven heads and ten horns, and seven diadems on his heads." This dragon gives power to the Beast in Revelation 13:2, "And the beast that I saw was like unto a leopard, and his feet were as the feet of a bear, and his mouth as the mouth of a lion: and the dragon gave him his power, and his throne, and great authority."

Could this red dragon represent The Welsh Dragon (Y Ddraig Goch), meaning *the red dragon*, a heraldic symbol that appears on the English Crown's coat of arms and the national flag of Wales. Also, could it represent The Royal Welch Fusiliers that was an infantry regiment of the British Army, part of the Prince of Wales' Division. It was founded in 1689. The regiment was numbered as the 23rd Regiment of Foot. It was one of the oldest regiments in the regular army, hence the archaic spelling of the word Welch instead of Welsh. The light infantry and grenadier companies of the Fusiliers saw bloody action at the Battle of Bunker Hill. The regiment participated in nearly every campaign from Lexington and Concord to Yorktown. The Welsh Dragon is also one of ten of "The King's Beasts" statues at Hampton Court, Greater London, England.

The first shot of the American Revolution on Lexington Green in the Battle of Lexington and Concord is referred to as the "shot heard 'round the world" and maybe it was the signaling of a new cycle. The American Revolution not only established the United States, but also ended an age (an age of monarchy) and began a new age (an age of freedom based on Christian values). It inspired revolutions around the world. The United States has the world's oldest written constitution, and constitutions of other free countries often bear a striking resemblance to the US Constitution – often word-for-word in places. As a result of the growing wave started by the Revolution, today, people in 144 countries (representing 2/3 of the world's population) live in full or partial freedom. The United States proclaims to the world that "Life, Liberty, and the Pursuit of Happiness" are fundamental natural rights endowed on every human being by the Creator and that we exist upon Christian principles and the motto "In God We Trust".

The US reminds me of Revelation 3:7-13, " And to the angel of the church in Philadelphia write; These things says he that is holy, he that is true, he that has the key of David, he that opens, and no man shuts; and shuts, and no man opens; 8 I know your works: behold, I have set before you an open door, and no man can shut it: for you have a little strength, and have kept my word, and have not denied my name. 9 Behold, I will make them of the synagogue of Satan, who say they are Jews, and are not, but do lie; behold, I will make them to come and worship before your feet, and to know that I have loved you. 10 Because you have kept the word of my patience, I also will keep you from the hour of temptation, which shall come upon all the world, to try them that dwell upon the earth. 11 Behold, I come quickly: hold that fast which you have, that no man take your crown. 12 He that overcomes will I make a pillar in the temple of my God, and he shall go no more out: and I will write upon him the name of my God, and the name of the city of my God, which is new Jerusalem, which comes down out of heaven from my God: and I will write upon him my new name. 13 He that has an ear, let him hear what the Spirit says unto the churches."

Could the creation of the USA be the original Templar plan?

The American Civil War Tribulation Cycle

About 80 years after the American Revolution Tribulation cycle, we have the American Civil War (April 12th, 1861 – May 9th, 1865). This was a civil war fought between states supporting the federal union ("the Union" or "the North") and southern states that voted to secede and form the Confederate States of America ("the Confederacy" or "the South"). The central cause of the war was "states' rights" and the status of slavery, especially the expansion of slavery into other territories.

The practice of slavery in the United States was one of the key political issues of the 19th century; decades of political unrest over slavery led up to the war. Disunion came after Abraham Lincoln (Republican) won the 1860 United States presidential election on an anti-slavery expansion platform. An initial seven southern slave states (Democrats) declared their secession from the country to form the Confederacy. After Confederate forces seized numerous federal forts within territory they claimed, the attempted Crittenden Compromise failed and both sides prepared for war. Fighting broke out in April 1861 when the Confederate army began the Battle of Fort Sumter in South Carolina, just over a month after the first inauguration of Abraham Lincoln. The Confederacy grew to control at least a majority of territory in eleven states (out of the 34 U.S. states in February 1861) and asserted claims to two more. The states that remained loyal to the federal government were known as the Union. Large volunteer and conscription armies were raised; four years of intense combat, mostly in the South, ensued.

During the American civil war, Liverpool England was the unofficial home of the Confederate fleet. Three significant acts of the war involved Liverpool:

The first act of the war - the first shot of the civil war was fired by a cannon made at the Lydia Anne Street Foundry in Liverpool.

The very last act of the war - Captain Waddell of the CCS Shenandoah walked up the steps of Liverpool Town Hall and surrendered his vessel to the Lord Mayor, after sailing 'home' from Alaska to surrender. The last shot fired in the conflict was by CSS Shenandoah on June 22nd, 1865, at a Northern Union whaling ship in the North Pacific Ocean.

The last official lowering of the Confederate flag - Was on CSS Shenandoah on the River Mersey at Liverpool overseen by the Royal Navy.

At the outbreak of war, the Northern Union fleet blockaded Confederate ports to prevent trade and supply of munitions of war. The Confederacy had no navy and proceeded to build one from Liverpool. The British government was officially neutral in the dispute not recognizing the Confederacy. Cotton importers Frazer Trenholm in Rumford Place acted as the unofficial Confederate embassy where operations were conducted. The Northern Union consulate was a few minutes' walk away in Tower Buildings, Water Street. Commander Bulloch of the Confederate Navy was based in Liverpool, whose prime task was to assemble and run a navy. He never returned to America after the conflict remaining in Liverpool for the rest of his life, now laying in Toxteth Cemetery. Britain's official stance was that the country, or its empire, was not to supply the means of war to the breakaway Confederate state. Liverpool ignored officialdom supplying what the Confederacy wanted against the policy and direction of the British government. Liverpool provided armaments and provisions of war of all kinds, together with merchant ships as well as man of war ships, complete with crews. Forty-two blockade runners, ships to outrun the Northern Union naval blockade placed on Confederate ports, were built on the River Mersey for the Confederacy, including the SS Banshee, the first steel hulled ship to cross the Atlantic. Could this British-Welsh founded port of Liverpool supporting the Confederate Navy be a reference to the red dragon of Revelation 12:3 and 13:2 similar to the American Revolution? Welsh Dragon (Y Ddraig Goch), meaning *the red dragon*, a heraldic symbol that appears on the English Crown's coat of arms and the national flag of Wales. The Welsh Dragon is also one of ten of "The King's Beasts" statues at Hampton Court, Greater London, England.

During 1861–1862 in the war's Western Theater, the Union made significant permanent gains, though in the war's Eastern Theater, the conflict was inconclusive. In September 1862, Lincoln issued the Emancipation Proclamation, which made ending slavery a war goal. To the west, the Union destroyed the Confederate River navy by summer 1862, then much of its western armies, and seized New Orleans. The successful 1863 Union siege of Vicksburg split the Confederacy in two at the Mississippi River. In 1863, Confederate General Robert E. Lee's incursion north ended at the Battle of Gettysburg. Western successes led to General Ulysses S. Grant's command of all Union armies in 1864. Inflicting an ever-tightening naval blockade of

Confederate ports, the Union marshaled resources and manpower to attack the Confederacy from all directions, leading to the fall of Atlanta in 1864 to Union General William Tecumseh Sherman and his march to the sea. The last significant battles raged around the ten-month Siege of Petersburg, gateway to the Confederate capitol of Richmond.

The war effectively ended on April 9th, 1865, when Confederate General Lee surrendered to Union General Grant at the Battle of Appomattox Court House, after abandoning Petersburg and Richmond. Confederate generals throughout the Southern states followed suit, the last surrender on land occurring on June 23rd. By the end of the war, much of the South's infrastructure was destroyed, especially its railroads. The Confederacy collapsed; slavery was abolished. The war-torn nation then entered the Reconstruction era in a partially successful attempt to rebuild the country and grant civil rights to freed slaves.

Jefferson Finis Davis was President of the Confederate States of America (CSA) from 1861 to 1865. Jeff F Davis CSA=666. Did he represent the first Beast in this cycle? Elkanah Brackin Greer took part in the earlier Mexican American War as a member of the 1st Mississippi Rifles, whose colonel was future Confederate President Jefferson Davis. He later became the Grand Commander of the secretive (KGC) Knights of the Golden Circle organization. The Knights of the Golden Circle was a secret society founded in 1854, the objective of which was to create a new country, known as the Golden Circle, where slavery would be legal. The country would have been centered in Havana and would have consisted of the Southern United States and a "golden circle" of territories in Mexico (which was to be divided into 25 new slave states), Central America, northern parts of South America, Cuba, Haiti, Dominican Republic, and most other islands in the Caribbean. Greer established KGC command post known as castles in East Texas and Louisiana. In the spring of 1860, Greer had become General and Grand Commander of 4,000 Military Knights in the KGC's Texas division of 21 castles. In October 1862, he was promoted to the rank of Brigadier General of the Confederate States of America. Elkanah Brackin Greer, KGC Commander-Brigadier General Confederate States. Brackin Greer=666. Was he the second Beast in this cycle? The American Civil War was among the earliest to use industrial warfare. Railroads, the telegraph, steamships, the ironclad warship, and mass-produced weapons saw wide use. In total the war left between 620,000 and 750,000 soldiers dead, along with an undetermined number of civilian casualties. President Lincoln was assassinated just five days after Lee's surrender. John Wilkes Booth was an American stage actor who assassinated President Abraham Lincoln at Ford's Theater in Washington, D.C. on April 14th, 1865. A member of the prominent 19th-century Booth theatrical family from Maryland, he was a noted actor who was also a Confederate sympathizer; denouncing President Lincoln, he lamented the recent abolition of slavery in the United States. Originally, Booth and his small group of conspirators had plotted to kidnap Lincoln, and they later agreed to murder him as well as Vice President Andrew Johnson and Secretary of State

William H. Seward, likewise, to aid the Confederate cause. Although its Army of Northern Virginia, commanded by General Robert E. Lee, had surrendered to the Union Army four days earlier, Booth believed that the Civil War remained unresolved because the Confederate Army of General Joseph E. Johnston continued fighting. Booth shot President Lincoln once in the back of the head. Lincoln's death the next morning completed Booth's piece of the plot. Seward, severely wounded, recovered, whereas Vice President Johnson was never attacked.

Could there be other references in this cycle to the prophecies John wrote about in the Book of Revelation? In 1861 Currier & Ives of New York, printed a tribute to commander of Union forces Gen. Winfield Scott, shown as the mythical Hercules slaying the seven-headed dragon, symbolizing the secession of the Confederate states. Could this represent the seven headed beast in the Book of Revelation? Revelation 13:1, "And I stood upon the sand of the sea, and saw a beast rise up out of the sea, having seven heads and ten horns, and upon his horns ten crowns, and upon his heads the name of blasphemy."

In the print General Scott is shown wielding a great club about to strike the beast. The beast has seven heads, each representing a prominent Southern leader. The neck of each Southerner depicted is labeled with a vice or crime associated with him. They are from top to bottom: Hatred and Blasphemy (Confederate secretary of state Robert Toombs), Lying (Vice President Alexander

Stephens), Piracy (President Jefferson Davis), Perjury (army commander P. G. T. Beauregard), Treason (United States general David E. Twiggs who in February 1861 turned over nineteen federal army posts under his command in Texas to the South), Extortion (South Carolina governor Francis W. Pickens), and Robbery (James Buchanan's secretary of war John B. Floyd, accused of supplying federal arms and supplies to the South).

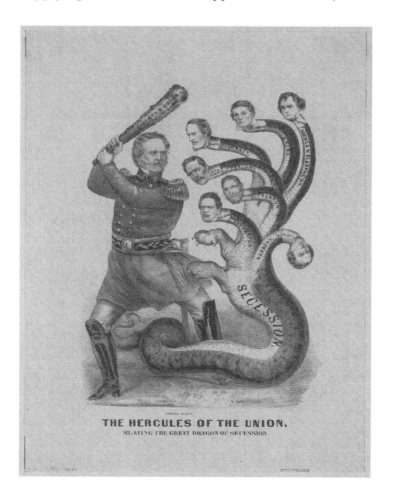

THE HERCULES OF THE UNION,
SLAYING THE GREAT DRAGON OF SECESSION.

The World War II Cycle

About 80 years after the American Civil War tribulation cycle the United States was thrust into World War II. This was a global war that lasted from 1939 to 1945. It involved most of the world's countries—including all of the great powers—forming two opposing military alliances: the Allies and the Axis powers. In a total war directly involving more than 100 million personnel from more than 30 countries, the major participants threw their entire economic, industrial, and scientific capabilities behind the war effort, blurring the distinction between civilian and military resources. Aircraft played a major role in the conflict, enabling the strategic bombing of population centers and the only two uses of nuclear weapons in war to this day. World War II was by far the deadliest conflict in human history; it resulted in 70 to 85 million fatalities, a majority being civilians. Tens of millions of people died due to genocides (including the Holocaust), starvation, massacres, and disease. In the wake of the Axis defeat, Germany and Japan were occupied, and war crimes tribunals were conducted against German and Japanese leaders.

World War II is generally considered to have begun on September 1st, 1939, when Nazi Germany, under Adolf Hitler, invaded Poland. The United Kingdom and France subsequently declared war on Germany on September 3rd. Under the Molotov–Ribbentrop Pact of August 1939, Germany and the Soviet Union had partitioned Poland and marked out their "spheres of influence" across Finland, Romania and the Baltic states. From late 1939 to early 1941, in a series of campaigns and treaties, Germany conquered or controlled much of continental Europe and formed the Axis alliance with Italy and Japan (along with other countries later on). Following the onset of campaigns in North Africa and East Africa, and the fall of France in mid-1940, the war continued primarily between the European Axis powers and the British Empire, with war in the Balkans, the aerial Battle of Britain, the Blitz of the UK, and the Battle of the Atlantic. On June 22nd, 1941, Germany led the European Axis powers in an invasion of the Soviet Union, opening the Eastern Front, the largest land theater of war in history and trapping the Axis powers, crucially the German Wehrmacht, in a war of attrition.

Japan, which aimed to dominate Asia and the Pacific, was at war with the Republic of China by 1937. In December 1941, Japan attacked American and British territories with near-simultaneous offensives against Southeast Asia and the Central Pacific, including an attack on the US fleet at Pearl Harbor which forced the US to declare war against Japan; the European Axis powers declared war on the US in solidarity. Could the dragon in Revelation 12:3 and 13:2 be represented by the culturally historic Japanese dragon? The Imperial Japanese Army Air Force gave some of their aircraft dragon names, for example the Mitsubishi Ki-67 bomber was called *Hiryu* (*Flying Dragon*) and the Nakajima Ki-49 bomber was called *Donryu* (*Storm Dragon*). The Imperial Japanese Navy and later the Japan Maritime Self-Defense Force named some of their ships after dragons. Notable examples are the World War II-era aircraft carriers *Hiryu* and *S?ry?* and the modern submarines of the *S?ry?* class.

Japan soon captured much of the western Pacific, but its advances were halted in 1942 after losing the critical Battle of Midway; later, Germany and Italy were defeated in North Africa and at Stalingrad in the Soviet Union. Key setbacks in 1943—including a series of German defeats on the Eastern Front, the Allied invasions of Sicily and the Italian mainland, and Allied offensives in the Pacific—cost the Axis powers their initiative and forced it into strategic retreat on all fronts. In 1944, the Western Allies invaded German-occupied France, while the Soviet Union regained its territorial losses and turned towards Germany and its allies. During 1944 and 1945, Japan suffered reversals in mainland Asia, while the Allies crippled the Japanese Navy and captured key western Pacific islands.

The war in Europe concluded with the liberation of German-occupied territories, and the invasion of Germany by the Western Allies and the Soviet Union, culminating in the fall of Berlin to Soviet troops, Hitler's suicide and the German unconditional surrender on May 8th, 1945. Following the Potsdam Declaration by the Allies on July 26th, 1945, and the refusal of Japan to surrender on its terms, the United States dropped the first atomic bombs on the Japanese cities of Hiroshima on August 6th and Nagasaki on August 9th. Faced with an imminent invasion of the Japanese archipelago, the possibility of additional atomic bombings, and the Soviet entry into the war against Japan and its invasion of Manchuria, Japan announced its intention to surrender on August 15th, then signed the surrender document on September 2nd, 1945, cementing total victory in Asia for the Allies.

Adolf Hitler was an Austrian-born German politician who was the dictator of Germany from 1933 to 1945. He rose to power as the leader of the Nazi Party, becoming the chancellor in 1933 and then assuming the title of Führer und Reichskanzler in 1934. During his dictatorship, he initiated World War II in Europe by invading Poland on September 1st, 1939. He was closely involved in military operations throughout the war and was central to the perpetration of the Holocaust, the genocide of about six million Jews and millions of other victims.

Adolf Hitler was born on April 20th, 1889, in Braunau am Inn, a town in Austria-Hungary (in present-day Austria), close to the border with the German Empire. He was the fourth of six children born to Alois Hitler and his third wife, Klara Polzl. In June 1895 his father Alois retired to Hafeld, near Lambach, where he farmed and kept bees. Hitler attended Volksschule (a state-funded primary school) in nearby Fischlham. The move to Hafeld coincided with the onset of intense father-son conflicts caused by Hitler's refusal to conform to the strict discipline of his school. Although his mother tried to protect him, His father beat him. This gave rise to an unforgiving antagonism between father and son. It's likely that Hitler, the pompous maniacal dictator Nazi Fuhrer of Germany, might have dropped his hated fathers name from his own and had any record of it covered up. Was Adolf Hitler the first Beast in this cycle? The number of his name Nazi Fuhrer Adolf Hitler (fathers name was Alois Hitler) Adolf A Hitler=666

Later Adolf Hitler moved to Germany in 1913, and was decorated during his service in the German Army in World War I. In 1919, he joined the German Workers' Party, the precursor of the Nazi Party, and was appointed leader of the Nazi Party in 1921. In 1923, he attempted to seize governmental power in a failed coup in Munich and was imprisoned with a sentence of five years. In jail, he dictated the first volume of his autobiography and political manifesto Mein Kampf ("My Struggle"). After his early release in 1924, Hitler gained popular support by attacking the Treaty of Versailles and promoting pan-Germanism, antisemitism and anti-communism with charismatic oratory and Nazi propaganda. He frequently denounced international Capitalism and Communism as part of a Jewish conspiracy. By November 1932, the Nazi Party held the most seats in the German Reichstag but did not have a majority. As a result, no party was able to form a majority parliamentary coalition in support of a candidate for Chancellor. Former Chancellor Franz von Papen and other conservative leaders persuaded President Paul von Hindenburg to appoint Hitler as chancellor on January 30th, 1933. Shortly after, the Reichstag passed the Enabling Act of 1933 which began the process of transforming the Weimar Republic into Nazi Germany, a one-party dictatorship based on the totalitarian and autocratic ideology of Nazism. Hitler aimed to eliminate Jews from Germany and establish a New Order to counter what he saw as the injustice of the post-World War I international order dominated by Britain and France.

The Holocaust was the genocide of European Jews during World War II. Between 1941 and 1945, Nazi Germany and its collaborators systematically murdered some six million Jews across German-occupied Europe, around two-thirds of Europe's Jewish population. The murders were carried out in pogroms and mass shootings; by a policy of extermination through labor in concentration camps; and in gas chambers and gas vans in German extermination camps, chiefly Auschwitz-Birkenau, Belzec, Chelmno, Majdanek, Sobibor, and Treblinka in occupied Poland. Germany implemented the persecution in stages. Following Adolf Hitler's appointment as chancellor on January 30th, 1933, the regime built a network of concentration camps in Germany for political opponents and those deemed "undesirable", starting with Dachau on March 22nd 1933. After the passing of the Enabling Act on March 24th, which gave Hitler plenary powers, the government began isolating Jews from civil society; this included boycotting Jewish businesses in April 1933 and enacting the Nuremberg Laws in September 1935. On November 9th-10th 1938, eight months after Germany annexed Austria, Jewish businesses and other buildings were ransacked or set on fire throughout Germany and Austria on what became known as *Kristallnacht* (the "Night of Broken Glass"). After Germany invaded Poland in September 1939, triggering World War II, the regime set up ghettos to segregate Jews. Eventually, thousands of camps and other detention sites were established across German-occupied Europe. The segregation of Jews in ghettos culminated in the policy of extermination the Nazis called the Final Solution to the Jewish Question, discussed by senior government officials at the Wannsee Conference in Berlin in January 1942. As German forces captured territories in the East, all anti-Jewish measures were radicalized. Under the coordination of the "SS" (*Schutzstaffel* a paramilitary Nazi organization) with directions from the highest leadership of the Nazi Party, killings were committed within Germany itself, throughout occupied Europe, and within territories controlled by Germany's allies. Paramilitary death squads called *Einsatzgruppen*, in cooperation with the German Army and local collaborators, murdered around 1.3 million Jews in mass shootings and pogroms from the summer of 1941. By mid-1942, victims were being deported from ghettos across Europe in sealed freight trains to extermination camps where, if they survived the journey, they were gassed, worked or beaten to death, or killed by disease, medical experiments, or during death marches. The killing continued until the end of World War II in Europe in May 1945. The European Jews were targeted for extermination as part of a larger event during the Holocaust era (1933–1945), in which Germany and its collaborators persecuted and murdered millions of others, including ethnic Poles, Soviet civilians and prisoners of war, the Roma, the disabled, political and religious dissidents, and homosexuals. After 1942, the economic function of the camps, previously secondary to their penal and terror functions, came to the forefront. Forced labor of camp prisoners became commonplace. The guards became much more brutal, and the death rate increased as the guards not only beat and starved prisoners but killed them more frequently. *Vernichtung durch Arbeit* ("extermination through labor") was a policy; camp inmates would literally be worked to death or to physical exhaustion, at which point they would be gassed or shot. The

Germans estimated the average prisoner's lifespan in a concentration camp at three months, as a result of lack of food and clothing, constant epidemics, and frequent punishments for the most minor transgressions. The shifts were long and often involved exposure to dangerous materials.

Transportation to and between camps was often carried out in closed freight cars with little air or water, long delays and prisoners packed tightly. Prisoners wore colored triangles on their uniforms, the color denoting the reason for their incarceration. Red signified a political prisoner, Jehovah's Witnesses had purple triangles, criminals wore black and green, and homosexuals wore pink. Jews wore two yellow triangles, one over another to form a six-pointed star. Prisoners in Auschwitz were tattooed on arrival with an identification number. Could these identifications be reference to the mark of the Beast in the Book of Revelation? Upon entrance to these death camps, prisoners were taken to the right or left by the guards for "showers" or work. The one's selected for the "showers" did not know that the shower room was actually a poisonous gas death chamber! I'm reminded of Luke 18:35-36, "Two women shall be grinding together; the one shall be taken, and the other left. 36 Two men shall be in the field; the one shall be taken, and the other left."

Paul Joseph Goebbels was a German Nazi politician who was the Gauleiter (district leader) of Berlin, chief propagandist for the Nazi Party, and then Reich Minister of Propaganda from 1933 to 1945. He was one of Adolf Hitler's closest and most devoted acolytes, known for his skills in public speaking and his deeply virulent antisemitism, which was evident in his publicly voiced views. He advocated progressively harsher discrimination, including the extermination of the Jews in the Holocaust. Goebbels, who aspired to be an author, obtained a Doctor of Philology degree from the University of Heidelberg in 1921. He joined the Nazi Party in 1924. He was appointed Gauleiter of Berlin in 1926, where he began to take an interest in the use of propaganda to promote the party and its program. After the Nazis came to power in 1933, Goebbels's Propaganda Ministry quickly gained and exerted control over the news media, arts, and information in Germany. He was particularly adept at using the relatively new media of radio and film for propaganda purposes. Goebbels's once said, "Think of the press as a great keyboard on which the government can play." Topics for party propaganda included antisemitism, attacks on the Christian churches and worship-like dedication to Hitler. Goebbels's also once said, "It would not be impossible to prove with sufficient repetition and a psychological understanding of the people concerned that a square is in fact a circle. They are mere words, and words can be molded until they clothe ideas and disguise." Could Goebbels be the second Beast? The number of his name Nazi Propaganda Minister Joseph Goebbels (abbreviation for Joseph-Jos) Jos Goebbels=666. In 1943, Goebbels began to convince Hitler to introduce measures that would produce "total war", including closing businesses not essential to the war effort, conscripting women into the labor force, and enlisting men in previously exempt occupations into the Wehrmacht. Hitler finally appointed him as

Reich Plenipotentiary for Total War on July 23rd, 1944. As the war drew to a close and Nazi Germany faced defeat, Magda Goebbels and the Goebbels children joined him in Berlin. They moved into the underground Vorbunker, part of Hitler's underground bunker complex on April 22nd, 1945. Hitler committed suicide on April 30th. In accordance with Hitler's will, Goebbels succeeded him as Chancellor of Germany; he served one day in this post. The following day, Goebbels and his wife committed suicide, after poisoning their six children with cyanide.

Hitler's first six years in power resulted in rapid economic recovery from the Great Depression, the abrogation of restrictions imposed on Germany after World War I, and the annexation of territories inhabited by millions of ethnic Germans, which gave him significant popular support. Hitler sought Lebensraum (living space) for the German people in Eastern Europe, and his aggressive foreign policy is considered the primary cause of World War II in Europe. He directed large-scale rearmament, and on September 1st, 1939, he invaded Poland, resulting in Britain and France declaring war on Germany. In June 1941, Hitler ordered an invasion of the Soviet Union. By the end of 1941, German forces and the European Axis powers occupied most of Europe and North Africa. These gains were gradually reversed after 1941, and in 1945 the Allied armies defeated the German army. On April 29th, 1945, he married his longtime lover Eva Braun in the Fuhrerbunker (an underground bunker safe from bombing) in Berlin. "Official records" say, less than two days later, the couple committed suicide to avoid capture by the Soviet Red Army and their corpses were burned. According to later US intelligence reports,

Hitler is rumored to have survived by faking his death with a body double corpse, escaping Germany and living out his life in South America. Many South American witnesses have testified that Hitler and also other high ranking Nazi war criminals lived there after the war. Does this mean Hitler was, and is not, and yet is? I'm reminded of Revelation 17:8, "The beast that you saw was, and is not; and shall ascend out of the bottomless pit, and go into perdition: and they that dwell on the earth shall wonder, whose names were not written in the book of life from the foundation of the world, when they behold the beast that was, and is not, and yet is."

Historians describe Hitler as "the embodiment of political evil". Under Hitler's leadership and racially motivated ideology, the Nazi regime was responsible for the genocide of about six million Jews and millions of other victims whom he and his followers deemed Untermenschen (subhumans) or socially undesirable. Hitler and the Nazi regime were also responsible for the killing of an estimated 19 million civilians and prisoners of war. The number of civilians killed during World War II was unprecedented in warfare, and the casualties constitute the deadliest conflict in history. I'm reminded of a Winston Churchill quote "Those who fail to learn from history are condemned to repeat it."

The 2020 United States Tribulation Cycle

And now we have arrived at 80 years after the
World War II cycle. The Bible says the warning
signs of coming tribulation is when you see
earthquakes, fires, floods, troubles and rumors of
war. These days we live in now are like that for
sure. The Bible says it's like when a woman is
having pregnant pains about to give birth. Matthew
24:6-22, "And you shall hear of wars and rumors of
wars: see that you be not troubled: for all these
things must come to pass, but the end is not yet. 7
For nation shall rise against nation, and kingdom
against kingdom: and there shall be famines, and
pestilences, and earthquakes, in various places. 8 All
these are the beginning of sorrows. 9 Then shall they
deliver you up to be afflicted, and shall kill you: and
you shall be hated of all nations for my name's sake.
10 And then shall many be offended, and shall
betray one another, and shall hate one another. 11
And many false prophets shall rise, and shall
deceive many. 12 And because iniquity shall
abound, the love of many shall grow cold. 13 But he
that shall endure unto the end, the same shall be
saved. 14 And this gospel of the kingdom shall be
preached in all the world for a witness unto all
nations; and then shall the end come. 15 When you
therefore shall see the abomination of desolation,
spoken of by Daniel the prophet, stand in the holy
place, (whoever reads, let him understand:) 16 Then
let them who are in Judea flee into the mountains:
17 Let him who is on the housetop not come down
to take anything out of his house: 18 Neither let him
who is in the field return back to take his clothes. 19

And woe unto them that are with child, and to them that nurse a child in those days! 20 But pray you that your flight be not in the winter, neither on the sabbath day: 21 For then shall be great tribulation, such as was not since the beginning of the world to this time, no, nor ever shall be. 22 And except those days should be shortened, there should no flesh be saved: but for the elect's sake those days shall be shortened."

Could "abomination of desolation standing in the holy place" mentioned in Matthew 24:15 be a reference to Pope Clement deGoth of the Catholic Church persecuting the Knights Templar's? In the World War II cycle, could it be a reference to the Catholic Church's agreement with the Nazi's called the Reich Concordat signed by representatives of both entities on July 20th, 1933? There is archived World War II film footage showing a Catholic Priest giving last rites at a mass open pit Nazi execution of Jews. Catholic Priest also helped Nazi war criminals escape Germany by giving them forged passports. In this current cycle, could "abomination of desolation standing in the holy place" be a reference to Catholic priest exposed as to sexually molesting thousands of children? Interesting to note Vatican Hill=666. In the Book of Revelation, the beginning of tribulations are four horsemen. The very first sign is the first horse, a white horse. Revelation 6:2, "And I saw, and behold a white horse: and he that sat on it had a bow; and a crown was given unto him: and he went forth conquering, and to conquer."

The white horse in cultures around the world represents good over evil. Freedom loving people all over the world see the United States as the good guys. Often the United States even tries to help preserve freedom and resolve conflicts between other countries. Also, the United States is the most powerful nation on earth. Could the rider that has a bow, but no arrows represent responsible power? Could the white horse represent the United States? The rider was given a crown. Could this represent the President? Also, the rider went forth conquering, and to conquer. What personality on the world stage today fits the description of conquering, and to conquer more than Donald J Trump? Could he represent the rider on the white horse? Interesting to note, the number of his name Donald J Trump=888. Wow, according to Gematria, that puts him in pretty good company. Could Donald J Trump possibly be like a Gideon sent to save us from the Midianites as described in the Bible? The Bible tells of how Gideon was given a great mission. Judges 6:12, "And the angel of the LORD appeared unto him, and said unto him, The LORD is with you, you mighty man of valor." (*Definition of Valor; "strength of mind or spirit that enables a person to encounter danger with firmness."*) Judges 6:14, "And the LORD looked upon him, and said, Go in this your might, and you shall save Israel from the hand of the Midianites: have not I sent you?" Judges 6:16, "And the LORD said unto him, Surely I will be with you, and you shall strike the Midianites as one man."

When President Trump set out to "drain the Swamp" in Washington he was surely, with no political party support, as only one man! It was like he was made CEO of a company where everyone else working there was stealing from the company. Now critics might say, how could Trump be like a Bible character such as Gideon, he is rude, crude and brags. The famous baseball player Dizzy Dean said "It ain't bragging if you can do it." Bragging to place yourself above others is bad but bragging to inspire success is good. Trump reminds me of a great football coach who is maybe coarse but loves his team, loves each player and is determined to win. Is he really rude when he calls a wicked person "wicked" or an evil person "evil" or a stupid person "stupid"? The Bible is infallible in telling us about fallible people. God often chooses fallible people to carry out his work like Gideon who was the least of his father's house, David with his adultery, Noah's drunkenness, Paul's argument with Barnabas, or maybe Trump's crudeness. President Donald J Trump is no doubt the most important and greatest President since George Washington! He comes at a time in the United States when everything on all levels is under evil attack. There is obviously a concerted plan, maybe by China or other global powers, to destroy the United States sovereignty, economy, stability and Christian morality. Christian morality is the foundation that made the United States the greatest and most powerful nation on earth. Trump introduced the term "Swamp" that represents the corrupt politically established Washington deep state shadow government. These people making up the "Swamp", including most Republicans and obviously all Democrats (referred to by many as Demonic-rats), have embraced evil in exchange for power, position and money. Possibly the "Swamp" act as officers taking their orders from global powers. The "Swamp" continually push fake "man-made climate change" that has been proven fake by (non-government funded) scientist. This "fake man-made climate change" facilitates nefarious control and manipulation of almost every aspect of life. They heavily borrow against our

47

national debt then distributes the money (fruits of our labors) through dummy companies and launder it back to themselves. They seem to deliberately want the United States bankrupt. This concerted effort to destroy the United States also includes using "Swamp" propaganda lies to produce racism. We all saw "Swamp" induced race riots in "Swamp" controlled cities causing murders and billions of dollars in property damage. For these riots the "Swamp" provided cans of gasoline, pallets of bricks, travel funding for out-of-town rioters to go there and funding for jail-bail. The "Swamp" has viciously demonized police and advocated for defunding the police. Could the "Swamp" be planning to replace police with a national Nazi Gestapo type police? The "Swamp" has illegally facilitated millions of illegal aliens to flood into our country to overwhelm the stability of our systems. The "Swamp" has introduced racism, sexual perversion and hatred of the United States teachings into schools, all of which are apparently to create division, lawlessness, anarchy, system failure and destruction. I'm reminded of the second horse mentioned in Revelation 6:4, "And there went out another horse that was red: and power was given to him that sat thereon to take peace from the earth, and that they should kill one another: and there was given unto him a great sword."

Trump campaigned to clean up the "Swamp". Voter support for Trump in 2016 was so overwhelming it rendered normal cheating methods by the "Swamp" insufficient and he won anyway. The "Swamp" would not use just normal cheating methods for 2020. From the time when Trump first became President in 2016, he has been under constant evil attack from the "Swamp" and the

"Swamp's" lying media 24/7. A United States President has never been treated as viciously as President Trump. The wonderful First Lady Melania Trump is the most beautiful First Lady ever, sorry Jackie O! She was also treated shamefully by the "Swamp" controlled media, talk shows and magazines. The "Swamp" has taken control of all major government institutions, all major media news outlets and medical healthcare institutions. The "Swamp" has infiltrated nefarious teaching material into our schools. The "Swamp" uses their control of the FBI, IRS and media to lie about truth and to persecute anyone who oppose their wicked agendas. Since 2016 the "Swamps" FBI, IRS and media have been persecuting President Trump and his family over false Russian collusion accusation lies. The DNC (Democratic National Committee), Obama, FBI and Hilary Clinton illegally created fake document lies to vilify and incriminate President Trump. These fake illegal document lies were presented to a federal judge to facilitate surveillance, sham investigations and sham impeachment. The "Swamp-media" knowingly pushed this fake Russian collusion lie 24/7. This lie and all the liars have now been exposed, but justice has yet to be served. "Swamp-media" even received a Pulitzer for this lie. The "Swamp" destroys everything that it touches and everything that touches it, even Pulitzer's. I'm reminded of John 8:44 where it says Satin is a liar and the father of lies. Nazi Propaganda Minister Joseph Goebbels said, "Think of the press as a great keyboard on which the government can play." He also said, "People can be convinced that a square is a circle if told enough times." How can it be that some people are so easily fooled? Mark Twain once said, "It's easier to fool people than to convince them that they have been fooled." It seems like Christians can clearly see through these deceptive lies. This ability is explained in Matthew 13:11-15, "Jesus replied to them, "To you it has been granted to know the mysteries of the kingdom of heaven, but to them it has not been granted. 12 For whoever has [spiritual wisdom because he is receptive to God's word], to him more will be given, and he will be richly and abundantly supplied; but whoever does not have [spiritual wisdom because he has devalued God's word], even what he has will be taken away from him. 13 This is the reason I speak to the crowds in parables: because while [having the power of] seeing they do not see, and while [having the power of] hearing they do not hear, nor do they understand and grasp. 14 In them the prophecy of Isaiah is being fulfilled, which says, 'You will hear and keep on hearing, but never understand; And you will look and keep on looking, but never comprehend; 15 For this nation's heart has grown hard, And with their ears they hardly hear, And they have [tightly] closed their eyes, Otherwise they would see with their eyes, And hear with their ears, And understand with their heart, and turn [to Me] And I would heal them [spiritually]."

Some say those of the "Swamp" take instruction and carry out plans from the "Globalist". The "Globalist" is said to be a powerful group that collectively control and shape world events. Others say it's just a conspiracy theory. In World War II early reports of Nazi death camps were called conspiracy theory. Even after the allied Soviet army liberated Majdanek death camp near Lublin, Poland in July 1944 and reported it, most did not believe. Is it conspiracy theory when it's carved in stone? Some say the "Globalist" may be the ones who created the

Georgia Guidestones, a granite monument in Elbert
County, Georgia. In 1979 it was commissioned to be
built by a man using the pseudonym R. C. Christian.
A set of ten guidelines is inscribed on the structure
in twelve languages. They are English, Spanish,
Swahili, Hindi, Hebrew, Arabic, Traditional
Chinese, Russian, Babylonian (in cuneiform script),
Classical Greek, Sanskrit and Ancient Egyptian (in
hieroglyphs).

The ten guidelines read like some kind of post-apocalyptic instructions. They are as follows.

1-Maintain humanity under 500,000,000 in perpetual   balance with nature.

2-Guide reproduction wisely-improving fitness and diversity.

3-Unite humanity with a living new language.

4-Rule passion—faith—tradition—and all things with tempered reason.

5-Protect people and nations with fair laws and just courts.

6-Let all nations rule internally resolving external disputes in a world court.

7-Avoid petty laws and useless officials.

8-Balance personal rights with social duties.

9-Prize truth—beauty—love—seeking harmony with the infinite.

10-Be not a cancer on the Earth—Leave room for nature—Leave room for nature.

Wow, maintain humanity under 500 million! That's only about 6% of the current 8 billion people on earth. Could this be part of some "Globalist" evil plan to depopulate the earth? Maybe this is part of that "Great Reset" we keep hearing about. Could it be that these "Globalist" considers the rest of us some kind of cancer using up   their earthly resources? Maybe they consider the rest of us like worker-bee slaves they no longer need because of robotic-manufacturing and artificial intelligence. I'm reminded of Psalm 37:12-16, "The wicked plots against the just, and gnashes upon him with his teeth. 13 The Lord shall laugh at him: for he sees that his day is coming. 14 The wicked have drawn out the sword, and have bent their bow, to cast down the poor and needy, and to slay such as be of upright behavior. 15 Their sword shall enter into their own heart, and their bows shall be broken. 16 A little that a righteous man has is better than the riches of many wicked. 17 For the arms of the wicked shall be broken: but the LORD upholds the righteous."

Maybe these "Globalist" wanted the "Swamp" to get rid of President Trump for sure this time because there is no doubt the 2020 Presidential election was stolen using election fraud many ways on many levels on a massive scale. Investigations have reveled evidence of election fraud enough to swing the difference many times over. If the truth was known, Trump probably got 100 million votes to the Democrats maybe 40 million. January 6th is the date that has been widely used for propaganda by the "Swamp" concerning the peaceful 2020 election fraud protest at the U.S. Capitol, falsely described as "the attack" on the U.S. Capitol that occurred on January 6th , 2021. Capital police removed barriers, opened doors and invited the crowd to enter the Capital building as a trap. The "Swamp" infiltrated, into the crowd, hostile agents posing as Trump supporters to create havoc and lure protesters into the building. Around 600 innocent protesters have now been tracked down by the "Swamps" FBI and jailed for trespassing. The "Swamps" 2020 election fraud effectively installed Joseph Biden as the Democrat False President. The conservative media and legitimate polls said Biden was not a popular candidate, and the only reason even democrats voted for him was because he had a D in front of his name! The number of his name D-Joseph Biden=666 (Democrat False President). Could Biden be the first Beast? During the Presidential campaign summer, we all saw 100's of thousands of people at Trump's rallies and by contrast, 12 people standing in a circle at Biden's rallies. We all saw Biden rarely ascend from his basement to give a campaign speech like a ground hog looking for his shadow. Revelation 17:8, "The beast that you saw was, and is not; and shall ascend out of the bottomless pit, and go into perdition: and they that dwell on the earth shall wonder, whose names were not written in the book of life from the foundation of the world, when they behold the beast that was, and is not, and yet is."

Biden was Vice President, is not now truly President, yet he is President! Could Biden be the Beast who was, and is not, and yet is? Also, there have been seven Democrat presidents and ten Democrat vice presidents since the World War II cycle.

32nd P- Franklin D. Roosevelt

32nd VP- John Nance Garner

      33rd VP- Henry A. Wallace

      34th VP- Harry S. Truman

33rd P- Harry S. Truman

      35th VP- Alben W. Barkley

35th P- John F. Kennedy

      37th VP- Lyndon B. Johnson

36th P- Lyndon B. Johnson

      38th VP- Hubert Humphrey

39th P- Jimmy Carter

    42nd VP- Walter Mondale

42nd P- Bill Clinton

    45th VP- Al Gore

44th P- Barack Obama

    47th VP- Joe Biden

46th P- Joe Biden

    49th VP- Kamala Harris

It says in Revelation 13:1, "And I stood upon the sand of the sea, and saw a beast rise up out of the sea, having seven heads and ten horns, and upon his horns ten crowns, and upon his heads the name of blasphemy."

One of these seven Democrat Presidents since the World War II cycle whose name still carries a lot of influence, getting votes even now, was John F. Kennedy. Although mortally wounded in the head by an assassin in 1963, his legacy lives on. It says in Revelation 13:3, "And I saw one of his heads as if it were wounded to death; and his deadly wound was healed: and all the world marveled after the beast."

Revelation 17:10-11 says, "And there are seven kings: five are fallen, and one is, and the other is not yet come; and when he comes, he must continue a short time. 11 And the beast that was, and is not, even he is the eighth, and is of the seven, and goes into perdition."

Is the number six king Clinton? Is number seven Obama? Is number eight Biden? It says number seven must continue a short time, like number seven Obama staying in Washington to run Biden's administration from the shadows? It says number eight is of the seven, like number eight Biden once being Vice president of number seven Obama? Democrat-Obama=666. Dem-B Clinton=666.

Revelation 17:1-6 says, "And there came one of the seven angels who had the seven bowls, and talked with me, saying unto me, Come here; I will show unto you the judgment of the great harlot that sits upon many waters: 2 With whom the kings of the earth have committed fornication, and the inhabitants of the earth have been made drunk with the wine of her fornication. 3 So he carried me away in the spirit into the wilderness: and I saw a woman sitting upon a scarlet-colored beast, full of names of blasphemy, having seven heads and ten horns. 4 And the woman was arrayed in purple and scarlet color, and adorned with gold and precious stones and pearls, having a golden cup in her hand full of abominations and filthiness of her fornication: 5 And upon her forehead was a name written, MYSTERY, BABYLON THE GREAT, THE MOTHER OF HARLOTS AND ABOMINATIONS OF THE EARTH. 6 And I saw the woman drunken with the blood of the saints, and with the blood of the martyrs of Jesus: and when I saw her, I wondered with great wonder."

Who could this harlot woman arrayed in purple and scarlet color and adorned with gold and precious stones and pearls be that sits upon the scarlet-colored Beast? Could it be False Democrat Vice President Kamala Harris? She has a political rise to power career that is stained by sex scandals. The number of her name VP-Harris=666. Kamala Harris was born in 1964. Three of the ten Democrat VP's (horns) have died since Kamala's birth; Lyndon B.

Johnson, Hubert Humphrey and Walter Mondale. Daniel 7:8 "While I was contemplating the horns, behold, another horn, a little one, came up among them, and three of the first horns were pulled out by the roots before it; and behold, this horn possessed eyes like the eyes of a man and a mouth uttering great boasts."

Could she represent the "Washington-Swamp"? Revelation 17:18 says, "And the woman whom you saw is that great city, which reigns over the kings of the earth."

Could the "Swamp" part of Washington, in this cycle, be Babylon? Revelation 18:2 "And he cried mightily with a strong voice, saying, Babylon the great is fallen, is fallen, and is become the habitation of devils, and the hold of every foul spirit, and a cage of every unclean and hateful bird."

Trump Administration Accomplishments

Starting January 20th, 2017, President Trump fought 24/7 with the "Swamp" to restore America to Her once greatness. Three and a half years later he had accomplished historical record gains in all categories. The following is a government archive list.

Unprecedented Economic Boom

America gained 7 million new jobs – more than three times government experts' projections.
Middle-Class family income increased nearly $6,000 – more than five times the gains during the entire previous administration.
The unemployment rate reached 3.5 percent, the lowest in a half-century.
Achieved 40 months in a row with more job openings than job-hirings.
More Americans reported being employed than ever before – nearly 160 million.
Jobless claims hit a nearly 50-year low.
The number of people claiming unemployment insurance as a share of the population hit its lowest on record.
Incomes rose in every single metro area in the United States for the first time in nearly 3 decades.

Delivered a future of greater promise and opportunity for citizens of all backgrounds.

Unemployment rates for African Americans, Hispanic

Americans, Asian Americans, Native Americans, veterans, individuals with disabilities, and those without a high school diploma all reached record lows.

Unemployment for women hit its lowest rate in nearly 70 years.

Lifted nearly 7 million people off of food stamps.

Poverty rates for African Americans and Hispanic Americans reached record lows.

Income inequality fell for two straight years, and by the largest amount in over a decade.

The bottom 50 percent of American households saw a 40 percent increase in net worth.

Wages rose fastest for low-income and blue-collar workers – a 16 percent pay increase.

African American homeownership increased from 41.7 percent to 46.4 percent.

Brought jobs, factories, and industries back to the USA.

Created more than 1.2 million manufacturing and construction jobs.

Put in place policies to bring back supply chains from overseas.

Small business optimism broke a 35-year-old record in 2018.

Hit record stock market numbers and record 401ks.

The DOW closed above 20,000 for the first time in 2017 and topped 30,000 in 2020.

The S&P 500 and NASDAQ have repeatedly notched record highs.

Rebuilding and investing in rural America.

Signed an Executive Order on Modernizing the Regulatory Framework for Agricultural Biotechnology Products, which is bringing innovative new technologies to market in American farming and agriculture.
Strengthened America's rural economy by investing over $1.3 billion through the Agriculture Department's Reconnect Program to bring high-speed broadband infrastructure to rural America.

Achieved a record-setting economic comeback by rejecting blanket lockdowns.

An October 2020 Gallup survey found 56 percent of Americans said they were better off during a pandemic than four years prior.
During the third quarter of 2020, the economy grew at a rate of 33.1 percent – the most rapid GDP growth ever recorded.
Since coronavirus lockdowns ended, the economy has added back over 12 million jobs, more than half the jobs lost.
Jobs have been recovered 23 times faster than the previous administration's recovery.
Unemployment fell to 6.7 percent in December, from a pandemic peak of 14.7 percent in April – beating expectations of well over 10 percent unemployment through the end of 2020.
Under the previous administration, it took 49 months for the unemployment rate to fall from 10 percent to under 7 percent compared to just 3 months for the Trump Administration.
Since April, the Hispanic unemployment rate has fallen by 9.6

percent, Asian-American unemployment by 8.6 percent, and Black American unemployment by 6.8 percent.

80 percent of small businesses are now open, up from just 53 percent in April.

Small business confidence hit a new high.

Homebuilder confidence reached an all-time high, and home sales hit their highest reading since December 2006.

Manufacturing optimism nearly doubled.

Household net worth rose $7.4 trillion in Q2 2020 to $112 trillion, an all-time high.

Home prices hit an all-time record high.

The United States rejected crippling lockdowns that crush the economy and inflict countless public health harms and instead safely reopened its economy.

Business confidence is higher in America than in any other G7 or European Union country.

Stabilized America's financial markets with the establishment of a number of Treasury Department supported facilities at the Federal Reserve.

Tax Relief for the Middle Class

Passed $3.2 trillion in historic tax relief and reformed the tax code.

Signed the Tax Cuts and Jobs Act – the largest tax reform package in history.

More than 6 million American workers received wage increases, bonuses, and increased benefits thanks to the tax cuts.

A typical family of four earning $75,000 received an income tax cut of more than $2,000 – slashing their tax bill in half.

Doubled the standard deduction – making the first $24,000 earned by a married couple completely tax-free.

Doubled the child tax credit.

Virtually eliminated the unfair Estate Tax, or Death Tax.

Cut the business tax rate from 35 percent – the highest in the developed world – all the way down to 21 percent.

Small businesses can now deduct 20 percent of their business income.

Businesses can now deduct 100 percent of the cost of their capital investments in the year the investment is made.

Since the passage of tax cuts, the share of total wealth held by the bottom half of households has increased, while the share held by the top 1 percent has decreased.

Over 400 companies have announced bonuses, wage increases, new hires, or new investments in the United States.

Over $1.5 trillion was repatriated into the United States from overseas.

Lower investment cost and higher capital returns led to faster growth in the middle class, real wages, and international competitiveness.

Jobs and investments are pouring into Opportunity Zones.

Created nearly 9,000 Opportunity Zones where capital gains on long-term investments are taxed at zero.

Opportunity Zone designations have increased property values within them by 1.1 percent, creating an estimated $11 billion in wealth for the nearly half of Opportunity Zone residents who own their own home. Opportunity Zones have attracted $75 billion in funds and driven $52 billion of new investment in economically distressed communities, creating at least 500,000 new jobs.

Approximately 1 million Americans will be lifted from poverty as a result of these new investments. Private equity investments into businesses in Opportunity Zones were nearly 30 percent higher than investments into businesses in similar areas that were not designated Opportunity Zones.

Massive Deregulation

Ended the regulatory assault on American Businesses and Workers.

Instead of 2-for-1, we eliminated 8 old regulations for every 1 new regulation adopted.

Provided the average American household an extra $3,100 every year.

Reduced the direct cost of regulatory compliance by $50 billion, and will reduce costs by an additional $50 billion in FY 2020 alone.

Removed nearly 25,000 pages from the Federal Register – more than any other president. The previous administration added over 16,000 pages.

Established the Governors' Initiative on Regulatory Innovation to reduce outdated regulations at the state, local, and tribal levels.

Signed an executive order to make it easier for businesses to offer retirement plans.

Signed two executive orders to increase transparency in Federal agencies and protect Americans and their small businesses from administrative abuse.

Modernized the National Environmental Policy Act (NEPA) for the first time in over 40 years.

Reduced approval times for major infrastructure projects from 10 or more years down to 2 years or less.

Helped community banks by signing legislation that rolled back costly provisions of Dodd-Frank.

Established the White House Council on Eliminating Regulatory Barriers to Affordable Housing to bring down housing costs.

Removed regulations that threatened the development of a strong and stable internet.

Eased and simplified restrictions on rocket launches, helping to spur commercial investment in space projects.

Published a whole-of-government strategy focused on ensuring American leadership in automated vehicle technology.

Streamlined energy efficiency regulations for American families and businesses, including preserving affordable lightbulbs, enhancing the utility of showerheads, and enabling greater time savings with dishwashers.

Removed unnecessary regulations that restrict the seafood industry and impede job creation.

Modernized the Department of Agriculture's biotechnology regulations to put America in the lead to develop new technologies.

Took action to suspend regulations that would have slowed our response to COVID-19, including lifting restrictions on manufacturers to more quickly produce ventilators.

Successfully rolled back burdensome regulatory overreach.

Rescinded the previous administration's Affirmatively Furthering Fair Housing (AFFH) rule, which would have abolished zoning for single-family housing to build low-income, federally subsidized apartments.
Issued a final rule on the Fair Housing Act's disparate impact standard.
Eliminated the Waters of the United States Rule and replaced it with the Navigable Waters Protection Rule, providing relief and certainty for farmers and property owners.
Repealed the previous administration's costly fuel economy regulations by finalizing the Safer Affordable Fuel Efficient (SAFE) Vehicle's rule, which will make cars more affordable, and lower the price of new vehicles by an estimated $2,200.

Americans now have more money in their pockets.

Deregulation had an especially beneficial impact on low-income Americans who pay a much higher share of their incomes for overregulation.
Cut red tape in the healthcare industry, providing Americans with more affordable healthcare and saving Americans nearly 10 percent on prescription drugs.
Deregulatory efforts yielded savings to the medical community an estimated $6.6 billion – with a reduction of 42 million hours of regulatory compliance work through 2021.

Removed government barriers to personal freedom and consumer choice in healthcare.
Once fully in effect, 20 major deregulatory actions undertaken by the Trump Administration are expected to save American consumers and businesses over $220 billion per year.
Signed 16 pieces of deregulatory legislation that will result in a $40 billion increase in annual real incomes.

Fair and Reciprocal Trade

Secured historic trade deals to defend American workers.

Immediately withdrew from the job-killing Trans-Pacific Partnership (TPP).
Ended the North American Free Trade Agreement (NAFTA) and replaced it with the brand new United States-Mexico-Canada Agreement (USMCA).
The USMCA contains powerful new protections for American manufacturers, automakers, farmers, dairy producers, and workers.
The USMCA is expected to generate over $68 billion in economic activity and potentially create over 550,000 new jobs over ten years.
Signed an executive order making it government policy to Buy American and Hire American and took action to stop the outsourcing of jobs overseas.
Negotiated with Japan to slash tariffs and open its market to $7 billion in American agricultural products and ended its ban on potatoes and lamb.

Over 90 percent of American agricultural exports to Japan now receive preferential treatment, and most are duty-free.

Negotiated another deal with Japan to boost $40 billion worth of digital trade.

Renegotiated the United States-Korea Free Trade Agreement, doubling the cap on imports of American vehicles and extending the American light truck tariff.

Reached a written, fully enforceable Phase One trade agreement with China on confronting pirated and counterfeit goods, and the protection of American ideas, trade secrets, patents, and trademarks.

China agreed to purchase an additional $200 billion worth of United States exports and opened market access for over 4,000 American facilities to exports while all tariffs remained in effect.

Achieved a mutual agreement with the European Union (EU) that addresses unfair trade practices and increases duty-free exports by 180 percent to $420 million.

Secured a pledge from the EU to eliminate tariffs on American lobster – the first United States-European Union negotiated tariff reduction in over 20 years.

Scored a historic victory by overhauling the Universal Postal Union, whose outdated policies were undermining American workers and interests.

Engaged extensively with trade partners like the EU and Japan to advance reforms to the World Trade Organization (WTO).

Issued a first-ever comprehensive report on the WTO Appellate

Body's failures to comply with WTO rules and interpret WTO agreements as written.

Blocked nominees to the WTO's Appellate Body until WTO Members recognize and address longstanding issues with Appellate Body activism. Submitted 5 papers to the WTO Committee on Agriculture to improve Members' understanding of how trade policies are implemented, highlight areas for improved transparency, and encourage members to maintain up-to-date notifications on market access and domestic support. Took strong actions to confront unfair trade practices and put America First.

Imposed tariffs on hundreds of billions worth of Chinese goods to protect American jobs and stop China's abuses under Section 232 of the Trade Expansion Act of 1962 and Section 301 of the Trade Act of 1974.

Directed an all-of-government effort to halt and punish efforts by the Communist Party of China to steal and profit from American innovations and intellectual property.

Imposed tariffs on foreign aluminum and foreign steel to protect our vital industries and support our national security.

Approved tariffs on $1.8 billion in imports of washing machines and $8.5 billion in imports of solar panels.

Blocked illegal timber imports from Peru.

Took action against France for its digital services tax that unfairly targets American technology companies.

Launched investigations into digital services taxes that have been proposed or adopted by 10 other countries.

Historic support for American farmers.

Successfully negotiated more than 50 agreements with countries around the world to increase foreign market access and boost exports of American agriculture products, supporting more than 1 million American jobs.

Authorized $28 billion in aid for farmers who have been subjected to unfair trade practices – fully funded by the tariffs paid by China.

China lifted its ban on poultry, opened its market to beef, and agreed to purchase at least $80 billion of American agricultural products in the next two years.

The European Union agreed to increase beef imports by 180 percent and opened up its market to more imports of soybeans.

South Korea lifted its ban on American poultry and eggs and agreed to provide market access for record exports of American rice.

Argentina lifted its ban on American pork.

Brazil agreed to increase wheat imports by $180 million a year and raised its quotas for purchases of United States ethanol.

Guatemala and Tunisia opened up their markets to American eggs.

Won tariff exemptions in Ecuador for wheat and soybeans.

Suspended $817 million in trade preferences for Thailand under the Generalized System of Preferences (GSP) program due to its failure to adequately provide reasonable market access for American pork products.

The amount of food stamps redeemed at farmers markets increased from $1.4 million in May 2020 to $1.75 million in September 2020 – a 50 percent increase over last year.

Rapidly deployed the Coronavirus Food Assistance Program, which provided $30 billion in support to farmers and ranchers facing decreased prices and market disruption when COVID-19 impacted the food supply chain.

Authorized more than $6 billion for the Farmers to Families Food Box program, which delivered over 128 million boxes of locally sourced, produce, meat, and dairy products to charity and faith-based organizations nationwide.

Delegated authorities via the Defense Production Act to protect breaks in the American food supply chain as a result of COVID-19.

American Energy Independence

Unleashed America's oil and natural gas potential.

For the first time in nearly 70 years, the United States has become a net energy exporter.

The United States is now the number one producer of oil and natural gas in the world.

Natural gas production reached a record-high of 34.9 quads in 2019, following record high production in 2018 and in 2017.

The United States has been a net natural gas exporter for three consecutive years and has an export capacity of nearly 10 billion cubic feet per day.

Withdrew from the unfair, one-sided Paris Climate Agreement.

Canceled the previous administration's Clean Power Plan, and replaced it with the new Affordable Clean Energy rule.

Approved the Keystone XL and Dakota Access pipelines.

Opened up the Arctic National Wildlife Refuge (ANWR) in Alaska to oil and gas leasing.

Repealed the last administration's Federal Coal Leasing Moratorium, which prohibited coal leasing on Federal lands.

Reformed permitting rules to eliminate unnecessary bureaucracy and speed approval for mines.

Fixed the New Source Review permitting program, which punished companies for upgrading or repairing coal power plants.

Fixed the Environmental Protection Agency's (EPA) steam electric and coal ash rules.

The average American family saved $2,500 a year in lower electric bills and lower prices at the gas pump.

Signed legislation repealing the harmful Stream Protection Rule.

Reduced the time to approve drilling permits on public lands by half, increasing permit applications to drill on public lands by 300 percent.

Expedited approval of the NuStar's New Burgos pipeline to export American gasoline to Mexico.

Streamlined Liquefied natural gas (LNG) terminal permitting and allowed long-term LNG export authorizations to be extended through 2050.

The United States is now among the top three LNG exporters in the world.

Increased LNG exports five-fold since January 2017, reaching an all-time high in January 2020. LNG exports are expected to reduce the American trade deficit by over $10 billion.

Granted more than 20 new long-term approvals for LNG exports to non-free trade agreement countries. The development of natural gas and LNG infrastructure in the United States is providing tens of thousands of jobs and has led to the investment of tens of billions of dollars in infrastructure.

There are now 6 LNG export facilities operating in the United States, with 2 additional export projects under construction.

The amount of nuclear energy production in 2019 was the highest on record, through a combination of increased capacity from power plant upgrades and shorter refueling and maintenance cycles.

Prevented Russian energy coercion across Europe through various lines of effort, including the Partnership for Transatlantic Energy Cooperation, civil nuclear deals with Romania and Poland, and opposition to Nord Stream 2 pipeline.

Issued the Presidential Permit for the A2A railroad between Canada and Alaska, providing energy resources to emerging markets.

Increased access to our country's abundant natural resources in order to achieve energy independence.

Renewable energy production and consumption both reached record highs in 2019.

Enacted policies that helped double the amount of electricity generated by solar and helped increase the amount of wind generation by 32 percent from 2016 through 2019. Accelerated construction of energy infrastructure to ensure American energy producers can deliver their products to the market.

Cut red tape holding back the construction of new energy infrastructure.

Authorized ethanol producers to sell E15 year-round and allowed higher-ethanol gasoline to be distributed from existing pumps at filling stations.

Ensured greater transparency and certainty in the Renewable Fuel Standard (RFS) program.

Negotiated leasing capacity in the Strategic Petroleum Reserve to Australia, providing American taxpayers a return on this infrastructure investment.

Signed an executive order directing Federal agencies to work together to diminish the capability of foreign adversaries to target our critical electric infrastructure.

Reformed Section 401 of the Clean Water Act regulation to allow for the curation of interstate infrastructure. Resolved the OPEC (Organization of the Petroleum Exporting Countries) oil crisis during COVID-19 by getting OPEC, Russia, and others to cut nearly 10 million barrels of production a day, stabilizing world oil prices.

Directed the Department of Energy to use the Strategic

Petroleum Reserve to mitigate market volatility caused by COVID-19.

Investing in America's Workers and Families

Affordable and high-quality Child Care for American workers and their families.

Doubled the Child Tax Credit from $1,000 to $2,000 per child and expanded the eligibility for receiving the credit.
Nearly 40 million families benefitted from the child tax credit (CTC), receiving an average benefit of $2,200 – totaling credits of approximately $88 billion.
Signed the largest-ever increase in Child Care and Development Block Grants – expanding access to quality, affordable childcare for more than 800,000 low-income families.
Secured an additional $3.5 billion in the Coronavirus Aid, Relief, and Economic Security (CARES) Act to help families and first responders with childcare needs.
Created the first-ever paid family leave tax credit for employees earning $72,000 or less.
Signed into law 12-weeks of paid parental leave for Federal workers.
Signed into law a provision that enables new parents to withdraw up to $5,000 from their retirement accounts without penalty when they give birth to or adopt a child.

Advanced apprenticeship career pathways to good-paying jobs.

Expanded apprenticeships to more than 850,000 and established the new Industry-Recognized Apprenticeship programs in new and emerging fields.
Established the National Council for the American Worker and

the American Workforce Policy Advisory Board.
Over 460 companies have signed the Pledge to
America's Workers, committing to provide more
than 16 million job and training opportunities.
Signed an executive order that directs the Federal
government to replace outdated degree-based hiring
with skills-based hiring.

Advanced women's economic empowerment.

Included women's empowerment for the first time
in the President's 2017 National Security Strategy.

Signed into law key pieces of legislation, including
the Women, Peace, and Security Act and the
Women Entrepreneurship and Economic
Empowerment Act.
Launched the Women's Global Development and
Prosperity (W-GDP) Initiative – the first-ever
whole-of-government approach to women's
economic empowerment that has reached 24 million
women worldwide.
Established an innovative new W-GDP Fund at
USAID.
Launched the Women Entrepreneurs Finance
Initiative (We-Fi) with 13 other nations.
Announced a $50 million donation on behalf of the
United States to We-Fi providing more capital to
women-owned businesses around the world.
Released the first-ever Strategy on Women, Peace,
and Security, which focused on increasing women's
participation to prevent and resolve conflicts.
Launched the W-GDP 2x Global Women's Initiative
with the Development Finance Corporation, which
has mobilized more

than $3 billion in private sector investments over three years.

Ensured American leadership in technology and innovation.

First administration to name artificial intelligence, quantum information science, and 5G communications as national research and development priorities.
Launched the American Broadband Initiative to promote the rapid deployment of broadband internet across rural America.
Made 100 megahertz of crucial mid-band spectrum available for commercial operations, a key factor to driving widespread 5G access across rural America.
Launched the American AI Initiative to ensure American leadership in artificial intelligence (AI) and established the National AI Initiative Office at the White House.
Established the first-ever principles for Federal agency adoption of AI to improve services for the American people.
Signed the National Quantum Initiative Act establishing the National Quantum Coordination Office at the White House to drive breakthroughs in quantum information science.
Signed the Secure 5G and Beyond Act to ensure America leads the world in 5G.
Launched a groundbreaking program to test safe and innovative commercial drone operations nationwide.
Issued new rulemaking to accelerate the return of American civil supersonic aviation.
Committed to doubling investments in AI and

quantum information science (QIS) research and development.

Announced the establishment of $1 billion AI and quantum research institutes across America.

Established the largest dual-use 5G test sites in the world to advance 5G commercial and military innovation.

Signed landmark Prague Principles with America's allies to advance the deployment of secure 5G telecommunications networks.

Signed first-ever bilateral AI cooperation agreement with the United Kingdom.

Built collation among allies to ban Chinese Telecom Company Huawei from their 5G infrastructure.

Preserved American jobs for American workers and rejected the importation of cheap foreign labor.

Pressured the Tennessee Valley Authority (TVA) to reverse their decision to lay off over 200 American workers and replace them with cheaper foreign workers.

Removed the TVA Chairman of the Board and a TVA Board Member.

Life-Saving Response to the China Virus

Restricted travel to the United States from infected regions of the world.

Suspended all travel from China, saving thousands of lives.

Required all American citizens returning home from designated outbreak countries to return through designated airports with enhanced screening measures, and to undergo a self-quarantine.

Announced further travel restrictions on Iran, the Schengen Area of Europe, the United Kingdom, Ireland, and Brazil.

Issued travel advisory warnings recommending that American citizens avoid all international travel.
Reached bilateral agreements with Mexico and Canada to suspend non-essential travel and expeditiously return illegal aliens.
Repatriated over 100,000 American citizens stranded abroad on more than 1,140 flights from 136 countries and territories.
Safely transported, evacuated, treated, and returned home trapped passengers on cruise ships.
Took action to authorize visa sanctions on foreign governments who impede our efforts to protect American citizens by refusing or unreasonably delaying the return of their own citizens, subjects, or residents from the United States.

Acted early to combat the China Virus in the United States.

Established the White House Coronavirus Task Force, with leading experts on infectious diseases, to manage the Administration's efforts to mitigate the spread of COVID-19 and to keep workplaces safe.
Pledged in the State of the Union address to "take all necessary steps to safeguard our citizens from the Virus," while the Democrats' response made not a single mention of COVID-19 or even the threat of China.
Declared COVID-19 a National Emergency under the Stafford Act.
Established the 24/7 FEMA National Response Coordination Center.
Released guidance recommending containment measures

critical to slowing the spread of the Virus, decompressing peak burden on hospitals and infrastructure, and diminishing health impacts. Implemented strong community mitigation strategies to sharply reduce the number of lives lost in the United States down from experts' projection of up to 2.2 million deaths in the United States without mitigation.
Halted American funding to the World Health Organization to counter its egregious bias towards China that jeopardized the safety of Americans.
Announced plans for withdrawal from the World Health Organization and redirected contribution funds to help meet global public health needs.
Called on the United Nations to hold China accountable for their handling of the virus, including refusing to be transparent and failing to contain the virus before it spread.

Re-purposed domestic manufacturing facilities to ensure frontline workers had critical supplies.

Distributed billions of pieces of Personal Protective Equipment, including gloves, masks, gowns, and face shields.
Invoked the Defense Production Act over 100 times to accelerate the development and manufacturing of essential material in the USA.
Made historic investments of more than $3 billion into the industrial base.
Contracted with companies such as Ford, General Motors, Philips, and General Electric to produce ventilators.
Contracted with Honeywell, 3M, O&M Halyard, Moldex, and

Lydall to increase our Nation's production of N-95 masks.

The Army Corps of Engineers built 11,000 beds, distributed 10,000 ventilators, and surged personnel to hospitals.

Converted the Javits Center in New York into a 3,000-bed hospital and opened medical facilities in Seattle and New Orleans.

Dispatched the USNS Comfort to New York City, and the USNS Mercy to Los Angeles.

Deployed thousands of FEMA employees, National Guard members, and military forces to help in the response.

Provided support to states facing new emergences of the virus, including surging testing sites, deploying medical personnel, and advising on mitigation strategies.

Announced Federal support to governors for use of the National Guard with 100 percent cost-share.

Established the Supply Chain Task Force as a "control tower" to strategically allocate high-demand medical supplies and PPE to areas of greatest need.

Requested critical data elements from states about the status of hospital capacity, ventilators, and PPE.

Executed nearly 250 flights through Project Air Bridge to transport hundreds of millions of surgical masks, N95 respirators, gloves, and gowns from around the world to hospitals and facilities throughout the United States.

Signed an executive order invoking the Defense Production Act to ensure that Americans have a reliable supply of products like beef, pork, and poultry.

Stabilized the food supply chain restoring the Nation's protein processing capacity through a collaborative approach with Federal, state, and local officials and industry partners.
The continued movement of food and other critical items of daily life distributed to stores and to American homes went unaffected.

Replenished the depleted Strategic National Stockpile.

Increased the number of ventilators nearly ten-fold to more than 153,000. Despite the grim projections from the media and governors, no American who has needed a ventilator has been denied a ventilator.
Increased the number of N95 masks fourteen-fold to more than 176 million.
Issued an executive order ensuring critical medical supplies are produced in the United States.

Created the largest, most advanced, and most innovative testing system in the world. Built the world's leading testing system from scratch, conducting over 200 million tests – more than all of the European Union combined.

Engaged more than 400 test developers to increase testing capacity from less than 100 tests per day to more than 2 million tests per day.
Slashed red tape and approved Emergency Use Authorizations for more than 300 different tests, including 235 molecular tests, 63 antibody tests, and 11 antigen tests.
Delivered state-of-the-art testing devices and millions of tests to

every certified nursing home in the country. Announced more flexibility to Medicare Advantage and Part D plans to waive cost-sharing for tests. Over 2,000 retail pharmacy stores, including CVS, Walmart, and Walgreens, are providing testing using new regulatory and reimbursement options. Deployed tens of millions of tests to nursing homes, assisted living facilities, historically black colleges and universities (HBCUs), tribes, disaster relief operations, Home Health/Hospice organizations, and the Veterans Health Administration. Began shipping 150 million BinaxNOW rapid tests to states, long-term care facilities, the IHS, HBCUs, and other key partners.

Pioneered groundbreaking treatments and therapies that reduced the mortality rate by 85 percent, saving over 2 million lives.

The United States has among the lowest case fatality rates in the entire world. The Food and Drug Administration (FDA) launched the Coronavirus Treatment Acceleration Program to expedite the regulatory review process for therapeutics in clinical trials, accelerate the development and publication of industry guidance on developing treatments, and utilize regulatory flexibility to help facilitate the scaling-up of manufacturing capacity. More than 370 therapies are in clinical trials and another 560 are in the planning stages. Announced $450 million in available funds to support the

manufacturing of Regeneron's antibody cocktail.
Shipped tens of thousands of doses of the
Regeneron drug.
Authorized an Emergency Use Authorization (EUA)
for convalescent plasma.
Treated around 100,000 patients with convalescent
plasma, which may reduce mortality by 50 percent.
Provided $48 million to fund the Mayo Clinic study
that tested the efficacy of convalescent plasma for
patients with COVID-19.
Made an agreement to support the large-scale
manufacturing of AstraZeneca's cocktail of two
monoclonal antibodies.
Approved Remdesivir as the first COVID-19
treatment, which could reduce hospitalization time
by nearly a third.
Secured more than 90 percent of the world's supply
of Remdesivir, enough to treat over 850,000 high-
risk patients.
Granted an EUA to Eli Lilly for its anti-body
treatments.
Finalized an agreement with Eli Lilly to purchase
the first doses of the company's investigational
antibody therapeutic.
Provided up to $270 million to the American Red
Cross and America's Blood Centers to support the
collection of up to 360,000 units of plasma.
Launched a nationwide campaign to ask patients
who have recovered from COVID-19 to donate
plasma.
Announced Phase 3 clinical trials for varying types
of blood thinners to treat adults diagnosed with
COVID-19.

Issued an EUA for the monoclonal antibody therapy bamlanivimab.

FDA issued an EUA for casirivimab and imdevimab to be administered together.

Launched the COVID-19 High Performance Computing Consortium with private sector and academic leaders unleashing America's supercomputers to accelerate coronavirus research.

Brought the full power of American medicine and government to produce a safe and effective vaccine in record time.

Launched Operation Warp Speed to initiate an unprecedented drive to develop and make available an effective vaccine by January 2021.

Pfizer and Moderna developed two vaccines in just nine months, five times faster than the fastest prior vaccine development in American history.

Pfizer and Moderna's vaccines are approximately 95 effective – far exceeding all expectations.

AstraZeneca and Johnson & Johnson also both have promising candidates in the final stage of clinical trials.

The vaccines will be administered within 24 hours of FDA-approval.

Made millions of vaccine doses available before the end of 2020, with hundreds of millions more to quickly follow.

FedEx and UPS will ship doses from warehouses directly to local pharmacies, hospitals, and healthcare providers.

Finalized a partnership with CVS and Walgreens to deliver vaccines directly to residents of nursing homes and long-term care facilities as soon as a state requests it, at no cost to America's seniors.

Signed an executive order to ensure that the United States

government prioritizes getting the vaccine to American citizens before sending it to other nations. Provided approximately $13 billion to accelerate vaccine development and to manufacture all of the top candidates in advance.

Provided critical investments of $4.1 billion to Moderna to support the development, manufacturing, and distribution of their vaccines. Moderna announced its vaccine is 95 percent effective and is pending FDA approval.

Provided Pfizer up to $1.95 billion to support the mass-manufacturing and nationwide distribution of their vaccine candidate.

Pfizer announced its vaccine is 95 percent effective and is pending FDA approval.

Provided approximately $1 billion to support the manufacturing and distribution of Johnson & Johnson's vaccine candidate.

Johnson & Johnson's vaccine candidate reached the final stage of clinical trials.

Made up to $1.2 billion available to support AstraZeneca's vaccine candidate.

AstraZeneca's vaccine candidate reached the final stage of clinical trials.

Made an agreement to support the large-scale manufacturing of Novavax's vaccine candidate with 100 million doses expected.

Partnered with Sanofi and GSK to support large-scale manufacturing of a COVID-19 investigational vaccine. Awarded $200 million in funding to support vaccine preparedness and plans for the immediate distribution and administration of vaccines.

Provided $31 million to Cytvia for vaccine-related consumable products.

Under the PREP Act, issued guidance authorizing qualified pharmacy technicians to administer vaccines.

Announced that McKesson Corporation will produce store and distribute vaccine ancillary supply kits on behalf of the Strategic National Stockpile to help healthcare workers who will administer vaccines.

Announced partnership with large-chain, independent, and regional pharmacies to deliver vaccines.

Prioritized resources for the most vulnerable Americans, including nursing home residents.

Quickly established guidelines for nursing homes and expanded telehealth opportunities to protect vulnerable seniors.

Increased surveillance, oversight, and transparency of all 15,417 Medicare and Medicaid nursing homes by requiring them to report cases of COVID-19 to all residents, their families, and the Centers for Disease Control and Prevention (CDC).

Required that all nursing homes test staff regularly.

Launched an unprecedented national nursing home training curriculum to equip nursing home staff with the knowledge they need to stop the spread of COVID-19.

Delivered $81 million for increased inspections and funded 35,000 members of the Nation Guard to deliver critical supplies to every Medicare-certified nursing homes.

Deployed Federal Task Force Strike Teams to provide onsite technical assistance and education to nursing homes experiencing outbreaks.

Distributed tens of billions of dollars in Provider Relief Funds to protect nursing homes, long-term care facilities, safety-net hospitals, rural hospitals, and communities hardest hit by the virus.

Released 1.5 million N95 respirators from the Strategic National Stockpile for distribution to over 3,000 nursing home facilities.

Directed the White House Opportunity and Revitalization Council to refocus on underserved communities impacted by the coronavirus. Required that testing results reported include data on race, gender, ethnicity, and ZIP code, to ensure that resources were directed to communities disproportionately harmed by the virus.

Ensured testing was offered at 95 percent of Federally Qualified Health Centers (FQHC), which serve over 29 million patients in 12,000 communities across the Nation.

Invested an unprecedented $8 billion in tribal communities.

Maintained safe access for Veterans to VA healthcare throughout the COVID-19 Pandemic and supported non-VA hospital systems and private and state-run nursing homes with VA clinical teams.

Signed legislation ensuring no reduction of VA education benefits under the GI Bill for online distance learning.

Supported Americans as they safely return to school and work.

Issued the Guidelines for Opening Up America Again, a

detailed blueprint to help governors as they began reopening the country. Focused on protecting the most vulnerable and mitigating the risk of any resurgence, while restarting the economy and allowing Americans to safely return to their jobs. Helped Americans return to work by providing extensive guidance on workplace-safety measures to protect against COVID-19 and investigating over 10,000 coronavirus-related complaints and referrals. Provided over $31 billion to support elementary and secondary schools.
Distributed 125 million face masks to school districts.
Provided comprehensive guidelines to schools on how to protect and identify high-risk individuals, prevent the spread of COVID-19, and conduct safe in-person teaching.
Brought back the safe return of college athletics, including Big Ten and Pac-12 football.

Rescued the American economy with nearly $3.4 trillion in relief, the largest financial aid package in history.

Secured an initial $8.3 billion Coronavirus Preparedness and Response Act, supporting the development of treatments and vaccines, and to procure critical medical supplies and equipment. Signed the $100 billion Families First Coronavirus Relief Act, guaranteeing free coronavirus testing, emergency paid sick leave and family leave, Medicaid funding, and food assistance. Signed the $2.3 trillion Coronavirus Aid, Relief, and Economic Security (CARES) Act, providing unprecedented and immediate relief to American families, workers, and businesses.

Signed additional legislation providing nearly $900 billion in support for coronavirus emergency response and relief, including critically needed funds to continue the Paycheck Protection Program. Signed the Paycheck Protection Program and Healthcare Enhancement Act, adding an additional $310 billion to replenish the program.
Delivered approximately 160 million relief payments to hardworking Americans.
Through the Paycheck Protection Program, approved over $525 billion in forgivable loans to more than 5.2 million small businesses, supporting more than 51 million American jobs.
The Treasury Department approved the establishment of the Money Market Mutual Fund Liquidity Facility to provide liquidity to the financial system.
The Treasury Department, working with the Federal Reserve, was able to leverage approximately $4 trillion in emergency lending facilities.
Signed an executive order extending expanded unemployment benefits.
Signed an executive order to temporarily suspend student loan payments, evictions, and collection of payroll taxes.
Small Business Administration expanded access to emergency economic assistance for small businesses, faith-based, and religious entities.
Protected jobs for American workers impacted by COVID-19 by temporarily suspending several job-related nonimmigrant visas, including H-1B's, H-2B's without a nexus to the food-

supply chain, certain H-4's, as well as L's and certain J's.

Great Healthcare for Americans

Empowered American patients by greatly expanding healthcare choice, transparency, and affordability.

Eliminated the Obamacare individual mandate – a financial relief to low and middle-income households that made up nearly 80 percent of the families who paid the penalty for not wanting to purchase health insurance.
Increased choice for consumers by promoting competition in the individual health insurance market leading to lower premiums for three years in a row.
Under the Trump Administration, more than 90 percent of the counties have multiple options on the individual insurance market to choose from.
Offered Association Health Plans, which allow employers to pool together and offer more affordable, quality health coverage to their employees at up to 30 percent lower cost.
Increased availability of short-term, limited-duration health plans, which can cost up to 60 percent less than traditional plans, giving Americans more flexibility to choose plans that suit their needs.
Expanded Health Reimbursement Arrangements, allowing millions of Americans to be able to shop for a plan of their choice on the individual market, and then have their employer cover the cost.
Added 2,100 new Medicare Advantage plan options since 2017, a 76 percent increase.

Lowered Medicare Advantage premiums by 34 percent nationwide to the lowest level in 14 years. Medicare health plan premium savings for beneficiaries have totaled $nearly 1.5 billion since 2017.

Improved access to tax-free health savings accounts for individuals with chronic conditions.

Eliminated costly Obamacare taxes, including the health insurance tax, the medical device tax, and the "Cadillac tax."

Worked with states to create more flexibility and relief from oppressive Obamacare regulations, including reinsurance waivers to help lower premiums.

Released legislative principles to end surprise medical billing.

Finalized requirements for unprecedented price transparency from hospitals and insurance companies so patients know what the cost is before they receive care.

Took action to require that hospitals make the prices they negotiate with insurers publicly available and easily accessible online.

Improved patients access to their health data by penalizing hospitals and causing clinicians to lose their incentive payments if they do not comply.

Expanded access to telehealth, especially in rural and underserved communities.

Increased Medicare payments to rural hospitals to stem a decade of rising closures and deliver enhanced access to care in rural areas.

Issued unprecedented reforms that dramatically lowered the price of prescription drugs.

Lowered drug prices for the first time in 51 years. Launched an initiative to stop global freeloading in the drug market.
Finalized a rule to allow the importation of prescription drugs from Canada.
Finalized the Most Favored Nation Rule to ensure that pharmaceutical companies offer the same discounts to the United States as they do to other nations, resulting in an estimated $85 billion in savings over seven years and $30 billion in out-of-pocket costs alone.
Proposed a rule requiring federally funded health centers to pass drug company discounts on insulin and Epi-Pens directly to patients.
Ended the gag clauses that prevented pharmacists from informing patients about the best prices for the medications they need.
Ended the costly kickbacks to middlemen and ensured that patients directly benefit from available discounts at the pharmacy counter, saving Americans up to 30 percent on brand name pharmaceuticals.
Enhanced Part D plans to provide many seniors with Medicare access to a broad set of insulins at a maximum $35 copay for a month's supply of each type of insulin.
Reduced Medicare Part D prescription drug premiums, saving beneficiaries nearly $2 billion in premium costs since 2017.

Ended the Unapproved Drugs Initiative, which provided market

exclusivity to generic drugs.

Promoted research and innovation in healthcare to ensure that American patients have access to the best treatment in the world.

Signed first-ever executive order to affirm that it is the official policy of the United States Government to protect patients with pre-existing conditions. Passed Right To Try to give terminally ill patients access to lifesaving cures. Signed an executive order to fight kidney disease with more transplants and better treatment. Signed into law a $1 billion increase in funding for critical Alzheimer's research. Accelerated medical breakthroughs in genetic treatments for Sickle Cell disease. Finalized the interoperability rules that will give American patients access to their electronic health records on their phones. Initiated an effort to provide $500 million over the next decade to improve pediatric cancer research. Launched a campaign to end the HIV/AIDS epidemic in America in the next decade. Started a program to provide the HIV prevention drug PrEP to uninsured patients for free. Signed an executive order and awarded new development contracts to modernize the influenza vaccine.

Protected our Nation's seniors by safeguarding and strengthening Medicare.

Updated the way Medicare pays for innovative medical products to ensure beneficiaries have access to the latest innovation and treatment.
Reduced improper payments for Medicare an estimated $15 billion since 2016 protecting taxpayer dollars and leading to less fraud, waste, and abuse.
Took rapid action to combat antimicrobial resistance and secure access to life-saving new antibiotic drugs for American seniors, by removing several financial disincentives and setting policies to reduce inappropriate use.
Launched new online tools, including eMedicare, Blue Button 2.0, and Care Compare, to help seniors see what is covered, compare costs, streamline data, and compare tools available on Medicare.gov.
Provided new Medicare Advantage supplemental benefits, including modifications to help keep seniors safe in their homes, respite care for caregivers, non-opioid pain management alternatives like therapeutic massages, transportation, and more in-home support services and assistance.
Protected Medicare beneficiaries by removing Social Security numbers from all Medicare cards, a project completed ahead of schedule.
Unleashed unprecedented transparency in Medicare and Medicaid data to spur research and innovation.

Remaking the Federal Judiciary

Appointed a historic number of Federal judges who will interpret the Constitution as written.

Nominated and confirmed over 230 Federal judges. Confirmed 54 judges to the United States Courts of Appeals, making up nearly a third of the entire appellate bench.
Filled all Court of Appeals vacancies for the first time in four decades.
Flipped the Second, Third, and Eleventh Circuits from Democrat-appointed majorities to Republican-appointed majorities. And dramatically reshaped the long-liberal Ninth Circuit.

Appointed three Supreme Court justices, expanding its conservative-appointed majority to 6-3.

Appointed Justice Neil Gorsuch to replace Justice Antonin Scalia.
Appointed Justice Brett Kavanaugh to replace Justice Anthony Kennedy. Appointed Justice Amy Coney Barrett to replace Justice Ruth Bader Ginsburg.

Achieving a Secure Border

Secured the Southern Border of the United States.

Built over 400 miles of the world's most robust and advanced border wall.
Illegal crossings have plummeted over 87 percent were the

wall has been constructed.

Deployed nearly 5,000 troops to the Southern border. In addition, Mexico deployed tens of thousands of their own soldiers and national guardsmen to secure their side of the US-Mexico border.

Ended the dangerous practice of Catch-and-Release, which means that instead of aliens getting released into the United States pending future hearings never to be seen again, they are detained pending removal, and then ultimately returned to their home countries.

Entered into three historic asylum cooperation agreements with Honduras, El Salvador, and Guatemala to stop asylum fraud and resettle illegal migrants in third-party nations pending their asylum applications.

Entered into a historic partnership with Mexico, referred to as the "Migrant Protection Protocols," to safely return asylum-seekers to Mexico while awaiting hearings in the United States.

Fully enforced the immigration laws of the United States.

Signed an executive order to strip discretionary Federal grant funding from deadly sanctuary cities. Fully enforced and implemented statutorily authorized "expedited removal" of illegal aliens. The Department of Justice prosecuted a record-breaking number of immigration-related crimes. Used Section 243(d) of the Immigration and Nationality Act (INA) to reduce the number of aliens coming from countries whose governments refuse to accept their nationals who were ordered removed from the United States.

Ended asylum fraud, shut down human smuggling traffickers, and solved the humanitarian crisis across the Western Hemisphere.

Suspended, via regulation, asylum for aliens who had skipped previous countries where they were eligible for asylum but opted to "forum shop" and continue to the United States.

Safeguarded migrant families, and protected migrant safety, by promulgating new regulations under the Flores Settlement Agreement.

Proposed regulations to end the practice of giving free work permits to illegal aliens lodging meritless asylum claims.

Issued "internal relocation" guidance.

Cross-trained United States Border Patrol agents to conduct credible fear screenings alongside USCIS (United States Citizenship and Immigration Services) adjudication personnel to reduce massive backlogs.

Streamlined and expedited the asylum hearing process through both the Prompt Asylum Claim Review (PACR) and the Humanitarian Asylum Review Process (HARP).

Launched the Family Fraud Initiative to identify hundreds of individuals who were fraudulently presenting themselves as family units at the border, oftentimes with trafficking children, in order to ensure child welfare.

Improved screening in countries with high overstay rates and reduced visa overstay rates in many of these countries.

Removed bureaucratic constraints on United States consular officers that reduced their ability to appropriately vet visa applicants.

Worked with Mexico and other regional partners to dismantle

the human smuggling networks in our hemisphere that profit from human misery and fuel the border crisis by exploiting vulnerable populations.

Secured our Nation's immigration system against criminals and terrorists.

Instituted national security travel bans to keep out terrorists, jihadists, and violent extremists, and implemented a uniform security and information-sharing baseline all nations must meet in order for their nationals to be able to travel to, and emigrate to, the United States.
Suspended refugee resettlement from the world's most dangerous and terror-afflicted regions.
Rebalanced refugee assistance to focus on overseas resettlement and burden-sharing.
85 percent reduction in refugee resettlement.
Overhauled badly broken refugee security screening process.
Required the Department of State to consult with states and localities as part of the Federal government's refugee resettlement process.
Issued strict sanctions on countries that have failed to take back their own nationals.
Established the National Vetting Center, which is the most advanced and comprehensive visa screening system anywhere in the world.

Protected American workers and taxpayers.

Issued a comprehensive "public charge" regulation to ensure newcomers to the United States are financially self-sufficient and not reliant on welfare. Created an enforcement mechanism for sponsor repayment and deeming, to ensure that people who are presenting themselves as sponsors are actually responsible for sponsor obligations.
Issued regulations to combat the horrendous practice of "birth tourism."
Issued a rule with the Department of Housing and Urban Development (HUD) to make illegal aliens ineligible for public housing.
Issued directives requiring Federal agencies to hire United States workers first and prioritizing the hiring of United States workers wherever possible.
Suspended the entry of low-wage workers that threaten American jobs.
Finalized new H-1B regulations to permanently end the displacement of United States workers and modify the administrative tools that are required for H-1B visa issuance.
Defended United States sovereignty by withdrawing from the United Nations' Global Compact on Migration.
Suspended Employment Authorization Documents for aliens who arrive illegally between ports of entry and are ordered removed from the United States.

Restored integrity to the use of Temporary Protected Status (TPS) by strictly adhering to the statutory conditions required for TPS. Restoring American Leadership Abroad

Restored America's leadership in the world and successfully negotiated to ensure our allies pay their fair share for our military protection.

Secured a $400 billion increase in defense spending from NATO (North Atlantic Treaty Organization) allies by 2024, and the number of members meeting their minimum obligations more than doubled.
Credited by Secretary General Jens Stoltenberg for strengthening NATO.
Worked to reform and streamline the United Nations (UN) and reduced spending by $1.3 billion.
Allies, including Japan and the Republic of Korea, committed to increase burden-sharing.
Protected our Second Amendment rights by announcing the United States will never ratify the UN Arms Trade Treaty.
Returned 56 hostages and detainees from more than 24 countries.
Worked to advance a free and open Indo-Pacific region, promoting new investments and expanding American partnerships.

Advanced peace through strength.

Withdrew from the horrible, one-sided Iran Nuclear Deal and imposed crippling sanctions on the Iranian Regime.
Conducted vigorous enforcement on all sanctions to bring Iran's oil exports to zero and deny the regime its principal source of revenue.
First president to meet with a leader of North Korea and the first sitting president to cross the demilitarized zone into North Korea.
Maintained a maximum pressure campaign and enforced tough sanctions on North Korea while negotiating de-nuclearization, the release of American hostages, and the return of the remains of American heroes.
Brokered economic normalization between Serbia and Kosovo, bolstering peace in the Balkans.
Signed the Honk Kong Autonomy Act and ended the United States' preferential treatment with Hong Kong to hold China accountable for its infringement on the autonomy of Hong Kong.
Led allied efforts to defeat the Chinese Communist Party's efforts to control the international telecommunications system.

Renewed our cherished friendship and alliance with Israel and took historic action to promote peace in the Middle East.

Recognized Jerusalem as the true capital of Israel and quickly moved the American Embassy in Israel to Jerusalem.
Acknowledged Israel's sovereignty over the Golan Heights and declared that Israeli settlements in the West Bank are not

inconsistent with international law.

Removed the United States from the United Nations Human Rights Council due to the group's blatant anti-Israel bias.

Brokered historic peace agreements between Israel and Arab-Muslim countries, including the United Arab Emirates, the Kingdom of Bahrain, and Sudan. In addition, the United States negotiated a normalization agreement between Israel and Morocco, and recognized Moroccan Sovereignty over the entire Western Sahara, a position with long standing bipartisan support.

Brokered a deal for Kosovo to normalize ties and establish diplomatic relations with Israel.

Announced that Serbia would move its embassy in Israel to Jerusalem.

First American president to address an assembly of leaders from more than 50 Muslim nations and reach an agreement to fight terrorism in all its forms.

Established the Etidal Center to combat terrorism in the Middle East in conjunction with the Saudi Arabian Government.

Announced the Vision for Peace Political Plan – a two-state solution that resolves the risks of Palestinian statehood to Israel's security, and the first time Israel has agreed to a map and a Palestinian state.

Released an economic plan to empower the Palestinian people and enhance Palestinian governance through historic private investment.

Stood up against Communism and Socialism in the Western Hemisphere.

Reversed the previous Administration's disastrous Cuba policy, canceling the sellout deal with the Communist Castro dictatorship.

Pledged not to lift sanctions until all political prisoners are freed; freedoms of assembly and expression are respected; all political parties are legalized; and free elections are scheduled.

Enacted a new policy aimed at preventing American dollars from funding the Cuban regime, including stricter travel restrictions and restrictions on the importation of Cuban alcohol and tobacco.

Implemented a cap on remittances to Cuba.

Enabled Americans to file lawsuits against persons and entities that traffic in property confiscated by the Cuban regime.

First world leader to recognize Juan Guaido as the Interim President of Venezuela and led a diplomatic coalition against the Socialist Dictator of Venezuela, Nicolas Maduro.

Blocked all property of the Venezuelan Government in the jurisdiction of the United States.

Cut off the financial resources of the Maduro regime and sanctioned key sectors of the Venezuelan economy exploited by the regime.

Brought criminal charges against Nicolas Maduro for his narco-terrorism.

Imposed stiff sanctions on the Ortega regime in Nicaragua.

Joined together with Mexico and Canada in a successful bid to host the 2026 FIFA World Cup, with 60 matches to be held in

the United States.
Won bid to host the 2028 Summer Olympics in Los Angeles, California.

Colossal Rebuilding of the Military

Rebuilt the military and created the Sixth Branch, the United States Space Force.

Completely rebuilt the United States military with over $2.2 trillion in defense spending, including $738 billion for 2020.
Secured three pay raises for our service members and their families, including the largest raise in a decade.
Established the Space Force, the first new branch of the United States Armed Forces since 1947.
Modernized and recapitalized our nuclear forces and missile defenses to ensure they continue to serve as a strong deterrent.
Upgraded our cyber defenses by elevating the Cyber Command into a major warfighting command and by reducing burdensome procedural restrictions on cyber operations.
Vetoed the FY21 National Defense Authorization Act, which failed to protect our national security, disrespected the history of our veterans and military, and contradicted our efforts to put America first.

Defeated terrorists, held leaders accountable for malign actions, and bolstered peace around the world.

Defeated 100 percent of ISIS' territorial caliphate in Iraq and Syria.
Freed nearly 8 million civilians from ISIS' bloodthirsty control,

and liberated Mosul, Raqqa, and the final ISIS
foothold of Baghuz.
Killed the leader of ISIS, Abu Bakr al-Baghdadi,
and eliminated the world's top terrorist, Qasem
Soleimani.
Created the Terrorist Financing Targeting Center
(TFTC) in partnership between the United States
and its Gulf partners to combat extremist ideology
and threats, and target terrorist financial networks,
including over 60 terrorist individuals and entities
spanning the globe. Twice took decisive military
action against the Assad regime in Syria for the
barbaric use of chemical weapons against innocent
civilians, including a successful 59 Tomahawk
cruise missiles strike.
Authorized sanctions against bad actors tied to
Syria's chemical weapons program.
Negotiated an extended ceasefire with Turkey in
northeast Syria.

Addressed gaps in American's defense-industrial
base, providing much-needed updates to improve
the safety of our country.

Protected America's defense-industrial base,
directing the first whole-of-government assessment
of our manufacturing and defense supply chains
since the 1950s.
Took decisive steps to secure our information and
communications technology and services supply
chain, including unsafe mobile applications.
Completed several multi-year nuclear material
removal campaigns, securing over 1,000 kilograms
of highly enriched uranium and significantly
reducing global nuclear threats.

Signed an executive order directing Federal agencies to work together to diminish the capability of foreign adversaries to target our critical electric infrastructure.
Established a whole-of-government strategy addressing the threat posed by China's malign efforts targeting the United States taxpayer-funded research and development ecosystem.
Advanced missile defense capabilities and regional alliances.
Bolstered the ability of our allies and partners to defend themselves through the sale of aid and military equipment.
Signed the largest arms deal ever, worth nearly $110 billion, with Saudi Arabia.

Serving and Protecting Our Veterans

Reformed the Department of Veterans Affairs (VA) to improve care, choice, and employee accountability.

Signed and implemented the VA Mission Act, which made permanent Veterans CHOICE, revolutionized the VA community care system, and delivered quality care closer to home for Veterans. The number of Veterans who say they trust VA services has increased 19 percent to a record 91 percent, an all-time high.
Offered same-day emergency mental health care at every VA medical facility and secured $9.5 billion for mental health services in 2020. Signed the VA Choice and Quality Employment Act of 2017, which ensured that veterans could continue to see the doctor of their choice and wouldn't have to wait for care.

During the Trump Administration, millions of veterans have been able to choose a private doctor in their communities.

Expanded Veterans' ability to access telehealth services, including through the "Anywhere to Anywhere" VA healthcare initiative leading to a 1000 percent increase in usage during COVID-19.

Signed the Veterans Affairs Accountability and Whistleblower Protection Act and removed thousands of VA workers who failed to give our Vets the care they have so richly deserve.

Signed the Veterans Appeals Improvement and Modernization Act of 2017 and improved the efficiency of the VA, setting record numbers of appeals decisions.

Modernized medical records to begin a seamless transition from the Department of Defense to the VA.

Launched a new tool that provides Veterans with online access to average wait times and quality-of-care data.

The promised White House VA Hotline has fielded hundreds of thousands of calls.

Formed the PREVENTS Task Force to fight the tragedy of Veteran suicide.

Decreased veteran homelessness, improved education benefits, and achieved record-low veteran unemployment.

Signed and implemented the Forever GI Bill, allowing Veterans to use their benefits to get an education at any point in their lives.

Eliminated every penny of Federal student loan debt owed by American veterans who are completely and permanently disabled.

Compared to 2009, 49 percent fewer veterans experienced homelessness nationwide during 2019. Signed and implemented the HAVEN Act to ensure that Veterans who've declared bankruptcy don't lose their disability payments.

Helped hundreds of thousands of military service members make the transition from the military to the civilian workforce and developed programs to support the employment of military spouses.

Placed nearly 40,000 homeless veterans into employment through the Homeless Veterans Reintegration Program.

Placed over 600,000 veterans into employment through American Job Center services.

Enrolled over 500,000 transitioning service members in over 20,000 Department of Labor employment workshops.

Signed an executive order to help Veteran's transition seamlessly into the United States Merchant Marine.

Making Communities Safer

Signed into law landmark criminal justice reform.

Signed the bipartisan First Step Act into law, the first landmark criminal justice reform legislation ever passed to reduce recidivism and help former inmates successfully rejoin society.

Promoted second chance hiring to give former inmates the opportunity to live crime-free lives and find meaningful employment.

Launched a new "Ready to Work" initiative to help connect employers directly with former prisoners.

Awarded $2.2 million to states to expand the use of fidelity bonds, which underwrite companies that hire former prisoners.

Reversed decades-old ban on Second Chance Pell programs to provide postsecondary education to individuals who are incarcerated expand their skills and better succeed in the workforce upon re-entry.

Awarded over $333 million in Department of Labor grants to nonprofits and local and state governments for reentry projects focused on career development services for justice-involved youth and adults who were formerly incarcerated.

Unprecedented support for law-enforcement.

In 2019, violent crime fell for the third consecutive year.

Since 2016, the violent crime rate has declined over 5 percent and the murder rate has decreased by over 7 percent.

Launched Operation Legend to combat a surge of violent crime in cities, resulting in more than 5,500 arrests.

Deployed the National Guard and Federal law enforcement to Kenosha to stop violence and restore public safety.

Provided $1 million to Kenosha law enforcement, nearly $4 million to support small businesses in Kenosha, and provided over $41 million to support law enforcement to the state of Wisconsin.

Deployed Federal agents to save the courthouse in Portland from rioters.

Signed an executive order outlining ten-year prison sentences for destroying Federal property and monuments.

Directed the Department of Justice (DOJ) to investigate and prosecute Federal offenses related to ongoing violence.
DOJ provided nearly $400 million for new law enforcement hiring.
Endorsed by the 355,000 members of the Fraternal Order of Police.
Revitalized Project Safe Neighborhoods, which brings together Federal, state, local, and tribal law enforcement officials to develop solutions to violent crime.
Improved first-responder communications by deploying the FirstNet National Public Safety Broadband Network, which serves more than 12,000 public safety agencies across the Nation.
Established a new commission to evaluate best practices for recruiting, training, and supporting law enforcement officers.
Signed the Safe Policing for Safe Communities executive order to incentive local police department reforms in line with law and order.
Made hundreds of millions of dollars' worth of surplus military equipment available to local law enforcement.
Signed an executive order to help prevent violence against law enforcement officers.
Secured permanent funding for the 9/11 Victim Compensation Fund for first responders.

Implemented strong measures to stem hate crimes, gun violence, and human trafficking.

Signed an executive order making clear that Title VI of the Civil Rights Act of 1964 applies to discrimination rooted in anti-Semitism.
Launched a centralized website to educate the public about hate

crimes and encourage reporting.

Signed the Fix NICS Act to keep guns out of the hands of dangerous criminals. Signed the STOP School Violence Act and created a Commission on School Safety to examine ways to make our schools safer.

Launched the Foster Youth to Independence initiative to prevent and end homelessness among young adults under the age of 25 who are in, or have recently left, the foster care system.

Signed the Trafficking Victims Protection Reauthorization Act, which tightened criteria for whether countries are meeting standards for eliminating trafficking.

Established a task force to help combat the tragedy of missing or murdered Native American women and girls.

Prioritized fighting for the voiceless and ending the scourge of human trafficking across the Nation, through a whole of government back by legislation, executive action, and engagement with key industries.

Created the first-ever White House position focused solely on combating human trafficking.

Cherishing Life and Religious Liberty

Steadfastly supported the sanctity of every human life and worked tirelessly to prevent government funding of abortion.

Reinstated and expanded the Mexico City Policy, ensuring that taxpayer money is not used to fund abortion globally.

Issued a rule preventing Title X taxpayer funding from subsiding the abortion industry.

Supported legislation to end late-term abortions.
Cut all funding to the United Nations population
fund due to the fund's support for coercive abortion
and forced sterilization.
Signed legislation overturning the previous
administration's regulation that prohibited states
from defunding abortion facilities as part of their
family planning programs.
Fully enforced the requirement that taxpayer dollars
do not support abortion coverage in Obamacare
exchange plans.
Stopped the Federal funding of fetal tissue research.
Worked to protect healthcare entities and
individuals' conscience rights – ensuring that no
medical professional is forced to participate in an
abortion in violation of their beliefs.
Issued an executive order reinforcing requirement
that all hospitals in the United States provide
medical treatment or an emergency transfer for
infants who are in need of emergency medical
care—regardless of prematurity or disability.
Led a coalition of countries to sign the Geneva
Consensus Declaration, declaring that there is no
international right to abortion and committing to
protecting women's health.
First president in history to attend the March for
Life.

Stood up for religious liberty in the United States
and around the world.

Protected the conscience rights of doctors, nurses,
teachers, and groups like the Little Sisters of the
Poor.
First president to convene a meeting at the United

Nations to end religious persecution.

Established the White House Faith and Opportunity Initiative.

Stopped the Johnson Amendment from interfering with pastors' right to speak their minds.

Reversed the previous administration's policy that prevented the government from providing disaster relief to religious organizations.

Protected faith-based adoption and foster care providers, ensuring they can continue to serve their communities while following the teachings of their faith.

Reduced burdensome barriers to ensure Native Americans are free to keep spiritually and culturally significant eagle feathers found on their tribal lands.

Took action to ensure Federal employees can take paid time off work to observe religious holy days.

Signed legislation to assist religious and ethnic groups targeted by ISIS for mass murder and genocide in Syria and Iraq.

Directed American assistance toward persecuted communities, including through faith-based programs.

Launched the International Religious Freedom Alliance – the first-ever alliance devoted to confronting religious persecution around the world.

Appointed a Special Envoy to monitor and combat anti-Semitism.

Imposed restrictions on certain Chinese officials, internal security units, and companies for their complicity in the persecution of Uighur Muslims in Xinjiang.

Issued an executive order to protect and promote religious freedom around the world.

Safeguarding the Environment

Took strong action to protect the environment and ensure clean air and clean water.

Took action to protect vulnerable Americans from being exposed to lead and copper in drinking water and finalized a rule protecting children from lead-based paint hazards.
Invested over $38 billion in clean water infrastructure.
In 2019, America achieved the largest decline in carbon emissions of any country on earth. Since withdrawing from the Paris Climate Accord, the United States has reduced carbon emissions more than any nation.
American levels of particulate matter – one of the main measures of air pollution – are approximately five times lower than the global average.
Between 2017 and 2019, the air became 7 percent cleaner – indicated by a steep drop in the combined emissions of criteria pollutants.
Led the world in greenhouse gas emissions reductions, having cut energy-related CO_2 emissions by 12 percent from 2005 to 2018 while the rest of the world increased emissions by 24 percent.
In FY 2019 the Environmental Protection Agency (EPA) cleaned up more major pollution sites than any year in nearly two decades.
The EPA delivered $300 million in Brownfields grants directly to communities most in need including investment in 118 Opportunity Zones.

Placed a moratorium on offshore drilling off the coasts of Georgia, North Carolina, South Carolina, and Florida.

Restored public access to Federal land at Bears Ears National Monument and Grand Staircase-Escalante National Monument.

Recovered more endangered or threatened species than any other administration in its first term.

Secured agreements and signed legislation to protect the environment and preserve our Nation's abundant national resources.

The USMCA guarantees the strongest environmental protections of any trade agreement in history.

Signed the Save Our Seas Act to protect our environment from foreign nations that litter our oceans with debris and developed the first-ever Federal strategic plan to address marine litter.

Signed the Great American Outdoors Act, securing the single largest investment in America's National Parks and public lands in history.

Signed the largest public lands legislation in a decade, designating 1.3 million new acres of wilderness.

Signed a historic executive order promoting much more active forest management to prevent catastrophic wildfires.

Opened and expanded access to over 4 million acres of public lands for hunting and fishing.

Joined the One Trillion Trees Initiative to plant, conserve, and restore trees in America and around the world.

Delivered infrastructure upgrades and investments for numerous projects, including over half a billion dollars to fix the Herbert Hoover Dike and expanding funding for Everglades restoration by 55 percent.

Expanding Educational Opportunity

Fought tirelessly to give every American access to the best possible education.

The Tax Cuts and Jobs Act expanded School Choice, allowing parents to use up to $10,000 from a 529 education savings account to cover K-12 tuition costs at the public, private, or religious school of their choice.
Launched a new pro-American lesson plan for students called the 1776 Commission to promote patriotic education.
Prohibited the teaching of Critical Race Theory in the Federal government.
Established the National Garden of American Heroes, a vast outdoor park that will feature the statues of the greatest Americans to ever live.
Called on Congress to pass the Education Freedom Scholarships and Opportunity Act to expand education options for 1 million students of all economic backgrounds.
Signed legislation reauthorizing the D.C. Opportunity Scholarship program.
Issued updated guidance making clear that the First Amendment right to Free Exercise of Religion does not end at the door to a public school.

Took action to promote technical education.

Signed into law the Strengthening Career and Technical Education for the 21st Century Act, which provides over 13 million students with high-quality vocational education and extends more than $1.3 billion each year to states for critical workforce development programs.
Signed the INSPIRE Act which encouraged NASA to have more women and girls participate in STEM and seek careers in aerospace.
Allocated no less than $200 million each year in grants to prioritize women and minorities in STEM and computer science education.

Drastically reformed and modernized our educational system to restore local control and promote fairness.

Restored state and local control of education by faithfully implementing the Every Student Succeeds Act.
Signed an executive order that ensures public universities protect First Amendment rights or they will risk losing funding, addresses student debt by requiring colleges to share a portion of the financial risk, and increases transparency by requiring universities to disclose information about the value of potential educational programs.
Issued a rule strengthening Title IX protections for survivors of sexual misconduct in schools, and that – for the first time in history – codifies that sexual harassment is prohibited under Title IX.
Negotiated historic bipartisan agreement on new higher

education rules to increase innovation and lower costs by reforming accreditation, state authorization, distance education, competency-based education, credit hour, religious liberty, and TEACH Grants.

Prioritized support for Historically Black Colleges and Universities.

Moved the Federal Historically Black Colleges and Universities (HBCU) Initiative back to the White House.
Signed into law the FUTURE Act, making permanent $255 million in annual funding for HBCUs and increasing funding for the Federal Pell Grant program.
Signed legislation that included more than $100 million for scholarships, research, and centers of excellence at HBCU land-grant institutions.
Fully forgave $322 million in disaster loans to four HBCUs in 2018, so they could fully focus on educating their students.
Enabled faith based HBCUs to enjoy equal access to Federal support.

Combatting the Opioid Crisis

Brought unprecedented attention and support to combat the opioid crisis.

Declared the opioid crisis a nationwide public health emergency.
Secured a record $6 billion in new funding to combat the opioid epidemic.
Signed the SUPPORT for Patients and Communities Act, the largest-ever legislative effort to address a drug crisis in our

Nation's history.

Launched the Initiative to Stop Opioid Abuse and Reduce Drug Supply and Demand in order to confront the many causes fueling the drug crisis. The Department of Health and Human Services (HHS) awarded a record $9 billion in grants to expand access to prevention, treatment, and recovery services to States and local communities.

Passed the CRIB Act, allowing Medicaid to help mothers and their babies who are born physically dependent on opioids by covering their care in residential pediatric recovery facilities.

Distributed $1 billion in grants for addiction prevention and treatment.

Announced a Safer Prescriber Plan that seeks to decrease the amount of opioids prescriptions filled in America by one third within three years.

Reduced the total amount of opioids prescriptions filled in America.

Expanded access to medication-assisted treatment and life-saving Naloxone.

Launched FindTreatment.gov, a tool to find help for substance abuse.

Drug overdose deaths fell nationwide in 2018 for the first time in nearly three decades.

Launched the Drug-Impaired Driving Initiative to work with local law enforcement and the driving public at large to increase awareness.

Launched a nationwide public ad campaign on youth opioid

abuse that reached 58 percent of young adults in America.

Since 2016, there has been a nearly 40 percent increase in the number of Americans receiving medication-assisted treatment.

Approved 29 state Medicaid demonstrations to improve access to opioid use disorder treatment, including new flexibility to cover inpatient and residential treatment.

Approved nearly $200 million in grants to address the opioid crisis in severely affected communities and to reintegrate workers in recovery back into the workforce.

Took action to seize illegal drugs and punish those preying on innocent Americans.

In FY 2019, ICE HSI seized 12,466 pounds of opioids including 3,688 pounds of fentanyl, an increase of 35 percent from FY 2018.

Seized tens of thousands of kilograms of heroin and thousands of kilograms of fentanyl since 2017.

The Department of Justice (DOJ) prosecuted more fentanyl traffickers than ever before, dismantled 3,000 drug trafficking organizations, and seized enough fentanyl to kill 105,000 Americans.

DOJ charged more than 65 defendants collectively responsible for distributing over 45 million opioid pills.

Brought kingpin designations against traffickers operating in China, India, Mexico, and more who have played a role in the epidemic in America.

Indicted major Chinese drug traffickers for distributing fentanyl in the U.S for the first time ever, and convinced China to enact strict regulations to control the production and sale of fentanyl.

Yeah, I know, that was a lot but, I had to list it for posterity. With all the censorship, this book may be the only record of President Trump's accomplishments that will survive. Wow, what a great job he did! I'm reminded of Psalm 1:1-3, "Blessed is the man that walks not in the counsel of the ungodly, nor stands in the way of sinners, nor sits in the seat of the scornful. 2 But his delight is in the law of the LORD; and in his law does he meditate day and night. 3 And he shall be like a tree planted by the rivers of water, that brings forth its fruit in its season; his leaf also shall not wither; and whatsoever he does shall prosper."

When the Covid virus hit, it turned the whole world upside down. I'm reminded of the fourth horse mentioned in Revelation 6:8, "So I looked, and behold, an ashen (pale greenish gray) horse [like a corpse, representing death and pestilence]; and its rider's name was Death; and Hades (the realm of the dead) was following with him. They were given authority and power over a fourth part of the earth, to kill with the sword and with famine and with plague (pestilence, disease) and by the wild beasts of the earth."

The Covid pandemic caused fear, suffering, panic, worry and to make things worse it also caused the churches to be closed, even for Easter. I began to notice people placing wood crosses in front of their houses, *just like mine*. I then noticed more and more crosses in many different areas. I thought about the lamb's blood over the doors to protect the Israelite's from the destroyer mentioned in Exodus.

I'm reminded of Revelation 9:4, "And it was commanded them that they should not hurt the grass of the earth, neither any green thing, neither any tree; but only those men who have not the seal of God in their foreheads."

This man-made virus was created by manipulating an existing virus that originates in bats into something more deadly. This process is called "gain of function". Sounds more like loss of mind! These bats remind me of Revelation 19:17, "And I saw an angel standing in the sun; and he cried with a loud voice, saying to all the fowls that fly in midheaven, Come and gather yourselves together unto the supper of the great God; 18 That you may eat the flesh of kings, and the flesh of captains, and the flesh of mighty men, and the flesh of horses, and of them that sit on them, and the flesh of all men, both free and slave, both small and great."

This deadly bat virus was created in a military biological weapons research laboratory in Wuhan, China. The creation, direction and means of funding came from Dr. Anthony Stephen Fauci, an American physician-scientist and immunologist serving as the director of the National Institute of Allergy and Infectious Diseases (NIAID) and the Chief Medical Adviser to the President. Could he be the second Beast? The number of his name Steve Fauci=666. Could China represent the Red Dragon in the Book of Revelation? China gave Joe Biden and his son $1.5 billion dollars through his hedge fund money laundering company. Wow, that's like hitting the lottery and winning a million dollars a year for 1,500 years! China also gave tons of money to all the major media news outlets in exchange for evil propaganda and censorship of truth. The media said this money was advertising (more like treason). No doubt why Trump called the media "the enemy of the people".

The Dr Fauci created China virus resulted in the US economy being shut down. Everyone just sits around in their houses, wearing there mask and mail ordering China merchandise using stimulus money (borrowed printing press money). All this has brought about hyperinflation, and it reminds me of the third horse mentioned in Revelation 6:5-6, "And when he had opened the third seal, I heard the third living creature say, Come and see. And I beheld, and lo a black horse; and he that sat on it had a pair of balances in his hand. 6 And I heard a voice in the midst of the four living creatures say, A measure of wheat for a penny, and three measures of barley for a penny; and see you hurt not the oil and the wine."

Today, because of this hyperinflation, it takes half a day's pay to buy a "happy-meal", but this has no effect on the rich. The Washington "swamp" made sure the public followed only Dr Fauci's instruction about his bat virus and they censored any alternatives to their narratives. The Washington "Swamp" reminds me of Revelation 18:2-3, "And he cried mightily with a strong voice, saying, Babylon the great is fallen, is fallen, and is become the habitation of devils, and the hold of every foul spirit, and a cage of every unclean and hateful bird. 3 For all nations have drunk of the wine of the wrath of her fornication, and the kings of the earth have committed fornication with her, and the merchants of the earth are waxed rich through the abundance of her delicacies."

Then Dr Fauci's financially affiliated drug companies presented vaccines that now everyone must take by mandate of Biden or lose their job and freedom. Could the vaccination be the mark of the Beast? The number of the word vaccination=666. Revelations 13:17, "And that no man might buy or sell, except he that had the mark, or the name of the beast, or the number of his name."

Mask were proven ineffective against viruses 100 years ago, but people are wearing their mask religiously. It's like telling school kids to get under their desk and put a book on their head to be safe from a nuclear bomb. I've seen people alone in their car or alone in their yard wearing a mask. One reporter said, "people cling to their mask like it was a Bible". Every day we all saw mask-wearing Joe Biden and Dr Fauci mandate that everyone must comply with the "wearing of the mask." Could the mask be the image of the Beast? Revelations 13:12-15, "He exercises all the authority of the first beast in his presence [when the two are together]. And he makes the earth and those who inhabit it worship the first beast, whose deadly wound was healed. 13 He performs great signs (awe-inspiring acts), even making fire fall from the sky to the earth, right before peoples' eyes. 14 And he deceives those [unconverted ones] who inhabit the earth [into believing him] because of the signs which he is given [by Satan] to perform in the presence of the [first] beast, telling those who inhabit the earth to make an image to the beast who was wounded [fatally] by the sword and has come back to life. 15 And he is given power to give breath to the image of the beast, so that the image of the beast will even speak, and cause those who do not bow down and worship the image of the beast to be put to death."

Wearing a mask only creates a warm, moist incubator for bacteria. Any virus is dangerous, but the first indication of suspicion concerning Covid-19 was when they changed the way death certificates are coded (recorded). Regardless of the primary cause of death, a person would be recorded as dying from Covid if tested positive. If a skydiver's parachute failed to open then he is

recorded as having died of Covid. This changing of how deaths are coded has no possible purpose other than nefarious. Could exaggerated false death rate data cause excessive fear and desperation, making the
general public more compliant and submissive? Could this excessive fear cause responsible skepticism to be replaced with hasty compliance? Could this cultivate future submission to a mark of the Beast vaccine. I'm reminded of Psalm 32:8-9, "I will instruct you and teach you in the way which you shall go: I will guide you with my eye. 9 Be you not as the horse, or as the mule, which have no understanding: whose mouth must be held in with bit and bridle, else they come not near unto you."

Now it's being mandated that we all must get vaccine shots and have proof of it to be employed, travel, be in public places, etc. Many corporations and companies have pledged their tribute to evil by complying and enforcing these mandates. To prove we have taken the mark of the Beast vaccine, the "Swamp" will want us to provide our "Papers" like Nazi Germany or by some "Passport" high-tech way. Bio-Implant=666. RFID Scanner=666. RFID Body Tag=666. E-Identity=666. Digital ID Chip=666. Many long time existing medications like Hydroxychloroquine and Ivermectin have proven to be more effective on Covid than vaccines but the "Swamp" controlled media censors any information about this. Under the direction and control of Dr Fauci, hospitals are financially forced into refusing use of these more effective medications. Doctors' jobs are threatened by their affiliated hospitals if they use these more effective medications. Some pharmacies even place themselves above doctors and refuse to fill prescriptions by the good doctors who prioritize the health of their patients over "Swamp" agenda.

The "swamp" seems to be now rushing to increase censorship and implement these mandates. This reminds me of Revelation 12:12, "For this reason, rejoice, O heavens and you who dwell in them. Woe to the earth and the sea, because the devil has come down to you, having great wrath, knowing that he has only a short time."

I'm also reminded of Revelation 14:9-12, "And the third angel
followed them, saying with a loud voice, If any man worships the beast and his image, and receives his mark in his forehead, or in his hand, 10 The same shall drink of the wine of the wrath of God, which is poured out undiluted into the cup of his indignation; and he shall be tormented with fire and brimstone in the presence of the holy angels, and in the presence of the Lamb: 11 And the smoke of their torment ascends up forever and ever: and they have no rest day nor night, who worship the beast and his image, and whosoever receives the mark of his name. 12 Here is the patience of the saints: here are they that keep the commandments of God, and the faith of Jesus."

If the "Washington-Swamp" is Babylon, then what about the good part of the United States of America? What about the great USA, a country founded on Christian principles with the motto "In God We Trust"? I'm reminded of the United States what Jesus told John to write concerning the church of Philadelphia in Revelation 3:7-13, "And to the angel of the church in Philadelphia write; These things says he that is holy, he that is true, he that has the key of David, he that opens, and no man shuts; and shuts, and no man opens; 8 I know your works: behold, I have set before you an open door, and no man can shut it: for you have a little strength, and have kept my word, and have not denied my name. 9 Behold, I will make them of the synagogue of Satan, who say they are Jews, and are not, but do lie; behold, I will make them to come and worship before your feet, and to know that I have loved you. 10 Because you have kept the word of my patience, I also will keep you from the hour of temptation, which shall come upon all the world, to try them that dwell upon the earth. 11 Behold, I come quickly: hold that fast which you have, that no man take your crown. 12 He that overcomes will I make a pillar in the temple of my God, and he shall go no more out: and I will write upon him the name of my God, and the name of the city of my God, which is new Jerusalem, which comes down out of heaven from my God: and I will write upon him my new name. 13 He that has an ear, let him hear what the Spirit says unto the churches."

What about all the people of the world? It says in Matthew 25:31-34 "When the Son of man shall come in his glory, and all the holy angels with him, then shall he sit upon the throne of his glory: 32 And before him shall be gathered all nations: and he shall separate them one from another, as a shepherd divides his sheep from the goats: 33 And he shall set the sheep on his right hand, but the goats on the left. 34 Then shall the King say unto them on his right hand, Come, you blessed of my Father, inherit the kingdom prepared for you from the foundation of the world:" Matthew 25:41 says "Then shall he say also unto them on the left hand, Depart from me, you cursed, into everlasting fire, prepared for the devil and his angels:"

We are surely living in dangerous times. The Bible gives us warnings about the coming tribulations in 2nd Timothy 3:1-4, "This know also, that in the last days perilous times shall come. 2 For men shall be lovers of their own selves, covetous, boasters, proud, blasphemers, disobedient to parents,

unthankful, unholy, 3 Without natural affection,
truce breakers, false accusers, incontinent, fierce,
despisers of those that are good, 4 Traitors, reckless,
conceited, lovers of pleasures more than lovers of
God".

Seems like a perfect description of the "Swamp"
and all who follow them. How did our country get
so bad, so fast? President Ronald Reagan said,
"Freedom is never more than one generation away
from extinction. We didn't pass it to our children in
the bloodstream. It must be fought for, protected,
and handed on for them to do the same".

The founding fathers had much to say about the
importance of Christian morality being the
foundation of freedom. The following are a few.

John Adams in a speech to the military in 1798
warned his fellow countrymen stating, "We have no
government armed with power
capable of contending with human passions
unbridled by morality and religion . . . Our
Constitution was made only for a moral and
religious people. It is wholly inadequate to the
government of any other." John Adams is a signer of
the Declaration of Independence, the Bill of Rights
and our second President.

Benjamin Rush, Signer of the Declaration of
Independence stated, "The only foundation for a
useful education in a republic is to be aid in religion.
Without this there can be no virtue, and without
virtue there can be no liberty, and liberty is the
object and life of all republican governments.
Without religion, I believe that learning does real
mischief to the morals and principles of mankind."

Noah Webster, author of the first American Speller and the first Dictionary stated, "The Christian religion, in its purity, is the basis, or rather the source of all genuine freedom in government. . . . and I am persuaded that no civil government of a republican form can exist and be durable in which the principles of that religion have not a controlling influence."

Gouverneur Morris, Penman and Signer of the Constitution stated, "For avoiding the extremes of despotism or anarchy . . . the only ground of hope must be on the morals of the people. I believe that religion is the only solid base of morals and that morals are the only possible support of free governments. Therefore, education should teach the precepts of religion and the duties of man towards God."

Fisher Ames author of the final wording for the First Amendment wrote, "Why should not the Bible regain the place it once held as a schoolbook? Its morals are pure, its examples captivating and noble. The reverence for the Sacred Book that is thus early impressed lasts long; and probably if not impressed in infancy, never takes firm hold of the mind."

John Jay, Original Chief-Justice of the U. S. Supreme Court, "The Bible is the best of all books, for it is the word of God and teaches us the way to be happy in this world and in the next. Continue therefore to read it and to regulate your life by its precepts."

James Wilson, Signer of the Constitution; U. S. Supreme Court Justice, "Human law must rest its authority ultimately upon the authority of that law which is divine. . . . Far from being rivals or enemies, religion and law are twin sisters, friends, and mutual assistants. Indeed, these two sciences run into each other."

Noah Webster, author of the first American Speller and the first Dictionary stated, "The moral principles and precepts contained in the scriptures ought to form the basis of all our civil constitutions and laws. . . All the miseries and evils which men suffer from vice, crime, ambition, injustice, oppression, slavery, and war, proceed from their despising or neglecting the precepts contained in the Bible."

Robert Winthrop, Speaker of the U. S. House stated, "Men, in a word, must necessarily be controlled either by a power within them or by a power without them; either by the Word of God or by the strong arm of man; either by the Bible or by the bayonet."

George Washington, General of the Revolutionary Army, president of the Constitutional Convention, First President of the United States of America, Father of our nation stated, "Religion and morality are the essential pillars of civil society."

Benjamin Franklin, signer of the Declaration of Independence addressing the continental congress in 1778 said, "Only a virtuous people are capable of freedom. As nations become corrupt and vicious, they have more need of masters."
"Whereas true religion and good morals are the only solid foundations of public liberty and happiness . . . it is hereby earnestly recommended to the several States to take the most effectual measures for the encouragement thereof."

We have to stop thinking in terms of Republican, Democrat, Conservative, Liberal or Moderate. We have to stop voting for these distracting labels and vote only Christian! There is no doubt the "Swamp" censors, docs, cancels, hates and attacks Christians...no matter the label. About being attacked, when you're "taking on flack", you know you're over the target! Jesus said in Matthew 10:22, "And you will be hated by everyone because of [your association with] My name, but it is the one who has patiently persevered and endured to the end who will be saved."

We must "stand" and put on the armor of God! The founders created a government that only works for and serves "WE THE PEOPLE" if it's a Christian government. Displacing the "Swamp" can only happen from the inside out. We must vote or appoint every government, judicial, educational, military, law enforcement and dog catcher position with only Christians. You don't have to worry about lies, fraud, corruption, lawlessness, greed or lust for power with a Christian. It has become an accepted occupational trait that a politician lies; accepting lies must change. For government or individual, change must happen from the inside out.

There are only two choices, Christian (Christ) or anti-Christian(anti-Christ). You are with Christ, or you are not; God makes the choice totally yours. 75% of the United States is Christian so, with "In God We Trust", odds are in our favor to win back the great USA.

Fellow Christian, stand strong and do not worry, Jesus is coming soon! Jesus said in Revelation 22:7, "And behold, I am coming quickly. Blessed is the one who heeds and takes to heart and remembers the words of the prophecy [that is, the predictions, consolations, and warnings] contained in this book (Bible)." Jesus said in Revelation 22:12-15, "And, behold, I come quickly; and my reward is with me, to give every man according as his work shall be. 13 I am Alpha and Omega, the beginning and the end, the first and the last. 14 Blessed are they that do his commandments, that they may have right to the tree of life and may enter in through the gates into the city. 15 For outside are dogs, and sorcerers, and fornicators, and murderers, and idolaters, and whosoever loves and makes a lie."

And what will it be like when Jesus comes? Revelation 19:12-16 tells us "And I saw heaven opened, and behold a white horse; and he that sat upon it was called Faithful and True, and in righteousness he does judge and make war. 12 His eyes were as a flame of fire, and on his head were many crowns; and he had a name written, that no man knew, but he himself. 13 And he was clothed with a robe dipped in blood: and his name is called The Word of God. 14 And the armies which were in heaven followed him upon white horses, clothed in fine linen, white and clean. 15 And out of his mouth goes forth a sharp sword, that with it he should smite the nations: and he shall rule them with a rod of iron: and he treads the winepress of the fierceness and wrath of Almighty God. 16 And he has on his robe and on his thigh a name written, KING OF KINGS, AND LORD OF LORDS."

Interesting to note; The United Nations placed a statue in front of their building in New York called "The Guardian of International Peace and Security". Does it represent the Beast described in Revelation 13:2, "And the beast that I saw was like unto a leopard, and his feet were as the feet of a bear, and his mouth as the mouth of a lion: and the dragon gave him his power, and his throne, and great authority."

The book of Revelation begins with Jesus, 80 years after his crucifixion and resurrection, appearing to the Apostle John and instructing him to write things of the past, present and future. Jesus said he was the alpha and the omega, beginning and the end. The sacrifice Jesus gave at his crucifixion was that he accepted total responsibility for all the sin of everyone onto himself, even though he was sinless, and then paid the price by suffering a torturous slow death on the cross. This sacrifice provides forgiveness of sins and life everlasting beyond death for everyone who personally accepts Christ as savior. Three factors lead up to his crucifixion; The Jewish High Priest Caiaphas had Jesus arrested and then sentenced him to death for blasphemy (for saying he was the son of God). Roman Governor Pontius Pilate then gives the crowd of people the choice between killing Jesus or a murderer called Barabbas, the crowd chose Jesus. Pilate then ordered Jesus to be crucified. The number of the High Priest Caiaphas is Kohen Caiaphas=666. Kohen is the Hebrew word for "Priest". The number of the Roman Governor Pontius Pilate is Gov Eques=666. Governor Pontius Pilate was known as an "Eques". On the third day following the crucifixion death, resurrection occurs, and Jesus appears to two of his followers in Emmaus. He also makes an appearance to Peter. Jesus then appears that same day to his disciples in Jerusalem. Although he appears and vanishes mysteriously, he also eats and lets them touch him to prove that he is not a spirit. He repeats his command to bring his teaching to all nations. He then ascended to be in heaven at the right hand of God.

I know it's hard to believe in supernatural things. Even Jesus with his miracles like giving sight to the blind, making the lame to walk and bringing Lazarus back to life from being dead 4 days, people of that time did not believe who he was. Even his own disciples did not believe who he was. Its sure not hard to believe the wickedness and evil we see all around us these days. Can we see evidence of God at work because people's sin has led to division in politics, media, healthcare, education, workplace, families and life in general? Is God separating the goats from the sheep? Is God separating the chaff from the wheat? Will enough people in this 2020 cycle repent and push back against wickedness in time? Will the truth about the 2020 Election fraud be revealed? Will the United States Supreme Court remove the Beast from power, and will it be in time? I'm reminded of Daniel 7:26-27 "But the court shall sit, and they shall take away his dominion, to consume and to destroy it unto the end. 27 And the kingdom and dominion, and the greatness of the kingdom under the whole heaven, shall be given to the people of the saints of the most High, whose kingdom is an everlasting kingdom, and all dominions shall serve and obey him."

If the Beast is removed from power, what about the "Swamp"? I'm reminded of Daniel 7:12 "As concerning the rest of the beasts, they had their dominion taken away: yet their lives were prolonged for a season and time."

Will people welcome Jesus into their hearts and return Jesus in the form of Revival or will Jesus return in person bringing the wrath of God? One thing is for sure, Jesus promised that he will return!

The Bible is much more than just prophecy. It is the living, breathing, loving words of God. This book only scratches the surface of the wonderful discoveries to be found in the Bible. Do you want to discover and know more? What could your insights reveal about the prophecies of the Bible? Matthew 7:7-8, "Ask, and it shall be given you; seek, and you shall find; knock, and it shall be opened unto you: 8 For every one that asks receives; and he that seeks finds; and to him that knocks it shall be opened."

So, pick up your Bible and invite Jesus to fill your soul with the light of his presence. Put on the armor of God and stand!

,

7d45f21c-5121-4d7d-9d7b-08c4cebe8ab4R01

Made in the USA
Columbia, SC
14 March 2023